DOWNFALL OF THE GODS
Clovel Sword Chronicles: Book 3

BY GORDON BREWER

CLOVEL SWORD CHRONICLES SERIES
SHIELD OF SKOOL (BOOK 1)
BATTLE FOR THREE REALMS (BOOK 2)
DOWNFALL OF THE GODS (BOOK 3)
CLOVEL SWORD CHRONICLES: OMNIBUS EDITION

PARANORMAL AND FANTASY
BEOWULF: CURSE OF THE DREYGURS
INFINITE LOOP
THE CURSE OF BLACKBANE

RAY IRISH OCCULT MYSTERY
A SHOT OF IRISH
(Ray Irish Occult Mystery)
DIE IF YOU WANT PRAISE
(Ray Irish Mystery Occult Book 2)
DRINK WITH THE DEVIL AT MIDNIGHT
(Ray Irish Occult Mystery Book 3)

NOVELLAS
CLOVEL SWORD SAGA: Volumes 1 - 2
SKELETONS OF NILGAVA: Clovel Sword Saga 3
DEATH STALKS THE RUNWAY: Ray Irish Mystery Case File #1
DEATH STALKS THE RUNWAY: Ray Irish Mystery Case File #1

DOWNFALL OF THE GODS
Clovel Sword Chronicles: Book 3

GORDON BREWER

Thorn Bishop Press
2020

Second Edition

Thorn Bishop Press

Cover Illustration Artwork © Dusan Kostic | Dreamstime.com

Cover Illustration Design: https://www.fiverr.com/oliviaprodesign ©Gordon Brewer

ISBN-10: 1-945590-23-8

ISBN-13: 978-1-945590-23-8

Visit the series website at

www.gordonbrewer.com

Dedication

To my son, Teige, for the friendly reminders and questions about my characters which helped push this final book of the series forward.

Also, special thanks to those readers who continue to send emails and posts in support of my work.

Contents

CHAPTER 1: BATTLE OF ERAN 1

CHAPTER 2: PRISONER OF ERAN 25

CHAPTER 3: BITTERNESS AND VENGEANCE 42

CHAPTER 4: UNDERWORLD RISES 60

CHAPTER 5: GRAVE OF HEPTARC..85

CHAPTER 6: PREPARE FOR WAR..110

CHAPTER 7: ROUTE TO THE SKY REALM 133

CHAPTER 8: YNYS GARRAID 159

CHAPTER 9: DEADLY ALLIANCE 186

CHAPTER 10: BLOOD OF HEROES 207

About the Author..237

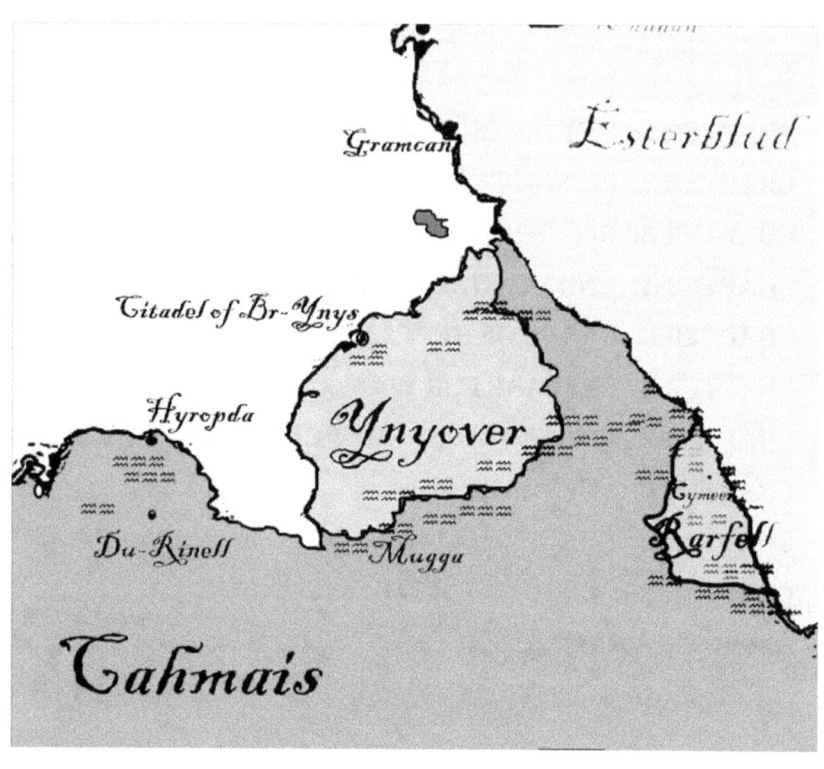

Chapter 1: Battle of Eran

The twin moons of Kamin cast a pale light on the forest floor, greeting the intruder who stepped from behind the *lellowtere* tree. A haunting melody of nature's songs coming from the *cruicads* and *tantals* suddenly stopped as the insects felt the presence of the fiend. A tall, bulky figure quickly picked up fresh scents, quickly setting off with purpose between the thin ranks of trees. Stopping occasionally, the massive white creature held up its head, sniffing at the air with a long muzzle exposing sharp black teeth. Directed by the smell of its prey, the hairy creature resumed its quad pedal gait. Using two stubby hind legs to propel its thick body forward, the underworld animal kept its balance by using large knuckles at the end of long, fur covered arms. Sharp claws curled up under the knuckles provided the underworld ogre with deadly weapons for use against its sometimes-armored quarry.

As the creature grew closer, it smelled the overpowering mix of wood smoke and cooked meat as it moved toward the aroma. It also heard several humans gathered around the supposed safety of their fire. The monster growled softly, keeping its mouth open to draw in the tantalizing aromas to guide it. The black eyes focused on the black silhouettes in the distance. Slowly, the hunter silently closed on the open patch of ground ahead. Sliding behind the final row of trees and crouched low, the fiend continued watching and listening while the men ate their meal.

Wet drool flowed along the sides of the closed muzzle as the waiting became too much for the creature. Suddenly, with a chilling roar, the Clovel rushed headlong into the camp. Landing upon the back of the closest man, the monster sank its large teeth into the neck of the armored fighter. The massive jaws crushed the victim's spine with a snap. Flinging its kill to the side, the hairy beast immediately sprang upon a large man got in hesitation between pulling his sword and running away. Large claws raked across the screaming warrior's belly, effortlessly cutting through the man's coat of chain mail like it was thin parchment. The monster went for the screaming man's neck as the prey fell to its knees. It finished the warrior off with a savage bite that ripped open the throat, instantly silencing the human.

Distracted by warm blood spraying across its muzzle, the Clovel felt the sudden agony of two swords cut into the creature's back. Howling with pain and rage, the monster spun around so fast its powerful arm backhanded a fighter who fell hard to the dirt. Jumping on the man, the enraged beast claws sliced through the metal helmet, along with the top of the dying man's head. The beast again felt another sharp strike from a warrior's sword, and it swung around again. The last of his prey scrambled away, trying to run away from the slaughter. Powerful legs pushed the creature forward, propelling it high in the air. It landed on top of the screaming person and sending the hunter and prey tumbling along the grass. As the man frantically struck out with his sword while he tried to crawl away, the monster's claws held fast. With an uncanny agility, the great beast lifted itself up, pulling the warrior high by his legs. It clamped its jaws around the victim's neck, nearly severing the head. The remains of the fighter in the green tunic convulsed as the monster let its prey fall to the ground. Turning slowly around the area, the Clovel sniffed around for any remaining threats, fresh gore dripping from the gaping, open mouth. The forest was silent again, but for the distant echo of hoofbeats as the ossanes continued their mad dash away from the area. Satisfied it was alone; the monster began ripping the armor and flesh of its prey. It's deep wounds were nearly healed when it sank its muzzle into the open belly of the last victim.

Unleashed upon human realms by an ancient, bitter god, the fearsome Clovel lived again. Created with foul souls from the underworld and using the miraculous waters of the Exyts Spring, the beast remained nearly impervious to weapons. As intended by the maker of the beast, word of the attack would spread, forcing the elders to acknowledge the return of the Guardians and their monsters. Terror from the underworld created the chaos necessary to bring down the Sky Realm and to install a vengeful master over all three realms of Kamin.

~~~

As the afternoon wore on, the sea breeze increased in its intensity across the bay of Eran. The Clovel Destroyer stood on the ramparts of the red stone fortress, paying little attention to the cooling breeze whipping his long brown hair. Instead, his rough right hand slowly kept the beat as he unconsciously slapped the sandstone used to create the small fort's solid walls. He was standing on the top walkway which connected the four square turrets of the fort, his hand tapping out the beat coming from enemy drums along the harbor of Eran. The perch gave the giant Esterblud warrior a full view of the activity across the area. Yet, at the moment, the man's thoughts were far away. Urith's scarred face remained thoughtful as he recalled his numerous voyages across the Maflow Sea. Since the time of his youth, dreams of adventure and new discoveries always beckoned him. From raiding enemy lands to f trade, the briny water provided the tribes of Esterblud an outlet for their warrior ambitions. Before the new burden thrust upon him with the Shield of Skool, the Clove Destroyer dreamed of leading an expedition into the unknown sea far past the lands of Regiussa. Old tales from the Skalds and stories he overheard during his youth claimed great riches and exotic spices awaited those who discovered the mythical lands far beyond the boundaries of the Maflow Sea. For a brief moment, Urith drifted back to his young self, listening intently and fantasizing about the world of islands with mountains going high above the clouds. Lands filled with dark skin people who drank from golden cups, living among exotic and deadly plants unknown to his people.

Soon the pleasant visions left him when he returned to the present. His gray eyes revealed the concern at the steady stream of Aberffraw troops coming ashore below his vantage point. Throughout the morning, the enemy fighters scrambled across the area, taking up defensive positions near the fort and steadily increasing their strength. The bay seemed filled with the ships of their mortal enemy, the kingdom of Cahmais. Several of the war boats lay beached upon the sand, deliberately driven ashore the day before. Stripping the ships of their timber, the enemy would use the wood for scaling ladders and other tools of war. For Urith and his comrades, any thoughts about their quest for the final piece of the Skool waited until the end of the upcoming battle.

Urith cursed the elders of the fort for their hesitation. In Esterblud society, the elders were looked up to for their wisdom and guidance. However, the few leaders who remained at the fort spoke as defeated men before the enemy even fully came ashore. In his eyes, the elders argued about petty little details, forgetting the need to strike quickly and boldly. Instead, the leaders of the Esterbluds waited in vain for their dead king.

The unfortunate news came in the day before. Brought by a tired and blood covered messenger from the south, the rider informed the people inside the fort about the gallant death of King Penhda during the massacre of the Esterblud army. Hordes of foul monsters from the underworld destroyed the army, butchering the living along with their leaders. While the news vindicated the prophetic visions of his companions, Fedelm and Mivraa, it meant the kingdom was in disarray. Two of the three main clans of Esterblud were missing the leaders needed to stop the invasion from the sea. Worse, some of those inside the fort could not believe monsters reached out from the underworld to slaughter the army of human on the battlefield. Instead, rumors of treachery circulated as some of the men who turned against Urith and those in his small group of followers.

Urith, along with his nephew Oslaf, were fugitives of the late King Penhda, thus tempting targets for the coming power struggle. On top of the concerns about the Clovel Destroyer, the elders were immediately suspicious of Fedelm who was foreign to their lands. As a *hakra*, or seer, the lovely woman's early revelations about the destruction of the Esterblud army were initially ridiculed by the men. A woman had little influence in the world of Kamin unless they held the strength of a warrior or used their cunning to manipulate those in power. The arrival of the messenger caused the elders to reassess her words. Urith remembered the grim satisfaction on Fedelm's face when the news arrived. However, he recognized the suspicions about the small group who followed him as rumors swirled inside the fort.

The warrior thought about Mivraa who remained silent while she listened to round after round of bickering during their time in Eran. A demigoddess, as well as a powerful warrior in her own right, the woman kept her identity secret to those in the fort. During the discussions, she sat next to Urith among the warriors. Her action sent glances of indignation from the men around the table. Fortunately, no fighter challenged the formidable woman's presence. Only later did Urith tell the other leaders around the table about the goddess of Haligulf in their presence. While this acknowledgment of her attendance caused most of the warriors to willingly accept her, it did not stop the bickering. Towards the end of the day, Mivraa leaned over, telling Urith that the men inside the fort were fools. The man nodded gravely, but he softly reminded her that he would be wary of any stories coming from two strangers and two outlaw Esterbluds if he was in their place.

It was evident the elders would not make up their minds as a group about what strategy the defenders of the fort should pursue. Some, like Wilgam, Urith, and Oslaf, sought an immediate attack while others opposed the idea, insisting upon defending the fortress. But the delay cost the defenders within the fort who were severely outnumbered. Just

4

as the enemy was able to surround the stronghold, the elders finally sent word to the tribal leaders in Cilgarran asking for more fighters to join their cause. Help would not come swiftly since the tribes in the north were spread across many areas of Esterblud. The situation left those in the fort with few options. Only a small amount of provisions remained since most were taken by King Penhda for his battle against Cahmais far to the south. A long siege would be impossible to withstand, and the lack of leadership did not sit well among the warriors.

While King Penhda considered Urith and Oslaf to be traitors, Wilgam asked for the two men to remain as free until a successor for the king was named. Seeing the dire situation in place, the elders reluctantly gave their blessing on the idea, stating the two men's fighting skills necessary to help those in the fort. The big warrior smiled when he heard the news, knowing the elders did not want to anger the Esterblud tribe coming to help against the Aberffraw. Both warriors were from the village of Cilgarran.

Limping from his still injured leg, the Clovel Destroyer crossed the ramparts while he struggled to hold his temper. Inaction in the face of an enemy gave him a bitter taste, similar to defeat. Unknown within annals of Kamin invasions, over forty *cuggles* and other types of ships filled the harbor. Each ship was unloading fighters and ossanes to smaller craft which carried them toward the beach. Further up the beach, the man watched a steady stream of villagers leaving the port town of Eran, the refugees taking their carts loaded with goods on the road past the fort, heading to Cilgarran. A few stragglers could be seen moving about in the large village. He hoped those who remained would leave soon. Seasons of warfare told him such people either ended up dead or as slaves when the enemy entered the towns.

Unconsciously, he rubbed the long scar running down the on his face as he thought about the events leading up to his arrival at the capital of Esterblud. Hanging on his back was the Shield of Skool, the formidable weapon of the gods. Nearly complete with only one piece remaining to be discovered, the shield, combined with his Clovel Sword and the amulet around his neck held enough power to wipe out the fleet before him. The thought sickened him. While the warrior realized the enemy would happily remove his head, the Aberffraw were only on the beach because of the lies and betrayals placed by those who wanted the shield. Urith understood better than most that this war came from the gods. He knew the deities of the Sky Realm and the underworld used the rivalries of kingdoms in their quest to stop him. The gods were afraid of the Skool and the power in the hands of a mortal. The immortals would be happy with the slaughter of people like him to ensure the Skool remained incomplete. That was the burden the Clovel Destroyer bore.

"You seem lost in thought," Oslaf's words broke his uncle's examination of the enemy and his own beliefs. Urith looked down the stone steps next to him as his nephew with Henther climbed toward the battlements.

"It's about time you decided to wake," Urith gave Oslaf a slight grin as he limped away, allowing them to enter the narrow walkway.

"I couldn't help myself, Henther kept me up all night," quipped the young warrior as he dodged the woman's slap at his head. The couple pulled next to Urith, smiling at each other. At first, their playfulness between his nephew and the former *docke* got under his skin, but the senior warrior grew to respect the ex-prostitute during their travel together. Steadfast and loyal, Henther carried many of the same traits as her father who Urith remembered vividly. Urith also believed he acted the same way when he met his wife, many seasons before. Once, he carried a similar feeling for Mivraa after they met as well. However, such genuine affection was fleeting now. Mivraa carried a fierce grudge against those in the Sky Realm. The need for vengeance forced the goddess away from her lover. No thoughts of the future were possible until the Skool was complete and the chaos coming from the underworld stopped.

Oslaf saw his uncle's pained expression. "The coming battle concerns you but why the worry. With the power on your back, the Aberffraw have no ability to defeat us. You control the Skool,"

Urith stared at him, anger filling his face. "Does that appear noble to you? To destroy many good and honorable fighters who have been lied to and sent by a corrupt king. Even worse, many of these warriors will follow their dead king if I use this Skool." The big man shook his head in disgust. "I've thought about this, and I believe this battle has been set up by the gods. Is it honorable to use a weapon against them which is meant to defeat gods?" He turned away, staring over the fleet. "I'm sure many of them would say the same as you if they had possession of the shield."

6

"But they are the enemy. Are you not Esterblud?" Oslaf asked, perplexed at the hesitation in his uncle. It was a side of the man he seldom encountered.

Urith nodded, lowering his head a moment before turning back to his nephew. "Of course and these fighters the beach are my mortal enemies. Our kingdoms fought over land long before you and I walked into battle. Now, let me ask you a question. Do you believe the gods use their monsters to kill only Esterblud or Aberffraw? Of course not! We've seen they send such beasts to kill everyone. It does not take a seer to understand these same gods are happy to have people slaughtering other people. Our journey in search of the Skool has convinced me that we have gods using men to create the carnage we find."

"No, hear me out," the man raised his hand to silence the coming protest from his nephew. "The deities are playing us for fools. Recently, all of us were forced into a fight with gods of the Sky Realm. The god Uugor we once gave offerings to in the temples. For your support, the god of the sea gave you that wound in your belly. And do you remember what that creature said he would do to your woman, Henther?" The giant warrior turned back to look at the ocean.

"Tell me the truth. Do you feel any need to worship these creatures now? These are the same entities we are told to pray for their blessings, to help us in our time of need." Urith went silent for a moment. "Why should I wish to kill others to receive the approval of such entities?"

"I've remembered how priests we're supposed to trust once begged the underworld god, Caruun, to trap the souls of my wife and my father in his underworld." He paused his voice nearly a growl. "The only help from the Sky Realm we have found comes from Mivraa. Now, would you take offerings to the temples for those half-brothers of Mivraa? These are the same ones who raped her and left her as food for the *ranqels.*"

Oslaf wanted to say something, but he realized his uncle was correct. The gods of the Sky Realm tried to kill all of them for the Skool on two occasions. He saw how much the demigoddess changed in the mountains of her torment. And, he remembered the small village of Hyropda, destroyed by the gods as their little group traveled through the town. Oslaf lowered head slightly, suddenly feeling a bitterness rise within him.

Urith's voice softened a bit when he glanced at his nephew. "It's good you remember what we've gone through. Now, ask yourself why

7

we are forced to fight these men from Cahmais? Who benefits from this bloodshed, human or gods? We already know both leaders who once ruled the kingdoms are dead. So any battle will only lead to more death and turmoil in our lands. And we tell ourselves if we die a glorious death, our spirits will live for eternity among those gods."

The big warrior spat on the stone floor under his feet. "I'm sure I don't want to see such creatures again, let alone to live with them. So, think of my words. Then, remind me who the enemy is." The giant Esterblud turned and walked away before Oslaf could reply. The nephew started to follow, but Henther grabbed his arm.

"Let him be. He has the world on his shoulders," the blond woman told him softly. "His words make sense. I wish more people would listen to him."

"Maybe, but those Aberffraw warriors will not hesitate to kill and maim as many of us as they can in the coming battle," he watched as his uncle went down the steps leading to the courtyard. "The fight that's coming will not be stopped. I hope my uncle doesn't forget that."

"He won't. From what I've seen, he'll always fight. It's in his blood, just like you. Right now, those from Cahmais make themselves the enemy. Soon they will realize the gods are the real foe." Henther smiled at him, but Oslaf just grunted, telling her that she did not really believe the Aberffraw would change.

"Ok, it is just hope," she said as she gave him a kiss on his smooth cheek. He smiled and put his arm around her, and he guided them along the stone walkway.

Not long after Urith stepped into the courtyard, the guards began shouting, pointing to a small group of enemy fighters walking toward the fortress. Looking out through the closed wooden grating at the entrance, Urith and Oslaf saw the small group of enemy warriors coming their way. The rest of increasing numbers of Aberffraw stayed back, waiting for more of their comrades. A few rowing vessels, each filled with more men and material, slowly made their way toward the beach from the bay, reinforcing the perception of overwhelming Cahmais strength building on the sand by the water.

Draca, an elder from the Eranis tribe, and Bucnar, a Gramcle clan leader, moved to the gate. They were council members to King Penhda and, as such, they would lead any discussions with the enemy. The elders told Wilgam, leader of the fort guards, to gather several men to escort them to meet the group of Aberffraw. Both of the elders stared at Urith and Oslaf when the two fighters joined them. While they said nothing against the giant warrior who made it clear he would be coming with them, their expressions revealed they were not happy at Urith's actions. Urith's past position as a leader of the *Geniht,* or kinship guard, gave him some authority, forcing the older men to remain quiet, despite their suspicions.

The small group went through the gates and underneath the lifting gate. Stepping past the trail which led to the village of Eran, the warriors walked toward the enemy leaders coming their way. The elders carried only their swords which hung on their baldric belts. By leaving their helmets and shields back in the fort, the leaders displayed their positions as peacemakers. However, Urith and Oslaf carried their helmets on their belts as well as their shields over their backs. Wilgam and his guards remained slightly behind the elders, each armed lightly as well.

As Oslaf walked with his uncle, he wondered what Urith was thinking. Generally, his uncle would not join in political discussions against their enemy. Oslaf took a quick glance back at the fort, catching a glimpse of Henther who was back at the top of the battlements. She stood next to Fedelm. He did not see Mivraa but assumed she was somewhere in the fortress, looking over their procession.

The two enemy groups met on the cusp of a small dune ridge. Six Aberffraw fighters, dressed in their full armor and brilliantly adorned in spotless blue tunics, stopped a couple of paces away as some of their brethren watched the meeting from the ridge behind. The enemy leader, his silver helmet decorated with the white and black *karker* feathers of the Aberffraw guard, went to the two elders who stepped forward from the rest of the Esterbluds. Urith, followed by Oslaf, veered away from the Wilgam and his warriors, placing themselves on the side of Aberffraw leader and his men. Uncomfortable with someone on his flank, the enemy leader gave Urith and Oslaf a glare. Urith returned his death sneer.

"We come to give you one chance to save yourselves," said the leader haughtily when he turned his attention back to the elders.

Draca remained unmoved by the man's words. "And who is foolish enough to land upon the lands of King Penhda?"

"I'm called Mycru, leader of this Cahmais fleet sent by the great King Asgurd." The man placed his hands on his hips staring

9

triumphantly at the group. When Urith grunted and spit on the ground, Mycru gave him another glare. "My king comes from the south with just punishment against your lands. I've been told by messenger, spikes holding the heads of those who resist already line the roads. However, I can give some leeway. If you leave the fortress before the sun sets in the east, my men will spare the lives of you and the villagers."

Wilgam and his men took offense at the Aberffraw words, immediately reaching for their swords and cursing. Urith scowled at the enemy leader and Oslaf quickly recognized his uncle rising temper at such words. Draca turned, telling his guarding party to remain quiet.

"And if we refuse this offer, what makes you think you can remain on our lands to siege this fort? Your ships cannot sustain your warriors for long." Bucnar, the other elder, spoke up. "Once your men have empty stomachs, we will be asking for your sword and surrender."

"Your eyes are getting old," Mycru laughed, "behind us are more ships filled with supplies. We have enough supplies to last the winter. But it does not matter, my overlord will join us soon where we will strangle your land like a snake. When the king arrives, his vengeance at the death of his son will be merciless. I recommend you save yourselves from this fate. I can be lenient, for the moment."

The look between the two elders indicated they believed the Aberffraw leader. They still doubted the messenger's words of the monster given to them the day before. The two old men were unable to hide their worried expressions. They showed their anxiousness as a large group of Aberffraw warriors moved away from the beach, heading toward the village. Urith and Oslaf eyes watched the enemy leaders who stood nearby while listening to the conversations. Both knew their enemy would be attacking the village to pressure the elders within the fort and to scavenge what might be left.

"So, we have a coward offering our lives?" Suddenly Urith spoke up loudly, to be heard over the murmuring conversations going on between the Esterbluds. Urith stepped closer to the enemy leader. "Apparently, you don't realize your king is dead, and the rest of your Cahmais army lies rotting in the sun."

Urith stopped about an arm's length away. "Now, since I'm a fair man as well, I give you a chance to call off your warriors heading to the village. You are being duped by the gods. The underworld opened and destroyed King Asgurd and his men. We receive this news last sunset."

The leader of the fleet shook his head smugly. "You think me a fool to believe such a tale? No doubt you are the jester for your people."

Urith's eyes narrowed at the insult. "I'm Urith. Perhaps you have heard of me? I'm the *wafaoil* who destroyed many of your Aberffraw fighters at Du-Rinell. They evaporated like the smoke in the wind. I ask you to remember this before you make the mistake of your life." He slowly put on his black helmet.

Mycru shook his head laughing as the men behind him growled and cursed. "It is a good joke giant man, but we are not fools. The great Lyncus came from that battle after he saved the reminder of our warriors from that evil magic brought by the goddess, Mivraa. She is now outcast among the gods for her work."

"Lyncus!" Urith gave a triumphant laugh, catching a glimpse of Oslaf putting his helmet on. "That little man lost to me in a fair fight on the beaches of Ynyover. Who do you think gave the *pitshog* his broken leg?"

The enemy's amusement suddenly stopped at the insult to the son of their king. His hand on his sword, Mycru grew angry at the abuse. "Your slight our great leaders is an insult to the gods who are on our side. The Sacred Overlord, Satres himself joins in our conquest of Esterblud. No longer can you hide behind the skirts of your women. No gods will protect you now."

His words about the Sacred Overlord had an immediate effect on the group of Esterbluds, in particular, Urith.

Mycru turned to Draca, coldly declaring he was losing his patience. "For the last time, do you surrender your fort to us? I will spare you this time, but I will not repeat myself."

Before Draca had a chance to respond, Urith spoke while he laid his hand on the pommel of the Clovel Sword. "The Esterbluds will not surrender to you. Leave this beach, or you will kiss the ass of Caruun when you reach the underworld."

The enemy's face turned red at the insult hurled at him. Mycru screamed for his men to attack as he started to pull his sword. He was only able to get the weapon about halfway out of the scabbard when Urith whipped the Clovel sword's long blade across the man's belly. Although armed with chain mail and leather, the sword sliced open the man's abdomen. As the enemy screamed from the hot pain as his entrails fell out, Urith swung around and landing the sword blade deep into Mycru's neck and shoulder. The Aberffraw leader had died before his body hit the ground while Urith held up his bloody sword triumphantly.

In the momentary pause, the fighters looked around in disbelief. In a quick instant, Urith started a major battle without the consent of the elders. But the fight was on as men suddenly rushed to attack while struggling to pull their weapons. Oslaf struck down the closest enemy who fell next to his leader, while others came at them. The enemy fighters tried to surround the Esterbluds who were blocking swords and spears with their swords, unable to pull their shields hanging behind their backs.

While the fighting quickly intensified, the two elders backed away. The other Esterblud fighters rushed forward, joining Urith and Oslaf in the center of the upheaval. One enemy warrior worked around Urith's side during the sword upon sword strikes, nearly ending the giant's life. The enemy rushed with his spear toward the Esterblud who barely escaped being skewered by the timely arrival of Wilgam. The leader of the fortress guards ended the life of the Aberffraw with a single stroke, cutting into the unprotected head of the enemy.

The retreating elders stopped Esterblud fighters coming from the fort to help their comrades. Forcing them back, the leaders began yelling for those to remain inside the fortress to prepare for an assault. The elderly men tried to run, but their youthful strides had long since left them. Neither man attempted to inform the small group of Esterblud fighters locked in combat behind them.

Seeing the retreat, Wilgam ordered his men into a defensive wall, yelling for Oslaf and Urith to join with them. Recognizing they had little choice, Urith, and his nephew pulled back, moving to the edge of the line while trying to keep the onrushing enemy from flanking them. The swelling ranks of Aberffraw enemy fighters continued their piecemeal attacks, forcing one of Wilgam's men to the ground where he was quickly hacked to death. Oslaf struck down an enemy fighter coming at him from the side, nearly falling to the ground when the man tumbled into him. The young warrior dropped to a knee, pulling his shield just in time to fend off a spear jabbed at him.

Nearby, two Aberffraw men rushed forward trying to ram their shields and spears into Urith. However, his deadly Clovel Sword came crashing down on the closest fighter, slicing through the wood and severing the man's arm. Unfortunately for the Esterblud, the other

Aberffraw ran into the giant, knocking Urith down to the sandy ground. As he prepared for the coming blow, Urith saw the glimpse of Oslaf sword slice deep into the back of the enemy's leg, the blow sending the Aberffraw to the ground, screaming while he bled to death.

Scrambling to their feet, both uncle and nephew rejoined the dwindling line of Esterbluds who fell back to the fortress. Some of the defenders were able to get their shields to help evade the incoming spears. However, the group heard the thick wooden doors closing after the elders reached the safety inside. Glancing back to see the entrance to the fort nearly closed, Urith caught sight of Fedelm screaming at the guards. The small woman jumped on the back of one man who was trying to push the gate closed while Henther was next to the prophetess, using a staff to help prop open the doors for the warriors outside. However, other guards quickly overwhelmed them, finally pushing the gates shut.

"Cursed old men, they've left us out here," yelled Wilgam when he saw their escape cut off. The fighter pulled around his shield in time to ward off a spear thrown at them. Oslaf swore loudly at the news, his belly beginning to burn from reinjuring his wound. Luckily, the attacks coming toward the line were uncoordinated as the bulk of the enemy struggled to run the long distance across the sandy beach.

Urith tried to parry a sword stroke; suddenly he felt the fire of a spear slice through his chain armor as two men attacked him. He let out a howl, savagely striking down the enemy warrior who attempted to push the shaft of the spear deeper. The weapon tip painfully hung in his flesh while it remained embedded in the chain mail. Hindering him when he backed up, the big warrior followed the line of fighters who finally reached the closed gate.

"Head over this way," a familiar voice yelled, and Urith saw the silhouette of Mivraa, standing near the corner of the fort. He immediately understood she had a way of escape.

"Go over there," groaned the giant warrior as he pushed Oslaf toward their escape. Moving back from the attacks allowed Urith to pull the Shield of Skool from behind his back. Almost immediately, he used the shield to fend off two spears coming at them from the small wave of attacking enemy fighters. Suddenly, Esterblud arrows and spears began to rain down from the fort into the group of Aberffraw warriors. The aerial onslaught allowed the remaining Esterbluds to move away toward the side of the fortress. Wilgam, taking a spear in the back, fell down. Urith and Oslaf ran next to his wounded friend. A lone Aberffraw foolishly closed in on the injured man, but Oslaf took the enemy down with a precise strike to the man's throat. Urith directed several of Wilgam's wounded men to the edge of the fort before he stepped in front of Oslaf who was pulling Wilgam to his feet. He used his shield to stop several incoming arrows and spears while he stood at the end of the defender's line. Sparks flew from the iron tips striking the Skool. Then, another round of arrows shot from the battlements above, sending the enemy attackers to the ground, dead and wounded. The covering onslaught of arrows allowed the last defenders outside the walls to reach the side of the fort. Fortunately, the attacking wave of Aberffraw warriors fell back, and the fighting came to a momentary halt as the enemy retreated out of range of the arrows.

Oslaf and Wilgam followed the remaining warriors to a line of empty barrels which they used for cover. Urith limped along, finally reaching Mivraa who waited, crouched at the end of the fort, holding her crystal spear.

"I don't know what you are doing here but it's good to see you," Urith told the demigoddess who did not return his smile. She looked over the others, pulling her shield from one arm.

"I'm here to save you again," she told him matter-of-factly, pointing to a thick rope hanging down along the wall. "Let me see that wound." She made the man turn. "This is getting to be routine every time you go to meet someone."

"Well, you could have just left the door open," Urith gave her his sneer smile which she didn't see. The woman slowly began to work to remove on the spear still stuck in the coat of mail.

Above them, Henther and Fedelm stared down at the group, waiting for the fighters to climb the ropes which they hung down despite the orders of the elders inside. Oslaf tied one rope around a protesting Wilgam, signaling for him to be hoisted into the fort. Another line came down, and soon most of the remaining warriors pulled themselves over the battlements. While Urith grumbled as the woman finally pulled the pointed tip free from his shoulder muscle, Oslaf waited.

"Get your butt on that rope. We'll be up soon enough," Urith growled at his nephew, before giving him a wink.

Reassured at the gesture, Oslaf started pulling himself up. "Just don't wait around too long. I might need you to tell me how to take a pee!" He called back.

Mivraa reached for the other rope help Urith climb the wall, but she stopped suddenly when she saw the giant warrior moving away from the wall. He stared at the thick smoke coming from the village.

"It's just a few of the enemy taking their vengeance out on the village. Anybody who is still in that village is a fool. Come on; let's get back to the fort. It won't be long until the enemy regroups and start coming at us again." Her tone was matter-of-fact. And it rubbed Urith the wrong way.

"No, those men are not warriors, just butchers of the unarmed. Their leader is dead, so now they will spread like parasites seeking out the weakest to terrorize. I've seen it before. They will strip the land and try to wait us out. We both know the coming siege will be long and painful. Any person who remains near us will be stripped of everything."

"There's nothing you can do." She reminded him.

To her surprise, the giant man stepped back to the hanging rope. He handed the end to her.

"No, I've had enough of this. We both know the war was started by gods who live to torment us. Since Oslaf and I landed on that beach back in Ynyover, we have been sent into one catastrophe after another." Urith's gray eyes grew dark as he recalled the long journey back to Esterblud. "And you know that the gods are always in the background, manipulating what happens to the people of this world."

"You cannot stop this, you are not a god," she reminded him, and he looked at her crossly.

"Maybe not," he conceded. "Still, we know something that most people don't. Those in that village will be sent to the underworld just like my wife. Butchered and killed by worthless men, those spirits left in that village will be unable to get to the Sky Realm. And for some strange reason, I think what's happening is related to the monsters we hear about. Who do you think should fix this?"

Urith slid his Shield of Skool over his forearm before he began a slow, limping jog away toward the village. He refused to acknowledge the protests from Mivraa or the cries from his friends looking down from the battlement above. His mind made up, the man felt a strange calm befall him. He swore he could hear his long dead wife whispering in his ear. She told him it was time to right the terrible injustices of the realms. Despite the pain in his arm and his back, the giant man felt a mounting fury fill him. A wave of adrenaline enveloped him. Death for a righteous cause turned into a searing flame of craving. He carried a desire for vengeance.

As she watched his deliberate pace toward the village, the demigoddess heard the voice as well. The woman recognized the sounds of the spirits since they often spoke to her. However, this voice was unfamiliar to the women. And the warrior goddess never heard a soul crying out for vengeance. The sound carried through shouts around her by men and females in the fortress above her. While the spirits of nature filled the three realms, those nearby remained invisible. Realizing they were hiding in the shadows of trees and rocks, the demigoddess listened to the words of hope and encouragement that one elemental gave a human and she felt the hair on the back of her neck rise. Suddenly, like the small cruicads who suddenly filled the air with their sounds, more of the elementals around the area began to repeat the words heard by Urith.

"Doltais!"

"Gcothrem!"

The air around her filled with the words as over and over again, the words kept repeating, justice and vengeance. The demigoddess looked around, sure that words could be heard by all. But those in the fort still only yelled for her and Urith to return. For the first time, she heard the haunting cry of the condemned spirits rang out in defiance the natural order around them. Shaking her head with disbelief, the warrior woman slid on her shield. Taking a deep breath, Mivraa slowly began to follow him into the village of Eran. She hoped her vow to keep Urith alive would not end in the coming fight.

Heavy smoke drifting across the beach meant only a few Aberffraw noticed the tall warrior walking to the village. The bulk of enemy fighters still regrouped along the beach near their ships. Those few enemy fighters who entered the village earlier focused their rampage near several burning buildings in the center of the square. Urith and Mivraa followed the main road past the small wattle and daub plaster homes to larger merchant buildings. Near the middle of Eran, the Esterblud fighter saw the first Aberffraw. So focused upon looting and terrorizing villagers, the men paid little attention to the giant warrior in a green tunic coming down the main street. Two men in armor laughed in delight as

16

they terrorized a merchant family who did not escape in time. As they beat a semi-conscious merchant who was bound to the pole outside the small shop using the flats of their swords, the two thugs stopped to lift mugs of heathmead in a repulsive toast to their host. Just inside the front door, the screams of the wife could be heard as men slapped and beat the naked woman who struggled against her defilement. Urith saw the couple's barely weaned child crying at the doorstep as he witnessed the madness.

The Esterblud said nothing was he walked up to the first Aberffraw, swiftly decapitating the man before the enemy could turn to face death. The other enemy fighter dropped his mug just in time to receive an uppercut from the blade of the Clovel Sword. The wicked slash from the metal sliced up through the dying man's jaw and sending his helmet tumbling into the air. Without a pause, Urith sprinted a few paces bursting into the building where he skewered a man in the back who was trying to mount the woman. Before the man's comrades could react, the Esterblud stepped over the dying man, smashing an Aberffraw in the face with his shield. There was a sickening crunch from the impact, and the man fell back into the wall with blood covering his staring face. Turning toward the last enemy, the partially naked man tried to surrender. However, on this day, Urith gave no quarter as he swung his sword across the enemy's chest, sending the opponent to the floor face first. The blood covered Esterblud walked out of the building, meeting Mivraa who carried her two-sided crystal spear at the ready.

"You might have saved one for me," the woman's sarcasm was evident.

Urith grunted, "You'll have plenty more before the sun rests." There was no humor in his face, his gray eyes fixed in a deadly fury. He quickly strode along the street, heading to the sound of more screams while the goddess of Haligulf took the time to cut the struggling villager free from his restraint. The man thanked her, asking for her name so he could give thanks to the Sky gods.

The demigoddess stopped, her eyes revealing the hate she carried to those gods. "You fool, I'm Mivraa. If I ever hear pray to that worthless scum in the Sky Realm, I'll come back and rip your heart out!" She hurried after the giant warrior, paying no attention as the stunned man stammered his thanks to her. He could not believe the anger he witnessed in demigoddess of Haligulf as his wife and child came running to him.

17

~~~

When Urith entered the village, Oslaf attempted to climb down from the battlements to join his uncle. However, he was stopped by the combined efforts of Henther and Fedelm. They reminded him about the Aberffraw warriors who gathered in various large groups on the beach as they regrouped. Men came from some of the beached ships, some carrying crude ladders as they gathered items to assault the fort. The women convinced Oslaf that he was needed there.

"I don't understand what my uncle is thinking," Oslaf confided to Henther. "I can only guess Urith didn't believe the Aberffraw would regroup so quickly after the death of Mycue," he sighed as pulled himself back from the stone ledge. "They are better fighters than we suspected."

As he looked over the battleground, he could not see either his uncle or the demigoddess in the smoke obscured village. The enemy on the beach remained focused on the fort.

"He must have something in mind because Mivraa followed him. Maybe he expected the enemy to break up and begin to go after him in the village," Henther wondered aloud. "But it seems too impulsive to be a clear strategy." Her comments reminded Oslaf, the woman probably knew as much as he did about the tactics of warfare.

"That's my uncle, curse the gods. We need to see how Wilgam fares. He'll be necessary for what's coming." Oslaf hurried along the top of the fort wall as the women followed on his heels.

The group found Wilgam in the open courtyard next to the entrance of the fort. He was in the care of a *mhoda*, a healer who just finished placing cloth bandages upon his back shoulder and on the man's leg wounds. Oslaf knelt next to the man, asking how he was doing.

"About as well as you I suspect," the leader of the guards told Oslaf who looked down at his belly where he saw the bloodstain from his old wound. The giant Esterblud's fight against Uugor, the sea god, not long before their small group arrived at the fort left Oslaf with an unhealed wound. It was now reopened during the brief but bitter battle earlier.

"I'll survive," Oslaf declared, "How about you? It looks like we have our enemy coming soon. I think they will send their men to attack us in revenge."

The warrior immediately struggled to sit up despite the protests of the healer. The man got to his feet, supported by Oslaf. "Why haven't my people told me of this?"

18

"Because I've taken over to defend this fortress," Draca said to the group as he stepped forward. The elder man looked at Oslaf directly. "Your uncle saw to it that we would have this battle, it is my responsibility to defend Eran for our king."

"I've been charged with the defense of the fort, Draca. You have no authority over me or my men." Wilgam confronted the old warrior. Shocked at the exchange, those who supported Draca expressed their anger by pushing forward with grumbles and threats. Within the Esterblud society, loyalties encouraged deference from the younger warriors. Wilgam stood his ground in spite of tradition.

"You are not well enough to lead the defense of this fort," claimed Draca as he looked around the fighters who gathered around the group. "Once we get our men organized, we can talk with the enemy again. Perhaps that fool Urith will kill himself in the village and allow us to save ourselves."

"What are you talking about, you feeble wench? You will not surrender this place to the Cahmais. Elder or not, I'll cut you down and drink from your skull," Oslaf started after the surprised Draca as some of the leader's tribe began to close in against the young giant.

"Enough," yelled out Wilgam as pushed in front of Oslaf as he grabbed the man's shoulder while pulling his sword. Pushing between the Esterblud and the elder, the leader of guards was quickly joined by his loyal men who pressed into the growing commotion.

"Everyone, back away now!" Wilgam shook with fury, his usual calm shattered by the infighting around him. He directed his anger at Oslaf and Draca. "I swear both of you will join me in the fight against our enemy or I'll have my men throw you in the vault to rot. Which will it be?" Momentarily stunned, the crowd around him grew silent.

"Well?" Wilgam stared at the elder who slowly backed down. Draca realized the numbers were not on his side in this encounter.

"As you said, you are charged with the defense of the fort. Until our king changes this, we will follow you." Draca had difficulty getting the words out.

"I'll fight with Wilgam and follow his orders," Oslaf stated aloud to emphasize his backing of fortress leader. The large man glared in the direction of some who muttered in the background about the Esterbluds who betrayed their dead king. For a brief moment, another exchange between warriors looked imminent until Wilgam suddenly ordered his men to their positions.

Disregarding the background talk, the leader of the fort forced himself through the crowd as he slowly hobbled to the narrow stairway. Wilgam gave orders to his men who quickly took off with others, heading to various parts of the fort. As he climbed the steps, Wilgam was helped by his closest comrade, Erran. Oslaf followed with Henther and Fedelm in tow. The two women noticed Draca remained behind, nursing his grudge against Wilgam. When the small group reached the battlements, they observed the smoke spreading rapidly from the docks. Racing from the waterfront by the ocean breeze, the flames jumped from one thatched roof to the next.

"So it starts," Henther stated to no one. Oslaf caught the woman's pale face and distant stare. It was evident his lover recalled a painful memory.

"Urith better get out of there soon," Fedelm whispered under her breath and Oslaf overheard the comment. He looked at her, and her face turned slightly red as she looked away. It was the first time Urith's nephew realized the depth of the seer's feeling about his uncle. He could not help but smile before turning back to the spectacle. But his smile quickly changed when he saw what Wilgam was looking at.

"I wouldn't worry about the village as much as those ships coming in."

The leader of the fortress gazed at a long line of shallow draft ships moving toward the beach. The single gray sails on each vessel puffed out wide by the push of the incoming breeze. Filled with more armed men, the blue of their tunics along with the glint of silver weapons appeared colorfully festive in the distance. However, the number of enemy fighters on the beach would soon be overwhelming. The sight gave everyone pause.

"With that many warriors, we will not last for many sunrises," Oslaf nodded to the beach where men began to dismantle one of the ships, using the wood to build various items.

"I've seen this before. The enemy realized they would have scarce building materials in this area after the village burned. They will dismantle some of their ships to make ladders, siege towers, and battering rams." Henther spoke louder this time, catching the attention of Wilgam.

The man turned to her, surprise evident on his face at her knowledge of the situation.

"How do you know such things? I cannot place your accent but what women know of siege battles? The last time a city fell to such an invasion was…"

"The great palace of the Vulthnal kings," the young woman finished the sentence for him.

"Yes, that's it. How do you know of this?" Wilgam stepped toward her.

Henther looked to Oslaf who shook his head slightly. The woman sighed. "It will come out eventually." She squeezed his hand before turning back to Wilgam and his man who stared at her. Curiosity and suspicion filled their faces.

"I'm the daughter of Kirowan, who led the defense of the palace against the Regiussa bandits. I know well what happens." There was defiance in her words.

There was initial disbelief in her statement until Oslaf interjected. "You can trust her word. She knew of the fight between Kirowan and Urith that gave my uncle his scar. Urith knows she speaks the truth. She has seen much in her time."

"But we know Kirowan lost the palace," Erran spoke up. "Why would we trust her word?"

"My father was betrayed by a *satgert* to put a ruler on the throne for his puppet. Kirowan would have saved that palace. I saw the entire siege and battle. I know what happens to those that lose the fight. Do you want to learn or die here?" The woman's anger flashed as she stepped toward Erran, starting to pull her sword from the scabbard hooked on her leather belt. The former *docke* appeared every bit the warrior as Mivraa at the moment.

Oslaf grabbed her arm, quickly moving in front of her. Wilgam suddenly laughed. "I have no doubts she is the daughter of such a great leader." He stopped and pointed to the beach. "But we need answers. What do you suggest we do about it?"

The woman did not hesitate. "You notice how close the ships are lined in a row coming ashore. Soon they will lie in a long line on the beach. When the tide drops, they will be stranded. The enemy doesn't care because they know they outnumber those in the fort. They intend to wait until they can breach the walls using those ships for building material. Do you agree?"

Wilgam nodded. "Yes, it is a good assessment. We are too many to flee without a slaughter and not enough to fight them head on."

"Then, wait until nightfall and strike their ships with fire." The woman's eyes lit up at the thought.

The men stared at her. Erran blurted out, "How do you expect us to walk through army? Do you want us to take a casual stroll along the beach with torches the whole way?"

Henther smiled sweetly, sarcasm dripped from her words. "I don't expect you to do much, but if you know of Mivraa's power to transform and hide, all it will take is some dry brush and lots of lamp oil. We can light up the night sky with their wood. Plus, they will still have some stores of food on those ships as well. If the whole thing goes up, how long can they last?"

There was a long pause as the group thought about her plan. It was both brilliant and risky.

"I pity the fools who try to return from the beach with the flames exposing them." Wilgam turned back to the view before them.

"That's why we need Mivraa to return soon." Fedelm blurted out. "This is one time I wish that demigoddess was here."

Oslaf watched at the village, the smoke and flames covering the area. Then, he saw the black helmet. Soon a glint of light came from a large warrior's shield as Urith stepped out of the smoke. Alongside him, the goddess of Haligulf strode with him, her auburn hair nearly red in the fading light. Behind them, a small line of people emerged as well. Men, women, and children moved swiftly trying to catch up with the long strides of Urith and Mivraa. The few refugees left in the village were following the couple up along a back path toward high ground.

"That crazy son of a *fealharan* is leading those people to be slaughtered. Look at those Aberffraw scouts watching them." Wilgam's disbelief evident, he turned to Oslaf. "What is your uncle doing?"

Urith's nephew could only shake his head as he replied. "I don't get it. My uncle must be playing by his own rules now. I just hope he knows what he's doing."

Hurrying along a steep path, Urith ordered the remaining villagers to move quickly. He recognized the trail they took would expose them to the enemy warriors. In fact, he counted on that fact since the Cahmais adversaries had only a few ossane available on the beach able to catch them. The rest of the army would be focused on their plans to destroy the Esterblud fighters inside the fort, not a few refugees trying to flee.

As Urith expected, several of the men got on the closest mounts and sped after the villagers. Urith counted three of the ossanes following the path while others went toward the burning village to see what remained. The Esterblud broke away from the small group of villagers, telling Mivraa to take the road across the ridge above them. He told her he would meet them at the fortress. The demigoddess paused as if she wanted to say something before she groused at the villagers to move faster.

Looking for the best spot to take on the fast moving enemy, Urith took several paces up where the path leveled off after going over a ridge. There, the man waited after pulling off his helmet to wipe the sweat from his forehead with one of the unbloodied spots remaining on his tunic. For the moment, he was out of sight of the oncoming ossanes and armored warriors, but he knew they would be coming fast. The mounts were galloping across the sandy soil toward him, and he soon heard the panting of the long-necked animals as they strained to haul their masters up the steep terrain. Putting his helmet back on, the warrior gripped his sword and adjusted his shield. Crouching as he moved a couple of paces to one side of the trail, Urith waited.

Just when the first rider reached the summit of the ridge, the Esterblud rose up, charging the man and his mount from the side. The Clovel Sword gave a slight humming sound as it arched high in the air, coming down on the shoulder of the Aberffraw enemy. The enemy warrior let out a surprised yell at the glancing blow which cut through his armor. Before the man was able to reach for his weapon, Urith quickly turned full circle using the momentum of his swing to embed the tip deep into the enemy's exposed side. The thin leather covering did little to stop the sword from killing the man.

As he pulled his sword from the first warrior, Urith felt another rider nearly on him, and he could not avoid the hammer blow of a club striking his helmet. The blow dazed the Esterblud, but his experience made his moves almost automatic. Following the sound of the second rider's ossane, Urith swung his sword low into the unarmored legs of the mount. The scream of the animal filled the air as it instinctively rose up, causing its rider to grab the saddle and lose his weapon. While the enemy held on to the seat, the Esterblud reached up to pull the man off the wounded horse. No quarter was given as Urith planted his foot on the fallen enemy's neck and jammed the tip of his sword through the eye socket of the man's helmet, feeling the death shudder under his boot.

The Esterblud warrior ran out of time as the final Aberffraw enemy decided to run his mount over Urith. The fighter and his mount closed so fast; the giant warrior could only throw up his shield in defense at the last minute. Urith's decision saved him. The charging ossane ran headlong into the nearly complete Shield of Skool. A lightning bolt shot out from the impact and the blast, along with the power of the large animal, sent the giant Esterblud flying across the ground. Landing hard on the flat rocks covering the area, Urith heard a bone snap in his arm holding his shield before he felt the wave of pain. Fortunately for Urith, his opponent was thrown completely from his mount, landing several paces away in the sand. Urith forced himself to his knees as his arm suddenly when limp and he snarled at the blinding pain. He watched as the enemy's ossane kicked briefly before dying from the shock of the Skool while the enemy quickly got to his feet. Grabbing his spear from the ground, the Aberffraw charged Urith who could barely lift his shield.

Forced to defend himself with his massive Clovel Sword, the giant warrior parried the wooden spear speeding toward his midsection. Striking away the spear, the agile opponent came in close and used the wooden handle of his spear to lash out at Urith's broken arm. The giant warrior yelled out at the pain, unable to defend his wounded area. The enemy quickly turned around to strike at Urith again. Seeing the weakness, the Aberffraw hit the wounded warrior's arm with a short sword he pulled from his belt. Urith sent a wild swing of his sword, but the enemy neatly dodged away. The smaller, quicker man ran in at Urith's wounded side again and again struck him with a sharp stab into the back shoulder. Urith suddenly sensed an opening from the man's tactics. The Esterblud dropped his sword arm, feigning he was heavily wounded by the last attack. Breathing hard, Urith called the man a coward for failing to face him head on. As he expected, the enemy warrior struck again from the side. However, this time Urith gathered all of his strength and lifted the shield with his broken arm while turning his upper body. As the Esterblud cried out in agony, his enemy ran his sword into the Shield of Skool. The electric bolt which shot out of the shield nearly evaporated the man's arm. Falling to his knees, the enemy warrior could only look up briefly before his head was removed by Urith.

Chapter 2: Prisoner of Eran

Outside the tall walls surrounding Citadel of Br-Ynys, Satres brought the cart to stop. As he looked at the important stronghold overlooking the Maflow Sea, the man felt a little like the first time he came to this place when he was younger. But he had little time for reflection. During the long ride back from Esterblud lands where he witnessed the destruction of his allies, the Aberffraw warriors, the Sacred Overlord mulled over a thousand different ideas. He needed a story to tell the Majireef Council. The debacle, which led to the death of King Asgurd and much of the invading force he joined, left the Sacred Overlord exposed and vulnerable. Satres had pushed through an unprecedented alliance with the king of Cahmais. That meant Satres understood many on the council might target him as a scapegoat in their ambitions. In the rough and tumble politics of the satgerts who controlled the temples throughout much of Kamin, this failure could lead him into disaster. As if he needed more trouble, many defeated Aberffraw warriors were streaming back into Ynyover. With so many of the Ynyover fighters missing after the slaughter, control of the kingdom would remain challenging. Despite the alliance, Satres realized he remained on borrowed time as tensions between the local militias and those Aberffraw who persisted in Ynyover could erupt into a conflict.

Flicking the reins, the Sacred Overlord goaded the reluctant *erba* toward the main gate. A few mornings earlier the man decided would play the victim to maintain his control of the Citadel. He was betrayed at the hands of the Cahmais king. By locking himself inside the fortress, Satres planned on consolidating his power using the guards loyal to the lands of Ynyover. With such a base, the overlord recognized his task of maintaining his power required the defeated Aberffraw warriors to come under his control. With King Asgurd out of the way, along with most of the leaders of the Aberffraw invasion force, the Sacred Overlord believed he could use the authority of his position to bring the Cahmais under his control. By the time, he reached the Citadel gates, Satres felt confidence in his plan rise. The Sacred Overlord's guard still managed the gates to his kingdom, and he could dictate a new fortune for his kingdom.

"Stop!" shouted one of the guards, quickly moving to halt the cart. When the man came close enough to recognize the thin man driving the vehicle, he immediately apologized.

"My apologies, my leader. I…thought, a trader, was coming to the gate."

"Look closer next time," Satres scowled. "Where are my advisors?"

The guard hesitated as he looked around quickly. "They are throughout the fortress, waiting for word of your….triumph." The man's words trailed off as he realized the uncharacteristic arrival must mean something unfortunate happened.

Satres gave the bearded man a cold stare. "You will keep any thoughts to yourself. Now, I want all of my advisors in the great hall immediately!" He watched with satisfaction as the guard immediately ran to the gate, announcing the arrival of the Sacred Overlord. Gathering his torn and dirty robes so he could step down from the cart, the leader of Ynyover rehearsed his coming speech during the short walk into the Citadel.

~~~

Near the border with Ynyover and Esterblud, Lyncus was not in a forgiving mood. The remaining son of King Asgurd focused his hatred of Ynyover with passing morning during his retreat back to Cahmais. While his small group men gathered up any remaining Aberffraw warriors, the barren land caused during their foray into Esterblud now threatened them with starvation. The sole heir to the throne of Cahmais might have been involved in the invasion, but he held the bitterness of defeat on one man. His humiliation along with the loss of most of the Aberffraw army, Lyncus placed squarely upon the head of Satres.

When Lyncus and his men arrived at the first small Ynyover village at the border, the leader of the Cahmais lands decided he would send a message to Satres. The local men quickly surrendered after they were overwhelmed by the Aberffraw warriors. As the eleven bound men stood before the new king of Cahmais, the rest of the village were forced out of their huts. As the woman and children gathered inside the line of Aberffraw warriors, the Cahmais leader began his revenge against the Sacred Overlord. He placed himself in front of the oldest man who was the only one wearing armor.

"Do you have family in this place?"

The old man nodded at Lyncus, his face suspicious and fearful. "I'm Betra, leader of the village."

"I don't care about your name or your hamlet." Lyncus turned to one of the few tribal leaders remaining in his army, a man called Vritgus. "Very well, put this man on an ossane and keep him tied to the saddle."

While Lyncus looked over the remaining prisoners, the older man was hastily shoved onto a mount. In his review, the leader of the Aberffraw noticed the militia was made up of only young boys. No doubt a good many of the real warriors of Ynyover died with their Aberffraw allies in Esterblud.

Finished with his inspection, Lyncus limped back to his ossane, stiffly getting on the mount. Guiding his ossane, he rode next to Betra, raising his voice for all to hear.

"This rabble of Ynyover betrayed my fighters on the battlefield. Each of you saw what came from the betrayal of our king by the Sacred Overlord who ran back to these lands on a cart. Will you join me to get our revenge as we travel back to our home?"

The yells and cries of revenge quickly filled the air until he stopped them by raising his hand. He pointed to several of his warriors. "You will hang these prisoners. I want them dangling from those trees." He continued, giving orders to another group of men, "Then, burn the village to the ground."

Even though he was bound to the saddle, Betra attempted to push his mount into Lyncus, pleading for his people. "Save this village, take my head as a sacrifice," the older man begged the young leader of Cahmais. The Aberffraw leader pulled his sword and gave the man a hard slap across the face with the side of his sword. The man's head lolled as he nearly blacked out, blood falling from his mouth at the blow. One of the Aberffraw fighters struggled to control the old man's ossane before he reached out to keep the prisoner in his saddle.

Vritgus asked Lyncus about the women and children as the rest of the warriors gathered around the small group. The ruler of Cahmais looked over the young and old, some of who were sobbing at the coming death of the captured men. The man recognized the fear in their eyes as he turned his horse toward the Citadel of Br-Ynys. However, his vengeance blinded him with hate as he turned away.

"I want the men with us as we reach each of these villages. Our kinsmen can do as they want with the villagers, the woman and children can be taken for slaves as long as they keep up." Lyncus looked down at Vritgus. "I want one person left alive to spread the word of my revenge against Satres. As I go to meet my enemy in the Citadel, we will give each village this same treatment. Those that live will remember the betrayal of their overlord."

His words unleashed his men who quickly hung the bound prisoners. As the unfortunates slowly died, their legs frantically kicking in the air, the Aberffraw rabble began their wanton destruction of the village. Woman and children were pulled down to the dirt to satisfy the cruel cravings of the men while the village huts went up in flames.

Lyncus forced Betra to watch the destruction for a while, then he slapped the back of the ossane, sending the mount speeding off toward the Citadel. As the rape and slaughter continued, the leader of Cahmais yelled after the man on the fleeing ossane.

"Remember to tell your overlord, Satres, that the King of Cahmais is coming for him. I'll have his head as a trophy when I get there."

~~~

Deep in the underworld, the figure of Caruun stood at the polished black altar near the spot that the Guardian re-entered the realms of Kamin. A green, luminous glow filled the chamber room where two beorhs held down the next victim, a strong man who fought savagely as they dragged him into the compartment. However, the monster's strength overpowered him, and now their victim lay on the cold slab of stone, loudly cursing them. Reppir, holding a large clay bowl half full of blood, stepped next to Kriell and placed the bowl in a carved out shelf under the slab. Razor sharp claws extended, the Guardian towered over the cursing man. With a single finger, the creature slashed the victim's throat. Shrieks and wails broke out from the men, women, and children bound to the walls of the chamber. Some screamed as they watched in horror at the thrashing body of the dying man. Other coming sacrifices simply cried in despair. One man, in near madness, lifted his head, his voice giving a strange cackling laugh at those to tried to avoid the sights and sounds of the carnage around them.

The chattering of the beorhs increased as the underworld creatures watched the blood follow the grooves cut into the slab, leading the hole above the bowl. Not long after the victim quit moving, the man's spirit stood next to his body, looking confused at what he saw. A demigod collector of spirits, known as Actita, pulled out his leather whip made of human skin. Quickly, the winged creature with snake-hair, lashed it around the unfortunate soul, dragging the soul from the room. Soon, the departed spirit of the dead man would be turned into another beast of the underworld.

After the blood finally stopped dripping, Reppir picked up the bowl and held it out to his master. Kriell took the offering and walked to a large mural on the wall of the room. Placing the cup of blood at the foot of the familiar, tentacle beast painted upon the rock face, the Guardian began chanting the words to the spell. Intending to release the rest of his kind into the world of Kamin, the creature sliced his wrist, cocking his bird-like head as he watched the black blood fall into the bowl.

Then, he waited. Cocking his head to the wall for any movement, the wall remained unchanged. Nothing revealed itself to the Guardian. After a long pause, the monster turned to Reppir.

"Get me another bowl."

The leader of the beorhs chattered something unintelligible to the ears of the human captives.

"I don't care if you want these prisoners for your beorh's entertainment. There must be plenty of fresh blood available. The gateway to the Great Void will be opened." The form of Caruun screeched out of his beaked face. "Now get me another sacrifice on the altar."

The leader of the underworld walked back to the black slab, waiting impatiently as a young female was dragged to her death spot. Kriell paid no attention to the hysterical creature begging for her life. He cut another throat, vowing he would fill the room with the blood of these wretched human things if necessary.

~~~

"Why did you have more of the enemy come after you? You could have sent the villagers on the trail up the coast and snuck back on your own." Wilgam's tone carried puzzlement and a bit of anger.

"I was not done with those cowards who pose as warriors. I'm tired of men with no honor. And I'm sick of explaining myself." Urith grimaced as a healer placed a splint on the warrior's forearm. His face and much of his upper body covered in sweat and blood, the warrior, leaned against the cold stone wall in the courtyard of the fortress. For the moment it felt good on his skin. Above them, the sky turned dark before his arrival back to the stone structure. His journey back to the fort took far longer than he expected due to the wounds he carried.

"You're a fool, Urith of Esterblud." Mivraa, her face red, nearly shouted at the man. The small group around the giant warrior went quiet.

"Are you trying to get yourself killed?" the demigoddess continued her wraith. "You have a duty given to you by the Fates to find the Skool, and you haven't finished that mission. Now you run into a village to save a few idiots who didn't leave. For what?"

Urith stared at Mivraa; his eyes harden at the accusations. "And you would leave those people to die? Why? Just because you are fixated on revenge; a sole purpose of destroying your father, Duwdamon. You have powers that most humans dream of. You are a half god. Still, you don't care about those people who look up to you. I'd say there is a vast difference in what we want. Don't lecture me on what I should do."

For a moment, he thought this woman would attack him. The man saw her hand tighten on her spear which hung on her belt.

"Fine, explain that to Caruun when you get yourself killed. I'm sure he will be happy to torture you for eternity in the underworld after such a dumb move." Her voice rose. "Look at you now. With that arm, you can't lift a shield. You can't even help stop the rest of those Aberffraw on the beach who will kill all of us." The demigoddess suddenly turned on her heel, her long auburn hair appearing fiery red as she passed the light of the lamp hanging on the wall.

"She's got a valid point," Oslaf stated after a long silence, sharing what others thought among the group. Urith glared at him before sending the healer away. As he stared at his nephew, Urith decided it was not the time to argue.

"Alright, she's could be right. But, don't tell me you would have left those people to be killed. I taught you better than that," Urith leaned back against the wall again, looking directly at Oslaf, who quietly nodded.

Urith shrugged. "Whatever I've done, it is over. We are in the same place as we started out the day, correct? So what have all of you been planning? I can tell you've been waiting for something." He grimaced as tried to gingerly move his arm to a more comfortable position.

"We are waiting for night. Then we are going to destroy those ships stranded on the beach," Wilgam told him. "A fire and the wind blowing across their decks will throw the enemy into confusion. We just need Mivraa's help with her invisibility cloak to get us close to the ships. I hope she's still on our side." He seemed worried about the demigoddess.

"I'll talk with her," Henther told them suddenly. "I'm sure she will help. It's not like she suddenly wants the Aberffraw to kill us. Since it's my idea, she can tell me whether she'll go or not." The daughter of Kirowan followed the path taken by Mivraa.

"You need to rest," Fedelm gently told Urith who shook his head.

"I'm fine. I can help," the Esterblud insisted.

"No, she's right. Get the healer to properly splint that arm and get some rest, uncle. We won't leave after the moons drop from the night sky." Oslaf offered his hand to his uncle who grudgingly accepted it. Limping away, Urith suddenly found Fedelm at his side. She took his uninjured arm and let him steady himself using her body while Wilgam and Oslaf watched.

After they had left, Wilgam turned to his friend. "Your uncle probably doesn't realize that woman cares deeply for him."

Oslaf considered the question for a moment. "I'm not sure. Ever since we saved her at Ynyover, Fedelm has stuck with him. I know Urith has forgiven her for her betrayal. She's become vital to helping him and what he seeks. But, if I had to guess, he's probably pushed such ideas out of his head for the moment. He's still taken with Mivraa."

"Yeah, but not the other way around it seems. The demigoddess looked to kill him earlier." Wilgam was joking, but Oslaf just nodded, his face remained serious.

"Mivraa is a goddess. She might have convinced herself that she really cared for him once, but I don't think so now. Urith doesn't see it, but I'm convinced somehow the woman wants to control the Skool more than he does."

The leader of the guards looked confused. "Why is that? From what I've heard, only Urith can carry the shield."

"I believe that's true, but she has changed. You've not heard, but I rejoined Urith after he and Fedelm rescued Mivraa. He said the woman was flayed alive by ranqels each night as punishment for joining us. This was after her brothers raped her and left their sister chained on that mountain." Oslaf led his friend away from the area, keeping his voice low.

32

"By the gods, they would do that to one of their own?" Wilgam wondered aloud. "I mean I've heard stories of the Guardians but not about the Sky gods."

"Now you know the truth. But what happened on that mountain changed the woman. Believe me; Mivraa would slit all of our throats if it got her the chance at revenge upon her father and brothers. I think that chance is the Skool."

"That's going to make me sleep easier," Wilgam replied halfheartedly.

"Don't worry about it. The Aberffraw may get their chance to kill us first if we make a mistake tonight." Oslaf's sarcasm did not help Wilgam's mood as they walked to the barracks where they would rest before their raid later.

When the twin moons of Kamin dropped behind the horizon to the south, a disparate group of new allies assembled on the far side of the fortress. The enemy warriors from Cahmais finally organized themselves during the day to fully surround the fort, leaving blazing campfires and torches to light the area. However, their lines of light were unable to extinguish all the shadows along the fort's various corners. Wilgam found a field in which the shadow ran from the top of battlements down to the ground at the back of the fort. The small group led by Wilgam and Mivraa huddled on the walkway, crouched low to ensure they could not be seen from below.

The one person missing from the group was Urith. Fedelm arrived late to tell them that the healer was still working on the large man's arm. She told them they should go without Urith.

"The night will end soon; we must leave now," Wilgam stated impatiently. "He is too injured to help us much anyway."

"I agree. We have enough warriors to make this work," Erran spoke up for himself and the rest of Wilgam's men. A murmur of agreement supported him.

"Alright, the plan is the same if Urith cannot make it," Mivraa's determination stood out like her armor which gleamed in the light of the torches on the battlements. "We will go over the wall individually, and you will stay close behind me so we can use my cloak to make it past the guards. From there, we will work our way through the grass and brush until we reached the beach area. I'll make sure any guards or lights along our path are removed."

She quickly took a long rope already tied off to a stone corbel hanging over the side of the wall. "Give me some time to make sure no one is around. I'll signal when I'm ready." Her voice growled. "And don't make a sound or you'll answer to me."

With her warning, the demigod scampered over the rock top and down the rope. Even in the dimness, Oslaf noticed Wilgam's annoyance at being overridden as the leader of the group. It was clear that Mivraa held little respect for anyone but Urith at this point.

While the small group waited, Oslaf took Fedelm aside, making sure he would not be overheard. "Urith wouldn't miss this if he lost both legs. He's still asleep. Am I right?"

The woman shot a glance around. "You saw him; he's in no shape to help. The Shield of Skool is useless unless he places it on his sword hand. I told the healer to give him some herbs to relax so they could bind his arm. He doesn't realize the leaves will knock him out for a while."

Oslaf stared at the woman. "Alright, I think you're right. I won't say anything to the others. You know Urith will be furious."

"Of course," she replied. "Urith believes he must be involved with anything that hints of danger with you."

Oslaf nodded, "You're right about that. When he finds out, it was my idea. Better to have him send his wrath my way." As the nephew turned back to the group, he quickly reminded her to be careful with her feelings. "Remember, Urith will never tell you his feelings. Mivraa thinks Urith is her man. She doesn't like to lose to anyone."

Fedelm smiled to herself as she followed him, "Neither do I."

When they joined the group, Fedelm noticed Henther standing next to the rope while holding a small stack of torches. The long sticks were specially made of sulfur mixed with lime under the guidance of Draca. Once lit, the flames, even if doused with seawater, would remain on fire. Oslaf sarcastically told Fedelm under his breath that the old man apparently decided Wilgam might get himself killed in the raid. It would make it easier to surrender.

"Alright, she's ready for us," Wilgam whispered to the group after spotting a green light flash from below. "I'm going down first, then my men will follow. Oslaf, since you are the biggest, you can make sure the torches stay with us by coming down last. Is that understood?"

"I'm coming," Henther announced forcefully. "It's my plan, so I'm going along."

"I agree," Oslaf low tone told everyone Henther would be joining them. He looked to Fedelm who said she was staying to keep an eye on Urith.

One by one, the group went over the top of the battlements, climbing to the darkness below. On the ground, Mivraa held the unwrapped cloak she generally carried around her shoulders. She ordered everyone to close in behind, given them a rope which was attached around her waist. As members of the team watched, the demigoddess said something under her breath. Suddenly, those of the group saw her disappear. Despite the warnings of this power, both Wilgam and Erran glanced at each other in surprise.

"I'll be out several paces ahead. Keep your mouth shut and don't lose your grip on the rope," an invisible voice hissed at them.

The demigoddess led them along a narrow footpath away from the fort. Each person in the group carefully followed along, trying to keep their feet from tripping over the person in front. Some felt especially vulnerable as they could see each other in the dim light while hearing the person next to them breathing. Even the soft sound of their boots moving through the high grass was amplified by their anxiety. As the invisible woman came close to a torch embedded into the ground along their path, the light suddenly and silently went out.

The small group made their way past the lines of sleeping men, warily bypassing the campfires that spread through the lines encircling the fortress. Twice they were forced to halt their progress. The first time, Mivraa nearly stumbled upon a sleeping guard. Without a second thought, she thrust her crystal spear tip into the man's neck, watching impassively as the man die. Within a few minutes, the demigoddess noticed the man's soul begin following them as they proceeded on to the beach. Before she joined Urith's cause, the leader of Haligulf would have guided the soul to the eternal paradise of the warriors. Now the spirits just wandered the places where they perished. The only other creature capable of guiding spirits was the Vanth known as Actita. The underworld demigod would eventually find this spirit and lead it to the underworld. Unwelcome now in Haligulf, Mivraa no longer concerned herself with the afterlife of her human side. Dead warriors would only burden her in the quest to seek retribution upon the Sky Realm.

"Let Caruun and Alrpan have them," she thought bitterly.

The group finally reached the shoreline, trying to avoid the many bonfires lighting the area. The one guard was quickly dispatched by the invisible demigoddess. The cluster of fighters moved into shadows of one beached vessel, already partially dismantled. Mivraa suddenly reappeared next to Oslaf after she pulled her cloak back over her shoulders.

Wilgam whispered they would take the sulfur sticks brought by Oslaf and spread out across the beach where they would toss the burning sticks on the decks of the ships. As the man started to hand out the torches, Oslaf suddenly noticed the ominous looking white clouds and flashes of lightning rolling toward them from the sea. Even in the darkness, the clouds swept low across the water, appearing like a tidal wall of water. Eerily similar to the storm front he recalled back in Cahmais which nearly killed them, the Esterblud fighter pointed out clouds to the huddled group. Before he could warn them, Henther spoke up quickly.

"Let's move and get this done. We can use the coming storm to hide us when we retreat back to the fort."

Immediately, the group broke up, fanning out across the beach to get the fires started. Unfortunately, they were too late. The blast of straight-line wind and rain struck the beach with a hurricane force. The wind pelted them with stinging torrents of water as they suddenly saw the wall of water heading at them. Before anyone could react, there was a flash and, in an instant, the wooden craft where they stood earlier nearly exploded by the lightning bolt that struck it. The force of the thunder along with the great winds sent the group running away, scattering them across the sand which strafed them. In ones and twos, lighting bolts struck the beached ships with the same catastrophic effect before the storm turned its strength against the town and the fort.

Across the beach, the combination of wind and lighting devastated the exposed army of Cahmais who suddenly found themselves in a torrent of destruction. The fighters tried to flee the area. In the chaos, men and ossanes ran, each looking for any place to provide shelter. The confusion allowed those in the Esterblud raiding party to flee with the enemy. Some of Wiglam's men found shelter behind a large dune where they huddled together, trying to avoid the howling wind.

Sent reeling by the first lighting strike, Henther and Oslaf struggled away from one of the damaged vessels. As the wave swell sent a massive

36

debris field toward them, they fell in the sand, barely able to get away from the surging tide. Heading to higher ground, the pair stumbled by three huddled Aberffraw warriors who suddenly recognized their enemy passing close enough to touch. However, the enemy left the man and woman alone, more afraid of the god's wrath.

Inside the fort, Urith woke from his herb-induced dreams when a stone tower on one corner of the fort fell from a massive electric strike. The sound of thunder and stone crushing some of the Esterbluds huddled nearby sent the man into a mad scramble. Grabbing his shield and leaving the tent where he was lying, the giant instantly found Fedelm trying to help one of the injured struck by debris falling from the wall. In the dim light, Urith noticed part of the structure wobbling unsteadily above her. Sensing the immediate danger, he stumbled as he raced to the woman, reaching her just as another powerful gust of wind and rain struck again. The massive blocks of stone came toppling down, and the man tackled the woman, sending them rolling away before the rocks landed on her. When they got up, she looked away after seeing only the exposed arm of the fort's defender she was helping. Amid the flash of lighting, she saw the mass of stone covering the corpse.

Urith pushed them away from the area, taking her with him inside an entrance leading to the storerooms below.

"We've seen this before. The gods are after us," he was nearly yelling to be heard over the din.

Fedelm only nodded, still thinking of the poor man she tried to help. Slowly she realized she was shaking from the rain and shock. Had it not been for the Esterblud she met only a season before, she would be buried under the rubble as well. The woman looked out at the storm, holding her hand over her eyes to see through the pelting rain. Urith was correct; the vicious nature of this massive tempest had to be the work of the Sky Realm against them.

While the pair watched the spectacle unfold in the sky above and the mayhem going on inside the fort, unconsciously, they held each other in a tight embrace. The blond woman suddenly realized the man held her in an embrace, his massive arm over her shoulders as he surveyed the heavens. At first, she felt a guilty feeling come across her before she dismissed it. Fedelm decided she was exactly where she should be.

~~~

Dawn of the next morning brought light to the devastation. Across the beach, shattered hulks and debris fields replaced the spots where ships sat the day before. The harbor itself appeared mostly deserted. The massive number ships which once filled the Esterbluds with dread were no more; many vanished within minutes of the incoming storm. Across the land leading to the fortress, a few bodies could be seen from those struck by debris in the heavy winds. But the army which once encircled the stronghold was scattered and broken. The object of the Cahmais army's invasion still stood on the hill, although the walls, like the people inside, were severely bruised and battered. Gaping areas of missing stone ran along the fortress on one side where the flanking turret fell. Slowly, people began to come out from behind the walls to assess the world.

Nearby, on the crest of a ridge, Alcarlic, the surviving son of King Penhda sat on his ossane, staring at the destruction. Like the rest of the few warriors who survived the devastating massacre in the valley called Awarware, the storms during the night which swept across the land left them weary and irritable. The food was scarce during their return from the south of the country, and the foraging left some of the small villages resentful the high-handed presence. Alcarlic was of the Eranis tribe, like his father and he had little patience for the Esterblud clans in the north. While his father generally welcomed bands of Esterblud and Gramcle which helped unify the kingdom, the son believed this to be a weakness. In his mind, his family and his clan provided the leadership to the Esterblud kingdom. To those of the Eranis tribe, it was natural for his father to be king since his people made up the largest part of the population and held more of the fertile lands. It was a mistake of history placing the Esterblud name on the kingdom. A mistake he had every intention of correcting once he established his rightful place as overlord for the kingdom, like his father.

His eyes wide in surprise at the utter destruction he witnessed below, the son of King Penhda did not see the expected a fleet of Cahmais ships to be in the harbor. They were gone. No doubt wiped out by the same storm they encountered, Alcarlic liked what he saw.

That morning, he and his men came upon a few Aberffraw warriors who tried to surrender after becoming separated from their comrades. After learning about the depth of the treachery within the Ynyover and Cahmais alliance, Alcarlic held little sympathy for his captives. He ordered his men to kill his prisoners, leaving only one alive to ensure the man's cooperation. After watching the cold-blooded butchery of his friends, the terrified Aberffraw prisoner quickly revealed all of the events which happened since he landed upon the beach. The prisoner then led the group back to the fortress.

Alcarlic finished his survey of the area, turning to the small group of warriors behind him. "Make it clear to all our people, kill any enemy who still trod upon our lands." The leader nodded at their captured prisoner who was quickly killed with a spear jabbed into the unfortunate man's neck. The vengeful son of Penhda galloped toward the fort.

When the group reached the front of the fortification, Alcarlic paid little attention the damage from the storm. Wilgam stood next to Urith and Fedelm, going over the events of the night before and trying to organize their people and begin the rebuilding. The group of mounted warriors quickly surrounded the trio.

"Alcarlic, it is good you have returned," Wilgam started to speak, only to be cut off by the rider.

"Seize him now," the son of Penhda pointed at Urith who was immediately knocked down as a rider ran his ossane into the man. Several armed fighters jumped down, tackling him before Urith could fight them. While they pummeled Urith with the blunt end of their spears and pommels of swords, Fedelm attacked the group using her short sword. Striking several of the unsuspecting fighters from behind, the woman wounded two men as more of Alcarlic's men entered the fray. They finally subdued the man and woman, beating them savagely until both fell unconscious. Even Wilgam was battered and held to the ground when he, belatedly, tried to stop the beatings.

"The king wanted that man arrested, and I expect his commands to be obeyed," Alcarlic told Wilgam as the man lay on the ground looking up at the mounted rider. The king's son turned to the people holding their new prisoners. "Put them in the cells. We will execute them later. The rest of you spread out along the beach. Kill any Aberffraw you find."

The son of Penhda rode into the fort determined to secure his position as the next ruler of Esterblud.

Down the road, many buildings in the town of Eran were gone, either through the work of the Aberffraw or the storm. A few remaining inhabitants emerged, already trying to rebuild their huts from the scraps of wood and debris left across the area. As she walked through the devastation, Henther saw the brutal capture of Urith and Fedelm.

Instinctively realizing Oslaf's reaction would be to attack, she ran to the blacksmith's shack where Urith's nephew was speaking with a trader about finding their ossanes. She pushed him around the corner of the shed which survived the storm, explaining what she witnessed. As she suspected, the young man reached for his sword.

"No, there are too many of them for you to fight alone. You will only get killed or captured," Henther told him as she forced the man to look at her.

The young man restrained his temper, turning back to look at the scene. "It must be what's left of King Penhda's fighters from the colors they wear. I'm not letting them get away with this," he scowled as he considered his options.

"Listen, to me. We can't find Mivraa, and your uncle is captured. You know you can't fight them all. There must be another way," she paused, trying to think. "Is there another place nearby where we can go and find help?"

Oslaf shook his head. "The only people who would help are the Esterblud people since the Eran tribe controls this area. The closest village would be Cilgarran. It's a full day's ride. They'll execute them before we get back."

"Why would they? No one can touch the Shield of Skool but Urith now. Besides, I saw Wilgam trying to help. His men won't assist them in hurting Urith. You know your uncle has some support in the fort. Plus, there are others who want to be the overlord, so they want to get to that shield as well."

The young warrior finally relented, insisting they must move quickly. Oslaf went to the trader who only had a single ossane left that didn't escape from the overnight terror. He finally convinced the man to trade the animal for his remaining koinon along with his shield. As the pair got on the ossane, they saw several of Eran warriors coming toward the village. Oslaf turned their mount to go in the opposite direction, taking the back path where Urith led the villagers to safety the day before. They rode hard, pushing the animal as it strained to carry its load up the sandy soil to the top of the ridge. From their vantage point, they saw no one was following them, and they slowed the pace toward Cilgarran. Following the narrow trail which took them through a thin forest of pines, their ossane suddenly reared back, snorting in fear. Oslaf got the mount under control, then spurred the animal forward cautiously.

"Our ossane is sensing something out of place. Keep your eyes open for anything strange," the warrior whispered back to his companion who nodded.

They didn't have to wait long. The couple entered a small clearing where bloody bodies lay on the ground while a few ossanes, with saddles still on, grazed nearby. In the middle of the carnage was an old woman with a brown cape and hood, her body bent, and frail. When she heard the ossane, she turned to them. Her wrinkled face smiled, but the only thing the riders noticed was the old hag was covered in blood and holding a gore covered spear.

"Well, I was wondering where you went. Where's your uncle?" Mivraa's voice came from the creature in front of them. In an instant, the goddess of Haligulf appeared, still covered in the blood.

"What happened?" Henther asked while Oslaf studied the scene.

The woman shrugged her shoulders. "They made a mistake. They tried to attack an old lady." Mivraa calmly walked over to the nearest ossane, whispering to the animal as she retrieved a leather bladder holding water. As she cleaned the blood from herself, she asked again about Urith.

Oslaf told her what he knew and explained his plan to return with Esterblud warriors to rescue Urith and Fedelm.

Finished cleaning, the demigoddess took the ossane by the reins, leading it to the couple. "Henther, you ride this mount, and the two of you will make better time."

"What about you," the girl asked Mivraa as she took the leather straps.

"I have my own work to do here. I'll see get into the fort at night and get Urith out of there." The demigoddess assured them.

"I'll stay and go with you," Oslaf exclaimed.

"And who'll convince your people to help Urith, a foreigner like me?" Henther slapped her lover across his head lightly. The woman slid off the back of their ossane.

The demigoddess handed the woman the reins. "If I don't get Urith out of the fort, Oslaf can destroy the place." Her voice had an uncanny, almost emotionless, detachment in the tone.

After Henther had mounted the ossane, they told Mivraa they would return as soon as they could. However, the warrior woman paid no attention, quickly transforming herself into the old hag and walking along on the trail to the village of Eran.

After the pair of riders had reached the main road to Cilgarran, Henther realized Oslaf had gone silent for a long while. She mentioned the odd feeling she had at the encounter with Mivraa in the clearing. He nodded, "I noticed that as well. Something else bothered me. I decided not to mention it at the time but did you see the dead men around her?"

"No, I've quit looking at their faces," she told him forcefully. "There's been too much death."

"That's not what I mean," he slowed his mount, and she looked at him. The expression on his face was a mixture of disbelief and disdain. "The dead were a combination of Aberffraw warriors along with some of the Eran warriors who rode with King Penhda."

"So what? I heard her tell you what happened."

"Since when would a man from Cahmais fight beside an Esterblud?" He asked, apparently believing he knew the answer.

"Well, maybe they one side saw the fight, and it became a battle between all of them. We've seen things get out of control before," the woman thought back to the bodies she saw, growing even more concerned.

"I didn't think so at first, but I'm sure she wasn't attacked. The bloodstains I saw on the Aberffraw were nearly dry. It was the blood from those Eran riders she was washing off. It doesn't matter what she says, they wouldn't bother to attack some old woman alone in a forest. Mivraa ambushed those men," he looked back in the direction they came.

"Do you know what you're saying? Mivraa is deliberately killing warriors. For what?" her face showed her disbelief.

"Do you believe those Aberffraw would have taken the time to kill the old hag while they are trying to get out of this land? Anyway, it would not take more than one man." Oslaf shook his head, convinced he was correct.

Henther stared at Oslaf, her mind trying to believe what he said. "But why would she do that? She might have done something against those men from Cahmais because one of them attacked her."

"Maybe," he conceded. "Except some of those men were struck down from behind, their wounds were on their backs. I think they were running away. And I noticed none of the weapons on the ground were blood stained. Only hers. How do you explain that? I've been in battles

42

with her before and seldom does anyone come out without a scratch. No, she must have lured them with her disguise to kill them."

"But, there's no reason she would need to kill those riders."

"Exactly. No reason at all," the young warrior spurred his mount forward. "Come, we have to get to Cilgarran as soon as we can." Trying to understand this terrible new side of a demigod, the warrior wondered what happened to the person he considered a friend.

Chapter 3: Bitterness and Vengeance

Inside the fort, Urith sat on the wet rock floor of his cramped cell. The compartment was too low for him to stand fully and he could reach the walls on either side by extending his arms. It was almost pitch black with a thin light trying to peek through the gap between the floor and a heavy wooden door. Cold and dank air made him shiver at times, even with his padded undergarments and tunic. Stripped of his weapons and armor, the man could only listen to the stillness of this isolated section of Eran's fortress. His arm ached under the makeshift splint, but at least it would heal if he survived that long. He knew this area was used to hold the condemned men, commonly traitors or murders. Yet, his mind was fixed on two things he considered more important. First, what happened to Fedelm and where was the Shield of Skool?

He remembered the young woman trying to help him when they were overwhelmed, but after that, it was blank. The warrior scratched unconsciously at the scar on his cheek, trying to guess what Alcarlic would do next. No doubt, the son of Penhda would attempt to replace his father as king. But the Council of Elders would be needed for such a decision. It would take several sunrises before the Gramcan, Eran and Esterblud tribe elders could gather for such a discussion in regular times. With the clans in disarray, Urith knew Alcarlic would try to take advantage of the situation. He was like his father, a capable leader with strong warrior prowess. Probably more ruthless than Penhda, Urith always believed the young man to be overly enamored with the politics and intrigue among those who sought power next to the king. In many ways, the young fighter was the opposite of Urith who once believed the goal of a warrior was renown among the other fighters along with an honored death while in battle.

As he considered the position he was in, he guessed Alcarlic would not try to execute him immediately. Once the son of Penhda learned more about the Shield of Skool, Urith felt confident Alcarlic would be coming to him. Any ambitious leader would want control over the weapon of the gods. The giant warrior rested his head against the stone wall, sighing at the thought. It was the curse of humans to always seek control over others. It wasn't like he never considered the idea. However, Urith really believed no such control would ever happen.

When he thought of the people he knew, each wanted their own bit of space and freedom. Maybe chaos was the natural state of humans. Tyranny, either through the gods or people, was only a way to delay the chaos. Control of individuals would only happen through ruthless actions which instilled fear. Yet, the man understood his heart could not turn so black. An encounter many seasons before with the goddess of the underworld convinced him of that fact.

His thoughts drifted back to the rest of his friends. When he woke in the cell, he called out, but no one responded. He guessed Fedelm must have been captured and placed in a cell somewhere else, too far away to hear his voice. The warrior hoped she wasn't dead. Maybe, they simply let her go since Alcarlic wouldn't consider her a threat. However, given the amount of reward on him and his friends, he examined the possibility that the Eran leader might use the woman as a bargaining chip with Satres. With the Sacred Overlord and his men joining with the Cahmais invasion of Esterblud, any obligations to return the *wafaoils* were gone. Still, the son of Penhda might take *koinons* to use in his quest to become king. Urith's eye's narrowed at the thought, vowing to kill Alcarlic if the man turned over Fedelm or anyone else to Satres.

Since he heard no one else nearby, the giant man wondered about the rest of his followers. He remembered Oslaf and Henther were near the village when he was attacked so they might have escaped. Mivraa, on the other hand, was nowhere to be found when he woke that morning. The demigoddess was probably working with the others, deciding on their next steps. He frowned when he suddenly realized Mivraa was the last one he thought about. His lover during most of the journey back to his homeland, he used to think of the future with her. That was no more. The distance between them was as wide as a canyon. She acted as she cared for him, but they no longer had the relaxed banter between them. Since her terrible experiences on the mountain side, the woman was changed. The goddess transformed into someone else, much like the person who might emerge from her magic shawl. Urith could understand why she became calculating, bitter, and aloof from any closeness. However, he could not fathom how to help pull her from the familiar darkness which he knew closed around her soul.

~~~

On the other side of the fort, Fedelm stood before Alcarlic. She held herself tall, refusing to back down to the man after he finished his tirade against the Cahmais.

"You are a foreigner in our lands. You have traveled here as an enemy of King Penhda." The muscular man stood over her. "Tell me why I shouldn't have you executed immediately?"

"Because I stood by your people and helped against the Aberffraw while you fell into the trap set by the underworld. While your army was trying to save yourselves from the monsters, we were fending off the enemies who nearly took your capital." The defiance in her words mixed with the shock and indignation coming from the crowd of men gathered around her.

Even Alcarlic expressed surprise at her words. "How could you know of this? You and your Cahmais allies must have given sacrifices to the underworld gods to destroy the Esterblud kingdom." There was a murmur of agreement among his men.

Fedelm rolled her eyes. "Are you so blind that you cannot see the truth? I know what happened because I saw the visions on the night of your escape. Explain how the Cahmais people would be an ally of the underworld? The same beorhs and *crubas* massacred both Aberffraw and Esterblud warriors on that ground."

"Quiet," he lashed out at the woman. "Your twisting of words cannot save you."

Wilgam stepped next to Fedelm. "This person speaks the truth. She came into this place and told the elders of this vision on the day their group arrived. Men like Draca did not believe her at the time, and now we have come to this. Besides, the woman is not who we should be taking with. Urith and Oslaf brought her along with Mivraa. Do you want to accuse the goddess of Haligulf of treachery as well?"

"Yes, I would. However, it seems Mivraa is no longer among us. And Urith's nephew is missing as well." The son of Penhda smirked as he looked around. He turned back to Wilgam. "You believe this woman. Does this mean you should be in charge?" Alcarlic's tone was menacing.

Wilgam glared at him. "You and everyone else understand that the elders among the clans will decide who will be overlord of this land. I warn you now. You might have surprised me by capturing Urith, but until a decision is made on who becomes the ruler of our lands, my fighters will follow my orders. You and your clan have no authority over me or my people."

Alcarlic moved toward the man, interceded by Draca who stepped between them. Others in the room were starting to take sides as well. Insults were hurled at members of the other tribes.

"Enough of this bickering," Bucnar shouted out to quiet the din, smashing his full mug on the table. The leader of the Gramcle tribe stood. "It is up to the all of the clans within Esterblud to determine our next overlord. Does anyone dispute that?" He glared at Alcarlic who remained quiet. The numbers were not on his side for the moment.

A warrior named Pecra stepped forward. "While I was against Wilgam when the Aberffraw arrived, he proved me wrong. We cannot stand against each other while we have enemies still in our lands. We need to begin rebuilding Eran and this fort. Until the council is brought to Eran to render judgment, I say that we have Alcarlic and Wilgam sit with the elders who remain to lead us for now."

The air remained tense until the Draca agreed to the proposal. "It is the best way for the moment. I have heard rumors that the Gramcan elders will be coming. Those people in Cilgarran will hear about the destruction of Eran from those villagers who left. We will have the Esterblud fighters coming soon."

"Very well, it is decided," Alcarlic suddenly interrupted. He pointed to Wilgam. "But I'll only agree if Urith and this woman will remain as prisoners until the new overlord decides. What say you?"

Wilgam realized the man left him little choice. Slowly he nodded.

"Good, let us think about the future." The son of Penhda pointed to one of his men. "Take the woman back."

As Fedelm was led away, she noticed Alcarlic quickly approach a large satgert who arrived after Alcarlic's men captured her. The scowl that the fat priest gave her gave the woman a chill. With the Sacred Overlord still after her, she was a pawn. It was something she never considered until that moment.

Pushed along, the woman entered the damaged courtyard where a limping man came next to the guard who escorted her. It was one of the fighters she injured earlier that day.

"I'll take the little wench," the man told his comrade who looked at the small woman briefly before nodding.

"As long as she gets to the cell," the guard said.

The limping man smiled as he grabbed her by the back of the neck with a calloused hand. "Oh, we're going to the cell alright. They say she's a healer. I'm going to have her fix something that's bothering me." Both men laughed as the wounded man forced Fedelm forward, placing a dagger in her back. The guard turned back to the hall.

When the pair reached the tunnel where the cells were located, the man pushed Fedelm into her cramped cell. He wrapped his arm around her neck in a choke hold and forced her to the stone floor. "Now, a little payback for what you did to my leg, you wench," he panted into her ear, sliding his dagger into his sheath, then struggling to remove his belt with his other hand.

She fought back, pulling at his long hair while she tried to twist away from him but his arm held firm. He slammed his fist into the side of her head, stunning her. As the rapist tried to pull her robe away, she heard a powerful voice rise up from behind her.

"Remove that man!"

In an instant, the weight on top of her was gone, and the woman turned over to see her stunned attacker being dragged away by men in scarlet robes. The man cursed at them.

"Make sure to hang him by his thumbs until Alcarlic decides what to do with him," the fat man in the same scarlet robe told his companions. She watched her attacker's eyes go wide with fear. As the two men pulled him into the passage, they heard him begging for forgiveness. Two more of the robed men entered the small cell next to the large man.

"I'm Feeral, hakra of the Esterblud kingdom," he told the woman as he slowly walked around the woman as if assessing her. "I've heard you came with Urith and are a hakra yourself. That means you are Fedelm, one of the wafaoils sought by the Sacred Overlord. As a defiler, I could have let the man have his revenge, then have you killed immediately."

Fedelm tried to stand, but one of the robed men forced her to her knees. "Alright, then why save me?" She stared at the fat man, the feeling of unease swimming over her.

"For several reasons," Feeral told her ominously. His round face remained sympathetic. "First, if you are a threat to Satres, then you might be useful to the new king of Esterblud. And, more importantly, you can tell us more about the shield Urith carries."

"You'll have to ask Urith about the shield. I don't know much about it."

He smiled, but his voice remained unpleasant. "Oh, don't mistake some fat around the middle for stupidity. You see I have heard of the many marvelous stories about your journey with Urith, some official and some just rumors, of course. If what I hear is even close to accurate, then you have insight about this weapon of the gods. Now, you can be assured, I will ask Urith about this Skool. But, as I remember the man, he can be quite stubborn concerning his duties to the overlord. I'm sure you can appreciate that some of his ideas are rather quaint." He sat down on a stool that was placed in front of her.

"So, I decided to ask you about this weapon first. If you please me in your answers, well, then I can be most accommodating. If not," the fat prophet paused, "well, some of my satgerts have great experience in persuading people to give us what we want."

"But I don't know that much. Besides, if you are a hakra, you recognize most visions come during sleep." The woman tried to reason with him, feeling a knot tighten inside her belly.

Now his smile turned foul. "Yes, yes, most times this would be true. Yet, you have had this insight already. Now, please let me know about this Skool."

The woman looked down. "I don't know anything."

The fat man sighed. "I see. I must say that stubbornness in you is not very fetching." He stood up from his seat. "It's a shame. I believe we will have to choose more compelling ways to help your vision along." He nodded to the other robed men who immediately pulled her from her kneeling position. "Let us proceed to learn what you know."

Feeral watched his men take the struggling woman from the cell. Another priest grabbed her long hair, painfully guiding the prisoner along the corridor. It was unfortunate he would have to hurry things along, he thought ruefully. While Urith could give up the information, he knew the man well enough to realize it would be a long, arduous process with no guarantee of success. The giant warrior might just let himself die, rather than say anything. Feeral believed this little *wafaoil* would be more useful to get the information he needed in the short amount of time that Alcarlic gave him. Also, Fedelm would be a great bargaining chip as long as she remained alive. The man was confident she would hold up under the torture, but he was willing to risk losing her as long as she gave him the secrets about the Shield of Skool that he needed.

The fat man slowly walked out of the cell with his hands behind him, thinking about his next steps when the echoed screams of the female prisoner finally started to reach him.

Urith heard the woman's screams as well, knowing instantly they were coming from Fedelm. Immediately he charged at the cell door, attempting to knock it down by the weight of his frame. It didn't budge, and the man fell back to the stone floor. As he got back to his feet, he saw Feeral peering at him through the bars.

"I was coming for you, Urith. No need to hurry." The fat man told him with a chuckle.

"If you are hurting her, I'm going to cut your heart out, my old friend," Urith growled at him.

Feeral's grin turned to a frown. "Yes, I do believe you might. That's why I brought some help." He unhooked the locked door and stood back as a small army of fighters and scarlet-robed men quickly entered.

The fight was brief and bloody for both sides. Urith managed to knock out one of his attackers while giving another a broken jaw before they finally subdued him. However, the big man got the worst of it, his splint shattered and his body was bruised and bloodied from the repeated punches and kicks. When Urith awoke he hung by his wrists, the broken arm throbbing with pain.

"I'm glad you are finally with us," Feeral told him as the warrior looked up. "This girl doesn't know much it seems. However, she did warn us of the power of the Skool. As you can see, I had them brought here to help with your memory." Urith saw the shield hooked to a long piece of board, leaning against the wall by a bench. The fat man stood in front of Fedelm who was hanging by her wrists as well, facing the stone wall. Her exposed, bloody back was covered with numerous welts and cuts. She was in a state of semi-consciousness, her head lulling as the sweat tangled hair covered her face. The fat hakra pulled her head up by her hair, slapping her face to try and wake her.

"You son of a docke, I will kill you. I meant what I said," the giant warrior struggled to pull the binding chain from the wall with his good arm. "There was no reason to hurt her."

Feeral walked closer to the bound man. "You are quite ignorant. You don't understand how a seer can use their visions, but I'm sure she will soon have the information we need. While sleep is usually the way such people receive their messages, it's well known within the Citadel that the spirits will communicate with those who are in great peril or duress." He looked back at the woman. "In her case, I need to speed this work along. The whipping she took will help her see the future. If this fails, we will increase the intensity of her pain."

"What are you talking about, you fat scum? She has nothing to do with my mission to the Citadel or Satres. She just saw a vision of Penhda and Asgurd being destroyed by the underworld gods."

The scarlet-robed man gave Urith a slight smile. "I see you haven't changed. You're still so sure of yourself, even when you are wrong. Your little journey to Ynyover meant nothing except for the shield you brought back to us." He stepped closer, his beady eyes bright. "Who do you think had Penhda send you on that trip? My visions saw you on that beach, starting your journey."

The hakra was no longer looking at Urith. He turned away as he put his arms behind his back, head down, "It was inevitable you would come back here. You know the person who controls this Skool will control everything," he whispered fervently, stopping to look at Urith. "Do you think you or Alcarlic can handle such power? Of course not, it must be someone like me. Someone who looks into the spirit world and realizes that god power will bring all humans under one ruler."

Urith started laughing which turned to words filled with scorn. "You are a fat idiot. Visions won't tell you anything about the Skool, only how to find its pieces. Fedelm has seen only glimpses of where it's located. Only one can control the shield, and it isn't you. That's me alone."

The fat man's face turned red, reminding Urith of an ugly erba. "You won't say such things for long. Soon, you will be telling me all that you know." He directed his torturers to the giant warrior. "Your broken arm will provide me all the pain necessary to get the information I want. Happily, you will end up a cripple with the damage to that arm. Then, I will make it my duty to give you back to Sacred Overlord as an invalid, an empty shell that was once called the Clovel Destroyer. Think about your fortunes after Satres gets hold of you."

Urith took a deep breath as he steeled himself for what was coming, vowing aloud he would kill everyone for what they were about to do to him.

~~~

Satres paced around the small meditation room where the statues of Caruun and Alrpan looked down. However, they remained oblivious to the man who asked for guidance. Around the room was adorned with rich tapestries of Vulthnal wool that hung from the tall walls. The fabrics, showing finely woven images of the gods, looked down on him. An aroma of scented herbs filled the room, but it didn't calm the tired man.

Since returning to the Citadel, the Sacred Overlord felt the world shrinking around him as he confined himself to the single tower housing his rooms and great hall. Dismissing all of his councilors after they questioned the wisdom of his alliance and the invasion of Esterblud, the overlord focused upon the small army under Lyncus. The Aberffraw warriors who survived the underworld were making their way to the Citadel to destroy him. The messengers and reports kept coming about the damage the Cahmais army inflicted upon his kingdom, destroying villages as they spent their wrath upon the populace. While leading a relatively small force, Lyncus rightly surmised that Satres had little options to stop him. The Sacred Overlord held only the loyalty of the Citadel guard to counter the Aberffraw and local militia who began to join against Satres.

Inside the fortress, the overlord heard the grumblings and whispers of those he thought loyal to him. Although Satres attempts to blame the disaster inside Esterblud on the Cahmais king, many members of the Majireef council indicated they believed the Sacred Overlord held much responsibility as well. The rumors were already reaching Ynyover about the underworld monsters unleashed on the humans and the inability of the hakra's to foresee the major events in the human realm. Satres realized his worst fears were coming true as the members of the council now looked him to be the scapegoat.

The morning after the first Aberffraw scout was discovered near the Citadel, Satres had two of the most vocal Majireef members executed. Leaving their bodies to hang just outside the gates, the Sacred Overlord believed his clampdown would strike fear in those who might oppose him. However, his fevered mind would not rest. Voices in his dreams informed him of another plot against his rule. Confident the Fates were telling him about treachery inside the fortress, the next day the man picked two of his loyal guards at random to be executed. While he watched the execution with glee, he missed the malevolent looks coming from some of his guards at his actions.

As the nights passed, Satres was found pacing around the halls, checking on the guards and ensuring the council members were in their bed-chambers. When the man received information that one member of the committee slipped out of the Citadel overnight, his reaction was swift. While his guards reported the leader was attempting to organize Ynyover defenses against the rampaging Aberffraw warriors, Satres had the council member executed when he returned. Inside the Great Hall, the man died by strangulation in front of the remaining council members. The Sacred Overlord left the hall assured he had just stopped another plot against him.

On the morning that Aberffraw arrived near the massive fortress, the morning breeze failed to cool the frenzied mind of Satres who was toying with the idea of executing more of council members, just to emphasize his control. He yawned, knowing he needed sleep but the Sacred Overlord realized sleep was becoming a precious commodity. Each night since returning, the man was overwhelmed by the stark nightmares which invaded his mind. The death of the half-naked woman holding the child repeated continuously in his half sleep. In the terrifying dream, the ghostly image of Dughorm sat in the seat next to the overlord as he whipped the erba pulling his cart. The ghost would sigh and moan, to wake the man every night. The man could not escape the images whenever he tried to sleep. There was a knock on the door, and his body immediately tensed, expecting more bad news.

"Enter," the tired man said as he walked into the bedchamber. The door opened, revealing a young guard who quickly told the overlord that Aberffraw warriors were sacking the town below the fortress.

Racing past the fighter, Satres quickly made his way to the battlements, taking the stone steps two at a time. When he reached the top, he stared down at the small city below, partially obscured by the rising black smoke.

"Where are the *comitatus*? Why hasn't the militia joined in the fight against the Aberffraw?" The Sacred Overlord demanded an answer from the single guard who looked at him blankly. Satres sent the man running after he threatened the guard with immediate execution unless the commander of the guards met him in the Great Hall by the time the Sacred Overlord got there.

The new leader of the Citadel's guards was waiting when the overlord entered the Great Hall. An experienced fighter, Ircia, replaced the previous leader killed by Urith. While quite competent in his duties, this commander of the guards was allied with some of the council who recently left the fortress. It left the overlord highly suspicious of the man. He carefully watched the armored man step to the elaborate seat where Satres sat, nervously drumming his fingers on the arm of the chair.

"You took your time getting here," Satres told him sarcastically. "What is the news about the village? Why do I not see any militia fighting these Cahmais scum who invade Ynyover?"

"You will recall many of the fighters in Ynyover left to join the Aberffraw invasion with you. Hardly any of these men returned. I'm told the leaders within the town attempted to negotiate, but they were slaughtered, and now the men under Lyncus are sacking the village. It seems some of the *comitatus* have joined with the Aberffraw in the pillaging of Ynyover. This is not unexpected given the lack of guidance coming from the Citadel of Br-Ynys," the armored man replied patiently.

The overlord leaned forward, "And what are you doing about it? We cannot hold Ynyover lands with these madmen sacking our towns and villages."

Ircia gave him a curious look. "I only lead a few guards within the Citadel. I'm unaware of any additional fighting men who remain loyal to Ynyover. Those people who could be used to help defend these towns and villages are joining against you. It is the responsibility of the Majireef council and yourself to find the army you need to drive out the Aberffraw."

"Watch your tongue, or I'll have it removed," Satres warned the man.

The leader of the guards did not back down. "You may order such a thing. However, I will guarantee such an order will not be carried out." He smiled affably, taking a deep breath. "Have you not recognized the changes within the Citadel? Locked away in your room, you failed to notice that none of the Majireef council remains in this fortress? Have you asked yourself where your loyal followers are? When you executed two of my guards, your stupidity caused the men who remain within the gates of this fort to give their loyalty to me. And I've made the decision that our loyalty of the Citadel guard is only to the defense of this Citadel, not a buffoon like you." The armored man turned and began walking away from the stunned Satres.

"Before you begin an unseemly rant, you would be wise to understand something. In reality, you are the Sacred Overlord in title only. You have no authority anymore. When most of the council left, you lost the land outside these walls. For the moment, you may stay here as a puppet. My men and I will keep the Citadel safe from the Aberffraw, and when they eventually leave, I will find the right person to restore Ynyover."

The man stopped suddenly, turning back with an evil grin. "By the way, if you give me another order, I'll hand you over to your lover boy, Lyncus. Remember, the guards always know about the dirty little secrets in this fort." Ircia's footsteps echoed as he exited through the double doors of the nearly empty room.

~~~

Outside the walls of the imposing Citadel, Lyncus sat upon his ossane. He was on the outskirts of the burning village, annoyed by what he looked at as the smoke obscured his view at times, forcing him to slowly move his mount along the road. Behind him, his men contented themselves with the slaughter, rape, and pillage of any inhabitants and their possessions. As they moved from village to village, his rabble became notorious for their brutally efficient methods, forcing many to flee before they arrived. Some of the militia came from smaller tribes, hostile to the Ynyover nobles. They quickly joined with the Aberffraw when they recognized their fate was in the hands of Lyncus. While he despised these local traitors as much as Satres, they were useful to his reign of terror. His allies quickly pointed out loyal followers of the Sacred Overlord, and those prisoners quickly learned of the thin man's vengeance.

However, when he looked at the object of his capture, Lyncus instantly recognized the odds were against him as he tried to think of a way to enter the fort. His force was far too small to overrun the substantial fortification on the top of the hill. And a siege would be nearly impossible now that his men pillaged much of the fertile areas of the small kingdom. While they controlled the port with tribal allies, a siege would be costly and, worse, left him vulnerable to other lands becoming involved. And if the Esterbluds came into Ynyover following him, he would be in a desperate situation. It was something he realized now. And the thought made him angry. He should have planned out his path before he began his march of terror toward Br-Ynys.

He heard the sound of an ossane galloping to him, the sound carried over the few screams still coming from the village and turned in his saddle to see Vritgus.

"I've had the men put everything of value, along with food stock into carts. We can walk their slaves back. I've got several lovely women to help warm the nights since their men are just spirits for Caruun now. Not very good fighters and they die screaming like cowards." The second in command spit in contempt at the slaughtered prisoners. Vritgus started to smile before he saw his leader return to staring at the fort. "I assumed you wished us to be ready for the return to Cahmais?"

Lyncus quickly gave the man a deadly glare. "I don't care about your slaves or the dead people. I want that *scunce* in the fortress disemboweled as I watch."

Vritgus remained calm, turning his gaze to the towering structure. "I'll be happy to do this. I just don't see them coming out to greet us like the leaders of this village did. How do we get in there?"

The son of King Asgurd gave a low humph as he returned his stare to the structure above. After a moment, he let out a deep sigh. "There must be a way since Urith, and his group of rabble entered that place to escape with Caestia. It is something I must think about."

"What are your orders?" His second in command asked quietly.

"I want the men to set up a camp just outside the walls, then they will scour every place around the Citadel to see if we can find a weakness."

"And, if they don't find something?"

Lyncus glared at him again. "Every place has a weakness. Your men need to be smart enough to find it or I'll hold you accountable."

Vritgus nodded slowly, thinking those women he captured wouldn't be of much use to him if he didn't find a way into the fortress.

~~~

Kriell's long tentacles draped over the throne of souls as the creature waited impatiently for the latest updates about the human realm. In his dark, gelatinous form, the soul stealer appeared sedate, almost inert except for the occasional image of one of the ingested gods showing through the black flesh. The souls of the underworld flashed like they were trying to pop out of their terrible prison, only to fade away again.

Kriell was slowly digesting their spirit energies. Soon, Caruun and Alrpan would evaporate into nothingness, leaving only their powers with the soul stealing entity once called a Guardian.

But the new master of the underworld thought nothing of his victims, its mind solely focused upon its next target. The Sky Realm was in chaos. With the loss of the god of the sea, the powers of Duwdamon grew weaker, even with the recharging energies of the Exyts waters. Since Kriell's underworld creatures started their wave of terror upon the humans at night, the symbiotic relationship between Sky realm and those who prayed to the gods grew tenuous. Satgerts found their faithful flocks avoiding the temples, the offerings from priests and faithful no longer sustaining the powers of the Sky Realm. Yet, down in his own realm, the spirits of the unworthy grew steadily, filling the underworld. The slaughter from the monsters unleashed at night kept the flow of souls coming into underworld realm. The turmoil coincided with increased need for violence and barbarity used by the human overlords of Kamin to maintain their grip on power. Events were proceeding exactly as Kriell envisioned when he stepped from the Void.

Yet, there was still one item to resolve. The Shield of Skool remained in the hands of the humans. While he knew the weapon was still unfinished, the master of the underworld remembered the power of the Skool. It blasted Kriell and the other Guardians into the Void, helping establish the current realms. The creature would not allow the instrument to again banish him into the blackness of ether.

"What have you learned," Kriell's voice came out in a warble when the creature god felt the Vanth enter the large beehive structure.

The creature named Actita cocked his head, the snake-hair squirming hideously. "The human's battle at Eran finished by the Sky Realm. The Skool resides there."

"What of the human who controls it?"

While Actita could not smile with a beaked mouth, his tone indicated pleasure. "The human's talk of destroying the man. They torture but not a good as me."

"Then, perhaps the humans will do our bidding for us." Kriell went silent for a moment as he considered the options. "Yes, maybe I will turn into Alrpan to help convince their priests to kill the man. Now, what else did you learn?"

"Mivraa came to a *sidhera* near the fort with spirits for me. She kills humans for sport like the Guardians once did." The beaked creature appeared confused by the change in the demigoddess of Haligulf.

"You spoke with her?" Kriell asked, and the Vanth nodded slowly.

"No longer cares of Haligulf. She told me she wishes for revenge. Asks if Caruun will help."

The tentacles slowly receded into the black body as the creature transformed into the underworld god known as Caruun. "This is fascinating information you bring. Find out whether she can prove useful to us. See what you can learn from her, especially what does she want? Caruun's memories which I carry inside tell me the woman is no friend of the underworld. I don't trust she would help us, even after what her brothers did to her on the mountain."

The Vanth cocked its head in birdlike fashion before bowing to leave. Kriell fully transformed into Caruun while he thought about the demigoddess and her sudden change of heart. Despite her human weakness, her knowledge could benefit him. The Guardian believed he understood the vulnerabilities of the Sky Realm yet it would be difficult to send his hordes into the area without help. But the idea of revenge against Duwdamon by using the sky god's half human daughter intrigued him. The creature decided she might provide him with the perfect means to a fitting retribution.

~~~

It was long after the twin moons of Kamin rose over Eran when Urith saw Dughorm. The ghost of his dead friend at first whispered, then he demanded the warrior to open his eyes. The giant man finally pulled himself from his semi-conscious state to see the spirit drifting next to him. Through the hazy glow of the dead man, Urith saw Fedelm was still chained to the wall like himself. She was unconscious, the blood stains on her back from the continued lashings now dried dark.

"You will not suffer much longer, my friend. Help will come." Urith shook his head, but the ghost remained.

"I've never seen you like this before," the warrior could only manage a whisper, his throat raw from his screams of pain.

The ghost took a seat on the wooden bench used by Feeral to watch the torture earlier. "No need to speak. Just listen." The ghostly image patted his robe, looking for something. "By the gods, I wish I still had my pipe. Oh, well." He looked up at the chained prisoner. "Since my death, I've become the oracle to the Sky Realm now. During my time with Duwdamon, I've learned much about the gods and their weaknesses. I've also seen events the Fates have in store. This priest called Feeral is correct about torture bringing the visions to the injured. But no one saw the great conflict coming except for me. More trouble lies ahead for you, but it's not what you think. Forget about your wounds and the suffering. Keep to your goal when you are released."

"I'm going to kill Feeral and those who maimed me." Urith forced a growl from his dry lips.

"That man is no matter. Keep your head because you will need all the allies you can find. Many will join with us." Dughorm leaned against the wall. "But that is not why I come. The fat man who tortured you and Fedelm doesn't realize the final vision of the Skool was already known by Fedelm." He looked over at her, smiling. "I have to give her credit; she is one special person to hold out like this. She knows where the last piece of the Skool resides."

"But she never told me," Urith croaked softly.

The ghost turned back to the warrior. "No, she understood you were not finished in Eran. While much remains centered on your path with the god weapon, the Fates have paths for others. Now, you must let others complete the tasks needed for the people of Esterblud. Your task is much too large for you to be conflicted. You must follow the path that this hakra gives you, only her. Do you understand me? It's vital to the future."

The big man nodded. "What about Mivraa?"

Dughorm looked at his empty hands. "She will return to you. Unfortunately, she has become dangerous to everyone, herself included. You know that revenge is her sole focus. It will drive her to abandon everything. Don't forget that!" The ghost shook his head like he wanted to forget a bad memory.

"Whatever she does, you must remember to follow your true nature of honor. It will help you to understand and do what is necessary when the time comes." The ghost paused. "One last thing before I must return. This is probably the most important. A Guardian has returned from the void. The gods who nearly killed you in the mountains are nothing compared to Kriell. This creature controls the underworld now, and he carries the disguises of Caruun and Alrpan, if not more. He will be after the Skool as it is the only thing powerful enough to stop him."

The shock on Urith's face was apparent. "What do you mean? I heard that name spoken but I don't understand. Why are not the gods of the Sky Realm against this one from the void?"

The ghost started to fade. "The entities of the Sky Realm are not smart enough, and the few gods left grow weak. I've told them about the Guardian, but it is now clear Kriell has already taken their future." His voice became ominous, and he vanished. "Heed my words; Kriell will destroy everything and everyone to achieve revenge and dominance of all three realms."

"No, don't leave," the warrior rasped out, but the figure was gone. He dropped his head, staring at the floor.

"Don't worry, I'm back." A familiar female's voice echoed in Urith's ear.

He looked up to see Feeral standing at the doorway. The fat man's face was ashen white. Beside him stood Brihar, the leader of the Gramcle tribe, and well known to Urith. Suddenly Feeral fell forward, after Mivraa pushed him, sending the fat man sprawling on the rock floor. The demigoddess stepped next to Brihar with a smug look on her face.

"Looks like you need some help," she said as she walked over to the Esterblud prisoner. "I found Brihar and his men coming to Eran. He wasn't happy with Alcarlic and these henchmen."

As the woman carefully unlatched the iron bands around Urith's wrists, Brihar entered with some of his men who unlocked Fedelm from her chains. One fighter held a spear on the back of Feeral who remained face down on the ground. Brihar stepped next to Urith.

"I'm sorry I'm late, my friend. The goddess of Haligulf nearly cut the man up, but he decided to cooperate now."

Urith groaned when the demigoddess unlatched the binding around his broken arm, and he tried to cradle the wounded appendage with his other hand. It was evident the arm was severely deformed from the torture. The agonizing pain nearly sent the great warrior to his knees while the woman and Brihar helped him to sit on the bench near the door.

"My men and I were delayed getting here from Gramcan. The other tribes of Esterblud are becoming restless since the news of Penhda's death so took extra time to spread the word about the Council of the Elders coming to Eran." The Gramcle leader explained as he directed his men to take the semiconscious Fedelm out of the room. "Take her to a proper bed and have a healer tend to her immediately," the man ordered.

He turned back to Urith. "Come, we will do the same for you."

Shaking his head, the giant warrior took several attempts to stand. When he finally was able to get to his feet, he slowly let his damaged arm dangle at his side. Walking to Feeral, he used his good arm to pull the sweating man from the floor.

"You wanted to control the Skool," Urith told the fat man, "now is your chance."

He quickly twisted the hood on the man's white robe, forcing the man up. Together, they moved to the shield hanging on the wall. Feeral had his men use a wooden pole to display the Shield of Skool like a trophy. The high priest pleaded for help, but no one moved to assist him. As two men stepped in front of the round object, Urith told the man to take the shield. Feeral refused.

"Pick it up and learn the power of the gods," Urith croaked out. Still, Feeral would not move, his wide eyes showing the fear. Urith's tight, twisting grip around hood caused the man to start choking.

Disgust filled Urith's face. "You torture for it and pray for it, but you're still afraid of it because you're weak. But now you must face this weapon you wanted so badly."

The large Esterblud heaved the satgert into the shield using his one good arm. Sparks flew when fat man encountered the Skool. Feeral stood, rigid like a statue, shuddering as the immense power ran through him. An instant later, the man fell to the floor, wisps of white smoke coming from the body. Urith calmly walked over the dead man and retrieved the god weapon. With practiced ease, he flipped the Shield of Skool over his back and hooked it to his baudrik belt.

"Now we can see the healer," Urith breathed out through gritted teeth. As he slowly hobbled out the cell, the group of Gramcle warriors quickly   moved   aside.

Chapter 4: Underworld Rises

Late the next morning, the tension among the clans within the fortress was palatable. Brihar could sense the anger and resentment coming from the Eranis warriors. The stares and mutterings were evident as he made his way through the courtyard. The man entered the small room where he found Urith standing by a small window. Despite his pale face and the dark rings around the man's eyes, the Esterblud appeared ready to travel. The mighty warrior wore his coat of mail and full armor, his Clovel Sword was sheathed on his belt, and the Shield of Skool hooked over his back.

Brihar was surprised to see Urith's green Geniht tunic, typically covering the warrior's coat of mail, replaced with a nondescript tan woolen cloth. The leader of the Gramcle tribe also noticed Fedelm sitting on the bench near the window. The woman had just pulled over a hooded linen shirt. While she moved slowly, the woman's pale face showed her determination as she appeared to be readying herself for a journey.

"Are you leaving before the Council of Elders assemble?" Brihar asked. "I must say that neither of you looks able to travel very far. You and she should take the time to recover."

Urith grunted, "We'll make do. The healer gave us herbs to help the pain. The clans of Esterblud can sort out who leads these lands. I have other business."

"I see." The tribal leader went to a table next to Urith where he picked up a *jamala* among the remains of breakfast left there. He took a bite out of the bittersweet fruit.

"I might have put the Esterblud kingdom in peril by coming to your aid with Mivraa last night," Brihar told Urith. "Many of those in this fortress believe I've sided against Alcarlic. But in my defense, I met the demigoddess right after she killed those satgerts who tortured you and Fedelm. When she asked where you were, I didn't think wise not to join her at the time.

"She can be persuasive," Urith replied diplomatically. "However, I've never seen you put off by a fight."

The stocky man smiled broadly. "No, I was mad when I found out what happened. Feeral deserved his fate. I knew immediately who put him up to it. These events give me an excuse to get back at Alcarlic." His expression went sober. "However, I hope it wasn't a mistake. Too many of our people are blaming others within Esterblud for the disasters. I've heard concerns about you and Fedelm. And I don't think your killing of Feeral will help your cause."

Urith looked at the splint covering his arm, his death sneer showing on his face. "I'm not diplomatic enough to let such things go. If I had my way, I would have flayed him alive first. But, like you said, that fat *calward* was just following what his master told him."

"I agree. That's why I'm wondering if you should leave. We need all warriors to back whoever becomes king. Esterblud cannot fall apart because of bickering tribes. I would think that anyone with the power you hold in that shield would be interested."

Urith shook his head. "My friend, you're missing the point. The Skool is not to force an overlord upon those of Esterblud. My path is not with my people or yours. I only came back to these lands to finish my mission for King Penhda. He is dead, and my work as a Geniht is complete. I will no longer wear the colors of a group that does not exist. Now I go where I'm called to finish the work given to me by the Fates."

"Some of the tribes may not want that," Brihar reminded them before he took another bite of fruit.

Urith gave him the death sneer again as his voice turned almost to a snarl. "Such people only want the power within the Skool to rule and terrorize. But let's be honest, do you think any of them can stop me? I may have let my guard down before, thinking I was among friends. Now, anyone who tries to stop me will face the Skool. I will finish what the Fates have given me, maimed arm or not."

Brihar nodded, knowing the Esterblud meant what he said. The stout man watched as Fedelm gingerly tightened her belt. His expression showed the appreciation for the woman's toughness when he remembered the wounds on her back. He turned back to Urith. "What then? What becomes of the holder to such power?"

"Such a question assumes I will survive." The giant warrior took the last fruit from the table, walking over to offer it to Fedelm. She shook her head. He turned back to Brihar.

"I have gods against me. If Dughorm is correct, there's a Guardian god among them who sends the underworld after me as well. I don't think the future is something I can worry about right now. Now finish that *jamala* so you can escort us to our ossanes. I don't want Alcarlic and his men to start something he'll regret," Urith explained to his friend before he took a bite of the fruit.

In the stables just in the fortress gates, Urith finally finished placing his saddle on his mount. Just outside the stable were several of Brihar's men keeping an eye out for any problems arising from Alcarlic's people. As he struggled with tying off the leather attachment, the giant warrior heard the distant sound of hoofbeats. Shouts from nearby Eranis men told him that a contingent of Esterbluds was arriving. He looked over to Fedelm who was already on her ossane, riding out of the open pen. Her expression confirmed what he heard.

"I don't know how large your village might be, but it looks like Oslaf has brought everyone with him," she told him hastily before she spurred her mount toward the arched entrance.

Finishing his work, the large man took the reins of the animal and slowly led the creature out of the pen. His arm was nearly useless from the pain with each slight movement. Urith thought about the arduous journey coming when he finally saw a long line of ossanes carrying warriors from Cilgarran with Oslaf leading them. He immediately noticed the black helmet of his young mentor, ready for battle. "I believe my nephew will be disappointed more than he realizes after we talk." Urith was smiling as he walked up next to Fedelm.

"Are you sure you want to do this?" She asked the man while he pulled himself up on the smelly ossane. "You know he's not going to like it."

Nodding, the man spurred on his mount to the gate. "I know, but he has little choice now. I have to do what's right for my people."

When the pair rode through the open gates of the fort, Urith waved to the line of Esterblud warriors who suddenly slowed. When the first fighters closed in around them, Urith recognized a familiar black helmet and shield held by a warrior riding next to his nephew.

"Pehnuwick, by the gods, what are you doing here?"

Urith's brother pulled off his helmet, his handsome face showing feigned resignation. Fedelm caught the gleam in the man's eyes at the sight of Urith. "I'm here to save your hide again brother. What did you do now?"

"Now, that's no way to greet your favorite brother. Anyway, it is great you are here. Those disappointed Eranis men behind me are waiting for people like you to show up for the council. You know, put all you diplomats into a room so you can figure out what to do with yourselves." His broad smile caused Pehnuwick to grunt. Fedelm suppressed a smirk at the similarity between the brothers.

"So, we came with the entire warrior population of Cilgarran for nothing?" Oslaf asked. There was disappointment showing on his face as he pushed back his helmet.

"No, I'm truly happy you have arrived, but you're just a bit late. Fedelm and I had some help from Brihar and Mivraa last night. However, it is wise you brought our people. Some will be needed for what's coming. Come, let's discuss this. Follow me."

Urith turned his mount, motioning his brother and nephew away from the group while Henther rode up next to Fedelm. The two women listened to the murmuring coming from some of the Esterbluds fighters around them who expressed their disappointment with the lack of an expected battle.

"Are you ok?" Henther asked the hakra. "You look to be in pain."

Fedelm nodded, "I'll be alright. I'm glad you're here. Did you see Mivraa?"

The woman shook her head as a dark expression crossed her attractive face. "No, not on the path we were coming back to Eran."

"What is it?"

Henther turned her mount and led the woman away from the warriors. She explained to Fedelm what she and Oslaf witnessed the day before in the forest outside Eran. Henther could see the hakra was not surprised. Fedelm told her about the changes she saw during their journey with the demigoddess.

"I'm not sure what is happening. Urith explained that Mivraa joined with Brihar to release us, but she never returned after they took him to a healer. I'm not sure Mivraa really knows what she's doing at times. If what you say is true, she might be a *brgensoc*" Fedelm shook her head as Henther thought about the term she used.

"Then the gods turned her into a brain sick person. No wonder Urith curses them." Henther replied.

Fedelm patted the neck of her mount, giving her a thin smile. "The more I know, the more I agree with him. However, the only thing I know with clarity is the next place to go. That's what Urith is telling his brother now." She was looking at the three Esterbluds, noticing how similar they were in their physique and manner. "Funny, in all this time together, I never thought about Oslaf's father. Urith always acted the part, I guess."

Henther gave a smirk as she thought about the woman's words. "You're right about that. I believe Urith basically raised Oslaf when Pehnuwick was chosen as King Penhda's personal diplomat. Even though I only met Oslaf's father last night, I knew right away he was Urith's brother. He's like a calmer version of the man."

Fedelm laughed as she thought about the image. It didn't fit from her point of view. Her smile faded as the men turned their mounts toward the women, quickly riding closer.

"Well, it's settled," Pehnuwick explained. "Oslaf will stay in Eran to help me. From what I hear, Wilgam and my son are the perfect leaders to rebuild. I'll work with Brihar and the other leaders to keep the clans from ripping the lands apart. Some of our people will be staying. I don't want Alcarlic to become too enamored with his idea that he will have his father's title."

The women noticed Oslaf was not happy with the news, but he remained silent as he rode off with his father and Henther. Urith watched the three join the rest of the Esterbluds before he turned to Fedelm. "Too bad, they are needed here. I believe we could use some extra help when we go to Ynyover."

The woman nodded, looking at him oddly. It was the first time she recalled the giant warrior even hinting he might need help. She wondered what he was thinking, but she knew he would tell her in his own time. The two riders turned to the south and began their long trek to the Citadel.

Oslaf glanced back at his uncle and Fedelm, still upset that he was staying in Eran. He wasn't paying attention as his father rode up after sending some of the Esterblud fighters to the fortress while sending others back to their homes.

"You do your people a great service by staying here," Pehnuwick said as he led the group to the fort. "My brother will miss your help, but he carries the burden of the Skool, not you."

"Maybe, but I still feel I can do more to assist him. Eran doesn't need me, he does."

Oslaf's father frowned. "Then, you are not thinking, and that shames me. Remember, it was Urith that told you to stay. He, like me, realizes you have the talent to help us bring Esterblud back together. King Penhda, for all his faults, was the hide glue that kept the tribes together."

"I would have thought you or Urith would be such a force now," Oslaf replied, raising his eyebrow slightly at the conversation. In the past, his father rarely spoke with such openness around him.

The large man smiled briefly. "No, Urith is not one to lead a land like ours. You know he never held such ambition, and he never liked the internal struggles of men competing for the king's attention. In fact, he would be content to be left alone and travel Kamin. He is a wanderer at heart."

"Well, you would be the natural fit," Oslaf persisted.

His father shook his head as he stopped his ossane. "Unfortunately, I am not. While I might have the ambition and the skills," the man smiled briefly, "I know I don't have the time."

"What do you mean?" The surprise in the young warrior's voice was evident.

Pehnuwick scratched at the few days' growth of facial hair, avoiding his son's eyes. "I know that I should have involved you in such matters before you left with Urith to Ynysover. However, I thought you would return sooner." He took a deep breath and stared at Oslaf. "The fact is I probably won't make it through the coming winter."

There was a stunned silence before Oslaf finally asked. "What are you telling me?"

"The aches in my belly grow worse. The healers who must give me herbs for the pain." He stopped. "Well, they say the rot inside will kill me before the spring."

Oslaf's mouth hung open for a moment as Henther glanced at him. She could see so much in his face. A range of emotions flickered through his eyes before hiding as his facade went up. It was a same reaction she expected from his uncle, Urith.

Oslaf nodded. "I wish I had known."

Pehnuwick gave his son a proud smile as he placed his hand on the young warrior's shoulder. "It is the Fates. Really, what can anyone really do? You have done me proud by staying. Now, honor me by keeping this knowledge to yourself."

Oslaf promised. "I will do all I can to assist you."

"Good, now let's find some heathmead and get the work started." The large, dying man spurred his horse, yelling back to them. "By the way, Henther's noble blood will come in handy when I get you two in front of a satgert soon. This Esterblud family needs proper grandchildren coming."

Her face turning red, Henther looked at Oslaf. "He's too much like Urith."

"No, Urith's too much like my dad." The young man corrected his lover proudly.

As the sun began to set that day, the elders and leaders from the three top clans of Esterblud met in the banquet hall in the fort. Those in attendance felt the tension from the three groups separated by the large tables arranged in a semi-circle from another where the leaders sat. Everyone knew Alcarlic would make a forceful claim to replace his father as the head of the country. The question for many would be the reactions from respected elders along with the other leaders. For his part, Alcarlic came to the meeting late, carrying himself confidently. The room filled with voices as the fighters realized the son of Penhda wore the ripped, bloodstain tunic of his father. Under his arm, the man carried the battered helmet he retrieved when he left the fields of Awarware.

Pehnuwick, sitting next to Brihar, narrowed his eyes while Brihar scowled at the display. Near the back of the room, Oslaf watched the proceedings with Henther at his side. Both were seated on the long bench not far away from Alcarlic. Oslaf leaned over to her, making a joke about Alcarlic but there was no humor in his face.

"I wonder if he decided to bring back the overlord's loin cloth as well?"

Alcarlic, paused, throwing a glare at Oslaf while several Esterblud warriors who were next to the couple started laughing, slamming down their mugs on the table in agreement. Oslaf held the stare back at the man.

Henther noticed the eye contact, and she leaned next to him, advising him to let Pehnuwick and Brihar confront the man. Oslaf remained quiet, but he would not stop his focus on the man who instigated Urith's torture.

The woman knew the young man next to her wanted revenge after hearing what Urith and Fedelm went through. However, she hoped Oslaf's father would find a solution before the warrior decided to retaliate. As the daughter of Kirowan, she recognized warrior honor and retribution. The fact that Pehnuwick was able to secure her a spot with the Esterblud warriors was an honor itself as she was one of the few women in the hall. The rest were serving drink and food, the cute ones trying to avoid the lecherous intent of some of the men. While these women were part of the clan families, the sights revived old memories. She recalled her time doing a similar type of work for pirates after her enslavement quickly turned into prostitution.   Abandoned after her father's death, she wore the yellow belt of the docke to feed and clothe herself. While Oslaf helped her give up the past, something she would always treasure, she worried about her precarious existence. She was an outsider in Esterblud. Even as a devoted daughter of a Vulthnal hero, Henther believed her background could turn into a problem for Oslaf in the future. As she looked at the young man watching the elders, the woman hoped he would never regret his decision.

After Alcarlic had sat next to three Eranis clan elders, Draca rose to address the room. He began by stating the kinship of the tribes must continue. "We cannot allow the Holy Overlord and his Cahmais ally to find us weak and divided. I ask for a seamless transition to the throne by someone that King Penhda himself would acknowledge is the heir apparent. That person is Alcarlic."

There was an uproar from the Esterblud and Gramcle groups at the words. Pehnuwick and Brihar both stood, signaling for their supporters to quiet themselves. Ivrsun, the oldest warrior from Gramcle, threw his mug on the floor near Draca, the heathmead splashing everyone near him.

"There's never been an heir to the throne of Esterblud. Only petty little men would think the Eranis tribe owns the throne. I say Brihar is the man." His quavering voice cracked as he tried to stand, the drunken old man threatened Draca. Brihar placed his strong arm on the man, advising him to sit. The stout man raised his arms, and the crowd grew silent.

"I lead men in battle. Those of you, who know me, understand that I don't crave the throne. I have spoken with Pehnuwick on this matter already. We are in agreement that only a trusted warrior who can unite all of us will be needed. Alcarlic is not that person."

The Eranis clan erupted at the words of the short, stout man. Alcarlic stepped toward Brihar. "Who are you to say that? Are you backing Pehnuwick as the new king?

The statement caused Pehnuwick to rush forward. "Alcarlic, listen well. Brihar knows I will not accept any offer to become king."

"Then, that would leave only me," the son of Penhda sneered at him. "I'm glad you see the wisdom of not challenging me."

Pehnuwick paused, looking like he might suddenly break the man's neck. Then, he smiled as he looked over to the elders. "In our recent discussion, Brihar and I have agreed to look past our clan loyalty. In doing so, we decided we must support someone who is independent of the former king's influence and thinking. With the darkness descending upon the land from the turmoil of the gods, we need people who can understand this new world, not carry around the garments of those who have been destroyed by it. I warn everyone in this room, if you make the wrong choice, this kingdom will fracture quickly." The brother of Urith stared directly at Alcarlic as he made his statement and the son of Penhda grew visibly upset. The crowd in the room remained mostly silent with a few murmurs of agreement.

"I ask the elders, do you agree with this strategy? Say so now or let us return to our clans."

As planned earlier, the elders of the Gramcle and Esterblud tribes quickly agreed to the proposal. "It's about time somebody gave some sensible ideas about this. Even the Eranis needs the other clans in the face of the danger coming," Ivrsun spoke up, glaring at the three elders of the Eranis clan who were visibly shaken at the sudden turn of events.

Pehnuwick looked back at Alcarlic. "Do you have someone like that within your clan?"

Not waiting for an answer, Brihar suddenly spoke up. "I call for Wilgam and Oslaf to step in front of all."

The crowd of fighters watched as the two surprised men came before the elders. Brihar announced the pair should be the two co-rulers of Esterblud lands.

"These men fought to save Eran from the Aberffraw. They joined together with the help of all clans within the fort. Can anyone deny that?" Brihar reminded those in the room. "Unlike some, they've proven themselves and have shown no ambition beyond what was best for all the clans. Can anyone doubt they would lead as one?"

Red with frustration and the slights directed at him, Alcarlic came toward Brihar. "Those two men failed to follow the orders of their king."

He pointed at Oslaf, "That one ran back to his village rather than face justice."

Before Pehnuwick could stop him, Oslaf rushed at Alcarlic, punching the smaller man in the face. "Pull your sword, you *calward*." Brihar and Pehnuwick grabbed him, pulling him away as the young warrior screamed out curses. "You tortured my uncle and my friend through that fat satgert. I demand *fealth* even if you don't have the honor, you son of a docke."

Chaos quickly filled the room as Alcarlic swiftly pulled his sword. The king's son pushed past elders to attack Oslaf while the young warrior was still being held back. Fortunately, the sword blow struck him in the shoulder, stopped by the chain mail he wore.

Brihar instantly released Oslaf who swiftly pulled his sword in defense. While men from the factions gathered around to watch, Brihar and Pehnuwick continued their attempts stop the coming fight, shouting at the Eranis elders to intercede. However, Alcarlic attacked again. This time, Oslaf parried the sword blow, coming around with his fist to strike the man in the face again. He caught a glance of his father. Pehnuwick quickly pointed his own sword at the throat of an Eran clan member who was about to join Alcarlic.

Taking a cue from his uncle, Oslaf smiled as the Eran leader shook off the blow to the head.

"You fight like a tavern maid," the Esterblud smirked at Alcarlic.

As he suspected, his opponent charged him with a wave of powerful blows which Oslaf countered. Alcarlic tried to feign a side step move, but the Esterblud recognized the ruse and waited for the right moment to embed the point of his sword into the man's thigh, just below the chain mail. The Eran yowled in pain. Oslaf quickly followed up with another blow from his fist into Alcarlic's nose. Blood spurted across the man's face, and the Esterblud followed up by slashing the sword arm of his opponent who dropped his weapon. Clearly at an advantage, Oslaf suddenly backed away as he lowered his sword.

"I should kill you, but you are not worthy of such a death." The young warrior turned his attention to the Eranis elders, yelling to them.

"Instead, I'll let Alcarlic explain to his clan why they would let a weakling lead their cause. Do you wish to follow this person?"

Recognizing the dismay on their faces, Oslaf knew Alcarlic just lost much of the support of his tribe by the quick defeat. The Eran fighters looked away in disgust, only a few attempted to help their leader get to his feet.

Oslaf turned away as he sheathed his sword while his father came next to him, nodding his approval. The warriors began to mill around, people still glaring at their rivals and opponents.

Suddenly there was a yell, and Oslaf turned to see Alcarlic closing in on him with a long dagger in hand. Before the Esterblud could react, a sword came out of nowhere striking the attacker across the face. As the body fell to the floor, Pehnuwick stepped in front of Oslaf, holding his bloody sword at the ready.

"We end this now. Is there another Eran clan member who wants to side with Alcarlic?" The crowd wearing the colors of the Eranis clan looked among themselves, but no one spoke up until Draca stepped in front of the sharp sword of Pehnuwick.

"Our people have reached an impasse." The elder turned to his warriors. "We now have a choice. Our clans can become bitter enemies. Then, we will rip the lands apart with hatred and revenge. Those who support Penhda would say it is the time." He paused as some of the men nodded, their faces filled with hate. The man stepped over the body and faced several of those who apparently wanted to continue the fight.

"Look down at our feet. Which of you actually believes that Alcarlic could replace Penhda?" Again the man paused. "I've seen much, and I say the son of Penhda was not worthy of such responsibility. Now that he is gone, we need a new leader. Can we find this person by fighting with the other clans?"

The old man slowly circled along the fighters lined up on the opposing sides. "I say to let one respected Eranis warrior into the group of Gramcle and Esterblud leaders. They can work together to unite the lands. Otherwise, we fight now.

Draca looked at Brihar and Pehnuwick. "I call upon the Gramcle and Esterblud clans. Can you add one from our clan? Give us your answer."

Brihar stepped next to Draca, extending his arm. "Draca, you give wise counsel. The Gramcle will accept any Eran who seeks to bring cooperation and security for all within the lands of Esterblud." The leader began encouraging his followers to support the idea as he clasped his hands together with Eranis elder.

Pehnuwick sheathed his sword, then the large man nodded at Draca and Brihar, "I support this as well and will ask my people to agree." He started clapping.

Draca raised his hands, and the clapping stopped. "Then, I will gather the Eran fighters to bring a worthy person who will help us in this endeavor." The old man told two of his family to remove Alcarlic's body before he walked toward the door. Slowly the rest of the clan began to follow him. While the tensions remained with sidelong glares, it was clear to all that the initial break between the tribes was averted for the moment.

"Well, you removed a large thorn from my side and nearly started a war among the tribes. I thought only Urith was capable of such a feat." Brihar scolded Oslaf lightly, giving him a grin before he turned to Pehnuwick. "We were lucky. It appears the Fates have given us a different path now, my friend, although I suspect you might have considered it before striking down that man. I believe the Eran will join with us."

Pehnuwick expression remained serious. "I did. It seemed the only path left to us for the moment. Alcarlic would have brought our lands to despair with his ambition. But, I will hold judgment until we know who the Eran wants to bring to this council. Then, we can see if Esterblud holds together or not."

~~~

Far to the south, Urith and Fedelm traveled the empty road to Ynyover. The pair remained silent for much of their ride, weary and fighting off the pains of their wounds by chewing on *creqweed*. The only sound was the hoof beats and the occasional snort from their ossanes. As they traveled through Esterblud lands, they found abandoned farms and villages, the people yet to return since being driven out by news of the Aberffraw invasion. Even the animals seemed afraid to show themselves. For her part, Fedelm worried about Mivraa. They had not seen or heard from the demigoddess. It was unusual for warrior goddess not to be seen since they left Eran. After leaving the fort, Fedelm told Urith about the carnage from the hands of the demigoddess against any warrior she came across. While he remained stoic at the news, she knew Urith was upset at the thought. However, he refused to say anything more, and it put Fedelm in a bad mood. It did not help that her numerous welts and cuts on her back felt the slightest movement of her clothing with every step of her mount. Unsure what to expect from Mivraa, she glanced up at the giant man who held his natural reticence. It was times like this when she wished he spoke more since it was seldom clear what he might be thinking about.

Urith noticed the woman continued to look in his direction, but he forced himself to remain silent. He had nothing to tell her which had any certainty. While he remembered clearly what the ghost of Dughorm said to him, the man remained worried about those who followed him. He was also distracted by his mangled arm more than he would admit. It continued to ache and throb. Despite his bravado at Eran, the warrior knew he would have problems holding and directing the Shield of Skool if they encountered any enemies. He might even destroy his own friends from the power of the weapon. On top of this, he felt he left a bit of himself behind when he forced Oslaf to remain at the fort for the Council of Clans. However, Urith knew his nephew needed to learn more than fighting in battle, things that Pehnuwick would teach far better than he could. Still, the loss of a good fighter, as well as Henther who gave valuable practical advice to the group, forced him to confront the lack of help. Perhaps the Fates now wanted to change his luck. He looked over and caught Fedelm's glance. He gave her his sneer smile, "You're too quiet without Mivraa around." He recognized the concern in the woman's expression.

"I was wondering if she was captured by Duwdamon," the woman told him.

The warrior shook his head. "I doubt it. She'll show up soon," his words lacked conviction. "While I have no doubt that she's plotting something against the Sky Realm, she still appears on our side. Her help saved both of us from Freel's hospitality. Anyway, I'm more concerned about where we are going. This track takes us through Awarware. Brihar told me about the underworld monsters coming into the lands at night in greater numbers. I'm willing to bet there is a *sidhera* near. If so, we might have a fight on our hands."

The woman nodded, "That could be. Do you think they will attack us?"

He shrugged, "Only the Fates know. The only thing I'm sure about is a strong feeling that someone is following us. And whoever it might be, they are skilled because I can't locate where they are and who they might be."

"Maybe it's Mivraa?" Fedelm thought aloud.

"I thought about that but why wouldn't she just come out?" Urith asked. "No, she would come to us. I believe that we must keep on our guard as we travel."

"What about your arm? Can you handle the shield?"

"I'll be good with this splint. I had the healer put sturdy pieces of wood around my arm and open up the straps on the shield." He looked at his arm, wondering if it really would make any difference before he asked about her back.

Fedelm gave him a quick smile. "We've been together long enough for me to know when you want to change the subject. My back is as good as your arm."

Urith returned her smile. "Then, it must hurt like *Phlege* fire."

~~~

The realm of the Sky Gods was quiet, unusually so. The water sprites regularly provided a refreshing chatter along the Exyts Spring. However, now they hid in the shadows in the human realm, avoiding the temperamental outbursts coming from master of the Sky Realm, Duwdamon. The servants to the gods realized the fundamental change sweeping over the upper realm, Frem the Exyts Spring waters through the temples, offerings and prayers to the gods waned which weakened all of those spirits sustained by the energies. The terror of the water sprites was only one indicator of the changes happening. The Sky gods remained in disarray with only Ecarca and Duwdamon still holding the Sky Realm. Those in the Sky Realm believed Unis and Uugor continued to travel to retrieve the Shield of Skool. While unseen by the master of the realm, Uugor occasionally arrived near the Exyts Spring to relay messages to Duwdamon through Dughorm. For his part, the Sky God sent out his elemental servants in search of his missing wife. However, many of the servants failed to return and those spirits which did return knew nothing of the goddess since her escape from Urith and his group. With their long absence, the leader of the Sky Realm became convinced that the goddess of the sky and her son must be plotting to control the god weapon. Even when Dughorm revealed his vision of Unis within the underworld, Duwdamon dismissed the idea out of hand. Casting god's Sybil aside, the Sky God instead relied upon Ecarca for his information, confident the god of land and soil could be trusted.

With his temper growing more volatile each day at his insistence that his family was subverting his will. The Sky god's faith in his son appeared correct for when Ecarca determined the location of the human carrying the Shield of Skool, Duwdamon used his powers to strike at the warriors of Eran. Now the Sky god waited for confirmation from the water sprites about location of the Skool. Confident of his success at killing Urith and his followers, Duwdamon would go among the human and retrieve the weapon. Once in his control, the Sky god would strike out at any betrayal to his authority.

Away from the wrath of Duwdamon, the spirits of Dughorm and Caestia walked along the path to the Fields of Awarware.

"Do you believe the warriors in Haligulf will accept your ideas?" Caestia was watching the ghosts of men fighting and dying on the field as they did each day. The father of Fedelm suddenly noticed some of the spirits he expected in the fields were not in the fighting.

"Yes, the nature spirits enter the Hall and they inform those inside about the events on Kamin. Other signs have reached the warriors of Haligulf as well. You notice each day fewer fighters are doing battle against each other. They feel the time for change is upon us." Dughorm's manner was lethargic, apparently resigned to the enviable. Caestia asked him the reason.

"I suppose I should find comfort that the Haligulf warriors will join us. However, the danger to all spirits in our realm is great, and Kriell has grown strong, perhaps too strong in the end." The god's Sybil slowed his pace as he thought; scratching at the stubble on his face he could not feel. "What I find interesting now are my visions which lead to a point in the future and nothing further. It is always to the tomb of Heptarc and the eventual terrible destruction. I see three whirlpools spinning out of control and racing to a place of dark and light. Somehow, gods, spirits, and humans are all caught up in this, yet there appears to be no answer for me. It is most peculiar."

"I'm sure something will come. You told me you see so much more now in this realm. And we have learned a great deal from the Guardian's own engravings embedded on the temples," his friend assured him.

"Perhaps, but I have a gut feeling the Fates are actually running this show now." The pair stood before the large entrance to Haligulf. "Nevertheless, we fight until the end."

Upon entering the structure, they immediately met the spirit of Heptarc who stood with several other renowned dead warriors.

"We have talked among ourselves, and we will do as you have asked," the greatest of heroes told their visitors. "The time to act approaches quickly. The sprites have said the human realm descends into chaos. It extends now into this realm. We have also noticed no warriors have joined us in Haligulf recently. Even with all of the death we hear about, the route into our eternity appears to be completely broken."

Dughorm nodded. "Yes, with Wurms killed by Mivraa, No demigod carries the spirits to this place anymore. The warrior goddess of Haligulf was cruelly treated by the Sky Realm gods. She appears to suffer from a fevered brain now. It is rumored she reaches out to the Guardian."

"We thought as much. Then, rumors we are hearing from our elemental servants are correct. The gods of the Sky are splitting, and Kriell has returned. It's too bad I wasn't able to destroy those Guardians the first time."

"I'm afraid so," Dughorm agreed. "Soon, the fight will come with the last piece of the Skool. The visions are clear. After that..." The spirit of the seer made it clear, the future was unknown.

"Will Ecarca agree to your plan?" Kirowan's ghostly spirit spoke up.

Caestia laughed. "He is not the sharpest point of a spear. Tell him he can regain his powers and he'll mold anything we want. Already, he slaves daily for us. Soon we will have all the forms you need, along with suitable weapons."

Heptarc smiled. "It will please many of us to be living again. The warriors will return."

Dughorm's face remained stoic. "Yes, but it will be fleeting. Probably the last time our spirits will remember this world."

~~~

Fedelm and Urith arrived on the outskirts of Calalhan, a small hamlet near where the massacre of Awarware took place. The sunlight nearly gone, the pair of travelers saw light coming through an open tavern window. Lights were coming from windows on a few of hamlet's buildings, giving them hope that some friendly locals remained. The pair hitched their mounts to the porch railing and entered the building cautiously. Inside, they found a single tavern keeper placing mugs down on a table where two hooded and black cloaked figures sat with their backs to the door. Urith went to the bar, waving the keeper over.

"Do you have room for two more?"

"Of course, Esterblud warrior, it's nice to see fighters loyal to our king arriving now. Terrible things continue since the Aberffraw left. But we have tough people here who have stayed." The tavern owner told him proudly. He was a medium sized man with poor vision, his eyes narrowed to a squint as he leaned over to see his visitors who were only an arm's length away.

Nodding, Urith started for an empty table when a booming voice crossed the room.

"Is that the sound of the Clovel Destroyer in our presence? Why does the bearer of the Skool come forth among us?"

Urith immediately stopped, looking at the cloaked figures at the nearby table that remained obscured by the hoods. "And what business do you have to know?" He asked suspiciously.

One of the figures turned, pulling his hood back to reveal a gray beaded face. Although lined with age, it was familiar. "Don't you know the Skalds anymore?"

"Narslac, by the gods, you're still alive." Urith cried happily. "Are you still running through the lands with your silly stories?" He stepped to the table, extending his good arm.

"Aye, my old friend, still listening to your exploits," the old Skald replied. Narslac took Urith by the forearm. The Esterblud noticed the man's missing arm on the other side.

Seeing Urith's expression, Narslac pulled back his tunic to reveal a stump where the forearm would have connected to the elbow. It was wrapped in linen.

"One of those nasty crubas got me while I was in Cahmais. When those attacks started from the underworld, every town ran a risk. We were nearly overrun. The monsters killed most of the Skalds who were with me. I can still swing a sword, but my shield no longer fits," he joked.

"Then, you will need to learn to move faster like I'm forced to," the Esterblud told him with a slight grin, nodding to his own wound. "That means we have a couple of cripples who are fighting against gods. It evens the odds."

Waving over Fedelm, the Esterblud took a seat on the bench. "What brings you to this land?"

"There are many reasons which we will talk about soon enough." Narslac nodded to the other hooded figure next to him. "You still remember, Arvim?"

Urith looked over at the young man who pulled back his hood. The face looked untouched by time despite their first meeting so many seasons before.

"What's the matter?" asked Arvim, the masculine voice turning into a cackling little laugh.

Suddenly, the figure transformed into Mivraa.

Dumbfounded, Urith sat with his mouth open, trying to reconcile what he witnessed. While he'd seen Mivraa's ability to change her appearance with the cloak many times, he never knew about her role as Arvim. He met the Skald was just after he lost his wife and father. Urith fought bandits with Narslac and Arvim at his side. Now he found out it was Mivraa who fought with him.

"You never told me," the warrior was nearly unable to get the words out.

"A girl has to keep some of her secrets," Mivraa's eyes laughed along with the rest of them for a moment. Then, Urith saw the dark overtake her again.

Narslac finished his drink before slapping the tall warrior on the back. "My friend, I didn't know until much later. It was our little secret from the world." He smiled at Mivraa. "Anyway, she was waiting here when I arrived. We thought we would have our little joke on you."

Pausing for a moment as he watched the demigoddess take a drink, Urith gave her a thin smile. "It is good to keep your humor in these times." He turned back to the tavern keeper, raising his voice as he ordered more drinks and food. The warrior noticed Fedelm silently sit across the table from him with Mivraa eying her like a *bater* on the hunt.

"We are going to the Citadel again. Did you know?" Urith asked Mivraa

She nodded. "I was waiting for you. I saw Dughorm, same vision as she had." Mivraa glanced at Fedelm again and went back to her drink. Her demeanor was different now, almost detached.

"Well, no visions here," Narslac piped up. "I got the word you were in Eran, and I was heading there."

"Why?"

"To tell the story of our world, of course," the Skald looked at him perplexed "You are quite notorious and famous depending upon the stories and who wants you to succeed. I follow the truth, and it appears you carry that on your back now."

Urith shook his head, "I'm not sure about that, but it's a burden for sure. My friend, I'm not sure it's a smart move on your part, but you are welcome to join us. Another skilled swordsman is appreciated, even if injured."

He shifted his focus to Mivraa. "How are you holding up?"

The woman looked startled by the question. "I have no wounds."

He smiled sympathetically. "All of us carry wounds." He paused briefly. "I meant about the visions. Do you know anything more about these monsters or what is happening in the underworld? Dughorm told me Kriell is the god behind this."

"Why would I know about that?" Her voice had an edge to it that everyone noticed. The woman's eyes darted among those at the table, then she calmed herself. "Sorry, I was thinking of something else. No, I don't have much to add. Dughorm's right, the Vanth came to me not long ago, gloating about his new master."

"You saw the Actita? When?" Fedelm suddenly spoke up.

Mivraa gave the woman a sharp glare, "Near Eran. He was collecting spirits. He's grabbing all he can." Fedelm cast a glance at Urith at the news.

"So, with Wurms gone and you no longer welcome to the Sky Realm, the Vanth is taking everyone, is that it?" The warrior asked.

"Yes," she agreed. "From what I can glean, Kriell's building an army of monsters in the underworld. Soon, the Guardian will have enough to overwhelm the Sky Realm." Urith thought he heard a hint of admiration in her voice.

"But he's using them in the human realm," Narslac spoke up as he pointed to his lost limb. "Are we to just become spirit monsters for this god that I've never heard of? He's worse than what we have."

Those around the table went silent. Urith wanted to ask more about the Vanth, but he started yawning after a moment. From the expression on the demigoddess's face, it knew she was not willing to talk now.

"Well, we have to complete one task at a time. And I'm tired. Let us rest and see what the dawn will bring for us." He stood, stretching as the others broke from their thoughts to take the short trek upstairs to a room. He saw the tavern keeper returning to the building. The squinting man had already received his koinons for the night, and he took their mounts to the nearby stable. Just returning, he bolted the door, leaving the group alone in the compartment.

Only Mivraa remained seated. Urith nodded for Fedelm and Narslac to leave as he watched the demigoddess drinking her heathmead. After the others left, Urith came closer to the woman.

"That heathmead is not very good. What is on your mind?"

"Nothing," she replied too quickly.

"When you wish to talk, I'll be there." The giant warrior turned to walk away.

"That's doubtful," the spite evident in her voice.

Instantly, Urith's anger rose, and he stopped, looking down at the floor. "You will recall I've tried and you've turned me away several times. Demigoddess or not, I won't be your wooden dummy to practice on."

He turned back to the table. "I cannot fathom the suffering felt by you or what goes on inside now. But I know this much. You cannot play on more than one side in this game. We are not allowed that choice. If vengeance is all you want, then go fight that battle on your own and leave the rest of us out of it. I can't worry about your reason but I must trust you will do what is right for all of us. Remember, real allies are hard to find, and the world we know is at stake. Now, the Fates gave me this burden, so I don't get the option to walk away. However, you can. And you will have my blessing either way, if you still find such things valuable." The man walked to the stairs where he paused, staring up into the darkness of the stairwell.

"It appears you need to make a decision. You're one of us or not. Time will soon run out for you to make your call."

Mivraa listened to his footsteps disappear upstairs, leaving the warrior goddess to face her demons in silence.

~~~

Shadows moved in the darkness, coming from the twisted *lellowtere*. Shuffling along with an inhuman gait, beorhs followed the Vanth toward Callahan. Actita followed the human who held the Skool to the village, and he intended to grab the weapons for himself. After witnessing the power of the god's weapon, the demigod son of Caruun began forming ideas of his own. While supportive of his new master, the last Vanth realized Kriell might not live up to the bargain they struck upon Caruun's demise. Actita decided the Guardian need not know about tonight's foray into the human realm. After his monsters had completed their work, the Vanth would have the power to ensure the bargain remained.

The group of creatures arrived outside the tavern, and the beaked face of the Vanth tilted his head as he confirmed the windows were dark. He knew humans were afraid of the dark, unable to see well, especially with no moonlight on this night. He and his creatures did not suffer from this shortcoming. The Vanth also knew, from observing Urith and his group, that surprise was needed to ensure the Skool was not used against them. Using low whistles to guide and direct the beorhs, the demigod crept to the door. Finding it barred, the creature backed away looking for another entrance. While all of the windows were small, only able to get a single fiend inside at one time, he recognized the thatched roof had only thin slates of wood keeping the thatch in place. The Vanth sent his monsters up the low-slung overhang over the door, silently climbing to the top using their sharp claws on the exposed post beams.

Fedelm felt something brush across her nose and she brought up her hand to wave it away. Something else fell on her closed eyelid, waking her completely. As she touched something that felt like straw, she heard a scratching noise coming from above. At first, she thought it might be *twarts*, little rodents running on the timbers supporting the roof, knocking down the thatch. Then she heard the same sound coming from another part of the ceiling. Just as she was about to wake Urith who slept on the floor near her, a loud crack came from above followed by heavy objects falling into the room.

Two of the beorhs fell on her, ripping at her with sharp claws as they immediately smelled her fear and warmth. This time, the woman had a short sword nearby, and she reached out, her hand clutching the pommel. The first monster she struck across the head, causing it to let out an inhuman screech. While the other creature tried to pull off the woman's clothes, she pushed the point of the sword into the beast's eye. Hideous smelling blood spurted across her as she felt the monster collapse over her legs.

For his part, Urith fought without his sword as two of the monsters landed on top of him and quickly tried to pull him apart by his arms. The warrior kicked out at the legs of one, sending the creature down closer. The man felt the pain shoot through his arm as the splint was being pulled away however he kept his focus, hammering the beast's head with his feet until he was released. The other beorh dragged him across the floor, still holding onto his good arm. The warrior struck out at the monster with his broken arm, aiming the ends of his splint into the face of his attacker. The trick worked, causing enough damage to get the creature to release his arm. Rolling away, Urith found his sword just as the beorh attacked him again. The Clovel Sword found its mark, impaled deep into the chest of the monster.

More of the beorhs jumped into the room as Urith grabbed the Shield of Skool and backed into the hallway. Terrified yells combined with the sound of savage fighting came from the room where Narslac slept. Urith pushed open the door to find the man nearly overwhelmed by the monsters. Four of the creature ripped and bit at him while the Skald tried to jab at them with the spear he grabbed. Urith sliced through the back of one, giving the Skald an opportunity to defend himself. The Skald quickly impaled another beast with his spear. Letting go of the weapon, he pulled a long dagger and stabbed at his attacker, while Urith finished off the last creature in the room.

However, just as they tried to catch their breath, they heard Fedelm shouting for help. Gathering in the narrow hall, they saw Mivraa at the top of the stairs, killing a monster while more of the beasts dropped from above. Several landed on the demigoddess who fell under their combined weight. Urith arrived first, pulling off one of the creatures while Fedelm buried her sword into it. The giant warrior got to Mivraa and dragged her from under the pile while Narslac pushed past to attack the swarming mob.

"Back up," yelled Urith suddenly as he pushed Mivraa behind him before dragging Narslac back to him. More beorhs came from the rooms, filling the narrow passageway as the group of human backed to the end of the tavern. Many beasts slowly moved to the group, clicking sounds emanating their excitement at the coming slaughter.

"We must attack," Narslac urged but Mivraa grabbed him, telling him to wait.

Urith painfully pulled his shield in front of him and muttered the words, *Da Umca Mivwar*, as the mob of attackers rushed forward.

The roaring blast of white light coming from the Shield of Skool blinded the humans. Urith fell to his knees from his arm's agony while trying desperately to maintain control of the weapon with his sword hand.

Instantly, the horde of evil filling the hallway disintegrated. Then, it was silent.

As the dust enveloped them, Mivraa gasped as she slowly slid down the wall, watching the spirits of the beorhs slowly transform. It was a sight she never witnessed before. She may have led the souls of the dead to Haligulf for such a long time, the woman never encountered balls of energy dancing in the air. Each orb held a nearly translucent face which showed no malevolence or hostility. The warrior goddess heard the voices as the spirit pass her, thanking her for their release. Transformed by the Skool, the demigoddess saw the humanity returned to the souls. The view, seen only by Mivraa, struck the woman harder than a sword blade. She began sobbing, tears falling down her cheeks.

At first, Fedelm started to confront the demigoddess after her first gasp, thinking Mivraa was suddenly sympathetic to the beorhs. Then, she realized the woman stared at something floating around her. Fedelm looked around her at the dust, but it was clear no one else could see what Mivraa witnessed.

"Something with the spirits?" the hakra asked, helping the demigoddess to her feet. Mivraa just nodded, unable to speak.

Urith was on his knees, grimacing as he tried not to move his injured arm. It took everything for him to control the power of the shield, hurting him far worse than he guessed.

"By the gods," Narslac exclaimed.

The rest of the group saw the reason for his comment. The narrow hallway was now an open spherical gap which extended into the early morning light. The floor and roof were gone along with the stairs and the far wall where the blast rays shot through. However, they had little time to reflect as the group heard the sound of more beorhs trying to scale up the wall behind them. This time the humans were ready when the remaining beasts came over the open top of the roof. While there was no room to maneuver in their space, Narslac speared one with his sword as the creature tried to jump down upon them. Another creature decided to jump on the group, only to be redirected in mid-air by Mivraa. The monster landed on its back on the floor below, convulsing briefly before dying. One of the beasts tried to reach down, grabbing at Urith's head but the man whipped up his Clovel Sword, implanting the weapon tip in the creature's neck. The group received a foul shower of black blood that caused Narslac to heave.

Then, it was silent.

As the humans listened and waited, Actita the Vanth started back for the *lellowtere* tree, clicking with his bird beak, directing the few remaining beorhs to follow him. Mivraa heard the familiar noise and immediately rose, looking for a way off of their perch. The floor below was too far to safely jump.

"Help me up to the roof!"

While confused, Urith and Narslac helped the woman scramble up the open roof line. She pulled herself above the thatch just in time to get a glimpse of the last beorh disappearing into the darkness of a nearby tree line. As she looked over the area, the demigoddess realized where the *lellowtere* tree must be.

"I recognized the Vanth's chatter," she explained. "They are leaving, back to the underworld." She slid down so the men could help her back to their corner of the second floor.

"They must have been going after Urith. Probably for the Skool. None of the other buildings look like they were attacked." She told them before stepping back down.

"That must have been why you kept thinking we were being followed." Fedelm looked at Urith. "They knew you were here with the shield."

The giant warrior nodded as he looked down at the wreckage below, left by the Skool's blast. The hallway floor was gone, leaving them on the second floor with no way to quickly climb down. "At least we survived this round. Let's figure out how we get to the ground."

While they looked around, Fedelm saw movement, and the tavern keeper carefully crept from his room located on the ground floor behind the bar. His face held the ashen look of shock and disbelief as he stared at them.

"Don't just stare at us, grab something so we can get down," Mivraa ordered him impatiently.

The man nodded and scurried away. Soon, he returned with several of the villagers carrying a long log, partially cut along the side to make boards. The group made their way down the makeshift ladder after the villagers placed it into position.

"Well, tavern keeper, I believe the monsters will no longer be coming in force for a while," Narslac who was the first one down, turned to follow the owner's continued gaze at the open hole in the side of the building. The Skald grabbed the man's shoulder. "Listen, man, wake up. The beorhs are gone, and the villagers can help you with your wall. Have a boy climb up there and return with our stuff."

As the man left to get more villagers, Urith stepped close Narslac. "Still planning on staying with us?"

The Skald looked at him, giving him a broad smile. "I wouldn't miss it for the world. Let's check the ossanes and get them ready for our journey."

After preparing their mounts, the two men were leading the ossanes back to the destroyed tavern when a small group of villagers came toward them. They were led by the nearly blind bar owner and Urith suddenly wondered if an angry mob might be coming. He was wrong.

"We wanted to thank you for destroying those creatures of the darkness. Here is food for the journey." The leader informed them as Fedelm and Mivraa came through the crowd holding the some of the packs and blankets. Two young boys carried the rest.

"I'm sorry for the damage to your building," Urith said. "I didn't have much choice."

"Not to worry, my friends and I will rebuild. More people will return, and soon our village will be like new." The man spoke confidently.

Urith gave him a brief smile before turning to mount his ossane. As the warrior watched the rest of his friends get on their mounts, he kept himself from telling the villagers the truth. Until the final piece of the Skool was found, there would be no peace for the humans.

The Esterblud spurred his animal and slowly began the trek leading to Ynyover. As he rode out of the village, he realized only Fedelm and Mivraa were with him. He looked back to see Narslac finishing his conversation with the group of villagers before speeding after them. When the Skald reached them, the big man with one arm was whistling a familiar tune about the great warriors.

"You seem pretty happy with what we just went through," Fedelm told him.

"Yes, that's true." Smiling broadly, Narslac steered his mount between Fedelm and Urith. He glanced over to the scarred warrior. "By the way, I let the villagers know who you are."

"That won't get you a heathmead out of them next time you're through there," Urith grunted.

"Don't you believe it. The villagers are calling you the new Heptarc." The Skald began whistling his tune again, ignoring the sour look that crossed the big warrior's face at the comparison.

Chapter 5: Grave of Heptarc

Outside the Citadel, Lyncus sat on his ossane while he watched the last three members of the Majireef Council still in Ynyover, walk to the massive entrance gates. One of the robed figures was his wife, Greach. Not particularly attractive, the woman carried an air of superiority. It went with her status as Aberffraw noble and the only woman as part of the council. With the ability as a hakra, the seer knew many considered her to be one of the shining stars of the Cahmais political class. Joining Lyncus' wife on the ocean journey were two nobles from his homeland, Osramc, and Crutcl. The trio arrived at Ynyover the night before on a ship sent by the satgerts of Cahmais who were reeling from the terrible nightly attacks coming from the underworld.

Lyncus was still seething at the turn of events brought by the group of Aberffraw nobles walking up the hill. The riders found Lyncus the night before. The Aberffraw leader and some his men, waiting at a barren table inside one of the few remaining undamaged buildings down the road from the Citadel. Lyncus and his men looked up from their planning at the unexpected visitors.

The stench of bodies, who still lay unburied as a signal to those inside the fort, assaulted the new arrivals as they sat at the table to explain their visit. Lyncus listened impatiently about the turmoil occurring within his Cahmais lands. The noble said they were there to prod the son of Asgurd back to their kingdom to take up his duties as king. The leader of the Aberffraw glanced at his subordinates, realizing his men would soon grow worried about the news.

After a while, Osramc and Crutcl returned to the ship where they could eat and sleep without the foul odors disturbing them. Greach had Lyncus dismiss his men so she could walk her back to the docks with him alone. She came to her husband with other news as well. The disastrous losses of men in Esterblud left his family in a precarious position.

"My husband, I'm here to warn you. This insignificant need for revenge blinds you to the needs of your people." Her words to him stung.

"What do you know of my revenge?" he stopped when he saw her raise her eyebrow. He forgot that her ability at foresight could be used against him. He wondered if she knew other deep secrets as well. It was not long when he found out she knew far more than he expected.

"The fealharan now are aligned against you. It appears the assassination of your brother rests on our doorstep." Her quiet, calm voice nearly unnerved the man when she told him the news.

"That is a scandal conceived by the Esterbluds," he responded quickly. "Everyone knows this."

"Not everyone," she purred. "I've heard fealharan have decided to search for the person who killed their leader in Cahmais. Word comes that they are using their contacts within the shipping guild. Somehow the man who led the assassins died outside of Uugara. Suspiciously, the dead man arrived on the same ship you came back on from Eernicia. While I'm sure it must be only a coincidence, my husband, those who are against you might decide to use it to their advantage. You see, little is unknown to the shipping guild and they have been known to take sides against overlords."

He looked at her carefully, but the woman continued, apparently oblivious to him.

"I come here to relieve you of this quarrel with Satres. A king would not be waiting at the gates of a faraway castle while his kingdom burns from the inside."

"You talk as if a decision is made."

The noble woman stopped and turned to him. "This was decided before I left Cahmais. People grow desperate for a leader, and some of the tribes outside the city have begun to criticize the Aberffraw leaders. You will return with your men and take charge of Cahmais. I will stay and keep Satres in line with our new kingdom."

Lyncus stared at her, unused to her forcefulness. "And what makes you think I will do as you suggest? I'm the king and your husband."

Her lips curled into a sarcastic smile. "Yes, you are my husband, knowing fully well that a woman cannot rule Cahmais. Too many of the leaders would never allow a female to rule them. But let me remind you that a man who beds other men is reviled. A person with such urges should cover his tracks better. The Cahmais law is very specific as to the punishment and nobles are not exempt."

He suddenly stopped, and the woman turned to him. "Do you really think your escapades with Satres and the other men would remain unknown to me? If so, you're a bigger fool than I thought." The woman's words hit the man in the pit of the stomach, and his eyes grew wide at the charge.

Lyncus remained quiet, and Greach continued her walk, forcing him to follow her as she continued.

"Since I know our marriage is to maintain power with my family name, I have no reason to spread such news. It would make my life difficult as well. But it is decided that you will return to Cahmais in the morning."

"And if not?" his voice threatening.

She didn't bother to stop. "Power doesn't come from being a fool. All of those in Cahmais will know of your past, and no one will support you, not even those nobles who live like you." The woman ignored the murderous look in her husband's eyes as she continued on the path.

"No need to plot my demise," she assured him. "Your secret remains safe with me but arrangements have been made should I fail to return to our home. How long do you think you will last after such news were to spread? I dare say, you would be executed in a very painful manner." The man stopped while he watched his wife continue on into the night.

As Lyncus watched the Citadel gates close that morning, he was tired. For the rest of his sleepless night, he mulled over his limited options and had come to accept his wife was the master of his fate for the moment. His revenge against Satres would have to wait. Still, it was a long way back to Cahmais, he told himself. No doubt he would have a plan ready for his wife she returned to him. Accidents were known to happen, and other noble women with less curiosity could be found. Turning his ossane, the future king of Cahmais looked at the small line of Aberffraw warriors ready to return to their homeland. Slowly, he led them on the trail away from the Citadel.

~~~

Inside the Citadel, not long after the Aberffraw left, Satres watched the few remaining Majireef Council members gathered around the table. Despite his overarching need for sleep, the Sacred Overlord felt a surge of excitement envelop him. Greach, the wife of Lyncus, sat across from the thin man while Osramc and Crutcl took positions on either side of her. Already informed from his guards that the Aberffraw were leaving, the Sacred Overlord welcomed the satgerts with his usual self-assured manner. After finding them in the Great Hall, Satres dismissed the guards and personally took the group of nobles to another room. As they journeyed down into the depths of the Citadel, the small assembly reached a place unknown to any of the guards. It was the secret room next to the *sidhera* where food and drink were already laid out on the table.

"This is an unusual room," Osramc spoke up, looking over the contents around them carefully. His expression was a mixture of uneasiness and surprise.

"Yes, you can be assured of that. This is one of the most important places on Kamin. Do you know that behind that curtain is the gateway to the underworld?" Satres calmly rose, walking around the table to the curtain which hung over the portal. He looked back with a smile at their surprised expressions.

"I'm quite surprised such illustrious seers did not know about my little secret," he smirked as he pulled back the red cloth which revealed a dark vestibule. "Would anyone care to enter?" he offered. Smiling to himself, he let go of the curtain. "No, I guess not. Not even the best of my council would risk a one-way trip to meet with Caruun."

"Let us discuss why we have returned," Greach interrupted impatiently, craning her neck to watch the thin man in robes staring at the dark alcove. "My husband has returned to Cahmais, and we are here to ensure our kingdoms remain on friendly terms."

"Friendly terms?" Satres glanced over to Greach as he walked back around to his chair. "You have an interesting way in which you describe the current situation." His eyes kept glancing at the curtain as if he expected Caruun to suddenly pop out of the dark. The Sacred Overlord went quiet, repeatedly yawning while nervously tapping the wood handles of his elaborate chair. His guests glanced at each other.

Satres gave a short laugh, coming back to the people in the chairs across from him. "Tell me, what do you see in the future? What threats require our friendly terms?"

"I'm not sure I understand your question," Greach told him.

"Come now, you and these other hakras who call themselves seers must have some visions you can share with me. I mean after your failure to foresee the death of Asgurd and these nightly invasions by the underworld, the Sacred Overlord should expect something of value from the Majireef Council."

"You should recall that the council was told by you that the invasion would happen. No advice was sought." Crutcl spoke up diplomatically.

Satres gave the man an evil look before suddenly smiling. "You're correct, my friend. Now give me your visions. Since you are all the remains of the Council within these walls, tell me the future."

"The bearer of the Skool remains alive and a threat," replied Osramc. "My visions show the shield he carries can bring down this fortress and he comes this way."

Satres continued to smile. "Should I be worried about this Esterblud? Why would he return again?"

The visitors quickly exchanged glances before Osramc spoke. "We are not sure. We see a tomb which is unfamiliar to us along with an army of stone warriors."

"You're telling me this man comes to the Citadel with stone warriors?"

"We cannot be sure. But it's clear this man is dangerous to you." Greach spoke up.

The Overlord stood and began to slowly pace behind his chair. "You stated you're here as representatives of Cahmais. As such, you have noticeably missed the bigger picture."

"What do you mean?" Crutcl asked. "The Esterbluds will build their army and invade your lands. Our kingdoms need each other."

"So, you see the threat from the North, land of humans sweeping down upon us. Yet I receive reports about nightly deaths caused by the underworld. Do your satgerts not cry in fear from these underworld monsters who are overrunning the night?" The thin man slowly walked around the table to the curtain again.

"But of course," Greach replied. "Our people grow fearful and expect help from the leader of the Satgerts. As you are the Sacred Overlord, this shows us how important it becomes to forget our kingdom's differences."

"The Sacred Overlord commands a nearly empty fortress, and the Aberffraw army travels to Cahmais with only enough strength to hold its own tribes in check," Satres told them as they craned their necks to watch him inspect the curtain again, turning to give them a brief smile. "No need to look so surprised, I have regular discussions with the trader's guild." He rubbed the velvet of the cloth in his hand. "Now tell me, what do your visions say about the underworld and Kriell?"

"Kriell? We don't know what you are talking about, my lord. The underworld is in turmoil like the other realms."

92

Satres nodded, glancing to see his visitors were looking away from him. Osramc was looking down at his white robe, picking lint off while Crutcl looked at the mug in his hand. The Sacred Overlord reached under his scarlet robe to pull a jagged edge dagger from his belt.

"Well, every night I've seen the visions of danger," he told them as he walked back to the table. "The dreams come to me from my lost friends. You ignorant fools, the Esterbluds are not the threat," the Sacred Overlord stated, watching the ghosts of Dughorm and Joenhip smiling at him as they floated along the wall. Satres stepped next to Crutcl and plunged the dagger into the neck of the man. Before the big Osramc could react, Satres had the man by the hair and slit the man's throat, blood spurting across the table. Greach screamed, sending her chair flying as she madly scrambled toward the door. She futilely pounded on the stone before turning around to see Satres calmly walking toward her. The woman ran to the other side of the small room, keeping the table between her and the crazy person with a knife.

"Little lady, running away won't stop what is coming." Satres cocked his head slightly as his eyes glanced at the curtain behind her. "It would appear Actita has a job for you in the underworld."

Suddenly Greach felt powerful arms grab her, lifting her from the stone floor. Screaming, she vainly tried to fight, frantically twisting and turning while she scratched at the strong arms which held her tight. Panic filled her eyes as she pleaded for help. Satres calmly sat in his chair while the Vanth turned with his prize and pushed past the curtain into the sidhera. Blue light suddenly enveloped the demigod and his human prisoner. Then, they were gone.

Satres sat in his chair, held his cup aloof in a toast to his two corpse visitors and took a deep drink. He invited the ghosts he knew he saw along the wall to join him at the table. His eyes followed their progress as they took the two open seats.

"Too bad for the wife of Lyncus." He turned back to the dead bodies. "If she were really a seer, you would think she should have known that was coming," his sarcasm filled the room. Swirling around the blood-red wine in his cup, he smiled. "I wonder how long the living can last in the underworld."

~~~

Greach's desperate pleas mingled with the screeches coming from the hordes of beorhs and crubas as the Vanth dragged the woman through

93

the tunnels. On several occasions, the demigod used his whip to force the beorhs back. Their natural instinct to ravage and rape was on full display within their domain. Once elegant and regal, the short journey transformed the noblewoman into a pathetic shell. Red, bloody patches on her head replaced the brown hair torn away by the monsters of the underworld. Nearly stripped naked by the beorhs, her flesh was covered with welts and scratches from the claws of her attackers who grabbed and mounted her before Actita was able to force them away from the human.

Taking his prize inside the vast beehive cathedral structure of the underworld, he placed the unfortunate person at the foot of the throne of his master. A black gelatinous form lay across the arms of the underworld throne, tentacles hanging over the arms like black ivy. Actita forced Greach to bow before Kriell as the Guardian swiftly wrapped its appendages around the woman while she screamed in terror. Her desperate echoes filled the air. The face of Alrpan suddenly emerged from the midsection of the glob, staring the woman into silence.

"I'm told you are a human seer," Kriell's hoarse voice came from the lovely face sticking out of the black glob. "Is this accurate?"

Her wide eyes showing the shock at the question coming from the creature who spoke with a perfect Cahmais accent, the woman slowly nodded her head.

"Then, you will help me learn about future." The black tentacles began crawling around Greach, quickly covering her legs and slowly started pulling her close to the creature.

"No," she cried as she fell back on the steps, struggling to stop the relentless pull of the suckers which dragged her slowly into the dark body while the face of Alrpan slowly disappeared.

There was one last desperate scream as the woman was ingested in the form of Kriell. Actita cocked his birdlike head, watching as the struggles of the woman to break free grew noticeably weaker. Her skin started to disappear while the movement inside the Guardian stopped. Before long only the skeletal form was barely seen, to be digested with the spirit of the human.

Reppir, the infamous leader of the beorhs suddenly appeared in the chamber. He bowed before the underworld master, his chatter was high pitched and excited. The black blob quickly understood the eagerness and his form started to change.

"You're correct. This is excellent news. Bring me our special guest now."

The figure of Caruun appeared on the throne amid the animated clicking sounds coming from one of the tunnels. With a nod of his buzzard beak, Caruun had two beorhs bring the woman to him. Struggling against the leather bindings around her neck, the blue hue of her skin looked ghastly under the green lights of the room. Unis, goddess of the Sky Realm and wife of Duwdamon, retained the youth and beauty she strove to project. However, her human body was covered with deep welts and cuts. The Sky Goddess received a far more brutal treatment by the beorhs than the human visitor earlier, only her godlike powers of renewal kept her living. To the people of Kamin, she was a symbol of love worship. Reppir, on the other hand, left the goddess among his creatures all morning to be used as they pleased.

"Caruun, my husband will come down and rip out your heart for this." Unis screeched at the figure sitting on the throne.

The vulture face looked at her unperturbed. "As I recall, you had the power of mind control. Somehow I don't sense that in you anymore. Come now, peer inside my mind." The underworld deity closed his eyes, waiting. After a moment he opened his eyes. "You're not trying. Should I send you back with my monsters for a while?"

Unis glared at him, then she closed her eyes. Kriell watched her as he felt the goddess trying to enter the mind of Caruun. The souls of those inside him suddenly tried to grasp at the mind reader. Unis fell back and screamed. She looked up at the Guardian from the floor, her eyes told him the truth. Her powers were nearly gone.

Kriell's mind reached out into the goddess, and she suddenly was overwhelmed. As the monsters watched, the body on the floor, twisted and shook, racked with searing pain and torments. Unis was gripped entirely by the Guardian whose vengeance on her was just starting. The creature began to beg for mercy, trying to pin the blame on her fellow deities. However, the master of the underworld laughed aloud while he plunged the creature into a mental state of extreme torture.

While he watched the body on the floor contort into positions which snapped the human bones, Reppir leaned next to his master. He informed Kriell the goddess was unable to return to the Sky Realm after losing her powers. Then, he offered the Guardian a hideous thought. The human body suddenly stopped receiving its excoriating torment.

"Your suggestion is a good one, Reppir. She might be useful to us still." The Guardian turned to the recovering Unis, who was unable to lift herself from the cave floor. "Normally, I would ingest your body along with your spirit. However, your powers are weak and not really of much use to me. Still, I will make you pay for your betrayal of the Guardians. Since our underground hordes have a use for you, you will be utilized for breeding some of the extraordinary creatures for which we will have a need."

The beorhs dutifully dragged the broken body away as the goddess of the sky screamed and begged to be killed. Kriell reverted to his black tentacle body.

"You did well finding me this so-called goddess. The one power useful to us is her ability to mend quickly. Put her to use immediately." Bowing, Reppir started to leave. "If you or the Vanth find more of these soothsayers, bring them to me. In the meantime, continue to send out our creatures at night," Kriell ordered as the black blob settled into the chair again. In his imagination, he saw himself standing in the ruined temples of the Sky Realm, and the thought pleased him.

~~~

The group from Esterblud finally reached the small village of Cuinal, just outside the Citadel. Slowed by the massive storms that flooded the lands which hindered their progress, the group stopped for several sunrises while they waited for the rivers to become crossable, the rains provided them with relief from the attacks from the underworld. Urith guessed the beorhs and crubas needed a fresh scent to track their prey, and the torrential rains combined with high winds kept the monsters from finding them. The additional time spent waiting on the river to subside also help them recover from their wounds. Fedelm's back wounds showed no infection. Narslac bore some deep cuts along his chest and multiple scratches around his neck. He had no signs of infection either. Yet, it was apparent that Urith's ability to grip using his hand and fingers of his shield arm had not returned, still crippled from the torture done to him. At least the intense, throbbing pain was subsiding under the splints. His positive reports told them that the man stoically refused to consider the injury to be permanent. Fedelm and Narslac watched Urith struggle to remove and hold the Shield of Skool with his splinted arm, but they continued to encourage him. Privately, they believed the Esterblud would come to realize the truth eventually.

Left unsaid among the small group was the tension between Mivraa and Urith at times. Combined with the occasional odd behavior coming from the demigoddess, the journey seemed extraordinarily long and quiet to the riders. At times, the demigoddess was like her old self, confident and jovial among her friends as they planned their next moves. But as the day turned to night, the woman would grow erratic. Her mood quickly changed to explosive, bitter and personal attacks against those around her before finally going into a cocoon of sullen silence by the time they went to sleep.

When they got close to the fortress, nightfall was coming fast, so Urith sent Mivraa to scout ahead along a path which ran at the base of the Citadel. The Esterblud warrior broke away to check out the village as Fedelm and Narslac remained behind, keeping watch over the area from a nearby ridge. Recent graves covered the ground, giving Urith pause as he considered the possibility that a current plague came through the area. However, when Urith got past the first huts, it became apparent only a few inhabitants remained. He quickly realized from the burned out buildings and signs left by the Aberffraw that it was the aftermath of vengeful warriors.

Noticing movement in a nearby hut, he silently entered the structure where he found a wife with two small children who cowered at his presence. Waving Fedelm and Narslac into the village, they soon joined him. Fedelm's presence convinced the terrified woman to tell her story about Lyncus and his men's push through the area. The grave outside the front door explained what happened to the husband while the hurt and fear in the woman's look told Fedelm all she needed to know about what the rabble did to the woman afterward. Mivraa came into the hut as the villager finished talking about her ordeal. The look on the demigoddess's face at the woman's plight sent a cold chill through Narslac. The Skald decided against telling Mivraa about the many slaves taken by the retreating army.

Assured that the Aberffraw were gone and the guards within the Citadel would not come down to the village, the group left the woman and her children with some of their rations. They had gone to the only other inhabitable building before Urith broke away again, telling them he wanted to search around the area where the port jutted out to the Maflow Sea. As he left the shack, he asked Mivraa about the Citadel guards, and she just gave a hollow laugh.

"Not many left there from the number of people I've seen on the ramparts. It's locked up tight so they must be afraid of something still."

Urith nodded, thanking her as he left. He got on his mount and moved along the road until he was close enough to see the guards who held the home of the Sacred Overlord. Almost immediately, he saw the line of ossane tracks leading away from the Citadel. For the present, with the enemy gone, it should be easier for them to enter the Citadel.

As Urith doubled back to scout the cluster of houses and buildings near the port, he saw guards in the distance. Even in the failing light, he recognized the clothing as Aberffraw. Suspicion immediately rising, he slid off his ossane and used the shadows of the trees lining the road to get close enough to hear the men talking. From their dialect, he realized they were locals carrying the robes and weapons of their former allies. Lyncus must have decided to return to his home, leaving the local tribes to keep the pressure on Satres, the Esterblud decided.

Urith returned to the village, and he approached the hut where he left his friend, he heard the sound of strange voices talking with Narslac and Mivraa. Pushing through the entrance, the warrior found Fedelm standing near the door, watching the two old men sitting across the table from his comrades. He immediately recognized their robes. They were members of the Malhair House trading guild.

"Join us, my friend. This is Kaoden and Rordan. Our honored guests have news." Narslac spoke with a hint of sarcasm when he noticed Urith.

The two guildsmen stared at the Esterblud, their pained expressions revealing their recognition of his name.

"Your reputation precedes you, Clovel Destroyer," Rordan told him.

Urith grunted. "Not all of them benefiting your guild I'll wager. If my guess is correct, you just came from the Citadel, kissing the ring of the overlord. Now you're probably down here cutting deals with his enemies."

The slight uptick of the old man's left eyebrow confirmed Urith's suspicion. But he waited for the guildsmen to make the next move. The trading guild had a well-earned reputation for knowing events by which they could profit from. Experience told him that this meeting was prearranged, no doubt word was out about his journey into this land. Given the price on his head, he surmised the guild might be interested in the koinons for his capture or death.

"We have come for your benefit," claimed Kaoden.

"Somehow, I will also wager there's a benefit to you as well. This ongoing invasion of the Aberffraw over the Ynyover people has hurt your trade here," Narslac interrupted. He smiled broadly at the sudden silence from Kaoden.

Rordan leaned forward, talking directly to Urith as the large man sat next to Mivraa. "Granted, we have an interest in stability. Our people believe you are here to fulfill your destiny. Perhaps we can both benefit from this exchange of information."

Urith exchanged a quick glance at his comrades who nodded in agreement. "Fine, let us hear what you have."

"Rumors swirl around Ynyover concerning the Sacred Overlord. After meeting him today, it was evident his grasp on reality suffers." He stopped at the unexpected giggle which came from Mivraa who placed her hand over her month to suppress herself. Her expression forced the visitors to pause.

"Even his guards no longer take orders from him," Rordan continued, trying not to stare at Mivraa as he spoke. The woman's auburn hair and black shawl reminded him of someone. "As we left, it became apparent that the head of the guard holds power over the Citadel now and he told us they will wait for the satgerts to come up with a new leader."

"And who among the satgert would dare challenge the Sacred Overlord? Didn't they support his invasion of Esterblud?" Urith leaned closer to the table, sneering at them. "I'm willing to lay koinons your guild took the koinons from both of these kingdoms to invade my homeland." He waited a moment for a denial, but none came.

"Alright, so now you reap the harvest you helped to sow." the big warrior's voice lowered ominously. "Get to the point."

"Very well, the point is this. Only the Majireef Council supported the war. And we have information that Satres's closest allies no longer support him. Three of them showed up recently by way of the Maflow Sea, and they have not been heard from since they met with the Sacred Overlord. Support for Satres is nowhere to be found. The local Ynyover tribes are split, but mostly they align with the Aberffraw for the moment." The old Guildsmen leaned back against his chair.

"And what does that mean to us?" Fedelm spoke up, coming toward the table. "I don't like where this is going." She looked at Urith, sensing the trap.

Urith smiled, leaning back in his chair as well. "While I don't have the wisdom of such learned men like yourselves, I agree with Fedelm. You are suspiciously vague at the wrong time. I'll give you one more chance to come to your point, or I might let my friends beat the information out of you. In case you didn't know, I'm running short on patience with men and gods at the moment."

His words and menacing presence caused Rordan to swallow hard as he felt his mouth go dry. He now recognized the woman seated next to Urith from paintings in the temples. Mivraa, the famed demigoddess of Haligulf stood by the side of Urith. It confirmed the information of their messengers. The fact also left the Guildsmen in a precarious position.

Cautiously, Rordan proceeded. "Your reputation is well known, and we do not mean to test your patience. Let us come back to the problem. Satres will not leave the Citadel, and the guards will not throw him out. It came to us that you might be returning to the Citadel to confront Satres for the bounty he placed upon your head."

"As well as the bounty on your friends," Kaoden spoke up cheerfully. "Assuming this is true, and you should force the issue, our guild is prepared to support your claim against Satres."

"You son of a *docke*," Fedelm fumed, nearly jumping across the table before Urith quickly intervened, getting her to quiet down. While he was doing that, Mivraa suddenly pulled her long dagger from her cape and slammed it into the wood in the center of the table. Narslac saw the panic and fear in the men across from the demigoddess. He could feel the chill going down his back as well as he watched her.

"Enough of this." Urith thundered, his Clovel Sword pulled from the scabbard with lightning speed, pointed at the throat of Rordan. From the expression on the guildsman's face, Urith wondered if the man wet himself

"You are asking us to remove Satres from his throne for you. No doubt, you have a plan to put in a Ynyover puppet, one of those traitors who kiss the belly of the Aberffraw. I will tell you this plainly. When I meet with Satres again, I will do this on my terms and not yours. Your hands are dirty with secrets, playing off the overlords against each other while your group grows fat and rich on the chaos. You helped cause the problems we see now. In my mind, you're no better than the gods who try to strike us down."

The shocked men remained silent, each carefully watching the engraved blade when it came close to them.

The scarred warrior paused briefly. "Now, I'll tell you what will now happen. We will enter the Citadel and have our meeting with the Sacred Overlord. Whatever comes out of that will not matter to either of you except for this. You will carry back a message to the shadow leaders you have."

There was a deathly silence in the room until Rordan asked what the message was.

"Your guild will cooperate with the tribes and leaders to rebuild the lands for all traders and merchants, or I will make it my mission to use the Shield of Skool to destroy each one of your trade centers, starting with the main one in Eernicia." He gave him his sneer smile to emphasize what he meant. "You know the power of the Skool from your spies so you can guess what will happen."

"You can't mean what you say," protested Rordan. "The people would rise up against you."

"Why would they?" Urith asked. "You have already told us that trade suffers. You live inside your centers but we've traveled through the lands, and we know what the farmers say. Food rots on the docks because the guild won't ship without bribes being paid. Merchants can't sell to the villages without a toll given to the guild. This is not the god's fault; the blame is on your guild."

Narslac spoke out as he agreed with the assessment. "Your guildsmen don't get out much. The people would gladly welcome Urith for the destruction of the Malhair Houses. You should know only the overlords keep you in business."

Rordan sighed, nodding as he slowly stood. His eyes remained on the sword tip. "Very well, we will take your message back."

As he and the other man reached the entrance, Fedelm slowly moved aside for them. "I would take his words very seriously," she cautioned them. "He does not make idle threats." She watched them disappear into the darkness before turning back to the group.

"Do you think they will come after you with the fealharan?" She asked. "Until Satres removes you from the list of wafaoils, the guild might decide to get rid of you."

That would be all of us, except for Narslac," Urith reminded her.

"Hey, I take offense at not being one of you defilers. Many nights I've sung songs to those who accuse me of corrupting the gods." The stout man smiled broadly as Urith laughed lightly. The bard retrieved a bladder of heathmead, taking a large swig before handing it to the warrior. "She's right, you know. Those men of the guild can't be trusted."

"That's the last of our long list of troubles," the Esterblud reflected aloud. "First we have to get into the Citadel using the path we took before. Mivraa and I will know the way. Then, we find the Skool, probably while avoiding the guards. I can't imagine we are welcome there even as we are against Satres."

"That is true, but we can always kill them," Mivraa spoke up, her eyes suddenly brightened. "That is a big fort, and Rordan mentioned many of the guards left with their tribal elders."

The Esterblud glanced at her, his eyes narrowed. "That may be true but who controls the fort when we are gone? Those militias who sided with the Aberffraw still control the port and main trail to Cahmais will only follow what Lyncus tells them. More bloodshed and killing in turmoil to control this place."

"I don't care," the demigoddess told him defiantly.

"The rest of us do," Fedelm came closer to the table. "We need allies on our side, not more dead. They just end up in the underworld now." The smaller woman stared at Mivraa, the last sentence dripped with sarcasm. It was not lost on the warrior woman.

"Fine, do what you want," Mivraa stood, quickly going to the entrance of the building. "Just remember you can't beat gods by getting soft. Let me know when you get a backbone," she stated as she threw open the ramshackle wooden door. The door crashed into the wall of the building with a loud bang and fell from its hinges. The demigoddess stomped away into the blackness.

Late in the night, the group searching for the final piece of the Skool found the tunnel leading into the Citadel. When Mivraa finally calmed down, she rejoined them, leading the way despite the darkness of the night and new obstacles along the way. Now, the narrow trail, which rounded the steep cliff faces protecting most of the fortress, was laced with rudimentary metal spikes. One ossane nearly threw Mivraa when it went lame stepping on the device. It's pitiful bleating from the wound forced the demigoddess to kill the animal with a single strike to the neck

102

with her crystal spear. Leaving the remaining beasts tied to brush, the group made the rest of the journey on foot. It took longer than expected to find the tiny hole in the brush along the steep cliff face.

Surprised that the entrance was unblocked and not guarded, Urith carefully slid the Shield of Skool over his injured arm and took the lead, pulling some of the *tribolrocks* from the bag attached to his belt. The green light bearing stones guided them through the tunnel. Expecting a trap at every turn, their progress was slow and methodical as the line of four made their way through. When the group finally reached the end of the tunnel, the wooden door was gone. Instead, they found bars embedded into the stone entryway.

"Well, that explains the lack of guards. Now what?" Mivraa sarcastically whispered from behind the others.

Urith peered around the cavernous area on the other side of the bars. He turned his head back to the group, his voice growling. "There are no guards, and these rods are not thick. Tell Mivraa to get her butt up here. Narslac can help me, and Mivraa can work on the other side. We should be able to pull them apart."

"I heard you," the warrior goddess groused at him, pushing herself past Fedelm.

She stood across from the Esterblud and the Skald, using both hands to pull on one of the bars while the two men used their combined strength to bend the other metal bar wide enough to get Mivraa through. After she had slid through the narrow opening, she worked with them to widen the entrance to accommodate the Esterblud's bulk.

Squeezing through, Urith fell to the ground with a grunt as he landed on the splinted arm. Mivraa paid no attention as she raced across the room to the large vault door which led to the next level. After he had got to his feet, the warrior was helped by Narslac into the stairwell.

"Nobody around here," she told them after carefully looking into the hallway past the large vaulted doors. "You still don't want to get to Satres first? We know this leads back to his chambers."

"No," Urith and Fedelm spoke at the same time. Mivraa raised her eyebrow, throwing a glare at the young woman.

"We follow the visions, like always," Urith grunted as he turned his attention to the room.

They entered a cavernous room which glowed with a pale misty-yellow light given off by rows of tribolrocks lining the walls. Urith glanced at Fedelm who was not reacting to the sight of the room which had a tunnel to the underworld *sidhera*. He liked her show of strength. The young woman was raped and abused by Alrpan and beorhs in the chamber only a season before. Now, the determined look on the woman's face revealed the inner toughness he respected.

A large tapestry with embroidered images of the underworld gods hung down the sidewall. On the slab where Fedelm once lay bound and abused, Urith started to search for a clue or message on the gigantic engraved stone as well as the hefty stones supporting the top.

"We must be in the right place. Most of these engravings are about the last battle fought by Heptarc," observed Narslac. "Much of it tells of thanks from the gods to Heptarc."

"Why would they put this here? A warrior's body is burned on a funeral pyre to release his spirit to Haligulf. And if this was an honor to him, why hide it down here?" Fedelm asked, looking at Mivraa who focused on the walls around them. The demigoddess briefly turned back to her companions.

"I guess Duwdamon would not allow any public display of honor from gods to a human. He was probably fine if the satgerts came down to pay homage. He's a jealous god." She shrugged before going back to staring at the Sky Realm images. Her eyes scanned across the engraved pictures of the temples and buildings she once called home. Whoever the artist, they accurately captured the coldness and sterile structures where the gods resided. The thought made her angry, and she turned away.

After a while of scrutinizing the slab and the rest of the room, the group became convinced they missed something important. They gathered around the block, trying to decide their next steps.

"What have we missed?" Urith asked. "The visions were clear. I saw this room and this slab."

"So, did I. And Mivraa stated she saw this place." the hakra agreed, shivering as she remembered the past.

"Then, what's missing?" Narslac was watching Mivraa who continued to look at the walls. It appeared something about the images were bothering her.

"Not missing, something has been added." The demigoddess came toward the wall, pointing at the picture of Haligulf about waist high from the floor. "There, by the gates of Haligulf. See that statue of Wurms across from me."

"That doesn't look like him," Urith commented, slowly moving to get a closer look.

"Exactly. The statue is Heptarc. I don't know why I never noticed before." The warrior goddess ran to the wall. "Leave it to the satgerts to throw a little mud at the gods. Whoever carved this must have decided to put the likeness of a human over the statue of a god. Those eyes seem to follow you."

"Well, that's interesting but what does it get us?" Narslac asked as Mivraa looked at the statue carefully.

"Maybe this," the woman replied as she pressed her two fingers into the eyes of Heptarc. Immediately, the floor shuddered under her feet, and a large stone tile lifted slightly from the floor.

The demigoddess smiled briefly at her surprised companions. "I just remembered a vision where Dughorm stood next to Heptarc. In the dream, Dughorm kept saying Heptarc must have been blinded by the betrayal of the gods. There was something in those glass eyes on the statue."

The group soon lifted the stone slab, leaning it against the wall. Below their feet, dust covered stair steps led into the darkness. Pulling out her tribolrocks, Mivraa started down, closely followed by Urith who gave some of the light bearing stones to his companions. The stairs were steep and difficult to navigate within the narrow passage before it leveled off. Barely tall enough for a short person to stand, the group proceeded forward in a line until they came upon a large chamber.

Coming into the room, their pale lights showed the round structure which went up several levels above them. Long green drapes, hung down along the walls. Each worn and dusty curtain held the silver image of one of the Sky Gods.

Narslac let loose with a whistle after the feeble light revealed an oblong silver box lying in the middle of the room. "Now this is interesting."

Unadorned and covered in dust, the box was about the length of a person's arm. It rested upon a stone pedestal.

"What did your visions tell you about this?" Urith asked Fedelm, who shook her head. Then, he looked over a Mivraa.

"It looks familiar, but I don't know what it means."

Narslac spoke up. "It's got to be the container of Heptarc's remains. The songs talk about the final resting place of the killer of Guardians."

"It's too big for an urn," Mivraa argued.

"Not for bones," The Skald replied.

Urith stepped next to the box. "Only one way to find out." With his good arm, he fumbled around, trying to find an opening. He then tried using both hands, but his shield got in the way, nearly knocking the box to the floor. Fedelm and Narslac rushed over to join him. Fedelm kept the silver container from sliding off the stand.

The Esterblud gave her a wink, his face turning red. "You just saved me from the wrath of Heptarc." He moved away from the pedestal. "Alright, since I'm still clumsy with this hand, one of you open it."

Narslac nodded to Fedelm as the woman repositioned the box. She took a deep breath and ran her fingers along the top edge until she found a place to grip the lid. After several attempts, the top slowly gave way and opened as the group slowly came together. The blond woman gave a gasp, causing the rest to crowded around. Peering in, they discovered a rusty staff being held by a skeletal hand. The scepter was nearly the length of a human arm, and the silver bulbous end was engraved with various symbols. The symbols were like nothing the people ever saw before. Urith moved closer to get a better view.

"Unremarkable, whatever it is," Narslac commented, his broad face showing a frown. "It's some type of a mace. Obviously, the hand must be from Heptarc. By why cut off his hand?"

"Maybe he went lame like me, Urith joked grimly. "Whatever the reason, that silver looks familiar." The Esterblud warrior reached out and pulled the staff from the container. The hand remained attached as Urith brought the mace around to the front of the Shield of Skool.

"Wait, it's already there," Mivraa yelled as she grabbed Urith's arm. "Your shield must have touched the silver top of the urn."

The group instantly turned to look at the shield on his arm. The demigoddess was correct. The last piece of the silver filled out the middle circle. The large silver disk of his shield held four words inscribed on the outer edges. *Sevethm*, the name for sovereign was located directly across from *gcothrem* which meant vengeance. On the other part of the circle, *regaligc* and *doltais* were on opposite sides, creating the term sacred justice. Each person stood staring at the object, suddenly feeling let down. After all of the turmoil, heartache, and death surrounding their search, their journey appeared at an end. The Shield of Skool was complete, but they really had no idea what to do next.

Narslac shook his head. "But why bother with the hand and mace if the Skool was on the top of the container?"

"When it broke apart is was sent across the lands. The Fates must have decided to have the builder of the urn use the metal of the god's weapon," Fedelm recalled the legend of the Skool. "I'll bet the hand of Heptarc was just a location marker like all the others. A way for us to find each piece."

Urith noticed Mivraa standing near one of the curtains. When he started to ask what she was doing, the demigoddess held up her hand.

"Quiet!" she hissed under her breath.

Everyone went silent with thoughts swarming among them that the woman warrior was about to suffer another bout of insanity. Urith crept closer to the woman. Then, he realized she was attempting to listen to something by the way she tilted her head. She pointed to the curtain in front of her. The Esterblud came close to the stone wall next to her. After a long stretch of listening, he was about to give up when he heard a distant voice. It was Satres!

"You hear it, too?" Mivraa asked with a whisper at his reaction.

Urith nodded, giving a death sneer as he pulled the curtain away from the wall. Immediately the old cloth fell apart, scattering a gray dust forcing both of them to retreat. When the dust finally settled, they began to inspect the stones making up the wall.

"What have you found?" Narslac softly asked as he and Fedelm crept next to them.

"A voice and I think it's Satres." Urith used his fingers to probe potential openings. "Must be some sort of trap door near here."

"If so, it's not been used for generations," Fedelm observed before beginning to help the search.

"We have what we came for, why not just leave here?" Narslac suggested, but the look Urith shot him quickly made the Skald change his tune.

"Maybe we should just go back and come in from the other side?"

Mivraa turned to the one-armed man. "Satres knows this place inside and out. The only place we know about is his bed-chambers. Those are far away from this place, located in the upper levels. Now, quit talking and help find a way through this wall."

It took a while for the party to finally discover the key through the entrance. A discolored stone, several paces away caught Mivraa's eye.

When she pressed the rock, the demigoddess felt it give slightly. Pushing harder, it finally moved, and they heard a grating rumble.

"There!" Urith noticed the crack running down the wall in front of him.

After several tries, he and Narslac were able to push the wall forward, revealing another tunnel. The two men carefully looked inside before Urith moved ahead, firmly reminding Narslac that Satres was the Esterblud's enemy.

The line of Citadel intruders followed the passage, eerily quiet except for the occasional bits of conversation which reached their ears. From what they heard, it was a dialogue the Sacred Overlord was having with other leaders. The echoing sounds grew more distinct the further they went through the winding passage. Several turns later, Urith came to another wall. He heard the source of the conversation coming from above him. Holding his tribolrocks up, he saw a small opening which carried laughter to them, along with the voice of his enemy.

"My friend, you are as mistaken in death as you were alive. The world will fall before the Guardians. Your soul, like the rest of us, will be used as playthings." Satres laughed again, and Urith immediately began looking for a way past the wall. His anger grew each time he heard the thin man's voice.

"Osramc, are you sick? Your wine sits untouched before you. You clairvoyants don't seem to have much of an appetite either. Oh, well, more for the rest of us."

While Urith and Narslac scanned the wall, Fedelm and Mivraa listened to the Sacred Overlord.

"What's that, Dughorm? You believe we'll have more company. I must say, the room is getting full, but I can always have more chairs brought in. It's unfortunate my guards have become such sullen beasts. Otherwise, we could be having this party in the Great Hall."

"Did I just hear Dughorm's name?" Fedelm whispered to Mivraa who nodded.

Fedelm was about to say more when Narslac found the way into the room. With a soft click, the wall slowly began to slide away. An opening, just wide enough to slide through, appeared. Silently, Urith made his way inside after pulling his sword. Instantly he smelled the decay. The room reeked of death.

"Why the Clovel Destroyer has joined our party." Satres beamed a smile to the warrior as he remained seated at the head of the circular table. "Please come in. Some of our mutual friends told me you would be coming." The overlord looked to his guests. "Everyone, may I present Urith, the famed warrior from Esterblud and master of the Shield of Skool."

Satres stopped momentarily as the rest of the group entered, turning his attention to the empty chair next to him. "My, my, you've been quite bad, Dughorm. You didn't tell me we would have such illustrious guests today." He said, beaming at Mivraa. "Oh, my and the Goddess of Haligulf joined us as well. All of came with one of my own satgerts, the little girl who betrayed me. What a group of adventurers to share their triumph." He paused, taking a drink.

Too bad it was for naught," he said.

Satres stood from his chair, then gave a deep bow to his new guests. He appeared quite happy to see them, adjusting and smoothing his scarlet robes. He picked up his golden cup in one hand and staff in the other.

Despite his hatred of the man in front of him, Urith kept staring at the other guests as he slowly rounded the table. The two rotting corpses sat in their chairs, greenish-blue colored faces stared at nothing, and dark brown stains covered their white robes where the blood dried. The other seats held bodies as well. In various states of early decay, two men dressed as Citadel guards held cups filled with wine in their stiff hands.

"Oh, that's right. I never introduced you to my staff." Satres informed them as his long, bony finger pointed out his guests. "Those men in blue there. Don't remember their names really but they were gracious enough to join after I sneaked up behind them. They really liven up the party." "The two Aberffraw representatives are all that remains of my council. Please say hello to Osramc and Crutcl." Satres lowered his voice, telling Urith not to pay attention to the fact the two dead guests were from Cahmais.

"And there's no need to figure out which is which." Satres gave a chuckle as he took another sip of his drink. "I'm afraid you missed the wife of Lyncus. It appears the Vanth had plans for her when he dropped by."

"And, of course, Dughorm and Joenhip," the Sacred Overlord nodded at the empty chairs. "Now that introductions are out of the way, what does Urith wish from me?"

For a moment, Urith was speechless along with the rest of his friends.

"You said Dughorm told you we would come. Did he tell you why we're here?" Mivraa spoke, marveling at the insanity she witnessed.

"But, of course. And I see by the complete shield held by Urith that you have the power of the gods. Joenhip told me of this event so many seasons before." He told them as his face went dark. "Rightfully, it should be mine, but the Fates have not been kind."

Instantly Satres smiled again as he began pacing behind the chair. "Each night, when I try to sleep, Dughorm comes to me. He tells me about your progress. In fact, he just mentioned your arrival here in the Citadel." He stopped and looked at one of the empty chairs. "You were holding out on me, my old friend. You've been giving me these visions for how long? That's right, not long after Colainn accidentally killed you. No, that's correct, I said accidentally. You knew I would never have ordered him to kill you." The Sacred Overlord looked back at Mivraa, the overlord's face showing his exasperation. "You see; he's always saying that to me. Now, where were we again?" He paused briefly, gathering his thoughts. "Oh, that's right. You believe yourself to be finished since you possess the final part of your quest. I know you think the Skool and the gods of the Sky Realm will keep the realms of Kamin safe. However, the underworld comes here to keep me informed as well."

He tapped his head. "I've seen both sides, and I know the Guardians will win. Then, our nightmares really will come true." Satres confided to his guests.

Satres stopped in front of an empty chair, staring down at the ghost sitting there. "Joenhip, I know you disagree with me. But it's inevitable. Why do you think I've stayed loyal to Kriell, even when he consumed my true love, Alrpan? I will remain with the winners of the coming battle, make no mistake. The Guardians will need me to guide the humans. Plus, only I can keep enough people alive for the returning gods to use as they want. It's all planned."

Fedelm shook her head at the transformed lunatic standing on the other side of the table. "Once, I believed in you. Now, you're entirely insane."

Satres glanced up at her briefly, his frown almost comical. "You are really not a fun person. This party grows dull with such company." He turned to Urith as he walked behind his chair. "So, now that you have your Skool, I believe its time for you leave in your hopeless task to save the world. Dughorm tells me you can do that in the Sky Realm now. Too bad you won't be staying long."

Urith's eyes narrowed. "Crazy or not, I promised that I would kill you for what you've done."

"Oh, that's right. I remember you saying something about that, so long ago. I nearly forgot." Satres smiled. "Unfortunately, that's not your decision."

Abruptly, the overlord pushed the large chair at Urith, causing him to back up. Satres ran to the wall behind him. With practiced precision, he made his escape through the wall while Urith get around the obstacle in front of him. When he reached the entrance, the wall was nearly shut. Urith shoved his shield edge between the stones. Mivraa and Narslac joined with him trying to pry the wall apart enough for them to pursue Satres. After several attempts, they finally pushed the door open enough to slide through.

As he left, Narslac grabbed an empty chair, shoving it into the closing door and followed the others as they raced after their prey. Urith took the steps inside the dark stairwell two at a time, following the winding path upwards. The voice of insane man sang a tune, laughing at them.

"Come on, heroes. I'm far ahead of you." Satres told them.

When Urith came out into the main hall through a secret panel, he saw the scarlet-robed man run past one of the Citadel's guards.

"Invaders have gotten in. Call for reinforcements." Satres shouted. Witnessing the invaders coming through the opening in the wall, the guard immediately blew into a small horn, calling out his comrades.

"We don't need this," Urith growled, then suddenly had an idea. "Stay with me." The warrior broke into a full sprint. As the lone guard pointed his halberd to impale the Esterblud, Urith lowered his shield. When the Skool met the pointed end of the guard's weapon, a small explosion shot out sending the guard and his weapon flying. Urith passed the unconscious man lying in a heap on the floor, climbing the stairs taken by Satres.

Urith finally came out of the winding stairway at the top of the Citadel. A few paces away, Satres sat on one of the battlements overlooking the valley below. He was staring at the Kamin sun starting to peek out from the horizon.

"You're slowing down." He mocked him with a sigh. "It's a shame the wrong man got the Skool. I could have done great things."

"No, you have no honor. You worship power." Urith told him as he walked toward him. The remainder of the group followed him out. Urith indicated for them to remain back.

"What you say is true. But, let's be honest. What does your honor get you? A place in Haligulf? Not anymore. You will become like the rest of us, only fodder for the gods. The beorhs will have their fun with you warriors, before and after death." The man's eyes were bright as he looked at Urith. "I recall a story about you trying to get your wife into the Sky Realm along with your father. Then, you found out the gods would not accept your methods, so they put your family into the underworld. Judging from my discussions with the Vanth, they were probably given as a special toy for Caruun and Alrpan." The Sacred Overlord gave Urith a sympathetic smile. "Now you work for the very same gods. The irony is delicious, wouldn't you agree?"

The giant warrior stopped. "I don't work for them. I work to prevent the chaos that kills us."

"My deluded adversary. There is only one way to stop the chaos. You must control it through power. Yet, you're so blind you will let the only weapon capable of defeating gods to become a tool of the ones you claim to hate." Satres stood up. "Anyway, my time is through. Kriell has won. I just wanted to see the sun rise one last time. It's really quite beautiful this morning."

Urith saw the purple rays becoming lighter across the sky just as the sun broke the horizon. The Sacred Overlord turned to the Esterblud. "I don't think I'll see the light much in the underworld."

Nobody moved when Satres jumped off the battlement, diving headfirst like he was jumping into the water. When Urith went to look over the edge, he could only see the darkness of the rocks below.

Chapter 6: Prepare for War

The death of Satres did not end the problems for the invaders of the castle. Shouts and the sounds of horns were heard, sending the group fleeing across the battlements to a corner of the Citadel. From there, they descended the circular staircase to another level. As they poured out of the stairwell, they ran into a small group of guards led by Ircia.

"Surrender!" the man demanded.

"That's not going to happen," Urith shouted. "Your Sacred Overlord is dead of his own hand. We are leaving as we have duties elsewhere. Stand away, and we will leave peacefully."

While some of the guards relaxed their stance slightly, Ircia remained unconvinced. "You play an old trick. The Sacred Overlord remains within our walls, under our protection. "

"He's telling the truth," Narslac insisted, keeping Urith from challenging the guards further. "Come Ircia, you know me. My Skalds and I have drunk with you in the village below. We tell you the truth. Satres went crazy and threw himself from the top of the Citadel. Your guard saw him pass running to the battlements."

"What you say may be correct, but I need proof. I cannot let the killers of the Sacred Overlord escape now." The leader of the guards pointed to his other guards who came down the tunnel behind the small group of invaders. Mivraa and Fedelm turned to face them, but they were trapped.

"Very well, let me reassure you. We had arrived before the sun set yesterday. Do you have men missing from before that time?" Narslac asked. Ircia stood up from his crouch, nodding.

"Aye, several of our men have disappeared."

"Then, let me take you to the hidden chambers where the *sidhera* sits, holding corpses of your missing men along with two of the Aberffraw council members. Will that convince you?" The one-armed man sheathed his sword and walked toward Ircia, who nodded and did the same.

"I will follow you with some of my guards. The rest will wait here for our return. Lead me to this place you speak of."

Narslac turned back to Urith, giving him a broad grin. "I told you I was needed."

Urith shook his head at the jest and grunted, "Just don't forget to return. You can find heathmead after we leave."

After the Skald and leader of the guards left, Urith gave a grudging smirk to Mivraa. "He's right, we did need him."

~~~

Deep in the Sky Realm, Ecarca was nearly finished with his work. The energy required for his work drained him by the end of the day. Now, as he looked over the clay figures, the god did so with a sense of satisfaction. Thousands of the statues stretched along the Exyts, each human shaped piece a copy of the next. The army of hardened clay figures was made in his image and Kamin's god of rock and earth was quite pleased with himself. It was a grand clay army. All that was left would be the power of the magical waters and the right spells to control the warriors of his creation.

Ecarca smiled to himself when he thought of how he duped the spirit of Caestia. To think the ghost of a human would believe himself smarter than a god was the highest of folly. In his eyes, the statue army surpassed any of the great temples built by the people on Kamin. Soon, he would transform them into the finest warriors since in the realms. Impervious to pain and fear, his legions would set things right throughout the realms. When he took control of the domains, the god of soil and rock decided he would send Caestia to reside inside the throne of Caruun. It would teach the human spirit some manners.

But, first Ecarca needed to refresh himself after the taxing efforts of the day. As the god moved toward the stream of waters that immortality to the gods, he heard a voice.

"The sprites were correct; you have been busy." Dughorm silently flew on the breeze, stopping next to one of the statues. The god watched the oracle inspect his work, resenting his presence but vain enough to want affirmation of his grand masterpiece.

"Yes, despite that lucky shot from the human, my weakened state does not stop me from creating perfection."

Dughorm nodded as he dusted the shoulder of the statue. "I can see your superior capabilities. Only a god could create such exceptional fighters. Soon, you shall have a force to be reckoned with. Duwdamon must be quite pleased to lead such an army into the underworld."

Ecarca scoffed lightly as he disrobed. "My father makes amends, not war. I will give life and lead these creatures." The naked god strode

114

to the middle of the narrow stream to lay in the chilling waters. As he let the water's powers return his strength, he glanced at Dughorm who walked to another statue.

"I see you have decided to follow the visions. That is good." The spirit looked over at the god who turned his head toward the sky. Dughorm quickly pushed an amulet of inscribed metal on the cloak of the clay, just like all the others. It left the impression of the word, *regaligc*. The God's oracle smiled to himself at the irony of word's meaning. Sacred was not a term he associated with the Sky Realm now.

"Tell me more of this vision, oracle. You have not spoken to me of such a vision." Ecarca spoke suddenly, causing the spirit to quickly turn back to the stream, hiding the amulet from the god's view.

"That is because your father dismisses such things in the many times I've tried to help. It is most distressing since my sole purpose is to serve the gods. Your guidance would be valuable."

Ecarca kept his focus on the sky, his words were careful. "That is because my father and I don't always see things the same way. He sits in the temple, rather than forcing the humans to give him the Skool. It is a weakness to rely on others when you have the power."

The oracle nodded, carefully avoiding a smirk at the way the god spoke. Dughorm knew only threats from Duwdamon forced the god floating in the water to go after the Skool in the first place.

"So I understand. Well, it's quite simple actually. The visions I've seen show a strong leader taking the helm of an imposing army of stone. The Realms will tremble at the battle which will ensue, bring a new world," the seer told the god honestly.

Ecarca sat up, the bluish hue of his skin returning as the water dripped from his long hair. "Your words interest me. Tell me more."

"I see the vast army sweeping out the monsters of the underworld. New masters appear as well. But this dream was not clear. You must remember, these visions are vague, not sufficiently clear as the participants help control the events." Dughorm continued to appear distracted by the next statue he floated to.

Ecarca said nothing but his face carried a sudden determination. Refreshed, the god lifted himself from the water, pulling the finely spun robe back over his body. Head down in thought, the god of the rocks left Dughorm who pushed the amulet impression into the next statue. The oracle smiled as he hummed the ancient warrior song.

~~~

As Urith and his comrades finally left the Citadel, Mivraa was missing again. Fedelm made a smart remark about how that was normal, and the Esterblud just grunted. However, his attention was on the winding road from the port which showed many riders on ossanes galloping to the fortress. When he recognized the warrior tunics, the Esterblud let out an oath, cursing what else might go wrong. The rider's tunics and hats meant assassins. He was about to reach for his shield slung over his back, but Fedelm's sharp eyes caught sight of the lead rider. It was Brihar wearing his green tunic. To everyone's surprise, the Gramcle clan leader was followed closely by a band of fealharans wearing their notorious tunics and brown leather bowl helmets with thick protective leather flaps. The assassins were highly skilled with a bow and knife.

"Did you save any for us to deal with?" Brihar asked grimly when he arrived. His sword showed drying blood.

Perplexed, Urith waited until more of the fighters came close. He noticed some Esterbluds and Eran clan members, along with the Gramcle tribe as well. Their clothes bore the bloodstains of recent fighting as well.

"You surprise me, Brihar. There is nothing here for you. Satres is dead."

The short, stout man smiled. "That is only one head of the serpent. Since we landed in the port, we have already disposed of the Ynyover allies of the Aberffraw. We now follow Lyncus who still lives. Those Ynyover dung eaters who gave him shelter will pay as well. Once we burn out these vermin within the Citadel, we go after Lyncus."

"Allied with fealharan?" Narslac asked, surprised as Urith at the sudden alliance of Esterblud and the assassins.

"The Aberffraw leader owes us a debt, and we will get repayment." One of the death creepers in the brown tunic spoke up.

"I'm Skart," the man told Urith. "Your leader Brihar realized the mutual benefit of our combined forces."

Urith stepped next to Brihar, giving Skart a sneer. "I smell Malhair guild behind your interest now." He turned to his friend. "Revenge is not the answer." Those remaining in the Citadel are not loyal to Satres or Lyncus. Such people are long gone. Those left remain faithful to the code we follow."

Brihar scoffed. "Those we just battled were loyal to the serpent. They were wearing the clothes of the enemy."

Still filled with the lust of battle, some of the men who surrounded small group began to push close. As they muttered threats and catcalls, some of the fealharan bandits agitated the situation with their shouts of revenge. Brihar tried to restore order over the din. Warriors, who were just allies earlier, started to shove and jostle those who spoke up for Brihar or Skart. At one point, a fealharan who tried to push by Urith made a fatal error. By pressing his ossane close to Urith, the mount and its rider came against the Shield of Skool.

The surge of electrical power went through man and beast, instantly followed by a shockwave. The small blast threw Urith forward into Brihar's mount, knocking him to the ground. Nearby, other people fell from their mounts when their ossanes panicked. Many fighters near the mini blast scattered.

Urith jumped to his feet with the Shield of Skool now attached to his injured arm. Banging his Clovel Sword across the front of the shield, sparks flew across the area. The men around him cautiously watched the spectacle.

"Pitshogs and *calwards*, you disgrace Heptarc's death. Each of you just kissed the ass of the underworld gods by your actions. "

The giant warrior jumped on top of the dead ossane's body which still smoldered. His eyes were ablaze with a touch of madness. "The Skool is now whole, and the power of the gods resides here with me alone. If one more warrior fails to heed my directions, I will turn you into dust now." He deliberately turned the shield at the men while they stared at the deadly object. He recognized the mix of fear and awe in most of their faces as they recalled the stories of the weapon in his hands.

"This shield is now *Regaligc*." Urith initially used the term for Sacred for those might oppose him. "My mission comes from the Fates to restore the balance to the realms. It is not a burden I wanted. But, no man," he stopped and gave his death grin to the leaders he recognized among the group around him. "I say no man will stop me from ending the chaos that descends upon the lands. I don't care about vengeance and revenge against the Aberffraw or Cahmais or any other tribe. The monsters which come from the underworld will be happy to destroy you and your families while you bicker among yourself. Only the Skool can allow us to survive the coming onslaught from the underworld."

He swung his sword across the shield one more time, sending another burst of sparks around him, causing the circle to retreat a few paces. "Now, together we can set things right in Ynyover. But this means we start by ruling as just people, not petty tyrants thirsting for blood."

Urith pointed to Brihar. "You are my friend, but you've forgotten your people helped build this fortress. I ask you. Do you want to destroy it or make it be something worthy of the Gramcle? Do you follow in the footsteps of Joenhip or not?"

Brihar glanced down as his face turned red at the chastising given by Urith. The crowd around him waited. Finally, Brihar turned to the group. "Urith speaks the truth. None of our clan would lead in destroying the Citadel." He said as he looked at Urith. "But they wish for the head of Lyncus and his followers on pikes like many of our relatives and friends."

There was a murmur of agreement in the crowd as they slowly moved closer. Urith stepped down and stepped over to Brihar. "In this, you and I have a common cause. The Gramcles, like all within the Esterblud lands, are justified in seeking the men who invaded. Just like those in Ynyover who have suffered as well. Now put away your weapons, and we can hunt down Lyncus."

Brihar nodded and ordered his men to put away their swords and spears. As they slowly complied, Urith spoke up to all.

"Time presses against us. We must find his path and move quickly before Lyncus returns to Cahmais." He looked around at the warriors. "If he returns to his lands, we don't have enough people gathered to get him out of there."

Brihar quickly agreed, making sure to cut off any hesitation among those he brought to Ynyover. "I say Urith is right. Let us cut off the Aberffraw by going through the highlands?"

Urith smiled. "That's a good idea. Don't forget, many Ynyover suffered under the Aberffraws. Let us try to get their support to help us. Is that agreed?"

Brihar looked at his followers. "I'm in agreement. Warriors of Esterblud, Eran, and Gramcle, you will follow Urith and me, or you will return home." Then, he rode slowly in front of his fighters, making sure each looked at him to agree.

Urith sheathed his sword as he spoke to Skart, "What say the fealharan leader? If you join us, you follow our path."

"As long as Lyncus pays, we follow you." The man's thin face remained expressionless.

"I thought as much. The guild is paying well." The Esterblud replied bitterly as he watched Mivraa pushed her way through, bringing Urith an ossane for the journey.

"I made my way to the other side of the Citadel while you were showing off you speaking skills. If you want to follow Lyncus, I know the route he took."

Urith nodded, suddenly realizing they were short two ossanes. He gave Mivraa a glance remembering only one mount went lame. However, the demigoddess paid no attention as she got on her mount. The warrior saw Fedelm fuming at the intentional slight by Mivraa. The woman whispered to Narslac about the lack of mounts, and the stout man's face was dark at the thought of being left behind as well.

Urith called out to Brihar. "My friend, do you have spare ossanes for my group? Apparently, we had two go lame on the other side of the Citadel."

"Yes, I'll have a man bring them. The dead in the port will not need them any longer." There was grim laughter at the joke.

"Actually, let me get them. I just realized that I need to go to the Malhair House first," Urith gave a grin as an idea came to mind. He pulled himself on the ossane and held out a hand to Fedelm. "Come, I'll need your help on this matter. You can bring back an ossane for Narslac."

The blond woman smiled, then pointed out his deadly shield on his back. The Esterblud warrior pulled off his shield, hooking it to his saddle and Fedelm joined him on the back of the beast. The Esterblud waved Mivraa and Narslac toward him after a quick conversation with Brihar. He noticed the demigoddess hesitated at first before finally walking back to his group.

"Brihar agrees to leave some of his men here," Urith informed them. "The rest of the fighters will join us to hunt down Lyncus."

"I'll make sure that my men work with this Ircia who runs the fortress now. We should have no problems. However, I don't think a few fighters can patrol the town and port." The stocky Gramcle leader told them.

"I agree. That's why I'm heading down to see the guild. I'll send word to my brother for him to join us here with men. He is the perfect man to help rebuild this place." Urith replied.

"You old *bater,* you're up to something," Brihar exclaimed.

"Just a thought," the Esterblud shifted in his saddle. "Pehnuwick knows many leaders throughout Kamin, and he has a reputation as a fair man. I will get him to come here and help the Citadel. What do you think?"

"It's risky. Can Wilgam and Oslaf handle Esterblud without his help?" The Gramcle leader replied.

"You're probably right about that. However, it would be only long enough to get the satgerts gathered for a new Sacred Overlord. He can bring help to guide Ircia who leads the Citadel's defenders. I think Ircia is a good man."

"It makes sense. You will need to hurry, it will grow dark soon, and we need to go after the Aberffraw now," Brihar reminded him.

Fedelm leaned over to whisper in Urith's ear who nodded. "I like that." The warrior looked over at Mivraa. "You know Lyncus's route. Can we catch up by using another trail?"

The woman's eyes narrowed as she looked at Fedelm. "Yes, over the old trail that runs through Ynysbeag. The same way you took to find Dughorm."

"Then, the goddess of Haligulf should lead the way for Brihar and the fealharans. I will speak with the guild leaders and catch up." Some of the men around Urith, including Narslac, spoke up in support of the idea.

Grudgingly, Mivraa accepted. She turned her ossane to the trail and spurred the animal forward. "Alright you warriors, see if you can keep up."

Soon, the sound of hooves filled the air as the men scrambled, racing away to catch their guide. Brihar and Urith exchanged knowing smiles before Urith turned his ossane to the port.

"Stay here, and we'll bring you a mount from the harbor," he told Narslac who nodded.

As they rode away, Fedelm leaned close. "Thanks for taking my suggestion. She seems to want you alone for some reason. I don't trust her anymore." She told him. "I mean, she's never betrayed us, but I know she would slit my throat if you weren't around."

Urith grunted. "I have my suspicions about her as well. But I cannot tell her to stay out of this now." He said. "Besides she is still valuable. I suspect she is our only link for getting into the other realms."

"But you know humans cannot go into the other realms," she reminded him.

"Says who? The gods," Urith scoffed, turning quiet as the mount came upon one of the dead Ynyover comitatus fighters who stood against Briahr's men earlier.

"This chaos must be stopped," Fedelm said somberly. "It's clear that humans piling up the dead are just adding to the hordes of the underworld. But I don't think this Kriell is intent on destroying our world. Otherwise, wouldn't he have already sent them out of the realm into ours?"

"I think Dughorm was showing us more than just the underworld," Urith told her as he spurred the ossane past the body. "The Skool is now complete. Once we get Lyncus, then I believe I will be entering the underworld with the shield. At least, that's what I think I saw in the dreams."

"I wish he was here to tell us." She confessed.

"You hakras are supposed to know it all." He laughed at his own joke when she gave him a friendly slap on the back of his head.

Stopping at the Malhair House, the pair saw several of labors and sailors taking the bodies of the dead to the beach. Urith walked to the small hut used by the guild as Fedelm followed. Inside, they found an ancient man sat behind a single table. He didn't bother to look up at the visitors as he read a scroll in front of him.

"We are closed." He said. "Take your business elsewhere."

Urith's eye's narrowed. In the blink of an eye, he took a long step while he whipped out his Sagrian dagger. Slamming the tip of the weapon through the parchment held between the ancient man's hands, the Esterblud growled out his reply.

"Messenger, take this to Kaoden and Rordan. They will send a message to all of the kingdoms stating the Sacred Overlord is dead, and the guild will ask for all loyal satgerts leadership to return to Ynyover to determine a new leader. Remind your masters that if they fail to comply with this, I will make it my mission to destroy this guild, starting with this place."

The old man's hands were visibly shaking when Urith removed the dagger.

"Now little man, since I know you dine on koinons, I will pay you to send a messenger to my brother, Pehnuwick. No doubt, you can figure out he is in Eran. You will tell him to come to the Citadel in Ynyover."

"Is...that all?" The ancient one asked softly.

Urith gave him his death sneer. "If you do that, I'll have no need to remove your head." The warrior threw the last of his money on the table. "Now leave and do your job." With surprising speed, the little man scampered out the door.

"You were a little hard on him," Fedelm commented. "You just needed to throw down a few koinons."

"It made me feel better," the Esterblud replied derisively. "These people remind me of *vensars*, always squawking even with they get the largest pieces of the carcass. Let's go find an ossane for you and Narslac. I don't want to let Brihar and Mivraa decide the fate of our friend Lyncus if they catch him."

After retrieving the mounts and scavenging some of the food bags from the docks, the group rode hard. When their beasts became winded on the narrow, twisting climb through the back trail, the riders dismounted and pulled them along to keep up the pace.

They reached the village of Ynysbeag; the first thing they noticed only charred remains of the stone signal tower on the outskirts of the village. Used to communicate to the Citadel, Urith guessed the Aberffraw came this way, leaving their mark with the destruction. As they followed the trail into the small town, the scenes of death and destruction greeted them. Now, with the enemy hurrying back to Cahmais, the rabble was quickly executing people and leaving only the largest buildings burned. The residents were able to save some of the nearby structures. The remaining residents peered out cautiously from behind the buildings at the trio coming through.

"Why?" Fedelm stopped her ossane suddenly at one of the dead men laying in the street. She recognized the body of Wiclam, the little man who guided her to Dughorm when they arrived at the village after joining with Urith. It seemed like ages ago that the little man tried steered her to the old blind man. She looked at Urith when he guided his mount next to hers. Narslac peeled away to one of the villager's he recognized.

"I remember him guiding you to Dughorm," Urith spoke. "The Aberffraw are not much better than beorhs now. Come, don't think about it. We'll have to check which trail they took. Hopefully, we can get to them before they do this to another village."

As the pair started down the main trail, Narslac spurred his mount to catch them. "We're not far behind Brihar's men," the Skald informed his companions. "The survivors told me that only a small group of Aberffraw came through earlier. They were just a few raiders who found this trail. It seems Lyncus has most of his men on the main road. The bandits who came through only bothered to carry off a few of the women after killing some of the elders who made the mistake of hanging around. The villagers suggested we could take a back trail to catch our people."

"Fedelm and I know that route. Anything else?" The Esterblud turned his mount, leading them between some of the huts to the trail.

Narslac pulled a flask from his saddle, taking a drink. "I asked about the underworld monster, and they told me the local satgert is telling people to remain inside the temple at night, with guards at the entrance. For the moment, only their animals are getting slaughtered."

"Well, at least that priest is smart. The temples are nearly always made of stone and narrow passages so easier to defend."

"That's true," the Skald agreed. "However, I get the feeling the locals would be happy if both the Esterblud and Cahmais kingdoms were destroyed by the underworld."

Urith grunted. "I can't say I blame them."

"From what I've seen, I doubt that Kriell will show mercy to any side." Fedelm offered ruefully as the trio went silent at her thought.

The darkness swiftly fell over the trio while they made their way down the treacherous path from Grimma to the main road toward Cahmais. By the time they reached the road, they could see nearby campfires. Unsure whether it was friend or foe near the camps, Urith left the group to investigate. Spying movement near the road, he saw the familiar colors of the guard's tunics and helmets. They were Brihar's men. The warrior retraced his steps back to his friends, and together, the group entered the camp. There were several campfires, but only one held the large tents of the leaders. Brihar came to them as they slid off their saddles.

"You made a good time. I wasn't expecting you until the sun rose."

"We took a short cut. We were hoping we might find Lyncus here." The Esterblud replied. "You have any idea how far ahead the Aberffraw are?"

The short, stout man gave him a grin. "Close enough to catch them before they can reach the border. My guess is, by the end of tomorrow, our scouts will have found them. The farmers and shepherds heard of the killings and enslavement by the Aberffraw. They are staying away, hiding in areas away from the main roads. While the Ynyover people don't like us, they are willing to give us information."

Thinking back to the last village, Urith nodded. "Narslac found the same in Ynysbeag."

"You should get some food and sleep. We will leave when the daylight appears." Brihar said as he yawned.

Urith nodded, feeling an overwhelming weariness at the suggestion. Nearby, Fedelm and Narslac were already working on removing the packs, saddles, and blankets from their ossanes. Urith took Brihar by the shoulder, moving them away from the others.

"How are you getting along with Mivraa?" The giant Esterblud looked around. "By the way, where is she?"

The leader of the Gramcle shrugged his shoulders. "She took off just after dark. She's hard to figure out. One minute she's a hard-driving leader, pushing the men on and cursing out those who are slacking. The next minute, we rest, and she eats alone, then takes off without a word." Brihar sighed. "Such is the world of a demigoddess I guess."

Urith nodded absently. "I suppose so. Let me know when she returns. I'll grab some food and sleep. If the weather holds we should move quickly."

The morning light brought the demigoddess to the camp where the warriors were nearly finished packing their ossanes. Urith squatted by the campfire, chewing on dried meat while warming himself. Narslac and Fedelm were away, filling the water bags.

"I see you found your way back," Urith observed the woman appeared exhausted. "You should have rested. We have a long journey today."

Mivraa glared at him with bloodshot eyes. "That's my business."

The Esterblud stood as she came closer. "No, it's all of our business. Even a goddess needs sleep to stay sharp." He noticed the bloodstains on some of her armor. "I'm hoping you found the enemy."

124

Her eyes narrowed, then she looked at the stains. "Yes, I found some enemies. Don't worry; their spirits won't be going anywhere."

Immediately, the giant fighter became suspicious. "With you and Wurms no longer filling Haligulf, there is no one left but the Vanths leading them to the underworld. We don't need more monsters. How about capturing them alive instead?"

Mivraa looked like she was about to say something, but she walked away to feed and water her ossane. Narslac and Fedelm returned, walking by the demigoddess who focused on her mount. Fedelm quietly told Urith that they saw Eran scouts gallop by, heading to Brihar. Urith forced himself to watch from a distance as the group of scouts spoke with their leader. The Esterblud finished his breakfast while keeping an eye on the conversation among the Gramcle fighters. Finally, Brihar got on his mount, trotting over to Urith.

"My fighters have seen the Aberffraw camp about a half day ahead of us. If we move swiftly, we should be able to see them before the sun sets."

Back on the road, the large group of fighters pushed their mounts hard as the followed the winding road. The thin forest on either side echoed with the sound of the cloven hoofs. Not far after they left their camp, they came upon a body in the road. It was a boy, younger than Oslaf, dressed in the blue tunic of the Aberffraw. However, his helmet had a pointed metal cap in the style of the *comitatus* within Ynyover wore. Brihar, riding next to Urith and Fedelm wondered aloud if it was one of the local militia's working for the Aberffraw. He was surprised since none of his men mentioned running into a scout of the enemy the day before. Urith glanced back at Mivraa who was staring at the body. The man spurred his mount forward.

Further up the road, they came upon the remains of merchant carts, still smoldering after being set on fire. Bodies beside the wagons were Ynyover traders. As they continued, the fighters came upon one small hamlet after another which held similar sights as the Aberffraw continued their murderous retreat to Cahmais.

When the warriors from Esterblud reached the outskirts of Yns Cearcal, the Great Circle, they came upon a band of Ynyover militia. At first, it appeared a battle between the two groups might break out. The blue tunics some of the Ynyover wore, and their steadfast defense of a trail leading to the Great Circle forced the Esterblud men to come to a stop. However, something in their manner caused Brihar to hold back his men. Urith with his comrades caught up as Brihar was talking with Skart, the fealharan leader.

"They don't look to be asking for a fight, but we can't bypass them, leaving them to cut us off." The stout Gramcle fighter said.

"Did you think of talking with them?" asked Fedelm with a sigh.

Urith smiled at the quizzical look the men shot at the woman. "She might have something. That road seems familiar. Where does it lead?"

"To Yns Cearcal," she replied. "You remember; I took you there before."

"That's right; you tried to get us ambushed there by Alrpan." The giant man winked to the blond who turned red.

"How does this help us now?" Skart spoke up impatiently, and Mivraa agreed with the fealharan.

Urith let out a slow breath. "Instead of a fight which will slow us down, even more, I'll go ask what they are guarding and see where their sympathies lie. Can you wait before we decide others must die?"

He spurred his horse forward, giving the assassin leader and Mivraa a glare. Brihar and Mivraa rode forward with the Esterblud. Fedelm stayed behind with Narslac who suddenly began to sing a Ynyover poem, loud enough for all to hear. His voice was rough and unsteady, making the notes of a sick *vensar* at times.

"It's times like these, I wish I could still play the lute," he told her after he finished. "I've seen times when the Skalds can help stop a war with our songs. Too bad, my friends are no longer among us." The woman hoped the man's friends sang better than Narslac or a battle could break out.

Urith stopped his ossane several paces away from the line of blue-clad men. Their leader stepped forward. He was an old warrior, his face ravaged with scars and one blind eye.

"You are in the wrong land, Esterblud."

"This is true. However, we may have a common cause. We are after those Aberffraw who ravage your lands." Brihar spoke up.

"That would be our concern," the scarred man replied. "Your people come through enough to think you own our soil."

"We are not here to fight you unless you favor the Cahmais cause. You wear the colors of the Aberffraw. Are you with this man called

126

Lyncus who destroys the villages of Ynyover?" Urith got down from his mount and stepped toward the man.

"We don't follow that cursed Aberffraw. I wear the tunic taken from one of the bodies recently killed near here. We have little after those from Cahmais steal and burn. No use giving clothes and weapons to the worms. However, our people stand against invaders now. We have decided we will not let invaders come and go as they please through our land anymore." The man's one eye widened as Urith came close. "You're the one they talk about; the scarred man with the god's shield."

"I'm called Urith," the Esterblud replied as he slid off his mount, stepping closer to the man. "Like you, I've been scarred by battle. We only seek to capture the leader of the Aberffraw. We will take him back to the Citadel for trial and punishment."

The militia leader laughed sarcastically. "Put that scum back in the hands of the Overlord. You might as well, kiss his ass first. Satres and his council are why my people suffer."

"Satres is dead. The Citadel is controlled by Ynyover people now." Urith decided not to mention Brihar's men at the port helping.

The man looked at him, then Brihar and Mivraa. "That's too good to be true." His tone was skeptical.

"We have little reason to lie about such things," Brihar told him. "What Urith says is the truth. I have but a few men in the port outside the fortress who are helping stop the destruction now. Once we catch the vermin who invaded our lands, we will leave this place. You have a warrior's oath on that."

The old man turned back to his men, yelling out the news. The cheer that came from the other blue-clad fighters showed their satisfaction. He turned back to Urith. "My name is Deijumb. If what you tell is correct, you will be surprised who waits near the Cahmais border for Lyncus and his men. He is not welcome in any kingdom now. Let us join your cause. The Aberffraw are not far from here."

Urith cast a glance over to Brihar who was visibly suspicious. "Why do your men not attack these Cahmais invaders when they came this way?"

"We only arrived at this crossroads last night. I've been rounding up whatever fighters I could find since many of our leaders were sent to Mugga on the orders of Satres. For the moment, the fort in Mugga holds the only loyal Ynyover leaders left. My group was directed to cut off any riders why might be coming from the Great Circle."

He pointed over to a young man dressed in a blue tunic, holding a Ynyover helmet. "My boy there just came back to tell us where this Lyncus is." A thought came to the man. "Say, on your journey this way, did you not see anyone? My other boy should have returned by now. I sent him to Ynysbeag."

Urith heard an ossane trotting away and saw Mivraa leaving. He turned back to the man. "Our group came upon the body of a boy this morning wearing the blue tunic. He had brown leather armor, and canvas pants like you wear. No one here knows how he died. It doesn't appear he made it to the village."

The one-eyed man's face remained unchanged, but Urith immediately knew the mask that crossed Deijumb's face. "That's too bad. Hopefully, he died facing the enemy. The gods will take him to Haligulf." He turned away, slowly going back to his friends. "We'll lead you to the Aberffraw. Then, you and your people can let us live in peace."

Urith walked back to his ossane. As he awkwardly climbed on the saddle, he accidently struck his injured arm, sending a wave of pain through his shoulder. When he watched the old warrior pull himself on the ossane held by his son, Urith realized the old man carried a far greater injury inside. Fedelm and Narslac drew next to the Esterblud.

"What happened with Mivraa?" the woman asked him.

Urith shook his head. "I just saw her ride away." He didn't tell them he thought he knew why.

"I've never seen her look like that," Narslac said. He didn't want to tell the others he saw the warrior goddess in tears as she left.

"She remains," Urith groped for a word.

"Confused," Fedelm finished his thought, her tone was hard, and Narslac raised his eyebrow at what they told him. He decided not to ask as Brihar came joined them.

The Gramcle leader waved the group forward, and soon they were following the Ynyover militia. Narslac saw Mivraa remained far behind the group, slowly following them. He told his friends who glanced back, but they remained quiet. The one son of Deijumb traveled ahead with several of the comitatus. The one-eyed warrior fell back, directing his ossane next to Urith.

"Tell me Urith, why the women in your group? I've never seen fighters travel with cup-bearers to battle."

The giant man laughed. "Cup-bearers? I've not had such a thought like that in ages. I once believed as you. But now," he shook his head. "Would you believe the auburn hair woman is Mivraa? One of the fiercest fighters you will know. I've seen her behead her half-brother, Wurms." He shifted his weight and pointed over to Fedelm. "This lovely lady next to me is called Fedelm. Don't underestimate her size. She has saved my life several times. The woman's a hakra as well."

"Enough of the tales," the grizzled man laughed at the description. He stopped when he saw Brihar and Narslac's serious expressions.

"I'm the Skald, and I'll tell you the truth. I witnessed both of these women kill beorhs who attacked us. They are not cup-bearers, and Mivraa is certainly not a peacemaker," Narslac told him firmly.

Deijumb went quiet for a while. Finally, he spoke. "Then, the rumors appear to be correct. You are the new Heptarc."

Urith frowned. "That is a tale that is not true. I'm only following where the Fates send me. I don't want what hangs on my saddle."

The old man eyed him. "If that is the Skool, many others would give their limbs for it."

"Then it would mean their death," Brihar spoke up. "I've seen a man try to take it, only to die a quivering death. The Shield of Skool protects Urith." The old man whistled at the news, then redirected his ossane around to the other side of Urith.

~~~

While the gods of the Sky Realm slept, there was an unusual silence in the great hall Haligulf. Where the great warrior spirits would normally be eating, drinking, fighting, and carousing with the pretty water sprites, now they listened intently to one soul. Heptarc stood on a table, holding a mug of heathmead made from the waters of the Exyts Spring. The many great fighting ghosts around him held the same drink in their hands.

"As you know, I bear the responsibility for creating the pact with the gods of the Sky Realm and Underworld. It is also my terrible mistake. Before I step on this platform, Dughorm told you what is coming to our dimension. Quite simply, the Guardians will return, bringing destruction and misery to our children, grandchildren and long lost families. It is not a tale of the Skalds. It is a reality now for us. I trust this seer of the gods." He paused as his voice still echoed across the silent chamber. The maker of the warrior code continued.

"The time is here for a decision. We can continue our eternity to fight as individuals, maybe to die at the hands of rivals only to return to these tables to drink ourselves into oblivion. Maybe the Guardians will let this continue, who can say." Heptarc shrugged. "Or, we can try to help our offspring to create a new realm. To fix the world as it should have happened the first time."

Murmuring swept through the fighters around the hall.

Those of you who remember our vows to our clans and lands, I'm asking you to join me to correct the wrong I brought. Our new forms wait by the water's edge. Once we enter these new bodies, we will be mortal again, to feel pain and die without a future. It is the risk I'm asking you to take. But, be assured, a great fight is coming for us. The biggest battle any of us will ever know."

The spirit jumped down from his perch and pushed through the crowd as a change swept over the room. Fighters suddenly felt a rush of adrenalin, something lost since their death. They also began to remember their families, long dead wives and children who never made it into their dimension. Their souls felt the overwhelming tug of raw emotions which disintegrated like their bodies. A roar slowly built in the hall and when Heptarc opened the massive doors, the avalanche of sound came with a new dawn as the waves of spirits swept across the Sky Realm.

~~~

The combined group of Esterblud and Ynyover fighters stopped near a stream, letting ossanes drink and their riders to fill water bags. As Urith squatted by the water's edge, one of the local scouts galloped by on his way to report to Deijumb. The Esterblud glanced over to see the young fighter talking with the one-eyed leader along with several of his comrades. Returning to filling his water bag, the giant man felt someone come close to him. Turning, he saw Mivraa sit beside him, staring at the water. He waited, but the woman remained quiet.

"Is something bothering you?" The man recognized the words were inadequate as he watched the bubble rise in the stream as the bag filled.

He expected the demigoddess to suddenly scorn him. Instead, Mivraa surprised him.

"Much bothers me." The woman told him, then she paused for a moment.

"I still see his face." Mivraa broke a twig, reaching down to swirl it in the water to break up the reflection of her.

Urith turned to her. "Whose face?"

"The boy on the road," she went silent again, and the man really didn't know what to say. He watched her twirl the stick around again.

"You've seen death before," he finally replied.

The demigoddess nodded. "But the faces don't stay with me. The human didn't deserve it."

Urith knew the answer, but he asked anyway, "Just another kill against a human opponent who could not match you?"

Mivraa nodded again, taking a deep breath. "I guess the old man got to me. I saw it in his eyes when you told him about the boy. Why did the fool send him on that road?"

The warrior shook his head. "Why would you kill a person who could not possibly win? Maybe it was to wake you?"

"Why?" she asked, he thought he saw a tear on one cheek, but she turned her head as she wiped her nose with her sleeve. "I'm beyond this. Emotions bring nothing."

"I have no idea why. But since the mountain, you seek the blood of others. I know this much. You're better than that vengeance you wish for. You and I have been part of too much death." He stopped, his mind going back to the first time they met. "Remember the time on the bridge when I first met you and Narslac. I can still feel the hate and bitterness of which came out of me on that day. Those bandits did not cause the deaths of my wife and father. But I wanted to butcher them, to make them feel my loss. That went on for a time for some crazy reason. While some might have deserved their death, others did not. Being a butcher does not stop the pain inside. In fact, I still wonder what waits for me after my death. The whole idea of Haligulf is gone for me. How can my spirit wash the blood I still wear from the suffering I cause?"

She stopped twirling the twig and threw the branch into the water. The demigoddess rose and began to walk away.

"We both have questions. Yes, I remember you on that day. I saw your madness and desperation," she told him. "I just hope my mind is not already gone."

Before he could reply, Mivraa quickly walked away, heading downstream. Urith thought about following her but realized she would need to answer the questions inside. Her life, like his, was part of a changing world which could become even more hopeless.

As his eyes followed her, he saw the demigoddess suddenly stop, peering closely at the foliage across the stream. Then, Mivraa quickly stepped through the creek to the other side where he lost sight of her in the brush. He thought about what he saw for a moment, then went back to finish his work.

On the other side of the stream, the warrior goddess carefully entered a thick grove of young trees and spiny brush. Inside, she sensed spirits watching her, but she couldn't see them. Suddenly, she turned, whipping out her spear as she expected something behind her. Only the green and blue foliage showed, covering the path she made entering the grove.

"The goddess of Haligulf is mighty jumpy." The breath of a woman's voice came from above.

Mivraa looked up and saw Spanca hanging upside down, the talons on her feet embedded into the thin trunks of two trees. Her nude green body camouflaged the woman among the canopy of leaves. "I thought I saw you come into this grove," Mivraa growled. "You're getting easy to spot."

The nature goddess blinked her yellow eyes several times. "Perhaps I wanted you to follow me. Not all of us who travel between realms are against you."

The woman warrior slid her spear back into her cloak. "I'll believe it when I see it. What do you want?"

"Rumors fly among the sprites that grow fearful, hiding in the lost lands within Kamin. They tell me that you are *brgensoc*, crazy from your time on the mountain." The upside down woman paused when Mivraa glared at her. "Forgive the pain of truth but remember I was born of a god raping my mother. There are not many of us left now. With the underworld beasts unleashed upon the lands and the death of gods in the Sky, should we not work together?"

The warrior goddess remained quiet. Fathered by Uugara, Spanca was worshiped primarily by the Gallaeci and controlled the local forests, crops, and forest creatures. While Mivraa took on many of the characteristics of her mother, the nature goddess carried more of the attributes of the god creature who fathered her. Along with her complexion and unusual feet, the woman had unusually long arms, perfect for trees. Yet, her face was attractive with angular features and full lips. Her long brown hair twirling, Spanca flipped herself over from the trees, neatly landing in front of Mivraa.

"You travel with the scarred one. I can help you. I know a way to the gods who fathered us."

Before the demigoddess could speak, the two women heard another voice.

"If she is not interested, I would be." Urith slide in behind the green goddess who turned with a startled cry which sounded like a wounded bird. The man smiled at her, hoping his death sneer would not send the creature running away.

"No need to fear. It's not often a man meets with two beautiful demigoddesses in such tight spaces."

Immediately, Spanca blushed, her face turning a shade of blue. She looked at the scarred man as he tried to keep from admiring her naked body. Despite her green hue, the woman was stunning, especially when she smiled at him. "The Clovel Destroyer is known for death, not flattery."

"I'm trying to change my ways," he said jokingly. Then he saw Mivraa's look, and he turned serious. "I noticed Mivraa hunting something, so I followed. Your conversation suddenly interested me."

"Don't mind him," Mivraa told her fellow goddess, her attention peaked at the new possibilities. "Tell us about your idea. We know something is coming and it seems to involve the Sky Realm."

Spanca waved them to come in closer. As she leaned in, she put her long arms around them and began whispering. "The one they call Kriell in the underworld has been seen near Yns Cearcal. It is said, the creature transformed into Uugor within the Great Circle."

"By the gods, I don't know how but Oslaf's wound must have killed Uugor. If Kriell stole the god's soul, does that mean he can get into the Sky Realm?" Mivraa asked, her mind reeling at the implications.

The nature goddess nodded, her face was grave. "The sprites that blow with the wind tell me so. Their souls are in torment. They hate the Sky Gods, but the nymphs fear the underworld nearly as much."

"You mean they have nowhere to turn," Urith said bitterly, and Spanca nodded. He remembered his dead wife's voice urging him to help the villagers in Eran.

Mivraa stared at the Esterblud suddenly understanding what she heard that day as well. The sprites sought a way to rebel against the Sky Realm. "So, how do we get into the realm without Duwdamon finding out? Some of those who watch for intruders will still give out an alarm if I try to enter."

The green woman smiled, and her eyes brightened. "I take you to Yns Cearcal and show the way. The spirits who protect the entrance will listen to me."

The warrior goddess broke away from the circle, excited. "We can go now."

"I'm going to finish with Lyncus first," Urith told her.

Mivraa flashed her temper, "Fine, I'll go alone."

"And do what?" The large man responded. "Can you fight Duwdamon by yourself? Only I carry the weapon that can fix this." He saw her anger rising, but he kept his voice steady. "Mivraa, nobody is saying you can't go after them. But I'm asking you to think first. If our past means anything, let me help. I don't want you hurt again."

Spanca took her sister goddess's arm. "He's right. I heard what happened. The Skool is with him. Use it for your justice." She turned the woman fighter toward her, her yellow eyes staring into hers. "For our justice, you know what I mean?"

Mivraa recognized the sorrow she saw in the green demigoddess told her much about herself. The goddess turned to Urith. "Let me talk with Spanca alone. Go back and get our ossanes and come for me. We will decide what to do when I return."

Urith nodded and left. True to her word, Mivraa was waiting by the stream when the Esterblud returned. Fedelm and Narslac came with him, although both showed their confusion at the secrecy. The giant Esterblud refused to discuss what he and Mivraa talked about as the demigoddess climbed on her mount.

Suddenly, Brihar whistled for them as the Gramcle along with the rest of the fighters galloped away. They followed the road toward Cahmais.

"We will see Lyncus by the end of the day if our scouts are correct," the Esterblud told her. Mivraa nodded and spurred her ossane back to the road.

"We will follow your plan," the woman told them.

"What plan? What's going on?" Fedelm asked, glancing over at Narslac.

"Mivraa found a way for the two of us to enter the Sky Realm. After we get Lyncus, we will go to Yns Cearcal." The warrior told them matter-of-factly. The stunned silence from their comrades continued for a while. Fedelm's face went sour at the words while Narslac looked at the stub of his one arm.

"We will come back and meet Spanca at the circle," Mivraa told the Esterblud who nodded.

"Have you got the nature goddess of the Gallaeci on your side now?" Narslac moved his mount closer to Mivraa who nodded. The Skald beamed a smile and laughed. "That is good news. I remember hearing about her, but few get to see her. They say she is beautiful."

Urith nodded absently while Fedelm gave the warrior a hard glare. Narslac smiled to himself.

"Well, I always wanted to see the Sky Realm but doing it while I'm alive will prove to be kind of interesting," the Skald reflected on the idea.

"What makes you think you're going in," Urith grunted. "The fight coming is between the gods and me. Mivraa has her own reasons."

The stout man suddenly grabbed the reins of Urith's mount, forcing him to stop. Narslac scowled at the Esterblud. "I joined with you to the finish. Friends we are and warriors as well. Like it or not, I'll be needed, and you'll not decide my fate."

Urith looked at his friend for a moment, before he took the reins back. "You're correct. It is not my place to stop you."

"You might as well get that idea out of your head for me as well," Fedelm came up beside the two men. "By my oath, I'm finishing this for my father."

Urith gave them a grin, knowing he lost the argument. "Let's try to get ourselves to the Great Circle alive first. Lyncus and his vermin will not be coming back with us willingly."

The fighting broke out when the militia of Ynyover stumbled upon the rear guard of the Aberffraw warriors. Instantly, men in blue tunics attacked other fighters in blue, creating a melee of yelling people and screaming animals. The slaves, still tied to the ossanes of their captors, their plight suddenly became even more horrific. The battling warriors ran over those unable to move out of the way, while Aberffraw fighters attempted to distance themselves from those attacking them using the slaves as human shields. Sword blows and spears flung against unarmed men, women, and children sent bodies to the ground where ossanes stomped and tripped.

Brihar's men arrived soon after the fighting started, and his men instinctively joined the battle. Seeing the plight of the slaves, many who came from Esterblud, the fearless leader called for his fighters to cut away the ropes binding the people to the ossanes of the enemy. Soon, prisoners who still survived scrambled away from the savage brawl.

Urith and his group reached the clash just after Brihar's men. The confused mass of bloody fighting by warriors wearing the different colors of tunics and armor made it difficult to understand who to help. Then, Urith caught a glimpse of a familiar silver helmet in the distance. Quickly throwing on his own black helmet and sliding his injured arm into the Shield of Skool, the man galloped off at full speed to his target. The warrior clamped his teeth, forced use his injured arm to control his mount while he pulled out his sword. His ossane jumped several bodies in his path, and he could not avoid running over a wounded warrior in a blue tunic. He wasn't sure if it was a Ynyover ally or one of the enemy fighters. But his focus remained on the last of his mortal enemies.

Lyncus didn't see the big opponent charging full speed at his small group of men. Surprised by the immediate frenzy of the fighting they stumbled into, the leader of the Aberffraw tried to regroup his fighters. He yelled for his men to press forward, attempting to exploit the inexperience of the Ynyover militia. However, the swirl of confusion and lack of warriors forced his thin line to fall back. Suddenly, out of the corner of his eye, Lyncus saw the Esterblud. Urith charged full speed into the small group of men around their leader.

The Clovel Sword whipped through the air, slicing through the metal breastplate of one man. As the man slid off his mount without a sound, Urith's follow through swing cut into another man's thigh as he passed. He didn't hear the man's screams. The big warrior tried to pull his sword up in time, but his mount ran right into the ossane that Lyncus rode. The headlong impact sent both men and animals falling to the grassy knoll.

Just before his mount struck the ground, Urith let loose of the reins and tumbled from his squealing ossane. Using the momentum, the warrior quickly rolled to his feet, next to a mounted Aberffraw. While the man tried to embed a spear into the Esterblud's belly, Urith threw up his shield which touched his opponent's leg. The surge of electrical power sent the man and his ossane to the ground, both dead before they hit the grass.

While Urith contended with those guards around Lyncus, the Aberffraw leader saw another small group heading his way. The head of the charge was a stout man in a green tunic, but Lyncus also noticed fealharan in the mix. He pushed two of his men, who lost their ossanes, in front of him.

"Unleash your spears on them," he pointed to the charging group who were nearly upon them as he backed away. Immediately, the deadly weapons were coming at Brihar and Skart. The Gramcle leader was able to dodge on of the missiles, but Skart took one in his shoulder. The force of the weapon striking him sent the fealharan tumbling off his ossane. Brihar continued his charge, sweeping through the warriors who were on foot. The warrior struck down one fighter with a battle ax he carried. The other enemy tried to move to the side, but he was run over by Mivraa who came speeding through, followed by Fedelm. Both women were heading to Urith who tried to push through a regrouped line of Aberffraw who attacked with spears and halberds to avoid the Shield of Skool.

The two women fighters struck the Aberffraw from behind, surprising the warriors who were battling the Esterblud. Mivraa took down one Aberffraw with her deadly spear. The golden hair woman following her, stabbed another enemy in the back as the man tried to turn his ossane. Urith grabbed man's shield arm as he turned his mount, embedding his Clovel Sword into the warrior's throat. The Esterblud pulled the dying man off the mount, trying to scramble aboard the ossane. Disregarding the excruciating pain of his arm, the fighter lifted himself on the moving animal.

Almost immediately he caught sight of Lyncus who was fighting for his life, his dwindling group surrounded by fealharans and Ynyover *comitatus*. The line of Aberffraw moved away, trying to reach their leader. Urith noticed Deijumb in the middle of the fray, urging his men forward.

"Let's get to Lyncus before the fealharan does," he told his partners as they came alongside him. Immediately, the trio took off toward the melee.

As they were galloping at full speed, Fedelm wondered about Narslac. Then, she saw the one hand man, charging hard from behind the line of Aberffraw. She instantly realized the Skald circled around the fighting, waiting from the forest for an opening. Fedelm yelled over to Urith, pointing at the charging fighter. Just as they were about to reach the core of the battle, the trio could only watch as Narslac swept behind Lyncus and slammed his shield into the man's back. The force of the impact sent the Aberffraw leader to the ground. With practiced ease, the Skald jumped from his mount, landing next to the stunned enemy and placed his sword at the man's neck.

"Yield now, or have your head removed," Narslac yelled at Lyncus as Brihar reached the two men.

Quickly the fighting fell away when the leader of the Aberffraw surrendered. His remaining Cahmais fighters, seeing their leader at the foot of the enemy, began to lift their arms in the air, dropping their weapons to the ground. A few pockets of men still fought as the remaining leaders tried to calm the blood lust.

Urith rode up on the now standing Lyncus who took off his silver helmet. Narslac had already taken away the man's weapons, looked up at Urith.

"I told you, you would need me." He said as his eyes danced with victory.

Urith sighed, shaking his head. He could see the Skald wasn't going to forget his words. Urith turned his attention to Lyncus who stared at him with hate in his eyes. The Esterblud gave his death sneer.

"Many deaths would have been avoided if I just killed you the first time we met," he said.

The thin son of Asgurd glared at him. "You were a fool then and remain one still. You've killed many using the power of the gods as without it. You're still a *wafaoil,* and the ancient code you live for is gone."

Urith stared down at the defiant man. "Perhaps, but your remaining ally, Satres, is quite dead. Killed himself by jumping off the battlements. So now, the rest of us can rebuild this world while you rot in the dungeons of the Citadel."

Lyncus looked over those who surrounded him and gave a bitter laugh. "These allies are rabble. Not fit to clean my outhouse. I'm the son of a king."

Brihar suddenly smacked the arrogant man in the back of his head. "Our agreement to return you to the Citadel doesn't mention in what condition you will arrive."

Skart gave a grim smiled as he stepped close, holding his bloody shoulder. "The fealharan are paid whether you are dead or alive. It might be easier just to remove his head and return it."

Lyncus glared for a moment, then suddenly began to smile. "You should start to worry about your condition."

In the distance, a line of blue-clad warriors rode at full speed toward the battlefield. Brihar and the others called out to their fighters to take up defensive positions. Narslac pushed Lyncus into his group of remaining warriors, helped along by the rest of his band. Urith went to Deijumb, who directed some of his men to surround Lyncus and his fighters.

"Will you join me to see if we can avoid a battle with these Aberffraw coming? They may not want to attack if they know who we have."

Deijumb carefully surveyed the line of blue fighters. He noticed they slowed their gallop to a trot as they approached.

"Well, it's a sure way to Haligulf if we can't stop it." Deijumb told him.

Urith grinned at Mivraa and Fedelm who overheard the conversation. "I think the goddess who rides with us will find be happy to lead us there."

"Don't go getting yourself killed before we get to the Sky Realm." She said with a grimace.

Narslac laughed, his booming voice carried across the field as he climbed on his mount. "Irony is not lost on the Fates. I say we all go along. Just to make sure Urith doesn't start something. Who knows? They might not want Lyncus back."

As the small group rode forward, Urith told Brihar what he planned. The Gramcle leader shook his head. "Now you sound like Pehnuwick." He looked at the line of the enemy who stopped many paces in front of them. "Well, if they come this way, I'll make sure Lyncus is the first to die. You can let them know that." Brihar said, deciding to remain with his men. He brought the wounded into his lines, using the Aberffraw prisoners to carry them. Some of the Esterblud and Ynyover prisoners helped as well. The fealharan tended to their own, staying close to Lyncus who stood defiantly smiling at the coming battle.

When the group led by Urith got close to the silent warriors on their mounts, they heard the squeaking wheels of a cart slowly coming up behind the line. Still too far away to see the wagon, those loyal to Urith instinctively slowed when they saw several leaders in blue tunics pull ahead of the others. Urith recognized one of the men coming.

"Is that Flacanus, I see?" Urith tried to read the man's face. "You're a long way from Du-Rinell."

"Urith, by the gods, I should have known you would be in the middle of this." Flacanus gave a brief smile before turning stoic. "My scouts tell me you hold Aberffraw fighters as prisoners. We will take them back to Cahmais."

The groups stopped only a few paces apart, each side looking suspiciously at the other.

"I believe that should not be a problem. You may have all but one. Lyncus remains with us. He has much to answer for."

Flacanus shifted in his saddle as several of his men grumbled. "I'm afraid that is not possible." He replied. "Much has changed in Cahmais upon the death of King Asgurd."

The sound of the wagon grew louder as it came in sight. No one but Fedelm paid attention as the large man driving the cart as the line of blue-clad fighters reluctantly opened a hole for the wagon to pass. She recognized the bearded man, growing concerned that he could end up in the middle of a fight.

Deijumb suddenly spoke up forcefully, "The one who brings death and slavery to my people is not going to become the king of your land."

Flacanus turned his attention to the one-eyed man. "You must be the one they call Deijumb." He said. "It was your people who informed us about the return of Lyncus. Therefore, the Ynyover know why he is needed."

140

Now Urith turned in his saddle to Deijumb. "What haven't you told us," he growled at the man.

The old man kept his good eye on the enemy in front of him. "Urith, I did not lie to you. I said you would be surprised by who would be cutting off the exit of Lyncus. Since I was unsure of your intentions, I kept the reasons to myself."

"Now would be a good time to let us know." Mivraa spat out the words at Deijumb before Urith could reply.

"I'll tell you," Flacanus told them. "There's a civil war about to break out Cahmais. The Aberffraw have run the lands into the ground. Now, the Gallaeci have taken over many villages since Asgurd has died. We need Lyncus as a hostage to ensure the Aberffraw who control the city of Uugara will listen to our demands."

"Now I'm confused," Urith told him. "I thought you are Aberffraw from your accent." The Esterblud saw the large man in the cart wearing a plain yellow shirt. Immediately the man questioned if his eyes were playing tricks on him.

Flacanus gave a brief smile. "I am. But I married into the Gallaeci. I want peace, not domination over the clan."

The cart came to a stop behind the line of Cahmais warriors.

Wearing a blue heavy wool trader's cape, Atheern waved at the group across from him. "Fedelm, my sweet lady, you remember me, don't you?"

"But of course, Atheern. However, I think you might want to continue on," she warned him.

"Nonsense now is a superb time to arrive. Come over and help me with something." The large man got down from his wagon, stretching as the fighters watched in surprised fascination at the brave Gallaeci merchant.

Fedelm glanced at Mivraa, then Urith. Both just shrugged their shoulders, unsure of what to do. The fair-haired woman spurred her ossane forward, and the Gallaeci fighters moved for her to pass. When she reached the back of the wagon, they saw her lean over as Atheern spoke with her briefly. The man struggled with a box in the back, then climbed inside. Soon, he handed her several clay mugs to the woman whose face lit up. After getting a few more of the cups, and with both hands full, Fedelm carefully guided her mount back to her group. While she gave the mugs to her comrades, the big man waved over the Gallaeci and did the same. When he finished, Atheern jumped down from his car with a large cup in hand. He came over next to Flacanus who stared at the mug he was given suspiciously.

"I find a good drink makes for better company," the merchant bellowed to the circle around him "I'm too fat to wander around." He waved at Urith and those near him, "Come in closer so we can talk."

With his mug in hand, the Esterblud cautiously directed his mount toward the cart. While he and the others came closer, the fighters in the blue tunics slowly converged around the wagon. Atheern climbed to his seat.

Still separated by a few paces, the two groups waited as the large man pulled out a cigar of *ulcath*, lighting it from the embers of wick that hung from a wire by his seat.

"Now, let us toast our fallen brothers with my best heathmead," the man leaned back in his seat. Dutifully, the men raised their mugs while suspicious of what they witnessed. Most of the men only took a swig of the drink.

Atheern looked at Flacanus. "You know I only get the best, drink up. Now, I overheard your dilemma. I would think it is smarter to talk this out since I see bodies already on this field. Don't you agree?"

The leader of the blue-clad men nodded. "Yes, we have a quandary. However, I don't think your drinks will solve the problem."

The Gallaeci trader laughed loudly. He turned to Urith. "Tell me, Urith. What are your plans for Lyncus? Is he to be put to death by you Esterbluds?"

Urith took another swig of his favorite drink. "No, those in our group have agreed to send Lyncus back to the Citadel. Is this not correct, Deijumb?"

The one-eyed man glance at the Esterblud then nodded. "Yes, it's agreed. As much as we would like his head on a pike, the new ruler of Ynyover should decide this. That is for those who gather in the Citadel."

"My brother Pehnuwick will have all of the satgerts convene to decide on his fate," Urith continued. "He is a fair man who will ensure all clans and tribes will be invited to join."

"Then, my people will say this is using the cover of the new Sacred Overlord to carry out the wishes of the Esterblud." Flacanus countered. "Such words will not help my cause."

Urith turned to him. "At Du-Rinell, you and I spoke as honorable fighters. Do you think I no longer follow that same path?"

The man looked back at his mug. "No offense meant. But chaos and bitterness change people's hearts. We cannot go to Uugara without Lyncus."

"Then, why not bring the Aberffraw to your table?" Mivraa suddenly asked. The men looked at her. She sighed. "It seems simple to me. Have Flacanus and some of his men go with you to the Citadel, they can make sure Lyncus remains under their control. There are more than enough Ynyover and Esterblud fighters to ensure this happens. Flacanus can send the word to the Aberffraw leaders who reside in Uugara, informing them they must send people to the Citadel as part of the agreement. In the meantime, the Gallaeci and the Aberffraw will need to determine how Cahmais will be ruled. That way, everyone will be forced to cooperate on the man's fate."

"Make sense to me," Fedelm interjected, hoping the bloodshed would stop. Narslac quickly agreed as well.

Flacanus looked to his comrades. Suspicion remained in their faces, and some of them shook their heads. It was clear; they would not make such a decision quickly. Atheern blew smoke from his smelly cigar. "Why don't you bring your Gallaeci warriors over to discuss as a group?" The trader offered. "Urith and his team can make sure those fealharan I see next to the Aberffraw don't accidently remove the head of Lyncus for their koinons. I hear the Malhair guild has more a large bounty on the man."

After additional discussions, the two sides agreed to the offer from the Gallaeci merchant. Urith and his friends returned to share the news with Brihar and Skart. Neither man appeared happy at the prospect of Cahmais fighters joining them. However, Deijumb pointed out the Gallaeci had no love for Lyncus.

As the two sides talked among themselves during the truce, Atheern drove his cart to the line of Ynyover and Esterblud fighters. He made the same offer of heathmead which the fighters happily took. Not long after that, Flacanus and a few of his men galloped to the warriors holding Lyncus.

"We have made a decision. We'll join with you on your trip to the Citadel. I'll send my men back with Cahmais with instructions one what to tell the Aberffraw."

There was a mixture of relief and trepidation at the news, but all agreed it beat the alternative.

Urith extended his arm to the Aberffraw after the man slid down from his mount. "Thank you for taking this risk. It is not easy for you."

"War makes for angry people." The old fighter told him. "However, I convinced my warriors that we will stand in a position of strength across the table as the ones who control Lyncus."

"Well, then you better explain to him since he appears to be in the dark," Brihar came up to Flacanus, nodding to the thin man intently watching them behind a line of Ynyover and fealharan.

The old fighter gave a slight laugh. "Yes, I just hope the Aberffraw believe he's still worth something once he is imprisoned at Br-Ynys." He walked over to give the news to Lyncus and his followers.

"You think you can handle those fealharan," Urith spoke under his breath to Brihar. The Gramcle leader considered the question for a moment.

"I think so. Just in case, I'll make sure that the Gallaeci realize it's up to the Cahmais fighters to keep Lyncus safe since many want him for their own reasons. That should be incentive to keep the guards watching the guards."

"You're a smart man," Urith said to him. "I thank you for your help. While I was upset you left Wilgam and Oslaf at first, you have shown me there are other options at times. I'm leaving you to finish the trip since I have duties elsewhere."

"I wish I could join you. I have a couple of things that the gods wouldn't want to hear from me." Brihar extended his arm and Urith grasped him by the forearm.

"I'll make sure they hear that," Urith said, giving Brihar a grin.

~~~

Next to the Exyts stream, the clay figures of an inanimate army stood. The spirits of Haligulf followed the stream which fed the Sky Realm springs and fountains throughout the temples. As they got closer, they were impressed by the work of Ecarca. Stepping next the clay statues, the warriors could feel a power in the clay binding the figures. Dughorm came front of the line, ironically noting the clay figures were modeled after the arrogant god who built them. He defiantly pushed the statue over. It fell headfirst into the water.

144

"Just remember the verse that Caestia told you. Once you walk into the stream, you will live again," Dughorm said to the spirits grouped around him. He entered the water and chanted the words over and over again. A glow enveloped him and his ghostly form twisted and turned, becoming a blue ball that hovered over the statue. Slowly the ball descended into the lifeless clay. After a long pause, the figure began to shiver, then jerked and shuddered. Suddenly, the powerful arms of the statue pushed the upper body out of the water, gasping for air.

Dughorm was alive in a new body.

Coughing and sputtering from the water he breathed in, the clay man lifted himself to his knees as the spirits closed around him, amazed at what they witnessed. He stood, forced to relearn how to use a physical body. Dughorm flexed his arms, enjoying the sensations of the sun warming his stone body.

"I wouldn't try swimming with this type of body," he joked grimly.

"How long will it last?" The spirit of Guthlaf asked. "I have much that I owe Urith and Mivraa."

Dughorm shrugged his shoulders as he moved his naked form from the water. "Given the coming onslaught I expect from Kriell; I don't think we can expect to survive, even in these strong shells."

He looked at Guthlaf. "Don't worry, Urith will find a way to set things right."

"By the gods, don't thrust all the weight upon my son." Uolven grew angry. "It's upon us as well. For too long, we've been the fools for following gods that aren't fit to be *dockes* and *calwards*. It's time to take Duwdamon down a peg or two."

Dughorm smiled. "My friend, I meant nothing of the sort." He told him. "Your son and his friends have done more than I believed possible. You know as well as I do, he has the Fates with him. I want to keep it that way."

"Aye, he's right about the Fates following the boy," Kirowan agreed as he remembered his first encounter with the young warrior so many seasons before. "Come on Uolven, let's give our young ones a chance to fix what we couldn't." Uolven nodded as he went to the next statue, pushing the spirit of Caestia aside.

Dughorm grinned when he saw what happened. He turned to the souls still floating around him. "Hurry, you need to get into your new bodies. Then, we go to the temples to arm ourselves."

Soon, the spirits of the greatest warriors of Kamin spread across the shoreline, each finding a statue for their new home. A line of quiet sculptures became a crowd of moving and talking figures. From a distance, the clay copies of the vain god who created the statues appeared identical. However, when the spirits looked at each other, they could recognize each individual brother in arms. Heptarc's scarred face, Kirowan's large ears, even Uolven's disfigured nose showed through the mold their spirits were encased in. As each clay man relearned how to use their new bodies, they marched along to the Sky Realm temples. The line moved in singles and pairs, each spirit now energized from the Exyts Spring water along with a sense of urgency. While they traveled, old comrades calmly talked about stories they recalled from the Skalds. Tales passed down over the ages concerning the end of the Guardians from the Skool came to life. When the fighters passed over the stone bridge into the main temple complex, the reeds which lined the water suddenly came alive with excited voices. The sprites came out of hiding, whispering among themselves at the unique sight which passed them. These spirits of the forgotten ordinary mortals who once inhabited Kamin recognized the clay men, giving cheer to the Haligulf warriors. Seeing a chance for deliverance from the chaos and betrayal of Sky Gods, the sprites rose up with prayers. Soon, the elemental spirits would leave the realm to spread the message to the human realm.

When the line of ancient fighters reached the inside of the Temple of Aedes, where a giant statue of the Sky God stood, Dughorm was already pushing back the massive doors to the long unused weapons vault. Even he was surprised by the strength his new form possessed since no mortal alone could have opened the vault. Inside, the warriors found dusty armor, spears and shields stacked high. Long before the Sky Realm gods, the Guardians created these instruments of war for their demigods. The tools of battle and slaughter against the mortals on Kamin would now be used to stop the Guardians.

Heptarc took a heavy shield and long sword from Dughorm and smiled. "Now, these weapons will be used for justice against the gods."

Caestia, now a clay man as well, stepped next to the great warrior, taking a short sword and breastplate which were covered in a silver sheen. "Just don't forget we will be outnumbered by hordes coming from the underworld. The Vanth has been busy for a while."

Nearby, bitter laughter broke out from Uolven. "Now is the time to set things right with Caruun and Alrpan after seasons of torment. Actita's head will be mounted on the wall of this temple if I have my way."

While the fighters pulled on their armor, some of them went into the temple and pulled down the curtains. They quickly fashioned robes using their daggers, the blue cloth reminding them of the finest wools tunics they wore in life. They took the clothes to the armory where they distributed to the other clay men. After making crude belts on which to hang the swords and dagger sheaths, the warriors pulled on the golden breastplates. Silver helmets showing the plumage of red feathers along the crest were passed around. However, the spirit men quickly cut off the adornments, loathing the idea of following the Guardians symbol. The men of clay spilled into the main temple, adjusting their garments and armor. Heptarc and Dughorm moved from under the massive statue of Duwdamon, walking among the warriors. Now they would wait for the next morning.

~~~

The small group of riders reached the fork to Yns Cearcal as the sun sank in the eastern sky. No one argued with Narslac who suggested they make camp before going to the Great Circle. The silence from the rest of the men and women was silent agreement at his idea. Bruised and battered from the fighting, they still carried the dry blood of enemies as well as their own. When they pulled off the main road, Urith noticed a campfire in the distance.

"Go ahead and make camp. I'm going to see what travelers we have nearby," he told the group, spurring his ossane forward. The warrior noticed that Fedelm remained with him as he rode further down the path. As they got close, they could see a small cart and two people by the roaring fire.

"Hello in the camp!" The warrior yelled out in Gallaeci, the language used in the area. He assumed the people were traders.

"Hello, Urith, son of Uolven. Come and join us," a voice replied in Esterblud. Urith gave Fedelm a confused glance.

"I think I know that voice," he whispered.

As they moved into the light, Urith recognized the portly little man wearing a red hooded cape.

"By the gods, Joclac! Is that really you? What are you doing here?"

The man stood as the two riders slid off their mounts. A blond woman rose with Joclac.

"Soma, you're here as well? Where is the child? Guthlaf should be a warrior by now." Urith smiled at his old friends as he stepped toward them. He grasped Joclac by the forearm. Then, Soma hugged Urith which caught Fedelm by surprise.

"It's good to see you as well, my friend. Come and sit with us for a moment. Then, we can call over your comrades." The round man told them.

The Esterblud shook his head. Like normal, he thought. The seer probably knew more about Urith's journey than he did. Urith introduced Fedelm.

"Fedelm, this is Joclac and his wife, Soma. You have to watch out for him, he's one of the greatest seers you've never heard of. I know I never spoke about these two, but he prefers it that way."

As the woman looked at the unassuming man with his broad nose and chin beard, she recognized the intensity coming from the man's bright eyes.

The man's wife reminded her of Henther, with her green, *bater*-like eyes. She was quite lovely, about the same height as Fedelm with auburn hair almost copper colored. Regal and thin, Soma carried herself with quiet confidence. Yet, something in the woman's manner hinted at a raw toughness inside.

"Again, you have overstated my abilities." The portly man sat on a log with his wife joining him. "You've been traveling with a seer like Fedelm for this long; you would think something would get through that thick skull. She's told you this many times. The visions of a hakra must be interpreted." The man smiled at her while she sat across from the couple. Urith struggled to sit next to her, his leg still bothering him.

"What a minute, how would?" Fedelm stopped herself in mid-sentence. She never heard of anyone able to retell conversations between people. Obviously, Joclac was a strong hakra with his insight and abilities.

"Don't mind him," Soma told Fedelm before she turned to Urith. "To answer your question, Unvel, stays with Joclac's brother and he is doing well. The boy is nearly as large as you now and he's ready to be a warrior." She paused, then looked at Fedelm again. "My husband is just showing off. Joclac likes to impress cute girls."

"Only you, my darling." The man's eyes brightened as he reached over to tickle his wife and she laughed lightly. He noticed the look Urith gave him and stopped. "Yes, I see the time is not right for such trivialities."

Pulling an erba skin bag filled with heathmead from behind him, then He took a large drink before he passed it to Urith.

"You are rightly surprised that I'm here. In fact, I had no plans on coming this way, but the separate paths we follow have suddenly aligned."

"How so?" The warrior had asked before he drank, handing the bag to Fedelm. She took a drink, trying to keep from shivering at the taste, catching a glance at Soma who smiled knowingly. Something in the way, Joclac's wife, looked at her and Urith bothered her.

"Spanca stopped by today. She told me that she waits at Yns Cearcal." Joclac continued. "However, that is only one door of two you must close. I assume you must know that by now?" He paused and saw the confusion in Urith's face as his answer.

"I see not. Well, let's get to the basics. The Skalds haven't sung of such things for many ages, so I'm assuming you don't know the origin of the Great Circle. There were three gateways between the three realms. They are the only places where the gods, demigods, and humans may enter and leave directly to any of the realms. These places are the only gateways with a direct path to the temples of the sky and underworld." He stopped to gather his thoughts.

"I've heard of such things during my training in the Citadel, but we were told they are just myths," Fedelm spoke up.

The short man smiled briefly. "It's not something the satgerts are eager to explain. Why go to a priest when you can go directly to the gods? That's not to say it's an easy or risk-free journey, even before the chaos now."

"It's always in threes," Urith noted under his breath.

"You noticed. This is important. Three is the Triad which makes things stable in Kamin. Well, it would have been once the Guardians were removed. However, Heptarc made a mistake. The fool didn't fix things at the time, and we're still paying for it." The man took another drink, nonplussed by the shocked look coming from the two sitting across the fire from him.

"Dear, you always do that. Tell them about the tree circles," Soma reminded her husband.

"Right! Well, you have Yns Cearcal, Yns Garraid, and Yns Rinell which made up the only places on Kamin where the Underworld and the Sky Realm meet with our world."

"Wait a minute; I've seen gods coming from behind twisted *lellowtere* trees?" Urith stopped him.

Joclac nodded. "Yes, the gods created a quick way to come to the human realm. Did you ever notice how the roots of the trees look like exact copies of the branches? The gods may come and go from such gateways but only from the realm where they call home. It's like the *sidhera*, which you know about. The gods and their children can come and go from those portals, but humans can only enter with help. Once inside, humans must be escorted out, or they will remain trapped forever."

"What about the circles?" Fedelm tried to get them back to the point.

"Yes, that's right," Joclac removed his pipe from his tunic. "You traveled to Du-Rinell, and you saw what was left. Where you found the first bit of the Skool was at Yns Rinell. Heptarc accidently split apart the weapon during the battle with the Guardians. He was on the right path, but he didn't see it. When they realized Heptarc would stop the Guardians, other entities from the void appeared. While the entities had less power than the Guardians, their lies convinced him to take on the Guardians at Du-Rinell. Duwdamon understood it would leave two places open for them to split the realms to be used as they pleased. Once they betrayed Heptarc, the Skool broke apart in the battle, and they made the world which was somewhat better. Since they have power over the elements of Kamin, it was not hard to have humans begin to believe the creatures were gods."

Urith shook his head. "So, lies and betrayals led us to this. Seems like those gods forgot about the first ones, the Guardians?"

Joclac put the empty pipe in his mouth, nodding.

"This means what to me?"

"That means you must close the last two gateways. Only then can the chaos stop." The seer told him.

"Why didn't Dughorm say this?" The warrior tried not to sound too skeptical.

"You don't understand, but the visions I receive have been extraordinarily vivid. This is unusual which gives me pause on how much I can reveal. Dughorm may know more or less, I'm not sure. But he must know you will be fighting those gods not yet consumed by Kriell as well as the old Guardian himself. Such a fight may call for supreme sacrifices. Those you care deeply about could stand in your way." Joclac leaned closer to his friend.

"When you left Dughorm's home village of Ynysbeag, he already knew it would die at the hands of Satres. Now, ask yourself this question. Why didn't he tell you? Because he is your friend and would gladly sacrifice yourself to help your friends. As difficult as this may sounds, sometimes being the champion is doing what's right for more than your family or your best friend. That may mean sacrificing others."

Joclac went quiet, knowing Urith faced problematic views at what he was told. Urith came from an upbringing where honor and sacrifice often meant dying to achieve immortality. It wasn't second nature for the man to just let others die when they could possibly be saved. He glanced over to Fedelm and saw how she watched the scarred man. It told him his visions about her were accurate as well.

"You're telling me that my burden will become heavier. It's one thing to kill a creature whose soul was mangled by the gods. It's another to say to me that people might suffer or worse for me to survive. Already, Fedelm and Mivraa have suffered terribly for this cursed Skool." The warrior shook his head. The conversation reminded him too much of the night that Dughorm told him about King Penhda's betrayal of Urith and his crew sailing to Ynyover.

"You have been hurt as well, my friend." Joclac reminded him.

"That doesn't matter." Urith sighed, standing up to allow himself to pace while he thought about his options. "Not only must I try to destroy gods; I must extinguish the gateways to these realms."

"What becomes of the realms when this happens?" Soma asked. Joclac looked at his wife and just shook his head.

The giant warrior paused from his pacing. "They will no longer exist. I know this, not from visions but I know it nevertheless. Tell me where this other place is at."

"Yns Garraid is an isolated place in the Mythroloy Mountains, far past the place where Mivraa was taken. It is near the lands of the unknown and a place where Ruggla resides. He is not a friend of the Sky

Realm or the underworld as I understand it." Joclac seemed troubled by his statement, but Urith let it go.

"I guess it's the Great Circle first. If I survive that, I can worry about this other place later." The warrior told Joclac who nodded.

The prophet sighed as he handed Urith the bag of heathmead again, "Exactly the correct strategy. Now, that is enough for you to think about. Go to your friends. You're welcome to bring them back and make camp here if you like. In the morning, we will join you as you go to Yns Cearcal. I've always wanted to see it."

The next morning, the entire group followed Urith as he led them to the gateway. Urith rode next to Joclac, who borrowed Fedelm's ossane. Mivraa and Narslac were close behind, trying to keep up with the seer's conversation. The demigoddess was upset with Urith for not explaining what Joclac revealed during the conversation the night before. Narslac agreed, but he was more interested in learning about the reclusive seer whose reputation was known by many in Esterblud. Soma and Fedelm were inside the erba driven cart.

At first, Fedelm was upset for being asked to give up her mount, thinking it was an intentional slight. After a while, she realized Urith was only trying to catch up with his friend as they rode together. During her conversation with Soma, she discovered how much the handsome woman knew about Urith. Fedelm was sure there was something between them in the past. Her interest peaked as the two women talked. Fedelm asked about Urith's past, and Soma opened up with unexpected candor. The devoted wife of Joclac was once a slave to the notorious Regiussan warlord known as Reppir. Soma went on to tell her about Urith's help getting her away from Reppir, explaining he took her with him to Esterblud where she met her husband.

"It sounds like Urith," Fedelm replied. "He's got a knack for getting into trouble."

Soma smiled, remembering her first ship crossing with him. "Yes, he does have that way. Of course, you know his first wife died at the hands of the gods. I think that was why he's never decided to try marriage again. When I knew him, I quickly realized he could not break himself of his anger and an almost desperate need for vengeance and violence. It was a death wish in a way."

152

Soma lowered her voice. "I've been watching you. While he has his temper, he's grown into a better man now. You could do far worse with more handsome men."

Fedelm turned red.

"I don't know what you are talking about. I'm here to get Urith through this. Besides, he still thinks of Mivraa."

Soma shook her head. "I know him far better than you can imagine. Joclac told me about the vision on the mountain when you held Mivraa. He also saw what she has done to herself in need for vengeance. Don't be a fool. I saw the way that man looks at you. It was the same look he once carried for me. Urith is protective of you, not the demigoddess. That should tell you all you need."

Fedelm couldn't argue the idea, but something else bothered her. "Why are you telling me this?"

Joclac's wife sighed as she watched erbas steadily slogging along the dusty trail. She looked to ensure nobody was listening to the women in the cart. "Urith was good to me and I believed in him like you do. However, he will not come out of the hard exterior he carries. Trust me when I say this, you will need to push inside, don't wait for him. That is the one piece of advice I can give you. I know this from experience. For all of his grunts, when he makes a choice, he cares deeply. However, he'll seldom show it. The ways of men are difficult to understand."

The blond hakra wanted to ask more, but she recognized the scenery. They were at Yns Cearcal.

"I'll take your advice, providing you will let me ask more in the future. Is it a deal?"

Soma, lost in the past, absently nodded. The riders in front of them suddenly pointed to the entrance to the Great Circle. The caravan of riders turned single file through the narrow opening between the impenetrable brush. Just inside, Spanca was waiting and smiled when Urith came in sight.

"The scarred man is ready?"

Urith nodded to her.

Mivraa pulled next to the other demigoddess who pointed to the manicured brush.

"Leave the ossanes here. The altar will scare them. I have already heard an alarm from the sprites who are warning of something wrong in the Sky Realm."

153

The wagon was too large to fit through, leaving Fedelm and Soma to walk inside. When they passed through the opening, both noticed the naked green woman next to Urith as the man dismounted from his ossane.

"Urith continues to find interesting people," Soma joked as they came closer to the group of riders.

The hakra next to her smiled thinly, "yeah, one demigoddess after another."

~~~

Dughorm stood before the oversized statue of Duwdamon inside the Temple. Filling more and more at home inside his clay figure, he looked over the tribute to a vainglorious entity with a frown. The sun was at its zenith, and the rest of the clay warriors were below in the vaults; waiting for the action they felt would be coming. As the Sybil thought about the last night's visions, he knew Urith and his friends were close. He also knew the enemies were just as close.

"What are you supposed to be?" The cold voice of Duwdamon came from behind Dughorm. He twirled the thin yellow mustache that hung down both sides of his mouth past his chin.

The old warrior turned to see the Sky God and his son standing beside one of the massive columns. "I'm the same person, just in a new shell. You see, I've grown tired of this realm and your foolishness. Kriell is coming so someone has to stop it."

"Father, I told you he was up to something," the god of the soil whined.

Duwdamon nodded as he floated closer to the Sybil. "I don't know what a human spirit might think, but one clay figure with a few measly weapons is hardly a threat to a god, let alone one of the Guardians. Besides, I can handle Kriell now."

"Oh, so now you believe me. I should be pleased that the great Duwdamon finally agrees with me." The sarcasm dripped with his words.

"You must think yourself quite intelligent. But soon you will know my wrath." Suddenly the sky grew dark and ominous.

"That would not be wise," Heptarc stepped next to the two gods. His long halberd pointed at them. Other clay warriors appeared from the vault, the noise of their armor echoing inside the temple.

"I could destroy you with a bolt of lightning," the Sky God's eye's narrowed.

"That might be true, but only if you bring this place down upon you as well. Besides, who will fight off the underworld? You and your dimwit son?" Uolven, his weapon at the ready, stood next to Dughorm.

The deity pulled out his godfire whip. "Kriell has no need to come to the Sky Realm. You fools cannot see that I've already made my agreement with him. He can do as he pleases with the human realm. The Guardian has no ambition for this realm."

"Then, you're a delusional fool," Dughorm gave a bitter laugh. "Did Kriell mention he gave your wife to the last Vanth for breeding? And what happens to the Sky Realm without the tributes from the human realm? Vengeance is all the Guardians ever knew. I find it amusing that you would believe them now." The warrior saw by the expression on Duwdamon's face that he wasn't surprised at the news. Clearly, the god was more concerned about the human usurpers inside his realm.

Suddenly, the sound of a thousand spirits screeching alarm came into the temple. Magnified by the acoustics, the noise caused the clay men to hold their hands over their ears. Almost immediately after, a roaring blast came to them as the gods and spirits looked out from the temple. Across the plaza, they watch as a white structure dedicated to the Sky Goddess no longer stood. Collapsed roof of stone sent up circles of gray and white dust. Coming out of the dust, hordes of underworld monsters scrambled across the stone plaza. The creatures were coming toward the Temple where Duwdamon stood.

"I believe you said Kriell had no ambition on this realm," Dughorm told the Sky God smugly. Duwdamon didn't respond as he watched his world falling apart. The look of disbelief on his face caused the old Sybil to shake his head. He wondered how they could have ever believed such creatures would protect them.

"We have our war. Now I say this is the perfect terrain for us," Uolven roared. Heptarc agreed, immediately ordering the clay fighters into a defensive formation. The heroes of Haligulf instinctively fanned out into lines using the top rows of stairs to the temple. Experience told them it was far better to play defense from a higher position. They waited as waves of creatures pressed forward, trying to climb the steep stairs which led up to the shrine from three sides. In the mass of underworld monsters, the warriors saw crubas, beorhs, and even the dreaded Clovels. Uolven, Dughorm, and Heptarc each took a side to lead the defenses. They walked along the lines, reminding the clay men of the weaknesses of these creatures. The finest fighters in Kamin history took no offense at the reminders coming from their comrades. Instead, the spirits of clay joked among themselves, or natural rivals placed wagers on who might be the first to perish. No one knew if their souls might continue or not.

The first wave of beorhs reached the lower steps, quickly scrambling up the stone steps. With a combined roar, the clay warriors fell into the attackers. The men of mud struck hard at the first wave of creatures, decimating them with practiced ease. Black blood of the monsters quickly covered the steps with the skeletal bodies. For their part, the fighter's blood spilled as well, gray and slick. The pain was felt by all sides in the bitter battle. As spears, swords, and axes did massive damage on the monsters, the claws, teeth, and beaks cut chunks out of the clay men. Uolven swung his long sword through one of the beorhs, and the body fall apart. However, a brief burst of blue light remained momentarily before quickly ascending into the ether above. The others in battle soon saw the same thing as creatures were slaughtered during the fighting. One of the clay warriors, overwhelmed by the crubas who eviscerated him, screamed a final oath and Dughorm caught a glimpse of the man's blue ball of spirit suddenly disappear into the heavens.

As the savage fighting between the righteous and the profane occurred, screams and chatter of inhuman creatures mixed with the primal cries of warriors creating a deafening roar across the temple complex. Suddenly, the sky went black, and light bolts spit out of the clouds. The flashes of electricity struck down groups of the creatures as the waves came across the plaza. When the bolts missed, the blast of energy still hit the ground, sending chunks of rock across the area which maimed anything nearby. Dughorm glanced back to see the Sky God gesturing with his hands and arms, trying to strike down the beasts with his weakened powers. The deity's thin face was lit up at the destruction he was causing. Next to him, Ecarca tried to replicate his father's success by opening a huge crack in the ground just in front of the second wave of attackers. Many creatures fell into the void. With a clap of Ecara's hands, the opening suddenly shut, crushing the unfortunates inside and a line of little blue balls of energy drifted away.

Coming out of the ruins where the temple to Unis once stood, Kriell watched over the battle. Transformed into the image of Caruun, the underworld deity was pleased with what he saw. The last two gods left for him to devour were surrounded just outside the temple of Duwdamon. It would be delicious irony for him to satisfy his vengeance upon the spot where the Sky God worshiped himself. The Guardian ordered the leader of the beorhs to send in more of the hordes coming from the fields. He would overwhelm the defenders with his masses of creatures.

"Make sure your monsters don't harm the two gods. They are mine," he told the leader of his hordes.

Immediately the beorh leader jumped down from his perch next to his master. Reppir formed his monsters into crude lines. The hideous spirit chattered out the orders, occasionally striking those of his army who failed to move quickly enough. More of the beasts came from the fields where they already committed cruelties upon the few remaining sprites who signaled their warnings. As servants of Haligulf and the rest of the Sky Realm, the elemental sprite's bodies had form and substance which the hordes of beorhs raped and ripped apart. Like the young and old innocents caught up in human wars, the servants to the gods could not stop their slaughter and their remains were scattered among the rocks and grass.

Reppir moved forward with his legion of skeletal creatures, sending the Clovel monsters scrambling forward to disrupt the first lines of the clay warriors. The white, hairy beasts with sharp horns ambled along swiftly. With long, saber-like front canines and jagged teeth, the monster was a walking nightmare, nearly impervious almost any weapon. The third wave fell into the mass of Haligulf warriors with a ferocity that pushed through the first lines of defenders. A fighter named Tarqirl fell under a Clovel who ripped off the shrieking man's arms in an instant. As the warrior's soul ascended, the old fighter Kirowan embedded his sword into the creature's eye socket while Dughorm swiftly removed the monster's head. A cruba struck at the leg armor of the Sybil causing him to back up the steps, hitting it with blows from his shield. Beorhs rushed at Uolven who embedded a spear into one after pulling it from a dead body of another lying at his feet. Another creature tore at the man's face, getting close enough for the old Esterblud to smell the rot. The clay man thrust his dagger up through the creature's chest, lifting the beast from the stone step. Uolven sent the dying body into other monsters rushing up.

About to enter the fray again, Dughorm suddenly realized the lightning bolts had ceased. Quickly looking back, he saw Duwdamon staring into the distance at the bridge which crossed the Exyts stream.

The god's face was filled with fury. Turning, the old hakra saw a small group running toward the fighting, and he smiled.

"Urith and the Skool are coming," Dughorm yelled out to those around him as he rushed up near the standing gods.

"Focus on the underworld." The clay man shouted at the god, pointing to the monsters that were nearly breaching several lines of defenders. Duwdamon gave him a glare, but almost immediately a shattering blast came from the sky. String near the temple, the lightning sent bodies of creatures flying into the air.

Not far from the explosion occurred; the small group of heavily armed human fighters came into sight. Urith and Mivraa crossed the bridge first with Narslac following close behind. Spread across the plaza before the two fighters was a sea of underworld monsters. At the top of a temple, they saw the warrior copies fighting the losing battle. The underworld creatures continued their push, crawling across their destroyed comrades. In places, they were nearly through the final lines of the defenders. Steps of stone closest to the group were damaged from the latest lightning strike. As the humans tried to grasp what they witnessed, their presence was immediately noticed by a small group of crubas who started croaking out warnings as they attacked. While the monsters were quickly cut down by the three experienced fighters, any surprise was lost.

Reppir, now in the middle of the plaza, instantly diverted some of his remaining horde toward the small group. The beorhs joined with their brother monsters and swiftly raced toward the humans. Urith recognized the danger immediately. Leading his friends to the temple steps where they could defend themselves, the human invaders ran as fast as they could while trying to avoid the bodies that littered their way. Reaching the steps of the temple, Urith slashed his way through the monsters still alive from the lightning blast. When Urith struck one of the monsters with his shield, the expected shock did not happen. Suddenly, the man grew worried as he hit the creature with his sword. Fortunately, the dazed creatures scarcely put up a defense as Urith and his group to cut them down. While he fought, the man noticed the blue balls of light which suddenly ascended into the sky with each dropping creature.

Mivraa waded into the creatures with relish, skillfully embedding her crystal spear into their backs as she climbed the stairs. Those who turned to her were impaled and thrown over her shoulder like toys as the demigoddess fought with a fanatical strength. The woman recognized the two Sky Gods at the top of the temple and pushed hard to reach them.

For his part, Narslac was not far behind, hacking down monsters who tried run up behind them. His battle ax was dripping with the black blood of the creatures. The man's face showed his excitement at the fight.

When Urith finally reached the first line of clay warriors, realized all of the fighter's faces were copies of Ecarca which confused him at first. Then, he heard the voice of his father.

"It's good to see you, Urith." A fighter stepped forward. His arm was gone. The rest of Uolven's body and armor were covered in black gore.

Urith instantly recognized the shadow of his dead father's face in the statue, and he was about to say something.

"Look out! They're nearly on you," Dughorm yelled out. At approximately the same time, Mivraa yelled out a war cry followed by Narslac who joined her.

The Esterblud turned to see the demigoddess stab her spear into a beast, only to slip on the steps, taking a hard fall. Behind her, a wave of beorhs and crubas came up the steps at them, their chattering noise deafening.

Urith held the Shield of Skool toward the oncoming monsters, bracing himself for the coming explosion. Deep inside, he was worried if the shield might fail in the realm now.

"Da Umca Mivwar," he said, waiting for pain that would come to his injured arm. Then, he felt the heat of the amulet on his chest inside the chain mail, and the blast of blinding light shot out from the Skool. The white flash instantly evaporated anything in its path, shooting far through the horde and into the plaza in a straight line. Urith yelled from the intense agony. Despite bracing himself on steps, the power of the light pushed him back, and his boots began slipping on the gore. Instinctively, Mivraa ran beside him and stood behind the man. In shock at what he saw, Uolven joined the demigoddess, helping to keep the Skool steady.

The deadly stream of energy hit untold numbers of creatures as the three people focused the beam down the steps and across the plaza. The ground shook when struck by the ray, sending up huge chunks of stone while the monsters instinctively tried to throw up their arms in defense before they were obliterated. The significant gaps were suddenly opened in the lines of creatures and the sky lit up from the orbs rising above. More of the beast filled in the gaps and those creatures on the other sides of the temples continued pushing forward, starting to overwhelm the defenders. Clay warriors near the Esterblud human while staying behind the Skool's beam. Dughorm ordered the living statues to reform their lines along the side of Urith.

Recognizing what they were doing, Urith forced his weapon's damaging light closer to the nearby fighting, attempting to cut down more of the creatures near the base of the temple. Below him, the man did not see Fedelm and Spanca who were running over the bridge toward him. The green woman wore only a golden breastplate and carried a small shield and sword. Likewise, the blond hakra had her short sword out. However, the sound coming from blast overwhelmed their desperate screams of warning as they suddenly recognized the threat behind the trio. Two gods near the top of the temple.

Duwdamon stealthily descended the steps along with Ecarca. The menacing look of the gods revealed their intent. Ecarca kept telling his father to strike them with lightning. However, the god of the sky shook his head. They would taste his vengeance. Godfire whip in hand, the deity moved in close. An instant later, the trio holding the Skool felt the whip wrap around them. Instantly, jolts of godfire electricity surged through the three people. Mivraa immediately recognized the pain, falling to her knees and sliding away on the steps. Uolven's mineral body instantly dissolved, the power overwhelming the spell which kept his spirit. The soul cried out to his son, but Urith only caught a flash of blue light when he briefly glanced back. The orb ascended skyward, leaving one person wrapped inside the whip.

Focused on holding the Skool's beam of energy, the giant Esterblud can only take the punishment. He felt the whip release only to strike him again. With an evil smile, Duwdamon yanked back hard on the godfire whip, and Urith felt like he would be cut in two. Nearly unable to control the Skool as the deity pulled, the shield's beam moved across a line of clay warriors fighting with monsters, instantly dissolving all in its path. Mivraa tried to attack the Sky God, but Ecarca intervened. Using the last of his depleted power, the ground beneath the demigoddess rumbled, and the steps began to fall away under her. She fell down several steps, landing hard on a pile of stone. Unfortunately for the god, Narslac came at him from the side. While trying to avoid the falling stones steps, the one-armed man flung his battle ax. The weapon struck Ecarca in the leg, sending the deity down upon the rock steps, screaming in agony. Fedelm made it up the stairs to reach Mivraa, reaching down to help the demigoddess to stand.

"Forget me, help Urith get that whip off of him," the goddess of Haligulf yelled, pushing the hakra away. Instead, Mivraa went after her father.

The blond woman instantly ran at the Esterblud who was visibly in agony, barely holding on. As Fedelm ran up the few steps, the woman remembered the amulet Imenal gave her. She put both of her hands on the Helios stone.

"*Teinidh cadhla*," she shouted as she reached Urith. Suddenly, the whip's power was gone, and the beam of destruction from the Skool stopped. The giant human collapsed. Fedelm barely caught him and struggled to them from falling down the steps. Together, they watched Mivraa and Spanca attacking Duwdamon. The remaining clay warriors went after the god of the realm as well.

The Sky God rose from the steps, suddenly sending down a bolt of lightning which struck near the two demigoddesses. Both tumbled away, quickly regaining their feet as they continued the attack. Duwdamon stared down at his offspring with contempt. Dughorm picked up a spear near his foot and flung it at the sky god. Unfortunately, he missed the moving deity.

"You dare challenge me. I will end this once and for all!"

Struggling to his knees, Urith noticed his opportunity. He pointed his shield toward the flying god. Fedelm told him to stop, but the Esterblud repeated the words which unleashed the weapon again. The discharge nearly pushed him down the stone stairs. Fedelm locked her arms around him, trying to use her small body as a counterweight to the force. Both slid across the slippery surface of black and gray.

Duwdamon saw the white beam nearly strike him, and he tried to fly out of the way. However, the energy of the Skool did remove some of the god's power, and the deity fell to the steps below. His human form began to fade. His appearance became the form the creature held inside the Great Void. Duwdamon's face turned skeletal with a large beak and deep sunk red eyes of evil intent. His thin arms and legs were sinewy like a bird, the legs ended with clawed feet.

161

Mivraa, spear held aloft, rushed at her prone father who used his remaining energy in his defense. At the same time, Urith focused the Skool's deadly ray toward the creature called Duwdamon. Suddenly, a lightning bolt shot down. The bolt from the sky intersected with the beam of light nearly on top of the Sky God. The massive burst of energies combined above the steps of the temple and sent out a shockwave of light and power. The Sky realm blast was larger than anything ever witnessed or experienced on Kamin.

Chapter 8: Ynys Garraid

When Urith awoke, he lay at the bottom of the temple steps, some fifty paces away from where he kneeled earlier. Stunned, grasping for answers, the man looked around the area. He saw Fedelm lying across a dead cruba near him. Trying to sit up, the man realized his injured arm was numb. He used his other hand to pull away from the remains of the crude split around the forearm which was in tatters. Next to him was the Shield of Skool, ripped off his arm by the force of the blast. Quickly he retrieved the weapon with his good hand, slinging it on his back after looking around the area. Nothing moved within his sight.

The warrior crawled over to Fedelm, his lame arm dragging on the ground. When he got to the woman, Urith felt his stomach drop as she appeared to be dead. A sense of relief washed over him when he saw her react slightly when he reached out to touch her face. She suddenly sat up, staring at him.

"Are you hurt?" she gasped out before he could ask the same question to her.

He shook his head. "No, everything works reasonably well," he lied. "How about you?"

Her face grimaced when she tried to push herself away from the body of the monster. "My hip hurts. I guess I was lucky." Her eyes widen as she looked across the area.

The dust was clearing around them, and the pair viewed the aftermath of the explosion. As far as the couple looked, the destruction was evident. The few ornamental trees around the area were broken over like the winds of a hurricane swept through. Bodies of monsters, some starting to move, were strewn across the plaza. The clay warriors were solid stone, frozen as they fell. The bodies lay in heaps, their missing limbs and heads providing grotesque monuments to the fighting. The temple itself was demolished, the roof and massive columns were blown over in a heap, their tops pushed away from the source of the explosion.

Urith struggled to his feet, immediately finding the Clovel Sword which lay at the foot of a standing statue. The dead Haligulf warrior was missing his entire upper body. Picking up his weapon, he sheathed it and returned to help Fedelm. The woman had pulled out a small water bag she was carrying under her cloak. She took a drink and poured some of the water on her hip.

"I stopped for some of the Exyts spring water. This should heal us quickly."

Urith reached out with his good hand. "Come on, we can do that as we look for the others. I'm not sure this thing is over. Those monsters could regroup."

She took his hand and rose to her feet, the pain still there from her injury. She realized by the way the Esterblud stood, his injury was far worse. "Nobody is regrouping quickly. Now hold still!" She ordered him impatiently as the woman stopped him. Carefully, she lifted his arm, wincing when his crushed forearm bones sag. She tried not to show her concern for his injury. The hakra poured some of the liquid across the skin, then made him take a drink.

"Now we can find the others."

Together, the pair made their way up the steps, stepping around the large chunks of stone and debris as they searched for survivors. They came upon the body of an unrecognizable creature first. Nothing more than a blackened skeleton of a hybrid like bird and human remained. Then they saw the whip handle still clutched in the clawed hand.

"That's got to be what's left of Duwdamon," Urith stated impassively as he rubbed his injured arm. It was healing but still numb and hung at his side. He quickly went down the stairs to where Mivraa was before the blast. Soon, he discovered the demigoddess.

Mivraa's lower body lay pinned under a massive slab of stone which once made up a step of the temple. Her eyes were closed. Urith knelt down, using his good arm to try to lift the stone. It wouldn't budge.

"Don't bother," he heard the weak voice of his friend and one-time lover. "Even the two of us together couldn't lift this chunk of rock. I always hated this forsaken shrine."

Fedelm came around the other side of the stone, kneeling to give the woman a drink. "This is the Exyts water," she told her. Mivraa immediately spat the water out.

"No, let me be. I felt that blast do something to me inside. My strength is gone. It's like I no longer have the powers of a demigoddess." She smiled at him. "It feels good to have nothing left from my father."

"I'll find Narslac!" Urith told her. "Between all of us, we'll get that step off of you."

Mivraa gave him a brief smile, shaking her head. "That will not work. The Fates have decided I will die here. Now tell me the truth. I must know that Duwdamon and Ecarca are dead."

Urith nodded. "We saw the Sky god's body. He will no longer torment you. I haven't seen his son."

"Then, I'm truly happy," the auburn hair woman told him. "I'm sorry I cannot do more to help you. You need to keep your focus on Kriell." She grimaced, then stared at her lover's face, telling him to remove his black helmet. The man complied, his rugged face showing the dirt covered sweat of battle. The scar he carried reminded her of something he once told her.

"You were right. Vengeance isn't sweet; it can leave a bitter taste in your mouth. I thought I was going crazy and maybe I was."

The Esterblud nodded as he watched the dying woman. "You were justified," he told her, and the demigoddess shook her head. "No, there was no reason to blame others for my torment. I can only hope my spirit remains to help those I wrongly killed in some way. It is the only way for me to atone for my actions," the woman stared at Fedelm. There was no bitterness in the look, and Fedelm reached out, clasping the woman's hand between hers.

"But, you know it doesn't make the pain go away," she paused as another wave of agony came from inside her. When it passed, she looked over to Fedelm. "I need you to leave. I must ask something of Urith in private." Uncertain, the hakra glanced at the Esterblud who nodded, his expression resigned.

"Go find Narslac," Urith told Fedelm as he knelt down. The woman left, and Urith again asked Mivraa to let him find help to remove the stone.

"You and I both know it's too late. That blast from your shield hit me, and I'm now mortal. This cannot be changed." She grabbed him by his tunic, her eyes bore into his. "I've seen many humans die on the battlefield. Somehow I always expected to lose my head, not die pinned under a piece of rock. Don't let me die a screaming death under this stone. Promise me that!"

Urith promised her, and she relaxed for a moment. "You must finish this for Kamin. Many spirits fought for you and died for you. Don't forget that." She reached out to clutch his leg when a wave of pain again racked her. "Now, you wouldn't let your ossane suffer like this, would you?" The woman asked through clutch teeth.

The giant warrior shook his head. His mind raced for a solution that could not be found. He started talking to her, telling her what he hoped the world might become. "There will be a time where you can look down upon those we leave behind and smile," he told her while the man forced himself to pull his long Sgian dagger from his belt. "I'm sorry," Urith told her.

Back to her old self, Mivraa smiled at him, then looked up at the blue sky above her. "Don't be. Now I can be escorted into the void when you shut the gate to this realm. I saw the blue orbs floating away and wondered where they went to. Now I get to find out. It might be better than I can dream."

Many paces away, Fedelm found Narslac alive. He landed far away from the steps, falling into the grass. Spanca was already with him and tending to some of her wounds. The blond woman noticed the green lady's color appeared much less vivid. She gave some of the healing water to both of them.

"How's Urith and Mivraa?" The Skald asked.

Fedelm said nothing for a moment, just shaking her head. Finally, she told him what she saw. "She is dying. Urith is with her."

Narslac got up from the ground. "I'm going to see her," he said and started to leave when he saw the Esterblud coming toward them. The look on the man's face told Narslac there was no reason to continue.

Urith paused, clearing his throat first. "Are you and Spanca well enough to for us to leave?"

Narslac nodded, then asked. "Did anyone see Ecarca?"

Urith looked around, "No, that's someone we shouldn't forget." The Esterblud moved up the steps to the flattened temple.

The god of the land was lying face down, looking a lot like the charred remains of his father. However, the creature still moved, slowly struggling to lift itself with one arm. The beaked face turned to look up at Urith, red eyes smoldering with hate.

The warrior gave the former god his death sneer. "Your power is gone so I won't bother to put you out of your misery. Instead, I'll leave you to your fate with the underworld monsters that will be coming soon. Have fun!

166

Urith stepped away from Ecarca, quickly rejoining the group below. "Grab your weapons and let's go. There is nothing left here. The souls of the Haligulf warriors are gone."

"What about the underworld creatures?" The Skald asked pointing to the movement of the beasts in the distance. While many were destroyed some of the creatures appeared to be gathering again. Then, Narslac caught a glimpse of the two monsters, leaders of the underworld, ahead of them on the trail back to the gateway.

Urith stepped past the Skald, urging him along. "According to Joclac, once the gateway is demolished, those inside the Sky Realm will be destroyed." Urith kept up the pace toward the bridge, his helmeted head lowered. As he hurried them away, the scarred man silently grieved for a good friend who died a bravely as any warrior he knew. His heart grew bitter at the Fates for what they forced him to do.

~~~

The figures of Caruun and Reppir suddenly stepped out of the opening near an altar after they returned to the underworld. They were inside a quiet chamber, near the main tunnel. Kriell was upset, and his silence filled the room. The Guardian still felt the effects of the blast which ripped through the area, diminishing his own powers immediately. While the creature from the Great Void knew nothing of fear, the threat of the Skool made him reassess the human threat. Leaving the remaining monsters in the Sky Realm was more than an inconvenience. It made the underworld master comprehend that it must understand what the person was trying to accomplish. Kriell witnessed the destruction of Duwdamon and Ecarca. That could only mean the carrier of the Shield of Skool would attempt to destroy his underworld realm as well.

Reppir, the beorh leader, remained behind his master, unsure what might happen next. He followed the underworld leader out into one of the main tunnels leading to beehive chamber where the trapped souls of Kamin existed. Despite the limited communication abilities of the beorh, the evil spirit inside knew he would need more souls to replace the losses in the Sky Realm. This would take time.

As if he read Reppir's thoughts, the Guardian laid out his next steps as he continued walking.

"You will have every creature in the underworld unleashed upon the humans at night. I expect anything living on Kamin to be afraid of leaving their homes."

The beorh chattered his approval, asking his leader about more beasts.

"Don't worry about that for now. Actita already is using the goddess to help add to your hordes. We have enough for the next steps. I want you to take a few of your creatures to find out where that human is going next. Have your crubas follow him. Once you know where he is going, you will come to me with that information immediately."

Reppir chattered about killing the human, and the figure of Caruun stopped walking. "Don't be a fool, he must be captured. The Fates have spoken, and I need that human alive. When the time is right, we will use his blood to put an end to this world and create a new one. Now, find him and make sure he doesn't get out of your sight."

~~~

One by one, the bruised and battered group exited from Sky Realm, coming out of a blue light next to the black stone altar in the middle of Ynys Cearcal. Joclac and his wife were sitting on a blanket, just finishing their meal when they saw Urith suddenly appear. Immediately, the couple realized something was wrong when the Esterblud continued walking passed them for several paces before he knelt on the ground. He was holding his injured arm, deep in thought. The rest of the group gathered around the couple.

"Mivraa didn't make it," Narslac told Joclac who nodded slowly as he continued to puff on his pipe. The Skald sat across from the seer.

Fedelm slowly sat down, gingerly finding a spot in the grass. Her hip still hurt, and she was thinking about Mivraa.

"I will be tough without her." The woman was overwhelmed with emotion which left her drained. It seemed like she and Mivraa traveled across Kamin over the last two seasons. They might not have been friends, but they were attached to the same goal. Silence filled the air. Like her, the rest of the group thought about the demigoddess and what lay in front of them.

Urith finally pulled himself to his feet, walking back to the quiet group. "Well, time to finish this," he told them as he awkwardly pulled the Shield onto his uninjured arm. While he said nothing, he was surprised his injury was not fully recovered. Instead, the bones were slowly hardening in an odd angle, and the numbness remained. The giant fighter went closer to the black altar and spoke the words which unleashed the Skool. In an instant, the blast closed the second door among all three realms. The ground roared and trembled beneath his feet as if the rock and soil were adjusting to the change. The realms had only one gateway left.

He went back to his friends, the air charged with energy. As he tried to sit next to Fedelm, she noticed his injury still hampered the way he moved.

"The Exyts Spring water isn't working like it used to. My hip is still not healed yet." She told them.

Joclac pulled his pipe, "I'm not surprised. The Skool probably drained much of the healing power of the water. Do you have more?" Fedelm nodded to the man, then asked Urith about his arm.

"It helped my arm a little, but it's still a mess," the warrior conceded. "I'll have to put a splint on the area again and hope for the best."

"Get some food first, and we will get that taken care of. It's a long way to the last gateway. With luck and what's left of the healing water, you'll be good as new," Joclac told him as he slowly got to his feet.

~~~

Several mornings later, the group of travelers reached the outskirts of Grimma with the massive Citadel perched like a guard above the village. The cart of Joclac and Soma, pulled by erbas, slowed their progress. The wagon was also a good place for Spanca to hide when needed. A naked, green woman was unusual even within the lands of gods and demigods. Still, the demigoddess of nature felt more a home within the countryside, so she often used an ossane to ride ahead, talking with the spirits she came upon. The extra time on the trail also allowed them to recover from their wounds. Fedelm used of all the remaining healing water on Urith's forearm which finally healed the bones. However, he still had little feeling in the arm, and the hand could barely grip anything. The woman knew the warrior was upset at the thought of being lame, but he said nothing. Instead, he grew quieter, seldom saying much to anyone.

When the group of travelers pulled to a stop, they looked over the village, it still bore all the scars of the Aberffraw destruction and few villagers remained. There was one change; the local Ynyover militia guarded the road leading to the Citadel. They pulled next to an abandoned ossane stable for water. While the guards remained suspicious of the ragtag group of foreigners, Narslac talked the men into giving a message to the Citadel inhabitants. Soon, Ircia and Brihar arrived.

"It's good to see you in one piece," the leader of the Gramcle clan.

"And you as well. It seems you and Ircia have an agreement," Urith observed.

"That is true. Cooperation is much easier now that we have Lyncus in our dungeons. It helps that those from Esterblud are leaving." Ircia responded slyly.

Brihar paused briefly at the comment. "Yes, our fighters will be leaving soon. Once, Pehnuwick arrives along with King Merkhan from Eernicia. We hear other leaders are coming as well."

"Good," Urith responded with his attention focused elsewhere. "We need supplies for us and the ossanes. Is that possible? Our group doesn't have much to trade with."

Ircia nodded. "Yes, I'll make this happen." He told them as he gave a guard the order. When the guard left, he turned back to Urith. "The Malhair House has become much easier to deal with. It seems a rumor is running around about their destruction at the hands of someone called Urith."

The man carrying the Shield of Skool said nothing, he only walked away leading his ossane to the water trough. Narslac and Fedelm walked over to the two confused men, quickly explaining what they went through at Ynys Cearcal.

"One gateway left, you say. Let my fighters and I come with you. I would love a chance to take out some of those wretched monsters." Brihar offered.

Narslac smiled at the offer. "I wouldn't turn down some help," he said. "But the big man is in charge." He turned to Fedelm. "What do you think? From what I can tell, he's not been happy about much. I don't think it's likely."

She agreed. "No, it's not likely but let me talk with him. I'll try to remind him of what Heptarc did in the past."

The Skald beamed a large smile. "You do remember those stories I told you during our journey."

Fedelm gave a brief grin as she walked away. She didn't want to tell him that Urith told her the story.

Urith was softly stroking the ossane's long neck as the animal drank from the wooden trough. Fedelm walked around to the other side, trying to see the man's expression.

"I heard your conversation," he told her, keeping his focus on the water.

"I thought you might have, but that's not why I came over. You've been too quiet since we left Ynys Cearcal."

"Not much to say," he looked up. "I can't plan beyond each sunrise at this point. Friends have died, and everything I once cherished is gone. I have no idea what I'm supposed to believe in. I cannot pray to gods that wish to destroy us and now they're nearly gone. Worse, I don't know what awaits us after this is complete."

She remained quiet as she thought. Fedelm had no answers for Urith. It would be the same for all humans when they finished.

"We saw the spirits go somewhere above the Sky Realm," Fedelm told him. "I know you saw your father again and he was able to help you. Perhaps we're not meant to know right now. You talk about the Fates. Maybe it's in their plan. I have to believe I will see my father and mother again."

He remained silent for a while as the woman dipped her hand into the water, stirring it with her fingers.

"You know, my father always believed that everything will come out to balance in the end. You ever play the game called *bolce*?" The woman asked. Urith nodded absently, remembering his unlucky streak every time he threw the round clay balls. His numbers never earned him koinons.

"He told me how much life reminded him of that game. We think that life is good when we roll the three balls, and our numbers win. Yet, he said we curse the balls and the world when we don't win. Nothing changed but how you tossed the balls. He always stated that in the end, nothing changes but your luck at the toss." She gave him a tired grin. "So far, what you call Fates has given us many hurdles, but it seems they remain with us." She looked up at him and their eyes remained locked for a moment. She knew he wanted to believe in what she was trying to explain. Urith's expression suddenly revealed a caring tenderness which gripped her. It was a moment she would not forget.

171

He finally broke the spell. "I guess everyone needs to be involved in what will come. As much as I don't like the idea of more people dying because of me, I suppose they need to make the decision."

Fedelm walked away, shaking the water from her hand. "I'll let Brihar know."

Later that day, the Gramcle leader and his two brothers joined the caravan as they headed down the road leading to Esterblud. Urith rode with Fedelm. The blond hakra was happy to see Urith didn't have the dark cloud hanging over his temper at the moment. Still, he kept quiet, looking at his injured arm. She tried to divert his attention by asking questions about Joclac who rode next to the wagon his wife handled. His answers were frustratingly short, so instead, she listened to Narslac who was nearby. The Skald was alongside the four new warriors who joined their group, regaling the fighters with tales of the past. Ever talkative, the one-armed man enjoyed his role of trying to keep spirits up among the travelers. Harlor and Micaq, brothers of Brihar, kept glancing back at Fedelm. At first, the lovely woman thought something was amiss in the way she looked or dressed. Finally, when they slowed their mounts to join her, she realized the two warriors were interested in something more.

The men struck up a conversation with Fedelm, and soon she began to enjoy the attention. Apparently paying no attention, Urith suddenly angled his ossane next to Joclac.

"Have you seen Spanca? She hasn't been back in a while," the big man asked.

"The demigoddess told me she would ride ahead and talk with Ruggla. I don't expect we'll see her until we get closer." The seer noticed the worry on the Esterblud's face.

"Good thing she's gone since we have more fighters with us now," Soma spoke up from her cart. "From the stories of the Gallaeci, she's a little temptress. I hear the woman uses men for her entertainment. She could cause problems among the fighters we have along."

"I believe my wife disapproves of the demigoddess. She's trying to get the lady to put clothes on," Joclac's eyes were bright in jest.

"That's not what I meant," Soma's face turned red, and both men smiled. "I'm worried if she causes our new fighters to forget about the rest of our journey. You said the underworld will probably start attacking even more now. We need the men to focus on their jobs, not a pretty little girl."

172

"No doubt, there's something in what you say," Urith agreed with her. "I'm not sure why she's even with us. But she's at least wearing the breastplate now. However, if you're worried about a temptress, Soma should start hiding inside that cart, and you let your husband drive the team."

The woman's face turned red as Joclac laughed in agreement.

"Oh, go away. You two never listen," she told the men. They pulled ahead, leaving her to grin at the compliment. Fedelm, with practiced ease, was able to disengage from her admirers and soon rode up next to the cart. She noticed the smile after overhearing a bit of the conversation.

"Urith is happier," she commented. "You must have a way to cheer him up."

Still grinning, the wife of Joclac disagreed. "No, he's always been like that with me. When we first met, I had a hard time trusting anyone, let alone a man. By the time we reached Esterblud, he had helped me over that. Too bad I couldn't keep him."

Fedelm thought she heard a note of wistfulness in the tone.

"What do you mean?"

"We were lovers. She grew quiet for a moment, carefully looking around for any eavesdropping. "Like I said, he did so much for me. And I fell for him by the time we got to Esterblud. For a while, I believed he thought the same of me. However, it was only a season after we reached Joclac's village that he wanted to leave on his next adventure. He only stayed because I asked him to. It was bad for him."

The woman was quiet for a while, remembering the good and bad of past events. "Finally, I convinced Urith to leave while I stayed with Joclac. Eventually, my seer got me to marry him."

Fedelm knew the woman was leaving something out. She told her so.

Soma nodded, remaining quiet. The sounds of the erba pulling the cart along with the snort from ossane were the only noise they heard for a while.

The woman driving the vehicle looked at Fedelm. "What I tell you will remain with us to the grave." Soma's expression communicated her offer was non-negotiable. Fedelm agreed, her curiosity now fully aroused.

"Of course, Joclac knew before Urith, and I ever reached his village that I was with child. Still, my husband, who knows so much about the future, decided I should be with him. My little man is an exceptional person. In some ways, he is better than Urith. There is no jealousy or concerns about my feelings toward Urith."

The blond woman went quiet on the news, remember Soma telling Urith about the boy she had who was nearly his size. "Does he know?"

Joclac's wife shook her head. "He never will, you understand that?" The tone of the woman's voice was clear, and again Fedelm nodded.

"I've been watching you. You know how to handle that Esterblud. If you and he both survive, I would think Urith could be married. It would do you both good."

"I don't know about that," the hakra was taken aback by the woman's forthright manner. She tried to make light of the statement. "I saw him looking at Spanca. Another demigoddess could be in the way."

"I doubt if you have to worry about that. Just remember to hang on. Heroes will not settle down in a little hamlet somewhere. After what Joclac told me about you, Urith won't do any good in some fortress among a bunch of nobles. He needs to find new paths to discover." Soma's knowing smile bothered Fedelm.

"Tell me something. Why did you not follow Urith, even with child? You are traveling into danger now with your offspring far away."

Soma's expression changed. "At the time, I was afraid. I thought I wanted a man to be there only for me. It was too much to expect of him. He's not an ordinary man."

Fedelm went quiet at the words. She agreed with the statement. However, Soma gave her a lot to think about and confirmed her suspicions about the wife of Joclac.

Out front of the wagon, Urith and Joclac were discussing the seer's visions. The Esterblud wanted to know more about what he would be up against.

"I don't know much about this Yns Garraid. Have you been there before?" Urith asked.

Joclac shook his head. "No, even the satgerts rarely go there since only a few mountain villages are nearby. I've heard of this Ruggla only in passing. He helps stop miners from accidently entering Caruun's domain. It's said, the demigod has a hatred of the vulture face underworld god. He helped forge the god's weapons from the heat of a volcano near the gateway."

"I've heard Alrpan has been known to entice Ruggla to do her bidding by sending the lava into villages. Then, again, she's had most of the gods in her chambers. At least that's the stories from the Skalds," Narslac joined the two men. "Good thing she is gone. Might make it easier to get the god of the mine's attention."

"I'm betting that Spanca won't have much problem with him," Urith said mostly to himself as he looked at his arm again. He didn't see the harsh glare that Narslac gave him at the comment. "Anyway, if the Fates remain with us, any ideas on when we should arrive at this gateway?"

Joclac pulled his smelly pipe from his mouth. "At least a dozen sunrises would be my guess. Nothing but small villages along the way, I'm afraid we won't have much help if we need it."

"That's normal," Urith told him. Narslac gave a friendly nod and a grunt in agreement.

As the day turned to night, the group of travelers finally reached a crossroads where a small hamlet once stood before the Aberffraw army came through. Only burned out husks of a few stone foundations remained in the desolate and abandoned area. A few scattered human bones could be seen on one side of the road, the grisly reminder of the unfortunates caught up in the murderous chaos of war.

Brihar suggested they make camp just down the road in a small grove of trees to the agreement of the others. Immediately, the Gramcle leader sent a few men out to scout for any food and water. While the rest of the group was unpacking, Brihar slid off his mount after stopping near Urith. He offered his condolences about Mivraa as Urith pulled his gear from the ossane.

"Narslac told me about what happened inside the Sky Realm. I'm sorry to hear of her death. From what little I knew about her, she was an excellent warrior." Brihar fished for the words.

The Esterblud continued working on the leather straps. "Yes, she was one of the best. I've never seen a braver person face death."

"It got me to wondering." Brihar paused, then began working on removing his own saddle.

"About what?" Urith asked.

"About Haligulf, what becomes of the spirits now?"

Urith stopped while he stared at the ground. He shook his head as his long hair covered his face. "I have no idea." He looked over at Brihar. "Did Narslac tell you about the blue balls of light?" His friend shook his head.

"All I can tell you is what I saw," Urith stated. "When the statues and the monsters were slain, orbs of blue suddenly went skyward from the bodies. Mivraa noticed this as well. She wondered what they could mean, telling me she would soon find out. I guess they were the spirits inside the bodies. "

"That's amazing," the Gramcle leader responded.

Urith agreed. "Once the last gateway is closed, I think a new world will come to light."

Brihar pulled off his saddle and walked by his friend. "Perhaps, you're right. But maybe it's not the world we want. Many liked Kamin the way we had it, even with chaos."

Urith, carrying his saddle, followed him to the open area where Narslac and Joclac were gathering wood to make a fire. "It appears nobody gets a say in this. I don't even know what to do except on those few times when soothsayers lay out a path. Maybe the Fates will let us know."

Laying out his blanket, Brihar nodded. "I see what you mean. But has that happened before?"

Urith's silence gave him the answer. Brihar watched his friend throw down his saddle before going back to the ossanes.

"I'm just worried about how to live to the next day," Urith said. "I'll let smarter people sort it out if we survive."

~~~

The morning brought a cold, steady rain to the lands as the travelers quickly packed up and restarted their journey. Brihar's brothers failed to find any game, but they guided them to the stream where the bags were refilled for the upcoming travel. With the sometimes-torrential downpours soon soaking their clothes, the line of riders remained mostly quiet. Each person was trying to stay as dry and warm as possible under wool hoods and capes. It was an unusual event to have such a cool breeze and steady rain during the dry season. Urith encouraged Brihar, and his men take the lead, trying to overcome his reluctance at having them join him on the journey. Narslac rode next to the fearless Gramcle leader. Urith wasn't far behind them, turning back to look at the cart where Joclac took over driving the team for a while as Soma remained inside the covered back of the wagon. He smiled to himself. The old seer still cared deeply for his wife, letting her stay dry. A smile crossed the scarred warrior face for a moment. Then, he saw the way Joclac was chewing on the stem of his pipe. Something was amiss. But, for this time, he stayed quiet.

Next to the large Esterblud was Fedelm, her small frame enveloped inside the large cape she wore. She was watching him, staying quiet as well. However, he knew her well enough now to recognize the signs. The hakra had something on her mind. Her green eyes told him.

"Alright, out with it," he told her.

"I don't have anything to say."

The man gave her his sneer grin. "That means something is bothering you. Come on, tell me what you're thinking about. Is it one of your visions?"

The blond hakra shook her head. "No, Joclac has those covered it seems. I've not seen anything about our journey when I sleep."

"Then, what is it? I saw that look before." He told her.

"Alright. It's the spirit of your wife. I've seen something about her."

The big man's eyes narrowed, and his voice went to a growl. "What have you seen?"

"Dughorm came to me again. He's still watching us. Don't ask me how he remains with us. I saw the spirits of the dead residing in a black throne. Dughorm told me they were the condemned of Kriell. For some reason, your wife is one of them. It seems the Guardian might be trying to come at you through your family." Her expression was mixed with sympathy and caution. She wasn't sure how the man might react.

Instead of his expected outburst, Urith took a deep breath, and she caught a glimpse of deep pain suddenly exposed on his face. To her surprise, he just nodded and went quiet, leading his ossane off the trail to the open field nearby.

Narslac noticed the warrior ride away, and he pulled around to talk with Fedelm. At first, she refused to tell him what happened but the Skald reminded her of his long association with the Esterblud. When she finally disclosed her vision, the stout man shifted uncomfortably in his saddle, making up his mind. Finally, he asked her a question.

"I met Urith right after he left his wife's funeral. Did he ever tell you what happened?"

Shaking her head, the woman said she knew little about the seasons before they met.

"Mind you I only heard about his anger with the gods from others over the seasons. However, I was there with the man after his wife's death. I'm confident the stories I heard are true." He gathered his thoughts, then began the story.

"The tale of the Clovel Destroyer begins when his wife, Earmis who was pregnant with their first child. She died in a tragic accident on their way to Gramcan with the body of his father in the wagon his wife drove. As he tried to deal with his grief, Urith decided Earmis deserved a place in the Sky Realm. So he put her body along with his father's on the funeral pyre at the temple shrine in Gramcan. At one point, he even made a satgert help him with incantations to ensure her passage to the realm. I heard that after he had left, the priests gathered together to make offerings to Caruun to capture her soul and torment her in his throne of pain for Urith's desecration of their temple. He must have found out about this just before the day I met him."

Narslac paused while he recalled the events so many seasons before. "I was with a traveling group of Skalds when met him in a tavern on the road back to his home." He told them. "Urith was quiet, acting like someone carrying darkness inside. Mivraa was with us at the time, transformed into a young man, like you saw when we met. Later, I found out she liked to use our Skalds to keep up with news in the human realm. Anyway, as we traveled together, we came to a bridge where a large gang of Aberffraw bandits stopped us. They were terrorizing the country at the time. And you know his way of starting something." He smiled at Fedelm.

"Let me guess, he made sure you had a fight." She suggested.

He nodded in agreement. "I thought we were well trained, but I'd never such speed and fighting skill, especially for a man with his youth." Narslac told them. "While he is intimidating with his size, it was the way he attacked that group forced the rest of us to pause, watching the spectacle. There was an unbelievable rage in him. It might have been the way the prisoners were being treated by the Aberffraw. To look upon that fight was a sight I'll never forget." His face turned dark at the thought.

"It was on that day when I recognized the savagery and brutality inside of him. I saw no mercy when I went to him after the fighting was done. When I went to thank him for his help and to advise that revenge was not suitable for a heroic warrior like him. I truly thought he would kill me when I drew close."

Fedelm listened to the tale, recalling her times when Urith fought. Narslac was correct. He carried a viciousness which was breathtaking at times.

"I understand," she said. "I probably shouldn't have said anything but Dughorm seemed insistent that I understand the vision. I hope it bodes well for us."

He gave Fedelm a sympathetic smile. "You did what you thought was right. So far, we've been guided well. Let Urith ride alone for a while. It's probably better for him."

Across the field, the warrior let the mount amble along a narrow path that ran somewhat parallel with the road. The animal stopped on occasion to fill its belly on the tender *vulgere*, growing wild in the unfarmed field. The Esterblud grappled with the emotions that crossed him like waves of hot salt water on an open wound. The man knew he could not bring is wife back, but he still blamed himself for her death and for her punishment. Back in Eran, he thought he heard her voice when the warrior went into the village. The voice gave him hope that all the sacrifices to gods and deals he made with many priests had finally come to fruition. Now, he was told that she was found and condemned inside the underworld. The man was confused and angry, unsure where to turn.

His ossane followed the trail into a thin forest which obscured the road. The sounds of the wagon continued to echo as his mount followed the path. Urith was lost in memories of the past, feeling quiet along despite the many friends only a quick gallop away.

"The scarred one bears too much, I think." Spanca's voice caught the fighter with surprise, and his instinctive reflex had the Clovel Sword nearly out of its scabbard when he saw the green lady. She was hanging in the tree next to him, her body partially covered with a simple cloth cape. Her brown hair drenched from the rain, she looked concerned.

He grunted, "just thinking. Are you spying on us or others?"

The woman suddenly beamed a smile. "I decided to look ahead and came back. The other women remain unsure about me, so I stay away to watch you. And I'm trying to see if those new men can find me. They haven't so they must not be valuable fighters."

The warrior wondered why she was playing such a game. "I don't know much about the Gallaeci ways; however, it seems odd."

The woman rolled her yellow eyes. "To see if they can overcome my challenges, of course. Any Gallaeci who are worthy enough to find me may share a night with me," she sighed. "None of these men are worth my time. I leave many hints, but still, they aren't able to capture me. It is lonely travel for me with all these men around."

He decided to turn the conversation. "Do you have any news for the rest of us?"

"Give me a ride, and I tell you." Without warning, she skillfully jumped down from the tree and sprang up onto the back of his ossane. The woman snuggled up close to the man, and he could feel her shivering.

"Bad signs are coming from the forest," she told him, her hot breath uncomfortably close to his ear. He inadvertently shivered as well, but her words got his attention.

"That seems to go with the territory. But what signs?" The warrior asked as he spurred the ossane forward.

"The seasons turn early. The birds are starting to fly away already. It is bad. I've never seen such fright in the animals." She wrapped her arms around him tightly.

"What does it mean?" Urith wondered aloud.

"Sky Realm is gone, and the gods are no more. The weather and earth look for a new master," She answered directly.

Urith wished she was wrong, but he had to agree. The balance of the three realms lay shattered with the death of the Sky Gods. He wondered what the destruction of the final gateway would unleash. As if she read his mind, the demigoddess breathed into his ear.

"Don't worry, giant man. Mivraa told me her visions, and you follow the right path. The goddess of Haligulf said you would be forced to make the choices nobody wants. She trusted you. Trust in her and the yellow hair girl." The green woman's voice was hauntingly far and so near like the peaceful sounds of the night.

"That's not my problem," he growled.

"Then, trust the dead spirits you cherish. They wish you to follow this through." The warrior stiffened. "No need to grow angry. Much has been explained to me about your past. The sprites who inhabit the land know of your turmoil. They also say other voices from the underworld are becoming louder."

Urith sighed at the puzzle. "Now what am I supposed to make of that?"

"I'm not sure," the demigoddess confessed. "I'm not a seer; I can only hear what the little spirits of nature tell me. But I would be careful of visions. The nymphs say bad dreams come from the Guardian."

Urith felt the woman wasn't telling him something. "Tell me, why are you coming with us? You are a demigoddess, worshiped by humans."

The pair emerged from the line of trees to see his group of followers on the trail. Disregarding his question, the woman kissed him softly on the earlobe sending an electric thrill into the man. Then, like one of the nature spirits he heard about, she jumped from the ossane.

"Where are you going," he turned to asked, but the woman was gone.

Her voice drifted out of the trees. "I'll find Ruggla again. Must make sure my warrior is welcomed in the mountains."

~~~

The weather was growing increasingly raw that day as they traveled deeper into Ynyover. The rain changed into ice pellets which rained down steadily from the dark gray skies. Cold and tired, the group of travelers saw the village of Gralwa come into view which offered a chance for warmth. However, the ossanes immediately began to snort, and bob their long heads, an early sign of panic as the group reached the edge of the village. At the split rail fence which nearly surrounded the town, they saw the reason for the ossane's reaction. Bodies covered the narrow main road. The group came to an immediate halt, and Brihar sent Harlor and Micaq around the edge of the village to look for signs of an ambush.

Urith edged ahead to the first building where he slid off his mount to inspect the ravaged body of a blacksmith. The partially naked body was missing an arm, and the ears were torn from the head. It confirmed his fears.

"The underworld monsters came through here," he told the others as he led his ossane further down the road. More mangled bodies revealed the extent of the gruesome massacre which included women and children. Nothing appeared to remain alive in the town.

181

Urith came to the mead house and tied off the ossane before he entered the small building. Stepping through the shattered doors, the warrior found the remains of a man and woman inside. As he walked to the back, he noticed Narslac was following him. In the rear of the tavern, the fighter found untouched dried meats and other supplies.

"Well, we won't starve. Let's take what we can carry," Urith told his friend.

Narslac cursed the underworld. "We should burn this place down. Nobody will return to this cursed place."

The one-armed man's words caused Urith to curse loudly. The man hurried out of the building, finding Brihar standing across the street, The Gramcle looked down at the body of a child, and the man's face was red with anger.

"Have your men look for a twisted *lellowtere* tree around here," Urith rushed up before Brihar could begin cursing at the underworld.

The confused Gramcle leader nodded and climbed on his mount.

"What are you thinking?" Fedelm asked, walking up behind the giant Esterblud.

"Narslac said we should burn this place down. It struck a memory with me," he replied.

"You mean those twisted trees Mivraa used to speak of?" She stopped. "You don't say that you're going to burn them?"

"I don't know why I never thought of this sooner but why not? Mivraa told me about those cursed trees that were the passage to both the underworld and Sky Realm. I say we just burn them and get the word out. Maybe that would stop some of this." The man's gray eyes were bright at the thought.

Fedelm hesitated. "I don't know. It seems like Dughorm would have brought that out in a vision before."

"Maybe it's time to quit relying on some of the dreams that are not actually clear and use our brain," the warrior replied. Then, he shook his head. "That's not really I meant. You and others have been very helpful. I'm just saying who knows what's the best path now? We already know that we have to close the last gateway that runs between all three realms. Can you tell me that Kriell can't come in through those trees tonight? Maybe those monsters we left in the Sky Realm found a way out? I'm saying we are not taking any chances."

The warrior heard Brihar shouting and waving at the other end of the village, and he told Fedelm to relay his idea to Joclac. Then, he ran down the road. Just outside the fence, he saw the twisted *lellowtere* tree where Brihar and his men stood. Immediately, he told them to burn it. He quickly explained after their stunned expressions. Brihar looked past the warrior to Fedelm and Joclac who walked up behind Urith.

"Do you think this will work? It seems pretty crazy to me."

The seer pulled out his pipe from under his cape. "Actually it could be a great idea, simple and to the point. I must be slipping for not seeing something like this before. Come, let's get it going so I can light my smoke." He smiled at the thought.

Fedelm reluctantly agreed. "Too bad it won't help this place. But I have an idea how we can spread the word. Is there a temple close by? Somewhere we can get a message through to a satgert?"

"I'm pretty sure there will be one at Hariwill which is only another day away," Micaq spoke up eagerly as he held a gaze on the blond woman. "It's the last stop before we get into the mountain. That is if the underworld monsters didn't already overrun the town like this place,"

"As I heard from Joclac, it was a bigger village. If we can't find a temple, we can have Brihar send you back to Grimma," Urith growled. His look showed his displeasure at how the Gramcle warrior was watching Fedelm. Brihar grinned to himself before sending his brothers to get firewood to put around the tree base.

"We'll take care of this," Brihar told Urith. "What about the bodies? I think should we spend some time removing them out of the road?"

"Dump them in one of the sheds and set it on fire," suggested Joclac. "With this rain, it's not likely we will burn the town. We can use the mead hall for a place to sleep tonight."

"Make sense to me," Urith told them, not envying the task ahead of them. "Too bad none of the Sky gods remain. I don't mind rubbing some salt in their wounds by using a funeral pyre for the dead who were never warriors."

It was late when the final bodies were stacked in the stable next to the ossane pen, and a torch lit up the dry straw. While the travelers gathered the corpses, Joclac sent his wife through the village looking for supplies. Fedelm eventually joined the woman, and they collected enough food for the rest of the trip. When they finished filling the wagon, the women watched the flames running up the tree while the women waited in one of the shacks.

"Perhaps this is the start to replacing all the destruction," Fedelm commented as she viewed the scene. It reminded her of tales about a lost world of fire.

"Let's hope so." Soma remained unmoved. "I left some food in the tavern along with some of the heathmead. Let's clean up before the men return from this work."

The hakra grinned, "And maybe we can get some of them to clean themselves."

"Good luck with that," Soma said. Fedelm laughed as she joined her walking to the building.

The next morning, the road to Yns Garraid was covered from overnight snow. Nobody heard of such weather during the height of the *Draenya* season, the time of planting and growing on Kamin. The storm confirmed the words of Spanca, and he mentioned his brief ride with the demigoddess to Joclac as the two men stepped from the tavern.

"I guess with the Sky God gone, we shouldn't be surprised. Still, these weather changes bode ill for all of Kamin. The crops will fail, and starvation will come soon if it doesn't get warmer quickly." The seer told him.

Urith nodded. "I guess we need to move quickly to finish what the Fates have started."

Urith took the lead as the travelers restarted their journey, their line of tracks the only prints on the quiet road. When they went by the still smoldering remains of the *lellowtere* tree, Urith noticed how the fire continued to burn down at the roots. While too late for this village, he hoped the death of the tree would put an end to at least one gateway. Perhaps if all of them were destroyed, humanity would have a chance against the underworld.

The snow fell slowly, flakes of white dropping down to cover their mount's long necks. As the day progressed, they begin to see the start of Mythroloy Mountains. The high peaks covered by the clouds, the mountain range blended in with the weather with its blue-gray rocks. Even the colors of the blue and green trees gave way to white and gray of the land around them as they got to the highlands. The weather turned colder, with the snowfall coming down heavy at times. Despite the slow progress, Urith looked at the snow as a potential advantage. The hordes of evil beasts would not be hard to track and quickly spotted amid the white background. For a moment he wondered about Spanca. Her green pallor would be easier to spot. The warrior smiled to himself when he thought of her surprise if Brihar's two brothers ever caught on to the demigoddess's game in this open country. Looking back, he observed the laughing Fedelm riding along with the brothers. A sudden anger surged through him.

"I would expect warriors to be scouting this unknown territory," he growled at Brihar who was nearby.

The stout Gramcle leader spurred his ossane next to the Esterblud. "They are young and infatuated. If you want to ride with the blond, then do it and have her make it clear she's attached to you. Otherwise, don't take your jealousy out on my family. I believe we will need all the allies we can find when we get into the mountains," he told Urith quietly.

The giant warrior glared at him but remained quiet for a moment. Finally, he nodded.

"You take the lead for a moment. I have an idea."

Brihar nodded, watching the warrior slow his pace to let Brihar's brothers and Fedelm's mounts draw close.

"Micaq and Harlor, I think I've done a disservice to you. Both of you should speak with Narslac about the tales of the Gallaeci so you can learn more about the demigoddess we travel with. She was telling me about some their strange customs the other day, and I believe you may have missed the signs she was giving out."

Urith gave them his snarling smile, glancing back at the wagon where Narslac sat on his ossane, regaling the trapped couple in the wagon about stories of the Kamin fighters.

The brothers looked at him suspiciously. "I'm telling the truth," Urith told them as he moved his mount next to Fedelm's. "I'll bet a koinon to each of you if Narslac can't tell you the story behind Spanca's challenges."

Quickly accepting the bet, the Gramcle warriors rode over to the cart. Fedelm watched as the big man next to her gave her a smug look.

"You're not going to admit it, are you?" She asked.

"Admit what?" He continued to stare ahead. "Spanca told me she left clues for them. They should know this. I just gave them an incentive."

"Maybe so, but you refuse to admit you are jealous." She told him with a slight grin.

Urith remained quiet, and she went silent as they pushed through a sudden burst of cold wind and heavy snow.

"You have no reason to worry," Fedelm whispered after the wind receded, leaving only thick snowflakes which deadened the sound around them.

"I know. But in my defense, I've gotten used to your company," Urith told her. "When we get through this, then we can talk about a future."

Fedelm smiled to herself. She guessed it was a close as he could come to the idea of loving another person at this point.

~~~

Far ahead of the travelers, a solitary figure rode on the back of a wild erba. Covered in several blankets taken from the last destroyed farm house she came across, Spanca shivered as she reached the high plateau between the two highest peaks of the Mythroloy range.

"I know we've not stopped for a while." She told the animal. "But soon, we be there, and I'll make sure you get extra food." The green woman smiled as the beast snorted several times in disagreement.

Spanca knocked snow from the hairy creature's neck, grinning as the erba shook its head. Riding bareback, her small round shield and gleaming sword clanked out a periodic chime with each step the creature took in the deep snow. Despite the snow cover, the green woman knew Yns Garraid was close, hearing the directions given to her in whispers by the few sprites that hid in the desolate area. Soon, she saw the dark opening along one cliff wall in the distance. As she drew closer to the perfect circle embedded into the rock, it became apparent to her that the enormous size could have only been made by the gods.

When the demigoddess finally reached the opening, the black void towered above her and the erba. The creature grunted its displeasure for getting so close to the gateway, and she patted the animal, trying to calm it.

"Spanca, the nature goddess of the Gallaeci," a booming voice echoed from the void. "The spirits spoke of your return."

She slid off the animal, her feet instantly feeling the cold of the deep snow with her thin talon feet. A dark figure moved toward her, remaining inside the shadow of the circle.

"I come ask you for help," she told the moving shadow. "Does Ruggla have an answer?"

A burly man stepped out of the darkness enough for her to see him. He was short with a long beard and massive arms which hung down past his knees. The demigod wore a black tunic and black leather pants. His gleaming red eyes looked her up and down as she felt a chill. The expression Ruggla gave her was the same as Caruun, his underworld father.

"I have little time for strangers who come to my lands." He said. "My spirits told you that before."

"You know of the chaos between the realms. It puts all in danger," Spanca said as the woman stepped inside the invisible barrier where the vast circle in the mountain stopped the snow. The air was warm inside the entrance.

"Of course, stupid little girl. Why do you return to tell me nonsense I already know?" He said as his broad face wrinkled up like he smelled an awful odor. He was covered in dust which gave him the look of a dirty miner.

"If you're so smart, do you know the human with the Skool comes this way?" Spanca lashed back at him.

Ruggla's expression turned curious. "I've heard something about this man from Esterblud. Are you saying he comes here now?" He asked.

"Do you mean a stupid girl knows more than you?" She smiled smugly as she leaned back against the curved wall, removing her blankets.

The short man grunted, his eyes remaining on her exposed shoulders and legs. "After my little helpers sent you away, I wondered if I might have been hasty. How are you involved with this?"

As the man sat across from her, Spanca told him about her journey with the Esterblud, making sure to emphasize the power of the Skool. She saw his eyes continued to focus on her body. While she talked, her eyes adjusted to the darkness inside the giant hole. She saw several small tunnels that ran deep into the pitch black. As he listened, Ruggla pulled a small pipe from a bag on his belt. Already filled with *xylox*, a pink weed from near the mines, he placed it between his thick lips. In an instant, he flicked his fingers, and a small fire came to life on his index finger which he used to lite the weed. Intrigued, Spanca stopped in mid-sentence to watch him.

Ruggla blew out harsh smelling smoke while his face remained unmoved by her words. "I might be isolated here, but I've heard of the Skool. You're not the only one who can listen to the words of the nature sprites who haunt the valley and caves. I also like my home here. You haven't said it, but this Urith plans on destroying this gateway, like the Great Circle. Is that not so?"

Her expression revealed the truth to him. "The Fates have sent him," she replied.

He scoffed at her. "Only those with power make the decisions, not some invisible chance. You've given your message. Is that all you come for?"

"I seek assistance from another demigod to stop chaos which hurts all. You've seen what is happening," Spanca told him, nodding to the snow outside.

Ruggla glanced outside and shrugged. "It doesn't concern me what happens to the humans."

"How can you say that? What of Kriell?" She asked as her eyes widened at his response. "You've heard of him from the sprites that are nearby."

"Of course, I've known of the Guardian," the demigod's face obscured from the smoke around him. "His slave, the Vanth call Actita came to this gateway not long after you left. He told me all about the new age coming. I said it doesn't seem any different than what I dealt with before."

"So you'll not help?" Spanca's face went sour.

"I've not said that. You've not offered me anything for which I should allow the humans to destroy my home. Tell me, if this person you are helping is unable to stop Kriell and his legions of the underworld, what becomes of the last demigods, like you and I?"

He fanned the smoke away to see her face. She said nothing, and he recognized the woman was considering the possibility for the first time. "I've been thinking about this," he continued. "I realize I need to have something that gives value to Kriell. Otherwise, the Guardian will just ingest me. His vengeance has no bounds, and we are offspring of the gods he is destroying. Actita told me as much. You might consider the fact that Kriell will do the same with you. I like living as a nearly immortal being, don't you?"

Spanca's look confirmed she had never considered what the underworld god might do to her.

"Now you arrive trying to enlist me to your side," Ruggla said mildly. "From what you tell me, the man called Urith carries the Skool, but he is injured. Is that right?"

The demigoddess nodded slowly.

"Then, it's hardly fair for you to ask me to help an injured person who might get me destroyed. What happens if Kriell learns of this meeting? It would make me a marked man. And you would find yourself in similar danger as well." Ruggla shook his head as if he was contemplating such a terrible idea.

Spanca inhaled suddenly. "Did you tell Actita of me?"

"I'm a reasonable person. No need to worry, I haven't told anyone of your travel," Ruggla assured her. "However, since the Vanth came by, I've had some time to consider my options. With Kamin in such a state, I think it's wise to have partners, especially someone who is a part-god like me. There are not many of us left, so we need to create more. Seems a logical step, don't you think?"

The woman felt a knot in her stomach as she realized what she was being told. He spoke a reality which could be her future. Spanca stared out at the cold where the erba scratched at the snow, looking for vegetation. "I have little to offer as a goddess of nature and a small clan of humans who worship me," the woman countered.

Ruggla watched her for a moment. Then, he stood and started for the closest dark tunnel. "Oh, you bring more than you realize. And I might have a solution for our mutual problem. However, that means you must join with me. That would mean starting right now." He paused. "Otherwise, you can return with your human friends, and I'll let you handle Kriell on your own."

When he reached the entrance, he turned and gave her a foul grin. "I've heard how you like to have the Gallaeci humans bed you if you find them as truly worthy. I always thought that such actions seemed beneath your status as a goddess. If you decide to partner with me, we can create offspring to ensure our survival no matter who wins. We can be overlords and masters of the humans under Kriell, or we can become next gods for these people if they somehow destroy Kriell and his many monsters. Either way, we will survive the coming end to Kamin. Otherwise, you and I have little value to the future world."

189

As the demigod disappeared into the tunnel, his words struck her like the blowing snow. "It's your choice, Spanca. Here it is warm and protected. Follow me to my chambers where we can get started on our new partnership. I suggest you think how the Guardian will react if you continue to help this Urith." His voice tapered off, but she heard his last statement. "I almost pity those fools who fight Kriell."

Spanca stood, noticing her hands were shaking. The woman stared out at the winter scene from inside the protected gateway. After a long pause, the woman took a deep breath and turned toward the tunnels. Spanca walked into the darkness.

Chapter 9: Deadly Alliance

The spirit of Satres kneeled at the foot of the throne where the black form of Kriell sat. Next to the soul, Actita re-wrapped his human skin whip before attaching it to his belt. Although he lacked a body, the former leader of the Citadel felt the pain of the whipping he took from the Vanth. It was another enchanted device given by the Guardians and used to punish and control those souls in the underworld. Kriell's hideous figure displayed nothing to indicate what it thought when Satres looked up.

You have no power for me to ingest, yet I let your spirit bow before me. Your primitive brain must be trying to grasp why I would do this? The voice of Kriell spoke inside the mind of Satres.

"It would seem I have some use to you. It appears you use the whip, no doubt, to ensure my cooperation." Satres replied aloud, trying to reveal nothing within his thoughts.

The black creature on the throne shifted to another position, tentacles falling down close to Satres. "Perhaps you are smarter than most of your kind." Kriell told him. "Yes, you might have a use. Providing you tell me about this human that carries the Skool as well as the others who follow him."

The former Sacred Overlord smiled at an opportunity before him. "Then, your need can be satisfied." He said. "Perhaps with my service to this new world, I might be useful in other ways. I noticed the creature that was once a human called Reppir works in support of you. Maybe my skills could be used to help you sow more chaos and suffering you inflict on Kamin."

"I could easily enter your mind to find all I need to know," countered Kriell.

"And can you tell what is true and what is fantasy? Surely you know about my hallucinations and delusions before I died. I am unsure of reality. Perhaps it would be a waste of your time." Satres suggested as he carefully stood, filling himself with the proud bearing of his past role as overlord.

"While not a seer, I did peer into the future about your coming. I knew you would become the master of the realms." Satres told him. "It was I who helped the underworld against the humans before you arrived.

Is it worth trying to understand my fevered brain when I'm willing to help?" Satres asked as he adjusted the tattered images of his clothing which he carried at death.

The black blob remained silent for a moment. Kreill's voice suddenly filled the cavern. "I find such things as deceit, treachery, and lust filling your thoughts. Those qualities led to your downfall. Yet, I can see your ambition remains." He said. "You wish to wield power over mortals. And now, I feel a burning desire in your soul for revenge."

Kriell went silent again, and Satres waited, unsure of his fate.

Finally, the Guardian spoke. "Tell me of all you know of this Urith and the ones who travel with him. If your information meets my expectations, I can give you what you want. If you fail me, I'll have Actita turn you into one of the *mungards* that prowl the swamps. Then, you can scavenge on the flesh of humans to satisfy your appetite."

Satres smile fell away as he bowed. "I'm happy to be your servant." His voice purred. "You will learn everything about the Esterblud and his comrades."

~~~

The blizzard struck the travelers in full force as they passed through the village of Hariwill. Like the last town, the underworld hordes attacked at night. When they entered the village, the heavy snow was already covering over the bodies. The frozen limbs sticking out of the blanket of white were the only markers to the dead.

However, a few brave defenders remained alive, holding off the monsters until dawn broke along with the blizzard. The battered defenders carefully emerged at the sight of the ossanes coming near the stone building. A large female satgert along with two male militia fighter and their families stepped out of the small temple. Urith noticed the blue stone structure was dedicated to the Goddess of Haligulf. He gave a brief smile at the thought of Mivraa and the irony of the Fates leading them to the village.

"Sorry, we're too late to help." Urith told them as he slid off his mount. "Are you all that remain?"

"It appears so," the woman replied, her fiery red hair quickly becoming covered in the white blanket of snow. "Welcome, visitors. I'm Micale, priestess to Mivraa's sanctuary."

Urith was silent as Brihar joined him. He decided not to mention the death of Mivraa to the woman. Standing before the two men, the plump woman carried a battle ax, her white robe covered in black blood of the monsters. Her round face looked tired, but her green eyes remained bright from the aftermath of the battle.

"We used the power of the goddess in our makeshift fortress during the fight," Micale told them. "My friends and I made offerings to Mivraa at sunrise in thanks for her help."

A tall man dressed in the brown leather armor of a militia fighter came forward. His blood-covered sword still unsheathed in his hand. "You're the first humans we've seen. I'm Jracar, and this is my family," he said, pointing to a small woman holding a well-wrapped child in her arms.

"We have remained close to the temple for warmth and shelter since those monsters left. Have you seen any others on your way here?"

Brihar shook his head, and Jracar's stoic face betrayed a hint of emotion. "We hoped some of our friends might have escaped during the night."

"Are there twisted *lellowtere* trees near here?" Urith asked.

The surprised satgert nodded toward a trail barely visible in the snow. "Along that path," she said.

"And the monsters came from that direction, correct?" He asked and the priestess agreed.

"Then burn it," Urith told her as he climbed back on his ossane. "And spread the word across the lands that every one of those trees must be destroyed."

"I don't understand. Stay and warm yourselves, you can explain what's happening." Micale urged.

Urith shook his head. "We must continue on. Your world will be overrun with monsters unless you destroy those trees."

"The road leads to the mountains, and there will be no shelter there." Micale told Urith, looking to Brihar for support.

"There's something in what she says. This weather is getting worse, and we might lose our way," Brihar reminded Urith as the cart carrying Joclac and his wife finally pulled into the village.

Urith squinted as he gazed through the blinding snow to assess the route. The road was covered, and the thin brush on either side of the trail stuck through limbs of blue and green vegetation in places.

"Do we risk it?" Fedelm asked the tall warrior, she shivered inadvertently under her starkts wool blanket.

193

Urith gave her his sneering grin. "Die of cold, or maybe we run into the underworld hordes." He said. "Either way, it's a risk. I say push on and destroy Yns Garraid."

"What do you mean?" The priestess spoke up. "You can't destroy the gateway."

Urith looked down at the woman. "Well, you might be right, but I'm sure going to give it a try." Spurring his ossane, he galloped away from the stunned woman.

"He's crazy," Micale told Brihar who nodded but stepped past her to get on his ossane.

"That's probably true," Fedelm agreed as she started to follow Urith. "But that Shield of Skool he carries allows him to get away with it most times. Good luck to you and your village."

"Don't forget to spread the word about destroying the *lellowtere* trees unless you want the monsters to return," Brihar told Micale as he waved the others in their group forward. He looked up at the snowfall.

"It appears a crazy man is one of the few hopes we have left."

~~~

Oswald stood with his father on the bow of their ship traveling to Ynyover. As he tried to avoid mentioning the man's obvious discomfort, the son recognized Pehnuwick's health was failing fast. The sun was setting in the east, and Oswald wondered if the captain would make the harbor before it became too dangerous. The ships of the Maflow Sea seldom attempted to enter the ports at night.

"He's running it close," Pehnuwick echoed his son's thoughts. "He must not want a dying passenger on his hands for another night." There was a brief smile on his lips at his joke.

"You're too tough to let go that easy," Oslaf assured him. "Besides, you have to stay around and finish the work coming. Urith must have set up something interesting to have called for you to come here."

"No doubt, my brother has me in another mess. While I wish you would have stayed in Eran, it is good to have you with me." Pehnuwick grabbed the rail as the ship reared up at the increasing swells. "The breeze has started to turn into us. I hope the wind doesn't stop us from making landfall tonight."

"Are you in a hurry?" Henther asked as she came next to the men. She handed a mug of heathmead to Pehnuwick. "Drink up. It'll keep the pain down."

194

"I don't need a healer," the big man grunted. He took the clay cup anyway and she winked at him.

"You sound like your brother," Henther chided him gently. "Now, since you and Urith always keep things bottled up, I'll ask the obvious. Why are you going to the Citadel?" She asked. "Brihar is already there to represent Esterblud, and those guild men you spoke with in Eran didn't seem to give you a lot of information. Just to help the satgerts convene to decide the fate of Lyncus. Others could have done this."

"That should be a forgone conclusion," Oslaf told them bitterly. "They should have hung him on the nearest tree."

"No, many in Cahmais will support him as the heir to their dead king. I think my brother realized this. The fact that Urith got him back to the Citadel without bloodshed tells me there is hope for a settlement in all of this destruction. The monsters coming out of the underworld might have finally jolted the overlords into realizing it's time to work together. Or be killed just for living." Pehnuwick took a long drink of the mead. His face screwed up at the taste. "You put *geju* root in the drink," he accused Henther.

The young woman smiled at him. "You can thank me in the morning when you sleep better. I'm tired of your pain keeping me awake."

Despite her brash statement, Pehnuwick grinned to himself before he took another drink. "In spite of your poor upbringing, you might be right about that." He confided as he winked back at her.

"Do you really think the attacks coming from the underworld are causing people to put aside these feuds among tribes? She asked.

Pehnuwick shrugged. "Let's just call it hope. The dramatic weather changes are probably helping as well. You've heard the satgerts we've spoken with. Other parts of Esterblud have the priests using the temples for refuge, not offerings. I think Urith realized that if we can get the priests and leaders of the tribes together, we might be able to fix this world."

"I would settle for just putting a little peace into the craziness. And that's only if Urith can finish," Oslaf interjected.

"You sound like a diplomat now," Pehnuwick teased his son.

Oslafy replied with a wry grin. "You might be rubbing off a little now. I hope Urith is still close enough to find out what's happened. I don't trust those in the Malhair guild."

"I don't either," his father agreed. "They always have their own agenda. However, you will remember that my brother has a way of leaving his calling card. I'm sure we'll know more when we get to the Citadel."

It was dark when the visitors to Ynyover made their way up the path as they walked away from the docks. Saying farewell to the captain who somehow managed to bring the ship into the harbor after the sun fell, the trio carried their rolled up blankets and canvas bags over their shoulders. Their leather boots slipped in the muck in the dim light of lamps which were hung on posts. Walking past an unconcerned guard who was dressed leather armor of local militia at the gate leaving the dock area, the man just nodded, his eyes following the handsome woman in their midst.

"It appears pretty relaxed around here," Oslaf commented.

"Looks can be deceiving," his father muttered as he grunted. Henther and Oslaf noticed him pushing himself through the pain.

"We should have gotten ossanes. It's too muddy," Oslaf protested, trying to find a less slippery place to walk.

Despite his heavy breathing, Pehnuwick growled at his son. "It's not a long journey. Don't act as I'm nearly at Haligulf just because of a little walk. I'm still strong enough to smack your head."

Henther laughed at the comment, nearly falling into the slimy muck.

"Alright, you too, that's enough." She told them. "Pehnuwick you let your son know when it gets too much. Is that fair enough?" Henther asked, smiling at Pehnuwick who just grunted.

They reached the Citadel gates just as the guards were closing the metal reinforced double doors. They were let in after Pehnuwick informed the guards he had come at the personal request of Ircia. An attendant, apparently roused from sleep, escorted the travelers to the leader of the castle guards. Ircia was waiting in chambers used by the former overlord, Satres.

"It is good of you to see us this late. My hearty greetings from the Esterbluds to your people," Pehnuwick said cheerfully as he immediately put on his diplomatic facade.

"It comes with the rebuilding here. I must tell you that the people of my lands are still mistrustful of the Esterbluds and Aberffraw. Kind words don't mean much with the destruction of our kingdom," Ircia replied steadily. "However, I agree with those who say we should come to a conclusion about my prisoner soon. I have several groups wishing for the man's head."

Pehnuwick nodded as he pulled one of the great chairs close to the fireplace. Oslaf noticed his father positioned his seat close to a small table. "Seems a reasonable idea and I can see your point," Pehnuwick told his host. "Please take so we can discuss what you and your men need. It was a long trip for me, and I'm not as young as I used to be."

Ircia pulled a chair across from Pehnuwick. He called one of his men into the room and sent him away to find them food and drink. Oslaf started to follow the guard out of the room when his father called him over.

"My son has become a co-leader of the Esterbluds with the death of King Penhda," Pehnuwick told Ircia. "He should listen to this discussion since he must agree to whatever terms arise. Our kingdom, like yours, must rebuild. Now is a good time to put our differences on the table."

As Oslaf pulled up a chair next to his father, he waved over for Henther to join him.

"She's my advisor," he told the startled Ircia. Ircia looked at the women, his eyes narrowed. Women were not invited to such important matters. Oslaf pulled a chair next to him for the woman.

"My friend, just remember that the world is changing," Pehnuwick told Ircia who nodded, suddenly feeling outnumbered. The group slowly began the discussion concerning the future of Ynyover, the Citadel and the kingdoms of Kamin.

During the long talks, interrupted by a servant carrying wine and bread, Ircia slowly began to warm up to the people around him. While he remained suspicious, he quickly realized they were forthright in their thinking. In fact, Ircia found much agreement coming from his guests about the concerns and necessities he laid out. Henther remained silent during most of the conversations, occasionally leaning over to whisper to Oslaf on points she believed were important. Oslaf dutifully brought her ideas into the conversation, giving Pehnuwick a chance to tease his son occasionally.

Just as the discussion finally turned to the subject of Lyncus, a guard suddenly rushed into the room. The man nearly tripped over himself attempting to reach Ircia. The Citadel leader's face went white after he heard the whispered message. Jumping to his feet, Ircia sent the guard out of the room and he turned to his guests.

"The underworld has entered the Citadel. Monsters are killing my guards."

~~~

In a cell befitting his status as a valuable prisoner, Lyncus sat on a makeshift, yet comfortable bed in the middle of the room. A small desk was pulled close to the side of the bed, covered with rolls of parchment. As he spent much of his time alone, the son of the late King Asgurd used much of his day, writing messages to his allies in Cahmais seeking relief from his exile. He also sent scrolls to other potential partners in the other kingdoms looking for support. While he suspected that his enemies within the Citadel might change their minds and seek vengeance upon him, the Aberffraw leader decided to play along with the charade of their quest for justice. The man realized that playing for time could only benefit him. He knew the chaos coming from the underworld, and he believed the Cahmais clans would finally understand only a strong leader would save their world. His wife would see to it that Lyncus was acknowledged as the only real choice for Aberffraw people as heir to the throne. Eventually, the Gallaeci would decide his fate was directly tied to their interests. Then, it would be a relatively straightforward matter of assuring the leaders of his lands of his sincere desire to right the wrongs of the kingdom. Pressure from the Cahmais people would ensure his survival.

As the leader of the Aberffraw contemplated his next moves, the familiar sound of a struggle grabbed his attention. Coming from the dark passageway nearby, Lyncus heard a muffled, strangled cry that immediately went silent. He knew the silence meant someone was dead. The man felt his anxiety rising as the shuffling sound of footsteps came closer. Peering through the small opening cut into the thick wooden door, the warrior could see nothing in the dimly lit area around his cell. But the sounds grow stronger, and finally, he saw three dark forms slowly coming toward his cage. Lyncus blinked his eyes several times, telling himself the hideous things walking his way were not there. The man backed away from the door, looking for something in his room to defend himself.

"Your eyes don't deceive you, my dear friend." The guttural voice was hard to understand, but the Ynyover accent seemed familiar. Lyncus heard what sounded like a claw created a slow scratching sound across the wooden door. The man instantly knocked over the desk, stomping on one of the wooden legs as he heard the lock of the door being turned. With a crack, the wood splintered under his boot, and the man grabbed the piece of lumber, ripping it away from the desk. It felt too small and light to defend himself.

"We'll let ourselves in," the dark voice stated as the door swung open. The tall figure entered first. Revealed in the lamplight, the creature's appearance caused Lyncus to instinctively back up against the wall.

The thing in front of the door wore the threadbare scarlet robes of the Sacred Overlord. However, the face was elongated like an ossane, the jaw hanging near the lower chest. The mix of sharp teeth stuck out from the large lips. Two dark black eyes stared from the top of the head. The skin of the creature had a muddy brown look.

"Don't you recognize your lover who has returned from the dead? I'm disappointed." Satres stepped to one side, running his long black claws along the rock wall. The raking sound filled the room as the other creatures joined him. They carried a similar appearance, but each was covered in a dark robe.

"That means you won't recognize these two other spirits of warriors who you hung as you rode through this land. When they overheard my discussion with Kriell, these spirits of the underworld jumped at the chance to join me in the Citadel."

"Wait, are you saying you have joined this Kriell? For what purpose?"

The creature slowly walked closer as one of the other monsters closed the door. "Our aim is revenge. I simply gave our master what he wanted, and he gave me this form to inflict my wrath upon those who wronged me. These jaws to rend flesh and talons so sharp I can slice through leather. Such a beautiful idea, don't you agree?" Satres licked his lips grotesquely.

Lyncus edged away, but one of the other monsters slid along the other wall to cut off any escape. "You mean you want to look this way? Have you gone mad?" The hunted man's eyes were wide with fear.

The beast that once was an overlord gave the man a strange look, tilting his head. "This body has become an instrument to instill the very nightmare you wish to escape."

The creature reached for Lyncus who slammed his wood club on the hand. Satres growled at the pain, pulling his hand back. Then he nodded, and the other monsters jumped on the man. Lyncus tried in vain to pound at the attackers, but they quickly pinned the screaming man to the ground. The monster called Satres grabbed the human by his long hair and painfully pulled him up, slapping him until the screaming stopped. The trio picked Lyncus from the stone floor and forced the man face down on the bed, ripping off his clothes. The monster called Satres laughed as Lyncus began to beg for his life.

"Oh, you will remain alive. After my friends and I are done with the delightfully, painful things I have in store for you, we will take you to the underworld to meet the master. You will be quite alive for the beorhs to use as they please. And you can meet your wife's soul down there. But you'll need to hurry since she won't last very long inside Kriell."

~~~

Pehnuwick carefully entered the dark passageway, holding his sword out while shining the lamplight ahead of them, encumbered by the shield he carried. Behind him, Oslaf and Henther silently followed. So far, the trio failed to find anything. While Ircia sent his men through the many passages and rooms within the upper floors, Pehnuwick led them in a check of the lower areas. He told Ircia that he and Oslaf would ensure Lyncus remained a prisoner. As they turned the corner, they came upon the remains of a Citadel guard. The body was covered in blood, the man's throat ripped out. Slowly, they moved past the remains, staring ahead for signs of movement. Getting close to the end of the tunnel, they heard the echoes of moaning followed by a tormented, hoarse scream that trailed away.

Oslaf closed to the side of his father, sword, and shield at the ready. The two men inched forward, following the sounds coming from behind a closed door. Just when Pehnuwick started to look inside the small opening, the door swung open. Dragging a bloody, half-naked human from the cell, two monsters stepped into the passageway. Screaming the warrior's battle cry, Pehnuwick's sword struck the first beast across the shoulder as the creature turned. Oslaf was right behind, impaling his sword into the face of another monster just as it dropped the body. Hissing like a snake, the dying creature fell. The third monster, dressed in a red robe, jumped at Pehnuwick. The beast sliced into the big man before he was able to defend himself, striking him in the shoulder. With incredible dexterity, the monster called Satres jumped over the wounded man, landing behind him. Just when Oslaf turned around, the underworld beast sliced at Henther, catching her as she was trying to stab at the creature with a spear. The sharp talons ripped deep into the woman's arm as Satres suddenly cackled in delight. Oslaf whipped his sword at the monster was, only to see the creature flip high over them like an acrobat. It landed next to the other wounded underworld creature, and they both attacked Pehnuwick.

The wounded Esterblud slammed his shield into the wounded beast, sending it back while he tried to stab at Satres. The monster was too quick, avoiding the sword and closing in to strike the Esterblud's injured shoulder again. Pehnuwick went to a knee from the attack, blood shooting from the deep wound, the monster called Satres let out a mocking chuckle.

"Fearless warriors, I will kill you slowly." It told them as he raked his claws across the stone for effect. "Cut you into little chunks. Oh yes, I will."

The two monsters attacked Oslaf, heading for the man while he stood next to his father. The younger man's quick reflexes caught the monster in the black robe, impaling his sword deep into the creature's chest. However, Satres found the young warrior's exposed flank, tearing past the chain mail and cutting into the man's side. Falling to the floor, Oslaf struck his head on the stone while he grasped at his wound, trying to staunch the bleeding. Lying on his side, his blurred vision saw the underworld creature attack Henther. The young man struggled to his feet, falling back to the floor.

Backed against the tunnel wall, the woman held the spear in front of her, her arm covered in blood, ready to impale the beast. Satres cackled again and whipped his talons across the spear. The wooden shaft weapon was cut in half, leaving his opponent nearly defenseless.

Just as the monster called Satres was about to jump at her, the creature suddenly paused, its head tilting oddly to one side. Then, Henther saw the sword tip push through the front of the creature's body, spraying black blood. Satres, the former overlord of Ynyover, fell face first to the floor, leaving the severely injured Pehnuwick standing. He slowly lowered the black blood covered sword; his face gray as the stone walls. Henther stepped forward while the older man struggled to remain upright. She reached him just as the man went down to his knees. Bloody and injured as well, Oslaf arrived knelt next to Pehnuwick.

"I'm afraid the mhoda were wrong. I didn't have as much time as they thought." Pehnuwick told Henther, and he closed his eyes forever, letting out a long death gasp.

Oslaf lowered his head, placing his hand on Henther's shoulder, feeling her body shake as she tried to stop her tears. Inside, the son of Pehnuwick silently wept with the woman for a while. He heard the prisoner stirring nearby, and the warrior stood. The man looked at the tortured man unable to recognize Lyncus. The naked prisoner was painfully turning over on the floor as Oslaf struggled to his feet. Long sections of skin around the Aberffraw's face, chest, and buttocks were gone, removed by the sharp claws of the monsters, while they abused and tormented him. The injured man tried to focus on the big man above him, his mind still reeling from the pain.

"I know you. You are the one saved by Urith." The prisoner said through clenched teeth.

Oslaf remained silent, nodding slowly. "Then, you are Lyncus."

The savaged leader of the Aberffraw gave a grunting laugh. "So you don't recognize me. That is almost funny." The prisoner groaned. "Listen, warrior. My time is done. Kill me, Esterblud. Let me seek my vengeance against Kriell and the underworld. By the gods, don't let me die slowly," the man begged, suddenly reaching out to grab Oslaf by the ankle, groaning from the effort. Even the battle-hardened young man felt a pang of sympathy for the dying man. But, he also remembered the man was a monster just like the others lying on the floor.

"Urith let you live, still believing in the Heptarc code. Yet, did you show mercy as you killed Esterblud and Ynyover people? I think you should suffer for your deeds, Lyncus." Oslaf watched the man's eyes widen at the horrible thought of a slow death. The Esterblud started to turn, then, with a quick, deadly sweep of his arm, his sword removed the head of Lyncus, sending it tumbling across the floor. Oslaf turned back to Henther.

"I'll let his spirit suffer as it tries to find the underworld."

~~~

"It's a good thing for you that I've tagged along this trip," Narslac boasted to his friend as he handed Urith a spare hooded cape he carried.

"Yes, you tell me that each day," the warrior responded dryly as he shook off the snow from his long hair before putting the woolen garment over his head. He winked over at Fedelm who rode next to him. Urith

202

couldn't see the woman smiling under the wrap covering her face before her thoughts quickly returned to the past night.

It was two mornings after the group of travelers left Hariwill. The heavy snow continued falling on the group as they got closer to Yns Garraid. The large, cold flakes stuck to the rider's clothes and their mounts, causing both human and ossane to try to shake off the powder on occasion. A gray sky continued to hide the mountains around them, but something within Fedelm still tugged at her, telling her they were close to the last gateway between the three realms. Her visions had also returned. However, the voice of Alrpan was now whispering in her ear at night. The sights she saw scared her, and they reminded her of visions about Awarware, the shallow valley where the Cahmais and Esterblud armies were massacred by the monsters of the underworld. The hakra tried to remain calm when she spoke of the dreams with Urith and the others. Unlike her thoughts of the past, the future showed quick images. But the scenes she remembered revealed terrible beasts, morphed into offensive caricatures of gods. In all the visions, the red blood of innocents filled the cups of the gods to drink. The scenes chilled the woman even more than the unseasonal snowfall. Fedelm watched as Urith slowed his ossane to fall back even with the cart. Joclac was sitting next to his wife who held the reins, goading the reluctant erba forward.

"Are you sensing anything this morning?" The giant warrior asked Joclac.

"At first, I thought it was not good with so much blood in my visions. Yet, I see an alliance coming before us, just like Fedelm is experiencing. The power of the demigods like Spanca and this Ruggla are useful to all of Kamin. I must admit, it's quite confusing to me, but I believe they are in alliance." The seer huddled under a blanket, trying to light his pipe. "Cursed weather," he finally gave up and placed the cold stem in his mouth out of habit.

"How much further?" Urith's tone showed his concern about the dreams of blood. It was never a good sign.

"I believe we will reach this place soon. I suggest letting Brihar know, just in case."

The big man nodded at his friend, looking at Soma briefly before he pushed his ossane hard through the deep snow to reach the other warriors.

"Joclac thinks we're getting close," Urith told Brihar as he rode next to him. "I believe we should get some eyes out ahead of us."

The Gramcan leader lifted his head, looking at the sky briefly. "We can't let any scout get too far ahead, or we might wind up losing someone."

"I agree, but with the threats we face, I think we should risk it. I would rather have someone looking out for any danger before we run into it. I'll push ahead. Just keep an eye on my tracks if I get out of sight. If the Fates remain with us, we should be alright." The Esterblud spurred his ossane on before Brihar agreed.

"Why does he think he leads this journey?" Micaq, the brother of Brihar, fumed under his breath.

"Maybe because he carries that shield," suggested the other brother sarcastically, then Harlor looked at Brihar, "Cursed if I'm following everything he says. You need to let him know that."

Brihar sighed. "I don't like it, either. He's always been that way. Urith is alway first in the fight if something comes."

"That won't do the rest of us any good. Unless Urith can get the shield on that injured arm quick enough, he'll end up dead first." Harlor pointed out.

"Yes, you're right," the Gramcan leader came to a decision. "I'll catch up with him. Just so he doesn't get himself killed first."

Brihar spurred his ossane forward, ordering his brothers to remain with the others and to follow their tracks.

As he rode ahead of the group, Urith welcomed the isolation for the moment. Tired and cold, the man kept pressing on; knowing the turmoil in his mind matched the chaos of Kamin. While he held that his path to destroy the gateway would lead to a stable world and hope for the people, his mind could not stop the questions and concerns which came to him about the future. Urith remembered the tales of the dark years when the Guardians placed demigods as rulers over the population. And the warrior knew from bitter experience how the strong often believed their superiority should extend over everyone. Humanity was awash with people who took advantage of the turmoil to become despotic rulers. Urith wondered if, in the end, whatever he did would really matter. If he survived, there was no assurance that the end of the gods would lead to anything better. He wasn't even sure what would happen to the realms once the gateway was destroyed. When he thought back to the village of Hariwill, it reminded him that, at least, the satgerts and the hakras help guide those unable to help themselves. He continued to ask himself, would that remain? So far, no clear answers came.

"Urith, slow up!" The words from Brihar startled the warrior. The Esterblud turned in his saddle to watch the Gramcan leader pull his mount close.

"Getting bored back there," Urith grunted.

"No, I'm tired of taking orders," Brihar stated to him bluntly. "You and the Skool are needed to destroy this gateway. Not much would remain of Kamin if you get yourself ambushed by the underworld."

The two men went quiet for a while. Finally, Urith sighed. "I suppose it's a bad habit of mine. Never did like hanging back."

Brihar nodded, shaking the snow off his helmet. "I know, and I just wanted to remind you. I should have just told you that my brothers are hanging out with Fedelm again. I figured that might get you back there."

"Is it getting that obvious?" The big man asked.

The Gramcan leader rolled his eyes. "It's been that way for a while now. She fought for you like a black *bater* protecting its young. You could do far worse."

"Agreed, but I'm not sure who'll be around in the future. Anyway, the underworld might just take care of this for me. That's what I told her." Urith stopped his mount as he thought he saw movement in the distance.

"What do you see?" His comrade asked.

"Not sure. I thought I saw a rider over there." The warrior nodded in the direction.

"Well, you're right. I see it as well. Let's find out who comes this way." Brihar spurred his ossane ahead in the deep snow, forcing Urith to catch up. It wasn't long before the pair of riders saw the green woman riding slowly atop her erba. Now covered in fur, leaving only her green face exposed, she wasn't smiling when the men rode up.

"I come get you." The woman told them. Urith noticed she seemed in a bit of a trance as she turned her heavy beast around.

"Entrance is this way." Spanca nestled down inside her furs, remaining quiet as the men glanced at each other. Urith ordered them to stop.

"With this snow, I can't see the others. I'll go back and make sure our tracks haven't been covered over. Wait here until we return." The giant man forced his reluctant ossane to retrace their path.

Soon, he found the small column and waved them toward his position. When they arrived, Micaq and Harlor were now riding on a single ossane.

"Micaq's mount broke its leg stepping in a hole. He had to kill it." Harlor explained.

Urith glanced at the heavy snow still falling. "It's a shame." The Geat fighter nodded. "I wondered if the snow might have covered our tracks. That's why I came back. But we have luck on our side. We found Spanca, and she knows the way to the gateway."

Urith turned around his mount, and Fedelm suddenly offered her mount to Micaq. The warrior glanced at Urith first and quickly accepted. Sliding off the ossane, the blond woman trudged through the snow to Urith.

"Well, give me a hand up. I want to talk with you," Fedelm told the puzzled man. He grinned and offered his hand, making sure he moved the Shield of Skool to the other side of his mount. The woman quickly joined him, trying to find a comfortable place on the leather back of the saddle while he led the column to Brihar and Spanca.

"Alright, what's on your mind?" The warrior asked.

Fedelm snuggled in close to him, whispering in his ear. "Trouble is coming."

The big man gave his sneer smile. "Like I didn't know that," he whispered back.

"No, I'm not joking. Something is very wrong. I was dozing back on the trail, and I had a vision of Dughorm come to me. I can feel him close to us, like a spirit looking down from above. He told me that we would need to reach down deep to survive. That was all he said, but the way he spoke has me worried. I think it's at the gateway."

Urith's face grew somber. He heard the concern in the woman's voice and his experiences with her warnings he now took seriously. But he wasn't sure what he could do about it.

"I believe you," he finally replied. "Joclac said he saw a vision of the demigods but wasn't sure what it meant. How about you?

"No, I've not seen such a thing. But your friend is a more powerful seer," she told him.

Urith shook his head. "I doubt that," he crooned. "But do you have any ideas on how we can avoid this?"

Fedelm remained silent, and her companion realized she didn't have any options. He placed his free hand on hers that were wrapped around his abdomen and gave a quick squeeze. "Well, we've been warned so now we have to be careful, I guess. But that's the way I always handle things," he joked grimly.

Fedelm kept silent, praying to the spirits of her mother and father.

After the column of ossanes and cart had reached spot where Brihar and Spanca waited, the group took a short break before they followed the demigoddess. Progress was slow as the cold blast of the wind and heavy snow took its toll on the animals and riders.

Finally, in the haze of the snowfall, the travelers noticed the dark spot on the mountain coming into view. As they drew closer, each person felt a sense of awe as the great circle loomed ahead. The rock face, covered overhanging snow, gave the dark hole the impression of a giant mouth, ready to swallow them. Narslac half-joked with Urith that he could see why the satgerts were loath to come to this gateway. The Esterblud wasn't paying attention; his focus was on the green woman guiding them. He noticed how Spanca kept looking around while avoiding the eyes of those in the group, even when the two young warriors tried talking with her. The demeanor change emanating from the carefree demigoddess bothered him. He pulled alongside the erba she rode.

"You seem lost in thought," he told Spanca.

She remained quiet for a moment before replying. "The scarred one should worry about his future. Kriell seeks you and Guardian is much stronger than sky gods."

"Funny you say that," Urith leaned over to brush off the pile of snow accumulating on his mount's long neck. "The story I always heard was the Guardians were kicked out into the Great Void. It seems they shouldn't be that powerful."

Spanca went silent for a while. "Maybe you've been tricked by your stories. Vengeance can make one powerful."

Urith nodded. "It can also make one lose sight of important things. I think Mivraa found that out. I've wondered why you haven't spoken of Ruggla. Have you arranged a meeting with him?"

The demigoddess nodded. "My brother demigod knows you come. He doesn't want the gateway destroyed. The man says he has a bargain for you," she said, staring at the giant tunnel in their path.

The warrior grunted, "We'll see if we can convince him. I thank you for arranging this for us." Urith turned his mount when he saw Joclac having trouble with his cart in the deep snow. As they rode away, Fedelm smiled at Spanca from the back of the ossane.

"I'm sure Mivraa would have approved of your help." Neither rider saw the green woman's expression change or the tears which Spanca quickly wiped away while her shaggy mount ambled along.

As the pair rode through the thick, heavy snow to the stuck cart of Joclac and Soma, Fedelm wondered about the dramatic change in the green woman. She was about to mention it to Urith, but the man pulled the ossane to a stop, quickly asking about the wagon.

"This stuff is just too deep for the erbas to pull us through," the seer was bent over, trying to scoop out the packed snow under the cart. He stood up, crossing his arms to put his hands under his armpits. "We're going to have to go on the backs of the erbas now."

Brihar and his brothers soon joined them while Spanca stopped ahead of them, waiting. Soma was already pulling some of the supplies from the wagon, ordering the men on horseback to come closer. Joclac unhooked the two hairy beasts in front of the cart, looking doubtful about riding one of the erbas. Narslac slid down from his ossane to help, suddenly coming up with a story from his vast collection which involved snowfall. There was a collective groan among the men as they quickly took on what supplies they could on their mounts. Leaving the cart behind, the group slowly began the final leg of their journey to Yns Garraid.

Nine cold and snow covered people arrived at the grand entrance to the underworld gateway just before sunset. Ruggla waited inside the large tunnel where the snow and cold could not be felt. The bearded demigod's eyes sparkled when he saw the large Esterblud, quickly noting the Shield of Skool hung on the saddle while a blond woman rode right behind the warrior. Spanca slid herself off the shaggy erba, quickly pushing through the snow to stand next to the bearded man as the others tried to tie off their mounts to the few large boulders not covered with snow.

"Come inside, my friends and warm yourself. We must get acquainted," Ruggla waved them forward with his massive arms. The demigod, still wearing his black tunic and black leather pants, looked very much like the miners of Kamin.

208

"It's a better welcome than I hoped for," Urith told Fedelm as he helped her down from the ossane. He fumbled with the Shield of Skool, but the wet leather attaching the weapon to the saddle had frozen. It was making it difficult to remove, especially with his one arm still not working as usual.

Brihar slid off next to Urith's ossane. "Nothing to worry about, he's only one demigod. Only has the power over the miner's tunnels."

Fedelm told him she wasn't so sure. "Something feels wrong here. But I can't put my finger on it."

Frustrated by the frozen leather, the Esterblud decided to leave the shield on the saddle. He was only a few paces away from the entrance. "Well, let's go find out what his terms might be. I've not found a demigod yet who doesn't have something they want." Urith told them.

Stomping through the white, wet powder, the line of travelers traveled the short distance to the invisible barrier. They stared above at the large round entrance, perfectly cut into the stone. Once inside, they shook the quickly melting snow from their clothing while Ruggla watched them, his pipe smoke filling the air.

"Yns Garraid welcomes the great heroes of Kamin," the demigod's voice came from behind the smoke which covered his face.

"You are a hard man to find," Joclac spoke up. "But your home is quite comfortable in this terrible weather."

Ruggla waved the smoke from his face as he took Spanca by the hand, leading the pair to sit on the edge of a large stone. "I understand you brought this weather when you destroyed the second gateway. Can you imagine what might happen if you damage my home?"

"Spanca must have explained that the gateway has to be closed." Urith suddenly interjected, quickly growing to dislike Ruggla. The demigod's manner reminded the warrior of an evil overlord named Reppir he knew back in Regiussa. "I assume you wish to ally with us. The threat from the underworld is far greater than the value of this gateway."

"Yes, let us come to an agreement," Joclac offered up. "I have seen the visions. The powers of the demigods, which benefit all of us, are coming together here at Yns Garraid.

There was an evil chuckle in the darkness behind Ruggla and Spanca. Immediately the ossanes and erbas outside the circle began to panic, their bellows coming through the barrier of the gateway.

"Of course, you had visions. Visions I wished for you to see." The figure of Caruun emerged from shadows. Behind him was the beorh, Reppir along with the beaked face Actita, the last Vanth.

Immediately, the humans whipped out their weapons. Urith instantly remembering his shield remained hooked to the saddle of his ossane several paces away. He slowly backed away, torn between his immediate urge to attack the three monsters in front of him and the need to retrieve the Skool.

Kriell, in his underworld god disguise, laughed at the armed men and women opposing him. "My heroes walked into my realm carrying their little weapons." The creature began chattering like a beorh, and his foul hordes appeared from the shadows. The monsters started jumping from hidden crevices above the travelers while Kriell and Reppir chattered out instructions to the growing throng.

Before the monsters grabbed him, Urith understood he'd been a fool. He immediately began running through the invisible barrier of the gateway. Rage filled him at his own stupidity for leaving the Shield of Skool behind. Instinctively, Fedelm joined him in his race. The pair ran to the frantic animals while Brihar and his brothers interceded against the overwhelming horde rushing at them.

Brihar sliced through several of the creatures, yelling for his brothers to give Urith some time. His sharp sword hacked into the chest of underworld monster only to have another slice his exposed arm with long claws. The warrior was overwhelmed, falling under the wave beorhs who pummeled him with rocks they carried. The Gramcle leader took two vicious blows to his helmet, falling to the floor as blood poured from his face.

The young brother, Micaq made the mistake of trying to defend Joclac and Soma as Reppir rushed forward. His spear struck the creature, but when Micaq rushed forward with his sword, several of the smaller crubas came from behind Reppir. The razor-jawed fiends focused their attacks on the young fighter who was unprepared to handle them. He struck one of the crubas but another bit into his leg sending him to the ground where two of the creatures quickly disemboweled the screaming man.

Reppir sent beorhs to capture Soma and her husband. With no armor and only their small daggers to defend themselves, the man and woman merely enraged the monsters, forcing Reppir to intervene before his creatures ripped them apart. The underworld fiends pummeled and beat the couple until they lay insensible on the floor, long scratches with blood dripping from their exposed skin.

Brihar's other brother tried to defend the retreating Urith and Fedelm. Quickly, stepping in the way of the monsters moving forward, the warrior fought valiantly and tenaciously against the beorhs. Able to pull his shield from behind his back, the fighter efficiently downed one creature after another until one of the beorhs dropped down on the man from above. The force of the impact sent him and the creature to the rock floor. Tumbling and rolling, the fighter embedded his sword into the monster, sending black blood everywhere. However, a few of the underworld monsters got behind him, striking him down with their handheld stones. Soon, the unconscious warrior was stripped of his armor and dragged over next to his brother.

Outside the entrance, the thick drifts slowed Urith and Fedelm as well as the monsters which poured from the gateway. Unfortunately, the frightened animals reacted to the fast approaching human by pulling against their reins. Just before he reached the terrified ossanes, Urith heard Fedelm yell out as a monster got to her. Glancing back, he saw her turning herself in time to kill a beorhs which knocked her down. Two more of the creatures were on her instantly. The Esterblud swiftly went back to remove the head of one as the woman viciously fought the other, screaming at Urith to retrieve the shield. Narslac joined her, and Urith turned back to his ossane, trying to calm the animal while it slid away from him.

Suddenly, he felt a blow to the back, then another. Whipping around his Clovel Sword, the man cut one beorh in half. Urith heard the animal next to him let out a bellowing scream, and he saw a monster digging its claws into the long neck of the mount. The animal fell into the snow, quickly dying while the warrior slammed his pummel into the head of attacking beorh who just killed his ossane. After he impaled the razor-sharp blade of his sword into the monster, the man angrily tugged at the shield. Urith lifted his arm to strike off the Shield of Skool; suddenly he felt a blow to his black helmet. Another beorh sliced its claws into the extended arm of the giant warrior, causing the man to yell out and the Clovel Sword fell from his hand. Before the Esterblud could turn to face his attackers, two more of the monsters struck him from the side. They forced him down into a drift as more creatures joined to beat the warrior with rocks and fists. Urith waited for the death stroke to enter his body as he   fell   unconscious.

Chapter 10: Blood of Heroes

Kriell, still in the form of Caruun, stood over the inert bodies of the travelers as they lay bound on the stone floor of Yns Garraid. Those who still lived were stripped of their armor and most of their clothes. The monsters quickly found out they were unable to touch the god weapon after two of the beorhs attempted to remove the shield. The Shield of Skool remained attached to the saddle, laying at the feet of the Vanth who carried the seat into the gateway. Actita placed the saddle in before Kriell who held the Clovel Sword by the baudrik belt removed from Urith.

"Mighty Guardian, you have your humans and the Shield of Skool before you as I promised," Ruggla stuffed more of the *xylox* weed into his pipe, smiling to his new master.

Kriell's beak face cocked to one side at the words, his black eye on one side of the head watching the demigod carefully. "Yes, this is nearly correct. The immediate threat is in control before me."

The underworld god chattered quickly with Reppir who nodded slowly. Actita overheard the conversation and immediately eyed the Clovel Sword in his master's hands.

The Guardian turned back to Ruggla who smiling contentedly at his new green companion. Spanca looked at the bound humans, avoiding her partner's gaze.

"My apologies, Master. It appears my new mate still has feelings for some of those at her feet. I believe you referred to them as your toys." Ruggla took a deep puff, trying to ignore the increased chattering among the beorhs while he wondered what Reppir told them.

The guttural voice of Kriell changed as the creature began to transform into the form of Alrpan. "I can feel her reservations at your plans as well."

Several blinks of the eye later, the image of the mistress of the underworld stood before them. Ruggla was stunned by the change, and he felt the atmosphere of the gateway change. The beorhs closed in around the group.

"Ruggla, you're quite right about my thoughts concerning the humans," a seductive voice came from the shapely woman form. Reppir slapped a few of the closest monsters, pointing and chattering to his creatures, sending them to work. The fanged brutes gathered up one bound human each. Most of the travelers were now fully conscious, each person desperately trying to lash out and resist. However, it was of little use. A human skin leather noose wrapped around their necks, bound to their ankles and wrists behind the back. Struggling caused the knot to close around their neck, choking them. The Vanth took the Clovel Sword from his master.

"You wish Skool with the prisoners?" Actita asked. The Guardian nodded absently, watching Urith being picked up. Alrpan immediately ordered the bound prisoners to be taken to the underworld.

"Make sure no harm comes to them. They are mine," Kriell told the underworld demigod who quickly nodded.

"What will you do with these?" Ruggla watched as the monsters picked up their prisoners.

"They will be used to bring forth the Guardians. We will return to a better time." Kriell's seductive woman's voice laughed an evil cackle, giving Spanca chills.

The green demigoddess watched as Fedelm was slowly being carried away, the woman's blue eyes wide. At first, Spanca believed the woman was upset at her betrayal. Then she saw all of the monsters staring at her and Ruggla, their chattering increasing. She took Ruggla by the hand, pulling him back to the invisible barrier to the outside world.

"We go, my partner. The animals take us far," the woman urged.

Confused, Ruggla turned to her. "I see no reason to leave." Then he saw a mass of monsters come between them and the entrance. The demigods were cut off from the outside.

"We have an agreement!" the god of the miners turned back to Kriell, his voice booming.

The female monster turned back and smiled. "I promised to let you live and I will. You are really just a human toy with a few powers. Not worth much more than those I'm sacrificing. I did notice how you and your little nature goddess decided to pair up and betray these humans. Because you might become a threat if you gathered more of your half-human brethren, I decided to change the arrangements."

Ruggla tried to protest, but Kriell held up a hand. "I cannot have any threats from lesser beings. However, Reppir gave me a suggestion which should provide us with a solution to our shared problem." The evil creature with the human form gave the man an evil grin.

Alrpan turned away, pushing through the line of animated underworld beings. "You and Spanca will need to entertain the beorhs for a while. When they are through with you, Reppir will make sure you and Spanca are added to the cave walls like our other guest. There you can live out your days as a toy of my creatures and remain no threat."

Ordering the bound prisoners to the tunnels, Kriell gave a quick chirp. Immediately the elongated faced hordes of monsters descended upon the demigods.

"You see, it's really an entirely logical solution," the Guardian couldn't be heard in the screams and chatter coming from behind.

The humans briefly witnessed the savageness events unfold as they were carried away on the shoulders of their underworld guards. When the beorhs ran at the two demigods, Ruggla attempted to save himself by throwing Spanca in front of him while he tried to escape. He only made it several steps before the other creatures were on him. The sound of cloth ripping and his shrieks could be heard as the chatter of the monsters died down momentarily as each excited creature shoved and struggled into positions to mount and torture their victims. It was a mass of sinewy monsters committing torture and gang rape upon their victims. Ruggla's howls of desperate rage and fear turned to whimpering pleas followed by screams as the man was lost under the swarm of monsters. A few paces away, a mass of bodies revealed only the bottoms of Spanca's talon feet as the thrusting, grunting bodies covered the sound of the woman's screams. Fedelm, remembering her own violations by the creatures, looked down, begging the spirits to help the poor female. Despite their betrayal, the blond girl could not believe Spanca deserved this.

Urith lost sight of the sickening displays when their capturers turned the corner of the darkening cave tunnel. Soon, echoes of more terrible screams followed them along with chilling beorh chatter. The bound prisoners tried to ignore the sounds. However, a burning rage continued to Urith as he locked eyes with the red-eyed Alrpan who joined the walk with them. He remembered the terrible underworld goddess he nearly destroyed at Du-Rinell. It seemed she was now back against him, even more powerful.

"Don't worry about them, human. They are demigods, nearly immortal. You should really thank me. For a while, my beorhs will have your two betrayers for their entertainment instead of your precious humans." The evil creature smiled as the leader of the beorhs came up.

The two monsters spoke their chatter language briefly. Kriell saw the puzzlement on the human's face at the exchange.

"Reppir believes the demigods will soon wish they weren't nearly immortal. I must agree with him." I'm not sure what I'll do with the other demigods. They have little us in my new world, so we'll probably let the *kronog* hunt down those who remain on Kamin."

Urith, recognizing the name of Reppir, suddenly cursed, calling the beorh leader the docke of Kriell. The enraged monster forced the guard to stop, then reached out with its claws and slowly ripped away a long piece of skin from Urith's upper arm. The warrior struggled, trying to twist and turn before finally letting out a howl of pain at the open, bleeding wound.

Kriell pulled Reppir way, sternly reminding the creature not to injure Urith further. The beorh chattered and pointed to Soma. The Alrpan's image turned to the human. "You wretched creatures forget you are quite vulnerable to pain. Knowing that I still need you Esterblud warrior, Reppir suggested I give him that woman you call Soma. It's unusual, but he remembers you and this woman he calls Chickle. He says you did him a great injustice in the past."

The beorhs took a couple of steps, grabbing the woman by her auburn hair and yanking her head back forcefully. Soma cried out, then went silent, her eyes showing her hate of Reppir.

Kriell cocked his head. "It's funny; nearly all of the beorhs have no memories. You must have made an impression." The savage god gave a thin smile. "Be happy, you're a human and will die when he's through. Then, your soul can serve my needs."

Urith couldn't see the woman from his position, but he cursed at Reppir again. He was responsible for Soma leaving her slavery. It was the Esterblud who gave the young woman the chance to change her life.

As the line of monsters continued carrying their prisoners deeper into the underworld, the group went quiet, leaving only the sound of dripping water and stomping of the beorhs feet to be heard.

"So what's your goal, you cursed one?" Narslac's voice suddenly echoed from the shadows ahead of Urith. "You strive to fill Kamin with monsters? Only a fool would destroy humanity to fill the lands with mindless creatures like these."

Alrpan's soulless eyes brightened. "Yes, the Skald who got away from my creatures. When your blood is drained from the body, I'll make sure your spirit is put into a very silent monster."

"Bold talk from a god who cannot see the light in front of him," Narslac replied.

Kriell's smile wavered slightly, but the figure of Alrpan walked faster to catch the one-armed man slung over a beorh. "Enlighten me you miserable one. Or should I enter your feeble mind?"

"The answer is quite simple enough. You need balance. The Guardians required it just as the people on Kamin. Heptarc realized this when he cast you out. Once all of the humanity is gone, what of your world then? How long while you immortals last without us?" Narslac told him confidently. The rest of the bound humans listened as they wondered what the Skald was driving at.

"Just like before. When the Guardians return, your species will be used as needed, of course." Kriell stated, growling now. "You're wasting my time."

"Really? Have you forgotten the Sky Realm is gone? Look outside; the world will soon be frozen over. Did you get Duwdamon's powers over the sky? Of course not, Urith destroyed him. And the power over the lands, it's gone as well." Narslac began laughing. "Some god you are." Kriell chattered instructions for the group to stop their journey into the caves.

"With the food gone from a frozen world, soon the only thing left will be the spirits. Not a balance and no one left to serve you," the Skald quickly continued as he saw Kriell's female face growing angry. "Your Guardian friends will surely want to come back for that. You were so focused on revenge; you're bringing Kamin down upon you. You'll be left with a ball of snow and mindless creatures to rule over."

Narslac took several smacks from one of the monsters carrying Fedelm, its claws leaving four deep wounds on the man's face. Wounded and stunned, the Skald lifted his head to spit at the creature. But he remained quiet as the group of fiends continued their journey deeper into the dark tunnels.

The followers of Urith arrived outside the altar room where Kriell attempted many human sacrifices to open the Great Void. Rotting bodies still filled either side of the large tunnel, overwhelming the people from the stench. The beorhs threw their prisoners to the tunnel floor at Kriell's command. A soft green glow from the walls illuminated the dead and the living.

As punishment for Narslac's talk, a beorh ran his claws down the bound man's back. Narslac cried out from the pain, causing two Clovels to come into the light at the entrance to the room. Their white fur showed the dark stains of blood from their rampages into the lands of Kamin. The hairy beasts sniffed the air with their long snouts, coal black eyes staring at their prey. Their canine teeth exposed, hoping for a chance to attack and devour those living creatures on the rock floor.

"A god who can't take the truth," Joclac suddenly spoke up, twisting his body to face the woman's standing over him. "I've seen your attempts at learning the future, Kriell. You ingested Greach to gain foresight. I'll bet koinons your attempts failed. Have you noticed you're not in the future?"

The underworld god, unused to such dissension, reacted violently. Alrpan's form kicked the man in his stomach. Then, the god turned away. The words were getting to the Guardian. Suddenly, it stopped, and the legs of Alrpan gave way to black tentacles which quickly wrapped around Joclac.

"You're correct, seer. It's just you who forgot something. I know who you are. We'll see how much I can learn from you."

Slowly, the suckers drug the struggling man to transformed lower half of Alrpan's form. The black globular body started moving across Joclac, the tentacles helping to pull the prophet through the slimy skin and inside the Guardian. Soma screamed, struggling to reach her husband. However, the woman's leather binds dug into her, and she could only watch helplessly as Joclac twisted and turned. Urith made a last desperate attempt to help his friend, rolling over closer where he was savagely kicked by Reppir. The leader of the beorhs dragged Soma next to the black entity, lifting her by her hair to witness the event. With the seer fully inside the spirit stealer, the horrified people watched as the victim finally quite moving while his skin disappeared. A red skeleton of her husband looked out with sightless eyes as Soma's pitiful wails filled the ears of the remaining humans. Fedelm stared at the black body, realizing she saw the spirit faces of Alrpan and Caruun among the others inside the horrible creature. Hope fell away and she began crying as well.

~~~

Many leagues to the north of Yns Garraid, a quiet and somber group of people stood in the freezing cold as the heavy snow flakes covered their woolen hoods. It was the morning after the monster's attack and the clouds hung low over the land. Outside the citadel, near the harbor, the crowd watched the flames rising from a makeshift funeral pyre where the body of Pehnuwick and those of the Ynyover guards lay. The small procession of people now included some of those needed to restore Kamin. Imenal, sent by the king of Eernicia, arrived by ship in with the early morning tide. He and Flacanus stood next to Oslaf, the young warrior paying no attention to the men. As a new leader of his tribe and half ruler of Esterblud, he felt lost, his brain in turmoil. He barely listened when Henther whispered in his ear at the arrival of Imenal.

Atheern, the Gallaeci heathmead trader, watched from the other side of the rising flames. The bearded man slowly walked next to Ircia, whispered reminding the leader of the Citadel about the ship from Cahmais which arrived after Imenal's vessel. Atheern glanced at the head of Aberffraw tribe, Berta, who waited nearby with some of his men. Informally becoming the intermediary between the Aberffraw and the Gallaeci tribes, the heathmead trader asked why the body of Lyncus was not on the funeral pyre.

"Lyncus was the reason for the attack on the fortress, and he died begging for mercy," Ircia refused to look at Berta as he nearly growled at Atheern. "He can have the body to do what he wants with it. It rests at the entrance with the bodies of the monsters. I lost enough men looking after that *calward*."

The large merchant slowly backed away, quickly realizing it would take more than his stocks of heathmead and fine wine to calm the resentments among the gathering leaders. He waved for Berta and his Aberffraw men to follow him, leading them up the hill to the fortress.

Later that day, the leaders slowly gathered in the Great Hall of the Citadel. The large rectangular table in the middle of the room had long benches on either side and the people entering took their seats close to allies and friends. Ircia directed the few men he had left to strategic positions at the corners of the hall, leaving only a couple of his most trusted men to patrol the towers after closing the massive gates to the fort. The leader of the guards had the foresight to bring in a few villagers to act as cooks and servants.

While preparations were being arranged for the people gathering, Oslaf stood in the snow at the top of a battlement. He was looking out at the dark clouds which covered the range of high mountains regularly seen from the vantage point. Henther stood quietly next to him, but her impatience grew from his silence and her cold feet. The man hadn't spoken since retreating to the isolated spot.

"What are you thinking?" Her voice surprised a nearby *vensar* who quickly flew away. After waiting for a while, the woman finally slapped his hood, knocking wet snow into his face.

"Curses, can't a person be left alone around here?" he wiped his face, suddenly realizing his hands hurt from the chill.

"Fine, when you grow up, come see me." Henther started to stomp away.

"Wait!" he turned to her. "That's not what I meant." He watched her come to a stop, still refusing to look at him.

"I'm not sure what I should be doing," he sighed. "It's easier when you know the enemy coming after you and you have a weapon in your hand. Curse the gods, I wish I was with Urith."

The blond woman turned back to him. "I don't think that's the problem. I think for the first time, you're afraid." Her words hurt him even though he knew she wasn't trying to belittle him. Henther walked toward him, her eyes glistened. "I'm going to tell you the truth. Can you handle it?"

Oslaf gave her a nod, his stomach knotting up.

"You are more like Urith than you think. For some strange reason, neither of you really fear death or the gods like the rest of us. Maybe it's your pride or training, or both. I don't know. But I understand you better than you think." She stopped, looking at his expression. "Do you agree with me?"

"Maybe," he replied slowly. He recognized some of the traits of his uncle. They had to have rubbed off after so much time together.

"There are a few things I know well, and one of them is to understand what is inside a person," Henther continued. "You and Urith are afraid of only one thing. It's something which changes your conceptions of the world. Neither of you can handle chaos because you seek order." She held out her hand which quickly covered with the falling snowflakes.

"It is not the chaos of fighting which I'm talking about. It's the turmoil of a different Kamin. You see it coming before you. The realms of Kamin are falling apart. It is something you cannot control this with your weapons or fighting skill. Oslaf, you need allies, and that means you must step forward to meet with others you don't know or even like. I believe you fear the work you know is needed, so the fighter inside wants to fall back to something familiar. But for us to survive, you need be like your father."

Oslaf looked at the beautiful woman who reached down inside of him and pulled out his secret for him to understand. He decided, he would never allow her to leave his side. The young fighter stepped forward and pulled her close to him, pulling back his hood again. Ignoring the cold drips of water that ran down the back of his next, he gave her a long kiss.

"Ok, I'll grow up." He told her when he pulled back. "Now, since you're my advisor, what's next?"

Henther smiled, giving him a kiss back, and then pulled his hood back over his head, "Remember you are the son of Pehnuwick and act as he would. Once you have the plan and gain the backing of your allies, then act like Urith and fight to the bitter end."

Oslaf and Henther were the last to enter the Great Hall within the Citadel of Br-Ynys. The nobles and emissaries representing most of the kingdoms around the Maflow Sea found their way to the table, and the noise was already deafening. Oslaf immediately went to Imenal, steering the badly limping man to a corner of the room for a quick conversation. Maimed by the gods, the satgert was an ally that Oslaf wanted to help guide them through the future discussions.

"Have you heard anything of my uncle?" The Esterblud asked.

Imenal gave him a nod. "Yes, my friend. He and the others must be very near Yns Garraid. I have received the news they went through the village of Hariwill, leaving word they were going to destroy the gateway. The priestess was shocked and sent word out to all the temples. She's also saying that the twisted *lellowtere* trees must be destroyed throughout the world."

"I can understand that. Those trees are where Mivraa used to move between the realms. What are your thoughts?" Oslaf glanced around to make sure they weren't overheard.

The satgert's face fell. "We will know soon enough. There is snow falling in the height of our hottest season, storms are destroying ships. If nothing changes soon, we will perish without any intervention by Kriell and his underworld creatures.

"Then, I believe we must start now to find ways to survive. I think we do that tonight." Oslaf told him.

Imenal remained cautious. "Some of those we need have not come. Some tribes may not realize Satres is gone yet. The turmoil has spread to other cities and villages. We cannot be sure who is in control. I just received word that Vulthnal is in a state of civil war, but their king sits inside of the temple. If what I heard is correct, King Barcal is praying to a god who no longer exists."

Oslaf nodded in agreement, remembering the young king during his time in Vulthnal. "Barcal relies on satgert who is corrupt. Both will find the land pulled from under them if they don't realize the trouble soon enough. What about King Merkhan? Your king was friendly with Penhda and our people for many seasons."

"I spoke with the king before I left for this place. He will follow my guidance." Imenal decided to give Oslaf something which weighed upon him since before he left the temples in Eernicia.

"But I must warn you about something I've seen. Dughorm came to me in a vision. He is warning that if Urith fails, Kamin will be destroyed."

Visibly worried, Oslaf put his hand on the man's shoulder. "Has he told you that he would fail?"

"No, but it is a warning, nevertheless. I believe we must find a way to help stop this Kriell, even if it means destroying any temple which might give him power." The Eernician leader appeared to carry the weight of the world for the moment with his thought. Oslaf realized what the man was saying. To destroy all references to the gods might be necessary. The young warrior could picture it in his mind. Wiping out all temples and structures to the gods, old and new, would be heresy. It would send many of the lands into further chaos and unrest.

"I hope we don't have to do this," Oslaf told the troubled man. "But, we must proceed like my uncle will fail. We must find allies that think like we do. We must gather any demigod to join with us, using their powers to stop what may come. However, I suggest we leave talk of such destruction until we have no choice. If it comes to that, we must have a steel spine to complete such work. Chaos or not, many will oppose such an idea."

The Esterblud warrior stopped, realizing he would be putting himself in such a role. It was something he learned from Urith.

He gave the satgert a thin smile. "Perhaps the Fates can still help us to overcome Kriell without such thoughts. Even better, we might get word of Urith's return. What do you think?"

Imenal gave the young warrior a contemplating look. "It is a difficult idea for you to believe Urith should fail. Because of the vision, I think we must take the path you are choosing. I will support your idea of a steel spine if necessary, which means Eernicia will do so. Merkhan is old, and his heirs are dead."

The lame man turned his friend back to the banquet table where servants sit down food and drinks. "Now let's get some of the more tenacious people I see at this table to agree as well."

~~~

When Kriell finished with Joclac, the god was fully transformed into its black globular form. It used its tentacles to slowly move to the entrance of the altar room while the monsters waited for their instructions. Urith watched as the god of the underworld passed through the small entryway with Actita close behind, carrying the saddle with the Shield of Skool. Reppir dropped Soma, following his master into the room. The weeping woman quickly curled into a fetal position, uncaring of her impending fate.

Urith noticed something move by the cave wall. Camouflaged by the dark shadows, he finally made out the outlines of a green skeletal creature whose spindly arms and legs were embedded into the rock. When the head lifted, he recognized Unis. The former goddess of the Sky Realm still retained the beautiful face which adorned many of the temples of Kamin. However, the eyes of the goddess instantly showed her insanity. The creature cackled one moment then began to sing an incoherent song before stopping to scream when a beorh came near her. The creature paid the goddess no attention and Unis went quiet, her head dropping. Whatever the monsters of the underworld did to the goddess, it was evident she was beyond any help.

Urith hated the goddess for her mind control and attempting to have the great warrior kill Fedelm. However, his vengeance fell away as he watched the creature. Instead, his rage began to rise. While knew he was

223

powerless, the warrior decided he would die with a fury built into his soul. Someway, somehow, he pleaded to whatever spirits remained to give him a chance, let him punish a spiritless fiend who believed it was a god. Urith remembered his past heartaches, knowing nearly each of them was caused by some entity whose only goal was to crush a person's soul, to make them toys for the gods. These were monsters, not gods. For humans to bow and pray to such things was the highest sacrilege in his mind. Such creatures must be destroyed, crushed by the very things they wanted to rule over. Then, the man heard a whisper in his ear. It was nearly unheard, but he felt it like a soft kiss from his wife.

"Be ready and have no mercy."

Suddenly the screeching laugh of Unis started again. "Spirits around me, betray someone else now. Yes, I see you." The insane woman began to hum an Esterblud war chant.

Fedelm was looking through the entrance into the altar room. From her angle, she noticed the Vanth suddenly stiffen. Actita began staring at the Shield of Skool attached to the saddle while sliding its long fingers along the baudrik strap holding the Clovel Sword on its shoulder. The creature glanced at Reppir who prepared the altar for the next sacrifice, absently nodding.

Next to the black table, Kriell transformed into a new human-like figure. Combining all of the poor spirits inside of the Guardian, the underworld god appeared now as an amalgamation of beast and human. The head of Uugor was perched on the tall female upper body of Alrpan and held up by muscular bird-like legs of Caruun. The long blond hair hermaphrodite creature walked into the tunnel, grabbing Urith by his leg and dragging the naked prisoner across rock floor. The Guardian chattered his orders to three of the beorhs who quickly followed their master by pulling the remaining humans into the room.

Inside, the prisoners saw the large mural on the wall, the tentacle Guardian image overlooking the black stone. Forced to their feet after a beorh cut the leather noose from around their necks, Narslac and Soma watched while Urith was forced on the altar by a Clovel while Kriell went to stand in front of the mural.

Struggling like a hooked worm, the Esterblud moved around the cold stone slab until Reppir slammed his hand into the man's abdomen several times. Gasping for air, the man could only get out a curse. Fedelm pulled to her feet by a beorh, tried to intervene. However, Kriell slapped her down, and then the monster wrenched her back to a standing position using her hair. Fedelm's yell was cut off as the underworld fiend grabbed her by the throat.

"You will watch the death of this weak man you follow." The Guardian forced her over next to the Vanth who held her. Kriell went back to the slab where Reppir gave his master the sacrificial cup.

"Once this human hero is sacrificed, my friends from the Great Void will return. No doubt, they will have some unusual ideas for what they will do with the rest of you." He turned to his victim on the slab.

"For this sacrifice, I will use your famous sword." Kriell's now handsome face smiled evilly when he saw Urith's surprise. "Oh, yes, your exploits are known from the memories of Alrpan and Caruun. You've always fought those who rule you. Now, Actita will give me this Clovel Sword, and I will use it to remove Urith's head. Your skull I will mount as a trophy upon my throne."

"May my vengeance come at you from a thousand directions," Urith spit out, suddenly struggling against the leather noose digging into his neck as the Clovel pushed down on the man's chest. Awkwardly pinned down on his back while his ankles remained tied to his wrists, his face turned blue.

Shaking his head, Kriell laughed. "I'll give you credit for stubbornness. Well, I'll have to cut your head off slowly so I can enjoy your death."

"Actita, bring me the sword," the god ordered.

The Vanth hesitated, listening to another voice at the moment. The blue orb of a spirit hovered near the creature when Actita entered the room dragging the saddle. At first, the underworld creature could not believe a spirit could remain unseen. Slowly, the creature started listening to the calm, soothing whisper which kept reminding the demigod of what happened to the other half-humans earlier. Unconsciously, the demigod slowly wrapped his hand with the leather made of human skin. It would protect him from the human sword.

"The Clovel Sword will protect you," Dughorm's voice grew more forceful. "Do you want the power of Skool to defend yourself? Sword in one hand, shield in the other, it's your only defense."

"Actita!" Kriell's voice rose above the soothing voice in the creature's head. "Bring me that Clovel Sword now!"

225

The Vanth cocked its bird-like face, one eye staring at the Guardian. The demigod now understood something Caruun and Alrpan missed. To be powerful, a god must control the weapons along with their human victims. Slowly, the Vanth pulled the Clovel Sword from the scabbard.

"No!" Fedelm cried out as the Vanth stepped closer to his master with the engraved blade gleaming in the green glow of the room.

Soma began sobbing again as Reppir placed the bowl under the hole where the blood of Urith would drip. The beorh leader went to the crying human, roughly lifting her head to witness the final moments. The evil soul within the monster was impatiently waiting to inflict all the torturous desires it could think of upon the former slave who outsmarted him in life.

So focused upon vengeance against the auburn hair woman, the leader didn't notice the beorhs behind Narslac edge past the prisoner to witness the sacrifice. The man slowly twisted and pulled on his cutoff arm. The leather painfully moved down past his elbow, quickly falling away and loosening its grip around the wrist of his good arm.

The Vanth held out the Clovel Sword to Kriell, neither creature noticed the bloodstone amulet around Urith's neck suddenly change color. Growing a brilliant white, the heat started to sear through the human leather. Immediately, the pommel of the Clovel Sword turned bright white under the leather bound hand of the Vanth. However, Attica continued to listen to the instructions coming from the whispering.

"You do to me like others," the creature's anger grew as it faced Kriell. Lunging forward, Actita embedded the sword into Kriell's middle. Howling in pain and rage, the underworld god backed away.

Reppir jumped at the Vanth, landing hard on the demigod. They struggled over the Clovel Sword, pushing hard against the black slab. Kriell backed away to the wall, his borrowed face showing the shock of the wound from the mighty sword. The god's body began transforming back to its black blob form.

The human sacrifice lying on the table felt his skin burning, smelling the charred flesh of the leather as the necklace burned him. He yelled out in pain. Beside him, distracted by the beorh and the demigod struggling for the sword, the Clovel released its grip on Urith to watch the fight. Suddenly, the noose broke free from around Urith's neck, and he felt his legs suddenly give. The man rolled over away from the Clovel, falling to the floor next to Reppir. The Vanth seized the opportunity to push the beorh over the Esterblud, tripping the monster back into Kriell.

Narslac, finally free of his bonds, slammed into the beorh next to him, forcing the creature toward at the Vanth. Instantly reacting, Actita swung the Clovel Sword into the monster, killing it as Narslac fell to the floor. Using his free hand to tug at the knot holding Urith's wrists, the Skald worked to release the man.

During turmoil around the altar, Soma, still bound by her hands, jump over the back of Reppir who was down on the floor. Trying to keep the beorh leader penned on the floor while Fedelm fell on top of the small pile to help the woman.

Freed of his fight, Actita quickly went to the Shield of Skool. Convinced of his power over the god weapon he carried the Clovel Sword in his hand, the Vanth reached down. When the demigod touched the Skool, he was motionless for a moment. Suddenly, the creature trembled and jerked before the electricity blasted Actita upward into the rock ceiling. The demigod slammed back into the floor, the Clovel Sword sliding noisily across the rough rock until it nearly brushed Narslac's leg. Actita trembled for a moment on the floor nearby the Skald, then quit moving.

The one-armed man finally untied the knot still holding Urith's wrists when the white-hair monster attacked. Bounding over the black slab on the orders of Kriell, the Clovel came down on top of the two men. The force of the beast landing allowed the Esterblud warrior to break loose and he quickly rolled away. Narslac was not as fortunate, the creature's claws dug into the man's upper body. Lifting the Skald up, the monster opened its massive jaws to rip into Narslac while the man cried out. Suddenly, the Clovel staggered, appearing off-balance. Then, black blood shot out of the monster's mouth, splattering his intended victim. Then, the nearly impervious monster pitched forward, dying as it hit the ground. Behind the creature, Urith stood with bloody sword in his hand.

Reppir finally flung off Soma, his claws ripping into the woman's back as she tumbled away. The leader of the beorhs chattering whails brought in two beorhs. The Esterblud whipped around with his sword, slicing the first monster across the chest. Instantly, Reppir attacked while Urith was trying to fend off the other creatures.

Fedelm shouted a warning and tripped Reppir with her bound feet. The beorh leader slipped down on the blood covered floor, giving Urith a chance to finish off the other monster, embedding his weapon through its body. The blond woman slid closer to help with Soma when she felt the tentacles of Kriell. She looked down, watching as the fiend began to pull the severely injured Soma inside the black body. Fedelm shrieked with fear as the creature from the Great Void used its tentacles to envelop the hakra's legs.

The Esterblud fighter had no time to defend himself, turning just when Reppir struck. Urith barely avoided the agile beorh's steel-like claws coming at his abdomen. Reppir's momentum continued forward, causing Urith to stumble over a dead beorh. Both human and monster grappled, trying to gain the upper hand on the bloody floor. The monster was stronger, but Urith used the slickness of the gore around him to keep the claws and teeth from impaling him, although he was sliced by some of the creature's claws. However, the man was unable to bring his sword against the creature. Finally, Reppir penned down the human, his claws digging deep into the warrior's massive arms.

The monster chattered a series of unintelligible clicks triumphantly.

Desperately looked around while the agony forced him to cry out, Urith saw his only chance. The man turned back to the beorh leader and spit in the creature's face. Enraged, the monster opened its elongated jaws, lifting its head to bite. When Urith felt the slight elevation of the monster off of him, he instantly rolled and lifted his body to one side. Reppir fell away, his head glancing off the Shield of Skool. When Urith slipped away, the electric shock ran through the monster momentarily, stunning Reppir. The underworld leader climbed to his feet as Urith found the Clovel Sword.

Sword in hand, Urith scrambled to his feet and gave no quarter. His first strike went into the monster's shoulder. A loud, wretched howl came from the beorh leader. However, the sound quickly stopped when the human warrior swung back around, sending the monster's head tumbling out of the room and into the tunnel.

While the Esterblud was in a fight for his life, Fedelm fought and kicked against the god trying to ingest her. While doing so, she shouted at the injured Narslac for help. Slowly the man turned over, his body and face covered in his blood. The one-armed man began to crawl at Kriell. The Guardian developed the face of Caruun upon his black body. The creature's beady eyes watched approvingly at the bloody fight between Urith and the beorh.

"Come to me human, so I may consume you was well." The thick guttural voice mocked Narslac as the man got to his knees. "You have nothing to injure me."

The voice caused Fedelm to stop fighting. Her mind reeled, trying to remember despite the fear she felt. The voice of her father came to her like a quiet passing breeze. She felt the warmth on her breast.

The Helios stone from Imenal!

Still haning around her neck, the hakra thanked her father as she remembered the words.

"*Teinidh cadhla*," the woman shouted as her legs grew numb, starting to be consumed.

Instantly the amulet became bright. Kriell's beaked mouth opened, letting loose a long shriek which caused the humans to cover their ears. Fedelm kicked and squirmed away from the retreating Kriell. Narslac crawled across the floor, quickly unbinding the blond woman before going to Soma. Fedelm tried to stand but her legs wouldn't cooperate, and she was forced to hang on to the black slab. She stared in horror as Kriell transformed into the hermaphrodite monster again. The Guardian god came toward her from around the slab. Narslac did not see what was happening as he rolled Soma over, trying to untie her wrists.

"Your amulet surprised me before, but it will not stop me now." The god slowly stepped around the sacrificial slab, smiling after glancing at Reppir who was on top of Urith. The Guardian turned its back on the fight, intent on forcing Fedelm back into the corner with the other humans.

"I will kill you slowly," Kriell told her, and the woman forced her unwilling legs to stand. Then, she saw the end of the beorh behind Kriell, and she smiled as Urith turned around.

"I think you better worry about yourself," the woman told the god.

Realizing his danger, the underworld deity suddenly looked around while a noise came from behind it. The Clovel Sword found its mark, impaling the Guarding in the chest. Kriell fell back, and Fedelm moved aside, letting the monster fall to the floor. Urith was already lifting the Shield of Skool, inserting his maimed arm.

"Finish that thing," the woman ordered him.

"I intend to." The Esterblud walked past her.

Kriell's black body returned, sliding quickly along the floor like an ancient sea monster. Its tentacles found the back wall where the mural of the Guardians watched over the room. The god of the underworld used the suckers of its limbs to climb the wall while the face of Alrpan appeared in the globular body, next to the still embedded sword.

"Foolish mortal, you made a poor decision. You forgot you cannot destroy me with your pitiful sword. The Skool without the sword is just a toy to me. I'm already gaining strength from the power within this weapon, enough to bring you to your knees." The voice of the hated goddess declared.

The scarred face warrior continued closing the distance to the godlike monster. He felt the stone of the amulet warming on his skin with each step, and he told Narslac to get Soma away. Seeing the look on Urith's face, the Skald scrambled to his feet, partially carrying and dragging the injured lady away.

Kriell suddenly tried using Alrpan's power of illusion, causing Urith's body to become wrapped in a searing fire. Steeling himself, the man kept moving.

"I've seen it before," he shouted as the pain intensified. Just a few paces away, Urith suddenly lunged forward, running full speed at the god. Shield of Skool in front, the Esterblud warrior slammed the weapon and himself into the monster on the wall.

Fedelm watched as the giant fighter held the Skool against the black form of the Guardian, electricity surging out of the weapon. The underworld god appeared to be gathering strength from the charge, causing the woman to suddenly doubt they could defeat Kriell. The Guardian's body grew larger, and the spirit's faces inside the fiend could be seen through the slimy skin. Urith lifted his free hand, grabbing the Clovel Sword.

"*Da Umca Mivwar*, you pitshog," the man growled.

The blast from the shield in the small room expanded into a massive shock wave that sent Urith flying across the top of the black slab. He landed next to the dead body of Reppir, near the entrance to the room. Fedelm was knocked over by the explosion, falling by the dead Vanth.

As the woman gathered herself, Fedelm glanced at the rock wall which now had an open hole where Kriell once stood. Evaporated by the blast, only black pieces of the creature remained, hanging on the edges of the dark hole in the wall. Nearly incoherent, Fedelm struggled over to the Esterblud, pulling the giant warrior over on his back. Then, she saw the blood. Coming from his nose and ears, the red rivulets crisscrossed the man's scarred face and closed eyes as his head lolled to one side.

She shook her head.

"You can't be dead!" her mind screamed.

Suddenly, Urith's eye flickered open. At first, he just gawked, breathing deeply and believing himself in the afterlife. Almost as soon as the warrior realized he wasn't a spirit, the stone floor shuddered beneath him.

A rolling sound like distant thunder echoed deep below the altar room, growing stronger with coming wave. Somewhere inside Urith's brain, he thought he should get away, but his body would not respond.

"On your feet!" Fedelm yelled into his ear grabbing his hand which still held the Clovel Sword. She pulled at him, her small size unable to move his heavy frame. "Curse the gods, get on your feet you *calward*!" the woman leaned over and slapped his face. She glanced at Narslac carrying Soma ahead of them into the tunnel.

The slap and curse finally started to pull the man from his daze. As she held onto his forearm, he painfully struggled to his feet, staggering around like a drunken man. Fedelm barely recognized his face, bruised and battered from the beatings and the blast. Avoiding the shield still hanging on his injured arm, she pulled herself under his right shoulder. Together, the pair stumbled out of the altar room as the grinding and shaking grew worse. When they reached the entrance to the glowing green tunnel, which took them back to the surface, the ceiling above them shattered, sending down rock and dust. Ahead of them, a massive boulder fell, cutting them off from their friends.

Narslac, still half carrying Soma, heard the grinding rumble coming from behind him and he turned just in time to see the cave in. The ground shook again, and the Skald turned back toward the surface, half pulling the woman along as he desperately tried to retrace their path to the gateway. The man kept the distraught and injured woman struggling forward, yelling and begging her to keep moving. As the pair went through the dust filled tunnel, they passed by beorhs and other monsters. The underworld creature's primitive instincts to survive sent the monsters into a panic. They ran past the humans, once knocking the pair to the ground, as the beast desperately tried to find places of shelter from the moving and falling rocks around them.

Finally making it to the entrance to Yns Garraid, the injured humans slowed when they saw many of the panicked beorhs near the invisible gateway. However, the monsters appeared more concerned with their own safety as large rocks fell from the top of the opening, sending them into nearby crevices to be crushed. Other creatures ran into the snow outside. Narslac stumbled upon the small mound of clothes and weapons, stripped from them earlier. He led the woman over where they quickly threw blankets over shoulders. Narslac slung a shield through his half arm and took a sword. He carefully turned to Soma, trying to keep from reopening his wounds. Her blank stare remained after another round of ground tremors stopped.

"Listen to me. Urith told me you are strong. We can stay here and die or try to survive outside." He tenderly turned her head to show her the direction. "Now you and I are going to be tough and survive. We are going that way, and I'm going to take out whatever stands in our way. You think of your children and getting back to them. I need you to do that." He smiled as she slowly nodded.

"Good girl," he said and immediately stood her up. "Let's go."

The pair followed along the wall as another round of quakes struck, this time even stronger. Trying to avoid the monsters while dodging the falling rocks, they came upon Ruggla. Only the demigod's exposed legs, along with the legs of two beorhs remained visible after a large boulder fell on them. Narslac led Soma around the rock mound, stepping on the clay pipe of their betrayer. Near the entrance to the snow, a terrible sound came from the tunnels as the ground above and below tried to press together. Instantly, the pair ran into the invisible barrier area. Several beorhs noticed them and immediately attacked.

Narslac turned to face the first monster, dispatching the beast with a sword thrust to the belly. As the other monster jumped at him, the Skald took it down with a swing of his wood and iron shield. Narslac heard the sound of a sword behind him and turned just in time to see Soma swing again into a third monster. Surprised at seeing the woman holding the heavy weapon, Narslac could only watch as the beorh fell to the cave floor. The woman continued to strike at the dying monster, black blood splattering her with each stroke. It took all of the man's strength to pull her away from the dead creature as the last beorh near the entrance attacked him.

While Narslac fought the monster, Soma entered the deep snow with bare feet and just a woolen blanket covering her body. She was following another beorh ahead of her. Oblivious to her cold feet and aching injuries, the woman's sole focus was the monster. Grimly smiling at the beorh's struggle in the deep snow, she took a straight line, moving to cut off the creature. The monster was oblivious to the woman behind it. Instead, the beast's eyes focused on the prey it followed, a figure with green skin.

After killing the monster that attacked him, Narslac followed Soma. He was surprised at the woman's sudden burst of energy until he realized she followed a monster. He struggled to catch her. His injuries and loss of blood drained him as the adrenalin of their escape began to wear off. His legs and feet quickly carried the bitter cold up to him. As he tried to maintain the pace, he cursed under his breath that they had no time to put on boots and trousers.

Narslac wanted to call out to the woman, but he didn't dare. The monster might double back to kill Soma. With her husband dead, the beorhs were the only target left for Soma. Then, he recognized another set of bloody footprints in the snow. They were left by Spanca who was dragging something.

The demigoddess stood next to the erba, frantically covering the large package partially wrapped in a green tunic. Winded from hoisting her load over the saddle, the exhausted, bloody woman sensed the beorh coming after her. Unarmed and covered only in a blanket she just pulled from the hairy beast, Spanca tried to left herself on the erba, but the beorh grabbed her first. The erba pulled sideways, its reins held tight to the rock. Spanca fell into a drift was the huffing and drooling monster stood above her. The woman rose, then fell back into the snow, resigned to her fate. The woman begged the beast to remove her head when it finished.

Then Spanca heard soft footsteps coming from the snow behind the monster. So intent on the demigoddess it hunted, the fiend failed to realize something hunted it. Starting to turn, the beorh felt a sword blade go through its neck, sending the elongated head at the feet of the prostrate Spanca. The body of the monster fell away, and Soma stepped closer. She looked down at a green woman, covered in her own blood from deep gouges of claw marks covering much of her breasts and belly. Deep puncture marks from their savage bites covered the woman's body. Large patches of the woman's skin were missing. Some of the beorhs tore at her skin or flayed the demigoddess alive after the others raped her.

However, Soma's face showed no sympathy or mercy. Her eyes were alight in blood lust.

"You are the betrayer who killed my husband; the *docke* who sided with Kriell. Prepare to meet your death." Soma's eyes gleamed as she lifted her sword high over the green woman.

Spanca slowly and painfully sat up for her executioner, tears streaming down her cheeks. "Let me get on my knees so you can remove my head and end this existence. I cannot go on."

~~~

After the tremor had separated them from Narslac and Soma, Urith and Fedelm tried to find another tunnel. As they passed the insane Unis, they heard the Sky Goddess screeching out a tune about Heptarc. Her words mixed gibberish along with various dialects of language neither of them heard before. Following Fedelm's lead, the dazed warrior stumbled along, nearly falling several times as the floor shook. Following a series of twisting turns, the pair suddenly entered the throne room of Caruun. Above them was the deep black stretching into what looked to be infinity supported by the beehive shaped cavern walls of spiraling black and white cubes gave the pair the feeling of vertigo. In the middle of the cavernous room was the throne of the underworld. A sudden jolt of the floor sent them scurrying to the platform where the throne of Caruun resided.

"Where can we go?" Fedelm's voice verged on hopelessness.

It appeared the Fates heard her when a nearby tunnel suddenly collapsed, sending billowing waves of dust toward them. Urith stared at the darkness above them, trying to avoid the unsteadiness he felt. He almost felt like the rock below them was lifting, but he could see the walls and caves around them were collapsing.

"I think we are stuck here," he stated calmly. Fedelm thought she heard a note of welcome to his statement. He looked down at her.

"I'm sorry."

She lashed out at the big man, pummeling her fists into his chest. "Curse You! How dare you give up?" Then, she stopped, her blue eyes showing the despair as the tears fell and Fedelm leaned against him.

"I'm sorry." She told him, suddenly forced to hold him for support as another severe quake struck below them. The woman noticed he wasn't looking at her.

Instead, Urith stared at the black and white throne covered in carvings and she looked at the hideous chair of stone. Engraved figurines were spirits left for special torment by the underworld master. When Fedelm looked at the chair, she noticed the carvings moving, each spirit pushing through their prison. Released into the air, the grotesque figures turned into blue orbs, slowly going skyward. As the spheres lifted higher, their light revealed the black ceiling closing down on them. The bottom realm of Kamin was coming together with the human realm.

"Reach the sky. Use the Skool!" The pair heard the voice of Dughorm at the same time.

"Curse the gods, I hate this thing," Urith told her as he lifted the Shield of Skool above his head. He pulled her close with his sword arm.

"Well, my friend Dughorm, you've left me with a cursed choice." Urith yelled into the darkness as the ground shook again. "We get crushed by the coming collapse, or we get flattened by all the rock which will drop on our heads if I use this thing." He looked down to Fedelm and gave her his sneer smile. "Your choice!"

Fedelm quickly wiped her eyes with her forearm and tried to smile. "I take none of those options." She stood on her toes and kissed his scarred cheek and he smiled.

Da Umca Mivwar echoed briefly just as the blast of energy shot upward. The man and woman held each other while they waited on their deaths.

~~~

When the gateway closed, the raging storms and snows affecting the lands quickly stopped. Across the kingdoms, people watched as the overcast clouds began to peel away. What they witnessed after the clouds retreated from sight left many of them in awe. Breathtaking beauty, high in the sky, the people watched thousands upon thousands of little spheres dancing among the winds. Some witnesses later told stories about a huge courtyard of stone structures floating among the clouds. Those who saw the sight claimed the stone structures suddenly turned into mists which quickly scattered with the orbs.

On the morning of the destruction of the realms, inside the vast Citadel of Br-Ynys, Oslaf and Imenal had just arrived in the Great Hall when they noticed familiar faces already sitting at the table. The men stopped in their tracks, dropping the rolls of papers they carried at the sight. Dughorm, Uolven, and Caestia along with many other dead warriors, friends and foes alike, sat around the large banquet table. As the ghosts held up their mugs of heathmead, their forms suddenly changed into blue orbs, ascending into the sky.

The Esterblud leader and the satgert stared at the empty table until Henther joined them. The woman could not understand why the two men looked so pale that morning.

~~~

The season of the harvest came to Kamin, long after the snows quickly melted following the destruction of Yns Garraid. Considerable damage done to the crops and animals left the lands barren of food and supplies. However, the weather became warmer, slowly returning to familiar patterns.

Oslaf stood on the wooden dock at Eran, watching the crews loading a cuggle for the forthcoming trip. The young man wore an elegant green tunic with the embellished figure on the front. The gold thread showed the image of an *Estercetus*, a sea serpent symbol of the combined clans of Esterblud. The symbol represented his status as one of the three leaders of Esterblud now. Wilgam and Draca were part of the council that ruled the lands. He turned at the sound of a cart coming next to him.

"My Lord, I've brought along enough heathmead to fill another ship." Atheern proudly declared as he looked down at the smiling king.

"You old Gallaeci trader, what makes you think you need that much?"

"I heard many tales about the savages and demigods in the unknown lands. They don't even know what a good drink is. I must remedy this." The fat, bearded man's eyes twinkled at the thought of selling his goods to the lands yet to be discovered. Oslaf laughed as he stepped aside for the man climbing down from the cart. He watched Atheern ordering several nearby people to help him unload the wagon.

"Why so happy?" A very pregnant Henther stepped next to the man.

"He's an interesting man," Oslaf turned to his wife. "He'll drive everyone crazy with his tales on that old Cahmais ship."

She noticed the slight melancholy in his voice.

"You wish to go on this adventure, don't you?"

Her new husband lightly rubbed his hand in a circle around her belly. "Every Esterblud wants adventure. But no, I have other responsibilities now."

"A bit more mundane than you're used to. It's only been a season since the downfall of the gods. You sure you're not going to get restless?" Henther's blue eyes searched Oslaf, looking for his reaction. He smiled.

"Don't worry; I'm more like my father now. This motley crew can regale me with their stories if they return."

"Who are you calling motley?" The familiar gruff voice came from behind. "I've still got enough parts left to cuff you upside the head."

Oslaf and Henther turned to see Urith and Fedelm walking to them, followed by the limping Imenal who was supported by Brihar. Like Henther, Fedelm's belly looked ready to burst with a child.

"I wondered when you might show up," Oslaf told his uncle. "And I'm not the trainee anymore. Cuff me, and you would be in a world of hurt."

Urith gave his sneer smile, and his gray eyes gleamed. "Yes, you are now the leader of our tribe and already becoming like the rest of those nobles. Let the others do your work."

Oslaf returned the smile and bowed to Fedelm. When he looked at his uncle, he realized the man in front of him had not changed, but then again Urith was a changed man. Outwardly, he still dressed as a warrior with his green tunic over chain mail and leather pants. The Shield of Skool hung over the man's back, and his Clovel sword remained in the scabbard at his side.

However, since he and Fedelm returned after using the Skool to cut through the collapsing chamber of the underworld, Urith's outlook on life appeared changed. Surviving the gods forced his uncle to see Kamin in a new light. The man no longer felt beholding to ancient traditions and cultures around the Maflow Sea. This expedition would be a small part of many things Urith sought to change.

"I'll see that Oslaf remains grounded," Brihar stood next to the young Esterblud warrior and Henther. "He will be like the brothers I lost."

The leader of the Gramcle somehow survived the skull fractures he received at Yns Garraid. The beorh's rocks may have left a noticeable depression on one side of the man's face, but Brihar was now the leader

237

of the Geniht guard who carried out the orders of the council. In his role as trusted advisor for Oslaf, Brihar would help keep the fractious kingdom of Esterblud united.

Urith stepped close to his friend, taking Brihar by the forearm. "Of that, I have no doubt, my friend. Fedelm and I have decided we will name this child Micaq in honor of a brave fighter." The large man suddenly looked around. "Have you seen Soma?"

"She is on the ship already with Guthlaf," Fedelm told him. "It appears your son is showing off for his mother. Be careful, the man wants to become a sailor."

Urith looked in the direction Fedelm indicated, catching sight of the large young man dressed in the leather leggings and blue wool shirt of a sailor. Guthlaf arrived in Eran with Soma only recently. Both son and father knew the truth now. After returning to Esterblud, Fedelm and Urith joined the auburn hair woman in the village of where they recovered from their injuries. At that time, Urith learned he had a son. Soma and Urith, with Fedelm's reassurance, determined Urith's best role would be as a mentor, so they decided not to tell the young man about Urith. However, the truth came out during their time together, helped along with the unforeseen reuniting of Soma and Urith as lovers.

"He'll be another work like Oslaf," Imenal commented as he watched the interaction between mother and son. "I'm glad Soma made it back."

"You and me both," Brihar told him dryly. Urith laughed at the statement while Imenal looked at them confused.

"You've been too busy with the Citadel, so you've not heard the story," Fedelm told Imenal. "Soma is the one that brought Brihar back from death."

"That's not entirely accurate," Narslac stated as the brave one-armed man joined the conversation. He was grinning as he confronted Fedelm. "Good thing you're not a Skald. Your stories would make us all look bad."

Looking offended, Fedelm took Urith by the arm. "Are you going to let him say such things?" she asked sweetly.

The giant man held up one hand in defense, "He has a right to his tales. Besides, you weren't there as I recall."

"That's right," Narslac immediately started recalling his tale to Imenal. "Soma and I discovered Brihar hanging over the back of an erba.

Nearly froze to death and blood everywhere but there Brihar was, all wrapped up in Urith's tunic. But I'll give Soma credit for healing the Gramcle fighter's wounds."

"As well as your own," Brihar reminded the Skald.

"True," Narslac unconsciously felt the area around his chest where the scars remained. His face went somber as he remembered back to the events. "However, it was Spanca who dragged you from the gateway to the erba. We thought you were dead. I'm not sure we would have found you when we escaped."

Brihar nodded, "The Fates were good to me on that day, despite losing my brothers. Do not blame yourself for nothing."

"What of Spanca? I never heard this story." Imenal asked.

Narslac turned to the satgert. "Fortunately, Soma is not a killer at heart. When I finally made my way through the snow, Soma held her sword above the demigoddess. I'll never forget the pain on her face at that moment. She wanted revenge and vengeance, but the woman realized none of that would come from killing Spanca." The Skald stopped, shaking his head.

"I finally got Soma to let go of the sword, and then I saw what those monsters had done to Spanca. They nearly skinned her alive, may the god's rot in the void." Anger grew in Narslac's voice. "I think when Spanca begged to die, it finally hit Soma. Both women suffered grievously on that day. We found Brihar after that. Spanca put him on the erba to save him."

"Where is Spanca now?" Imenal voice broke a bit, his expression showing awe at the tale.

"She's still recovering, and we left her with Micale in the village of Hariwill," Narslac said. "The priestess is quite taken with helping her. I believe after Micale heard about Mivraa's death, the woman needed some type of focus for her world. That reminds me of an idea I had. I think sanctuary for the demigods would be a perfect substitute, don't you, Imenal?"

The large satgert immediately agreed to Narslac's idea, telling the man he would insist on the priests to help spread the word of this new sanctuary. As the new Sacred Overlord of Kamin, Imenal carried considerable influence despite the turmoil caused by the destruction of the realms. The man understood the world around them was changing dramatically. Soon, Oslaf and the Sacred Overlord would begin their journey to the other kingdoms around the Maflow Sea to establish the new order. Imenal held no illusions to the challenging work in front of him.

"We must go," Urith interrupted the conversation. "The tide won't wait for us." He pressed his hand around the forearm of Imenal, who returned the handshake of his friends.

"Good fortune to you, uncle," Oslaf told Urith.

The warrior nodded, giving his nephew a grin. "Just remember to keep training. You never know when you might need it."

As Urith and Fedelm boarded the *cuggle*, they met Soma as she left.

"How are you holding up?" The warrior reached out to hold her, taking Soma in his arms.

"I'm fine. Please take care of our son. When you return, you and Fedelm's son will have a brother." The woman patted her stomach. Fedelm watched them, unfazed by what she heard. While Kamin tradition expected for one man to have only one wife, both women came to the conclusion that they did not need to hold onto the old ways. Instead of competition to force Urith into a decision, the women found a way to become wives to a single man. The warrior and the auburn hair woman still held something special between them and, gradually, Fedelm learned to approve. During the conversations and occasional arguments among the trio, it became evident Urith's passion for Soma remained just an intense as his feelings for Fedelm. The blonde hakra kept reminding herself that, in their insane world, jealousy and possessiveness based upon the old ways would not make their lives better. Fedelm would be with Urith on his journey. To her, that mattered more than how many children he might father with another woman.

Urith remained an adventurer at heart. A tenacious fighter, his passion for those he loved came out once a person grew to know him. Soma's observations were correct; Urith could not be expected to just settle in a village to live out his existence. But, he did need a place to call home when he returned. After learning of her pregnancy, Fedelm thought hard about her options and she made her choice.

Soma released the large man, touching his scarred face lightly. The auburn hair woman stepped in front of Fedelm, giving the smaller woman a hug. "Are you sure about this? You could stay with me when your little one arrives."

Fedelm shook her head. "No, I've made up my mind. It's a good choice for all of us. I will follow Urith into the unknown with his son."

Soma nodded, understanding what the blond woman told her. "Take care of yourself and the little one to come. I look forward to your return." The woman quickly stepped down the gangplank to the dock. She didn't turn to look back, quickly passing Imenal and Brihar who watched her. In a world dominated by laws and rules dictated by men, should something happen to the explorers during the voyage, Soma would have another son of a renowned warrior to help her through the future.

After the ship had sailed, Urith stood on the stern, just past the nearly empty quarterdeck. He watched the familiar tall landmarks of Esterblud gradually fading into the background of green and blue vegetation. The man suddenly felt the presence of Fedelm.

"You know, Soma was right. You should have stayed to have our child. Together you and Soma could raise the brothers. It's not fair to force you along," the explorer spoke from his heart.

"You did not force me. I made the decision with that knowledge. I would not do well waiting for you to return, if at all." She replied stoically. "We all make our choices in life. I'm content with my decision." Fedelm took his hand. "I'm actually excited by the prospects. You have a good crew and something to strive for. Now you will have two more sons to build a better world."

He turned his head as the wind whipped his long hair. She thought she noticed a bit of gray as he gave her a roll of the eyes. "Excited is not what I would call it. Soon we will pass Regiussa on our way into the unknown sea."

"After what we just went through, it should be quite peaceful." Fedelm gave him a smile to go with the sarcasm. "If not, you always have the Shield of Skool on your back."

Urith's face went somber. "No, it won't be used, that I can promise."

Puzzled, she stared at him. "Then, why bring it along?" Nobody but you can touch it."

With a practiced smoothness, the warrior pulled the shield from behind his back, holding it in front of them. The medallion in the front gleamed in the sunlight.

"*Sevethm, Regaligc, Gcothrem, Doltais,*" he read the inscriptions aloud.

"Sovereign, sacred, justice, and vengeance," she repeated the words.

"I've had this thing on my back and a lot of time to think about it. Does our new world need a weapon from those creatures who thought they were gods over us?" He was asking her and himself the same question.

"That shield has saved us a few times," she replied, her blue eyes remaining on the pieces of wood and metal.

"Yes, and killed many that might not have deserved it. I will not use this weapon against anyone we might come across during our journey. I don't believe I'm a god." The Clovel Destroyer suddenly released the object from his hands. The Shield of Skool hit the water at an angle, sliding down under the waves. The couple watched the weapon of the gods quickly disappear from sight. They remained quiet, listening to the straining and creaking sounds coming from the ship and sails as they moved through the water.

Urith turned her away from the edge of the ship. "You know the only tales about the unknown sea come to us from shipwrecked people they've found in Regiussa. I hope we don't find ourselves in that position. It was bad enough the first time we met."

Fedelm slid her hand around the crook of the explorer's big arm. "I agree, but we don't have the gods against us any longer. Let's hold that memory for ourselves and our son to pass down to his children."

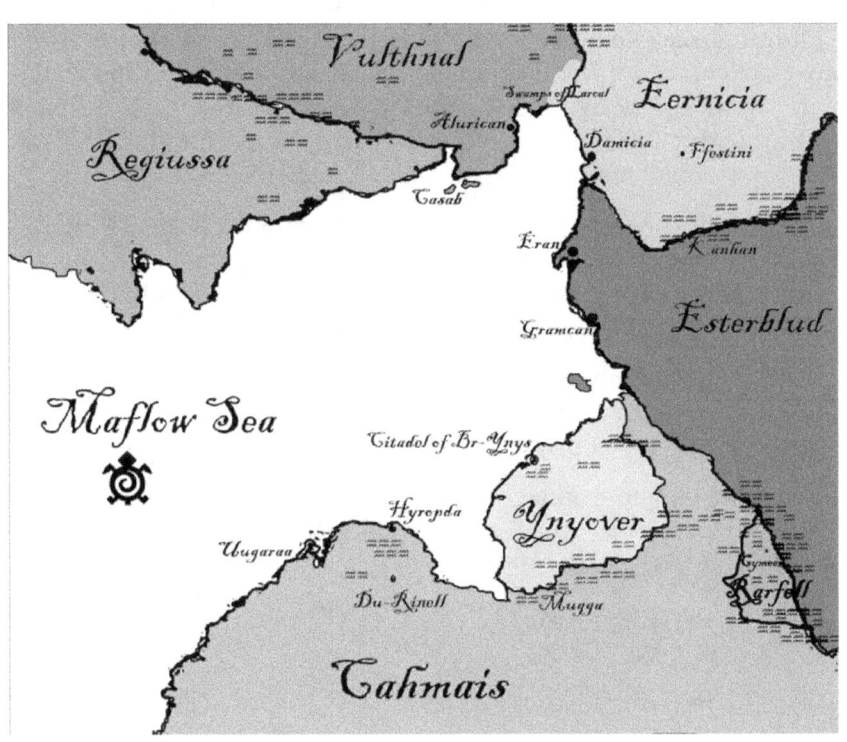

About the Author

Gordon Brewer is the pseudonym for a professional geek, history buff, and full-time dad who took up a challenge from his son to finish his first novel and enter the world of writing. Raised on a farm in Kansas, the author spent nearly five years in the US Navy traveling to 12 different countries during this time. After his discharge, he received his BS degree with majors in History and Political Science.

Over the next twenty years, Gordon focused on the business and IT world. His experiences left him with a need to explore wide-ranging interests in multiple genres, each with historical consideration given to the characters and settings.

Residing in Tennessee, he often uses his family and friends as unfortunate guinea pigs, where they listen to his tales, no matter how poorly conceived they may be.

You can find out more about the author and upcoming books, along with his other works at www.gordonbrewer.com.

www.ingramcontent.com/pod-product-compliance
Lightning Source LLC
Chambersburg PA
CBHW052030020726
47501CB00004B/1332